To the Zionsville
Community Library,
Best wishes!
Dane Starbuck

To Love an *African Violet*

Dane Starbuck

Pati Sparks, *Illustrator*

Don't Rescue!
I'm Reading a Great Book

little island press

Published by little island press, 11950 Pebblepoint Pass, Carmel, IN 46033 -
www.littleislandpress.com

in association with
IBJ Corp. Contract Publishing, 41 E. Washington Street, Suite 200,
Indianapolis, IN 46204 - www.ibjconpub.com

The characters and events in this book are fictitious. Any similarity to real
persons, living or dead, is coincidental and not intended by the author.

Cover photo - Mark Fredericks
Illustrations - Pati Sparks

Library of Congress Cataloging-in Publication Data

Starbuck, Dane (1956)
        To Love an African Violet / Dane Starbuck

        ISBN 0-9745673-5-3

        © 2005

For Bev

Philippians 1:3

*And with deep appreciation to the late Elizabeth Goodrich Terry
for her support in helping to make this book possible.*

Who that cares much to know the history of man, and how the mysterious mixture behaves under the varying experiments of Time, has not dwelt, at least briefly, on the life of Saint Theresa, has not smiled with some gentleness at the thought of the little girl walking forth one morning, hand-in-hand with her still smaller brother, to go and seek martyrdom in the country of the Moors?

. . . Many Theresas have been born, who found for themselves no epic life, wherein there was a constant unfolding of far-resonant action; perhaps only a life of mistakes, the offspring of a certain spiritual grandeur, ill-matched with the meanness of opportunity; perhaps a tragic failure, which found no sacred poet, and sank unwept into oblivion. . . .

Here and there a cygnet is reared uneasily among the ducklings in the brown pond, and never finds the living stream in fellowship with its own oary-footed kind. Here and there is born a Saint Theresa, foundress of nothing, whose loving heartbeats and sobs after an unattained goodness tremble off, and are dispersed among hindrances, instead of centring in some long-recognizable deed.

George Elliot
"Prelude," *Middlemarch*

Margaret Mahoney Reuben

Rev. Francis Tannen, S.J.

Eugene O'Connor, at age twenty-two

Rosemary and Hastings Hamilton

General Albert Mubarsoi

One

T he hideous nightmare of my struggle with General Albert Mubarsoi for my life—and Margaret's—was interrupted by a ringing phone. Who could be calling at this hour?

"Professor O'Connor, this is Donna Pauley. If you hear me, please call the office. It's an emergency and no one can find you! Don't worry about your 8:00 o'clock exam. Professor Coldren is covering it. Please call immediately!"

The voice blared from the telephone answering machine in my bedroom. I found myself draped asleep across the reclining chair in the living room. As I opened my eyes the sun, shining through the east window, blinded me. I rubbed my eyes and glanced at the digital clock. It flashed 7:45 a.m. I couldn't believe the time.

I ran to the bathroom, took care of the necessities and bolted out the back door. Tom Coldren wouldn't know that the classroom for the test had been changed, and he didn't have the exams, so I just had to get to the university as quickly as I could. No time to call or change clothes.

After the hurried commute, I parked in the faculty parking lot beside Ballantine Hall. I ran up the stairs with the exam papers to the third floor and entered room number 354. It was a classroom in the back east corner of the building near some testing offices. There I found them--my students in Journalism 101. They chatted among themselves as if this was just another class and not the last day of their first year of college. How could I have overslept? It was probably due to grading too many tests the night before.

The two hour examination passed quickly. The students completed the test and trickled out of the classroom. I stared out of the third story window, looking away from the sun and out over the central campus that is known as the "Meadows." Suddenly Melanie Steinberg, one of my brighter students, broke the stillness.

"I just wanted to say, Professor O'Connor, how sorry I am to hear about what happened to Elizabeth Brownlie."

I could tell that Melanie was waiting for me to respond, but I was clueless as to what she meant.

"What about Elizabeth?"

"You don't know, Professor? They found her dead at the bottom of Eigenman Hall early this morning. It was the lead story on WIUS. We were all surprised when you showed up. We thought that the test might be cancelled. Apparently," Melanie looked away from me and stopped talking.

"Apparently what?"

Melanie whimpered. "Apparently Elizabeth jumped from the top of Eigenman last night."

"My God!" I screamed.

Eigenman Hall, a graduate dormitory, was fourteen stories high. There had been a handful of students over the years who had leaped from the top of the building in distress over academic difficulties or a failed love affair.

Most of the students in my first year journalism class knew Elizabeth. As my graduate assistant, she had taught for me earlier in the semester when I had attended academic conferences off campus. What my students wouldn't have known is that Elizabeth was also my goddaughter. Melanie stood quietly with her head down.

"Thank you for telling me, Melanie," I finally said, in a daze. I reached out my hand and touched her on the shoulder. It was a token effort to try and make some connection, to show some recognition for her efforts to console. All the other students had now gone. I gathered up the blue books and looked one more time out of the east windows towards the Meadows.

As I walked out of the front entrance and down the steps of Ballantine Hall on the campus of Indiana University, I couldn't help but notice, in some perverse way, how beautiful a May morning it had become. My senses seemed extraordinarily sharp and everything around me—the colors of trees and flowers, the chirping of birds, the fragrances of lilac bushes—vibrantly filled with sight, sound, and smell. The bushes and trees were green, lush, and slightly dripping with moisture from rain the night before. The beauty of the morning seemed to intensify, not lessen, the numb, deadening feeling that had come over me.

I walked along the sidewalk between Beck Chapel and the Union building. The small graveyard next to the chapel was positioned to my right. The graveyard's older headstones leaned from rain that over the years had loosened the soil around the markers, causing them to list from their own weight. I crossed the arched bridge over the Little Jordan River. The stream's narrow banks were swollen from the previous night's downpour. Time seemed so much later than 10:30 a.m. I next attempted to enter Ernie Pyle Hall, the building that contained the journalism faculty offices and classrooms. Excited students exited the building, momentarily preventing me from entering.

I finally arrived at the faculty office on the second floor. The head and torso of Donna Pauley, the department's office manager, appeared from behind her desk. She held in her hand a paper clip that she had apparently just picked up off of the worn carpet. Donna's face wore an exasperated expression.

"Professor O'Connor, I've been trying all morning to locate you," she said. "Where were you?"

The examination room had been changed a week before by the department head and reported to the students, but I had forgotten to pass on the notice to her or anyone else in the department.

"I assumed you knew about the room change for the final," I said, lying.

"No, I didn't know," Donna retorted. "We've had several people out looking for you."

I was too upset to think straight and tossed the exam papers in the chair next to Donna's desk.

"Where do they have Beth? One of my students said that the campus radio station reported she jumped from the top of Eigenmen Hall."

Donna got up, took me by the upper arm, and led me down the hall away from the department foyer. "The police have the area cordoned off where she fell, Professor," she said. "There's to be an autopsy."

"But why an autopsy?" I asked in a whisper. "Do they think it wasn't suicide? Maybe Elizabeth fell. Maybe—"

Donna gently grasped my upper arm again. "Professor O'Connor, the police found a suicide letter."

Suicide? Beth was so stable, so sure of herself and what she wanted. Not suicide. It wasn't possible.

Donna sighed and looked at me with a frown. "There are two men here to see you. The first is an investigator from the Bloomington Police Department. His name is Lieutenant Allen Peterson," Donna said, handing me his card. "He's in your office now. I thought it was best that I let him in. I hope it was all right."

"Gene," interrupted Jack Roberts, a fellow professor in the department, "I just heard about Elizabeth Brownlie. So sorry, Gene."

"Just learned about it myself, Jack," I said in the hallway. "We're looking into it."

"What a great gal. It's just terrible."

I nodded, acknowledging his sympathy and looked back at Donna. "Who else is waiting? What does he want?"

"I don't know for sure, Professor, but I don't think it has anything to do with what's happened this morning with Elizabeth. He's insistent that he see you and he says he'll wait however long it takes. He's out front now in the lobby area."

"Please tell him I'll be with him as soon as I can."

Donna nodded and turned on her heels. I ran down the long corridor to my cramped faculty office. When I threw open the door, the man waiting inside jumped up from his seat.

"Excuse me," I said. "Didn't mean to startle you." I reached out my right hand to shake the officer's. "My name is Eugene O'Connor. I'm sorry you've been waiting so long."

"Allen Peterson, Professor. Bloomington Police Force," the officer replied. He pulled out his wallet from his back pocket and flipped it open to show his ID. We exchanged a couple more comments and I sat down behind my desk.

"I understand Elizabeth Brownlie was your teaching assistant," the lieutenant began. "Had you noticed any changes in her recently? Anything that would have caused her to want to kill herself?"

"Then you're certain it's a suicide?"

"We've not ruled out anything, Professor. We've just begun the investigation."

"Then no," I answered. "It just seems so contrary to her nature. Elizabeth was very discouraged that work on her dissertation hadn't gone any better. Then there's the matter of her recent break-up with her boyfriend, Paul Chamness. He recently moved to Cincinnati. Have you been able to get hold of him?"

"Not that I know of, Professor. I imagine that will be someone else's responsibility. Do you know why they split?"

"Paul recently took a job in Cincinnati. Procter and Gamble, I think. Apparently he and Elizabeth hadn't talked it over before he accepted the position and she was hurt that she hadn't been consulted."

"Any history of violence between the two of them?"

I fussed with papers on my desk. All of this was so strange and nerve-racking.

"Paul's a terrific guy," I answered. "Can't imagine that there's a violent pulse in his body."

"What about her dissertation? You said she was having trouble finishing it."

"Yes, Elizabeth was having trouble, but not to the point of killing herself over it. She's been teaching too much and not spending enough time on her research. Elizabeth didn't teach for the money but she wanted the classroom experience."

Peterson nodded and jotted something down on a beat-up, spiral ring notebook with no cover. Light reflected off of his bald head. He looked about sixty, with a large double chin and bags under his eyes. I leaned against the old radiator in my office and sighed.

"When did you first learn about Elizabeth's death, Lieutenant?"

"I received a call this morning around 5:30 from the department. I was asked to come in early this morning to start the investigation."

"But who contacted the authorities?"

"Don't know. I was just given your name and asked to come and talk with you."

A terrible thought came to me, causing me to blurt out. "Has Elizabeth's mother been contacted, Lieutenant?"

The officer looked up from his notebook. He ran his tongue over his teeth. "Don't know, Professor. Just in case she hasn't, how can she be reached?"

I jotted Irene Brownlie's name and telephone number on the back of his business card and handed it to the police officer. Through the cracked door, I saw several students pass outside my office. I walked over and closed it.

"How long have you known Miss Brownlie?" the lieutenant continued.

"All of her life. Her mother and I have been friends since grade school in the 30s. We grew up in the same small town of Lisbon, just east of Muncie. That's where Elizabeth is from, too. She graduated from the local high school in 1978."

"So Miss Brownlie was more to you than just your teaching assistant?"

"Definitely. Her mother asked me to be her godfather after

Elizabeth's own father passed away when Elizabeth was sixteen."

"Godfather? I'm not Catholic, Professor, but I thought that to become a godparent a person had to be appointed at the time of the child's baptism."

"I'm not Catholic, either, Lieutenant, but technically you're right. My relationship is nothing formal, nothing registered with the Church. Nonetheless, I've taken her mother's request very seriously."

I felt my stomach churn. The thought of Elizabeth lying in some morgue made me sick. The detective put down his pencil and stared at me.

"She's an only child," I continued. "Her mother still lives in Lisbon and she has an aunt in Lafayette," I said slowly, regaining composure.

"It sounds like Miss Brownlie and you were extremely close."

"As I just said, Lieutenant, she was more than my teaching assistant. After her father died, I was there for her."

"But was your relationship with her in any way more than that, Professor? I mean, was your relationship ever romantic in any way?"

"Are you asking if I was banging my goddaughter, Lieutenant?"

"Banging?" he said. "That's an interesting British expression. I'm not sure I would have used that strong of word, but since you did, we're you?"

"Of course not!" I replied. "Why would you even insinuate that?"

Lieutenant Peterson's sagging face turned red and he was obviously embarrassed. It was good to see a man about my own age still capable of blushing.

"I have to cover all the bases, ask the standard questions," Peterson said, back-peddling. "Should this ever come up as we look into this situation further, I can at least report back that I asked the question. That's all."

Donna cracked opened the door and then closed it again

when she saw that we were still talking.

"Professor, do you know of anyone who held a grudge against Miss Brownlie? Anyone who would want to do her harm?"

"Let me make Elizabeth come alive for you, Lieutenant. She was upbeat, cheerful, generous to a fault. She would rescue a stray cat, take it to a vet and have it cared for and then find it a home. At the end of every semester, she would come to me and just be in agony that she had to give a student less than a C grade."

There was a brief pause while the lieutenant jotted in his notebook, causing me to ask, "The office secretary told me that they're going to do an autopsy. Do you know why?"

He shook his head. "I'm sorry I can't give you more information, but like I said, we've just started the investigation. I appreciate your time. Someone from my department or from the Indiana State Police will be in touch with you soon."

And that was it. Lieutenant Allen Peterson shook my hand, walked out of the office and disappeared. I sat dumbfounded. Here I was closer to Elizabeth than probably anyone but her mother, and I knew absolutely nothing other than that she was dead—presumably from suicide.

"Professor O'Connor," Donna Pauley said from the doorway. "Is there anything I can get you?"

"Can you see if there's a copy of this morning's *Herald-Times* in the faculty lounge?" I asked.

I reached for my address book again to double check Irene Brownlie's work number when Donna came back into my office. Then I remembered someone else was waiting to see me. Donna handed me the newspaper and read my mind.

"Professor, the gentleman out front introduced himself as Nigel Reuben." Donna handed me his business card. "He told me he's from Morocco. He said he flew in unexpectedly last night. He said you didn't know him but that you and one of his relatives—an aunt, I believe—were once very close friends. He won't leave without seeing you."

"Tell him I'll be right out."

My mind swirled and I felt lightheaded. I remembered then that I hadn't had any breakfast. Donna escorted me to the foyer where the other stranger waited. I had obviously rushed right past him in my haste to enter the office and learn about Elizabeth.

Two

The man was tanned dark brown and dressed in a gray tailored suit. He was medium height with distinguished looking eyes, graying temples and thick, shortly cropped brown hair. He extended his hand.

"I'm Nigel Reuben, Professor O'Connor," he said smiling.

"I apologize for the wait, Mr. Reuben," I replied. "I had a final examination to give this morning and there's also been a personal tragedy."

I felt numb again, and then I realized I was still holding the stranger's hand. The situation was awkward, but he tried to dismiss it as a gesture of intended cordiality.

We walked down the hall and into my office. As we entered I became embarrassed by its messy appearance, something I had been oblivious to when speaking with Lieutenant Peterson. I apologized about the appearance, but Reuben simply dismissed it with a smile. He suddenly seemed nervous. I gestured for him to have a seat and he did, crossing his legs and revealing expensive leather shoes. He looked familiar, but I couldn't place his face in any context.

"I overheard your secretary this morning, Professor," Reuben began. "She was on the telephone for quite some time trying to reach you."

I paused. "My goddaughter, who happened to also be my teaching assistant, was found dead this morning outside her dormitory. I'm still in shock over it. An investigator from the local police department was just here asking questions. You may have seen him leave."

Reuben nodded. "I'm very sorry to hear this, Professor." He

looked sincerely concerned, then perplexed. He started to say more, but I stopped him when a thought came to my mind. I jumped from my chair, jerked open my office door, and ran down the corridor to Donna Pauley's desk and asked her to get Bob Zimmer on the phone as soon as she could. Zimmer, editor of the Bloomington *Herald-Times*, was a colleague and friend. I returned to my office, intrigued by the stranger's visit.

"I gave your secretary my card, Professor O'Connor," Reuben began. "As she may have mentioned to you, I'm from Tangier, Morocco, where I own an import-export business."

"An interesting part of the world," I said. "I spent a few days in Tangier covering an international conference in 1968. I'm sure it's much different today. Are you British, Mr. Reuben?"

"Not a Brit, Professor O'Connor, although I lived in England for a number of years at boarding school and university. No, my father was Irish, though I only lived in Ireland as a small boy."

He squirmed in his seat and smiled. "I arrived in Indianapolis last evening. It was a twenty-two hour trip from West Africa."

"So you didn't travel from Tangier, Mr. Reuben?"

"No. I've been in Cape de Leone the past few weeks on some business," he said. "I'm also working on some family matters as well," he added, as if an afterthought.

I'm sure I would have been quite interested to learn of his business and family connections to West Africa had I not already received the terrible news about Elizabeth that morning. I responded matter of factly. "I lived in Cape de Leone for several years, Mr. Reuben."

Reuben nodded. "Yes, I know."

"It's a terrible time for the country, isn't it?" I continued. "Of course, when hasn't it been a terrible time? Do you think that Albert Mubarsoi will have any serious opposition from Josiah Kimba in the upcoming national election?"

Reuben's eyes brightened. He seemed surprised by my mentioning Mubarsoi's name.

"At seventy-two, Mubarsoi is still quite a force," Reuben

answered. "If the election goes forward, I think he'll win in a landslide. Most of Kimba's followers are in hiding due to all the unprovoked attacks that government troops have exercised outside of Grand Bassa. Still, it's Mubarsoi's son that I'm worried about."

"Isn't it ironic that Albert Mubarsoi named his son Angel?" I said.

Reuben nodded. "Actually I think it's quite fitting, Professor. In my mind he's the *Angel of Death*."

We both smiled at one another, acknowledging immediately a kinship in sentiment towards this West African thug and his equally brutal son. Reuben seemed to be a man of integrity and high intelligence, but this was purely speculation. Why in God's name had he come halfway around the world to see me? I called for Donna to get us both some coffee. He took a sip and then said.

"I imagine my appearance here this morning is a bit puzzling, Professor O'Connor. I could have cabled you, but since you don't know me, I felt I had to come here and meet you myself."

"I see," I replied, "And what exactly did you come to see me about, Mr. Reuben?"

"I've come to take you back with me to Cape de Leone. I have tickets for us to fly out of Indianapolis this evening at 6:00 p.m."

Reuben stated this as calmly and matter-of-factly as if he had said the coffee was too strong or that he preferred button-down Oxfords to other dress shirts. I'm sure my mouth must have dropped open, causing Reuben to continue.

"I can only imagine your surprise, Professor," he said, looking out the window, "but, you see, I'm Margaret Reuben's nephew. You, of course, knew her by her maiden name of Mahoney. My aunt is near death and she fully understands that her time is short. My Aunt Margaret has asked for you several times in the past few days. She has begged me to come and bring you back to Cape de

Leone to see her before she dies. I know that this news is a shock, particularly now."

My mind swirled with images: Margaret Mahoney—fair, Irish complexion, lovely brunette hair, compassionate, perfume in the jungle—and dead!

"Mr. Reuben, it's totally impossible for me to leave Bloomington today or tomorrow or any time this week."

"You must understand, Professor O'Connor, my aunt is on her deathbed. She begged me—"

"Sir, if you are truly Margaret Mahoney's nephew, then you know that your aunt was killed by Albert Mubarsoi thirty years ago. What you say is impossible! I saw her myself dangling from the end of a noose. I'll always remember that awful day as surely as I'll remember the sorrow of this one."

I felt like I was in the Twilight Zone. Everything in my world was spinning. I hadn't had the dream about Margaret's death for years. What were the chances of my having it again just this morning?

I moved to open my office door, but Reuben remained seated. He then pulled out from his inside breast pocket a paper folded in half lengthwise. He unfolded the paper and placed it firmly on top of my grade book.

"Professor, she isn't dead. This is an article about my aunt when she gave a generous gift last year to her former secondary school in Dublin. Please see the photograph of her, Professor," Reuben said, pointing specifically to the picture in the upper right hand corner of the page. "She hardly looks to have been in her grave for thirty years."

The date printed on the bottom of the article was September 1988, about nine months before. The picture was of an elderly lady with silver-streaked hair, deep wrinkles around her mouth and eyes, but with a soft, assured smile. *This is not Margaret Mahoney*, I thought to myself. Then I realized that I hadn't seen her since she was a striking and radiant woman in the late-1950s.

"Mr. Reuben, I can't go anywhere with you."

He interrupted. "Within the past two days I have traveled six thousand miles, crossed parts of three continents, and one very wide ocean to see you. You must understand the seriousness of the matter I bring before you."

Unmoved, I stared at him and then Reuben's face became animated and his voice gruffer.

"Professor, as I remember my aunt telling me, a young and naive American arrived at her front door one day in 1952. She lived then in a small, isolated village named Burguna that was located on the southeastern fringe of Cape de Leone, West Africa. This young man came from a small town in the States. He announced he was the new Christian missionary who had arrived with nothing because he had been robbed in Dakar, Senagal."

Reuben went on to tell me about my history in Cape de Leone, making me feel even more as if I was in a dream or a Rod Steiger movie. He spoke in detail about my life as a teacher at the village school established by Margaret and a Jesuit priest, about my involvement in a terrible civil war and about me being expelled from Cape de Leone in the late 1950s. I was dumbfounded after listening to Reuben's short recitation. It was obvious he knew much about my life. And my mind again swirled with images of Margaret, of the small things that remain after the love of my life had been taken from me—her love of Irish tea, her wonderful laugh and the sweet, self-deprecating humor she used to apologize for her mathematical ineptitude and her inability to carry the simplest of tunes.

"Professor O'Connor," Reuben responded in a softer, more compassionate tone. "I wouldn't ask this of you except that I can't recall my aunt ever making such a request, not of me or anyone."

He stood, looked out the window and then back at me. "Aunt Margaret is dying of ovarian cancer. She only has a few days, perhaps even less, to live."

I pondered momentarily and then answered. "As you can see, Mr. Reuben, this has been a very upsetting morning."

I began to plead that Elizabeth's death and his sudden, unanticipated appearance couldn't possibly cause me to leave with him. But he interrupted me again, ignoring my excuses.

"Can I call you early this afternoon, Professor?" Reuben requested. "That would still give us time to drive to the airport. You don't need much. I've made all the arrangements to provide you with an airline ticket, visa, money, personal items. We'll fly into Grand Bassa via New York and Paris. You just need your passport and a couple of changes of clothes."

I felt helpless, compelled in an odd way. I told him I would give it serious thought and then wrote down my home telephone number on a business card and handed it to Reuben. He left and then Donna Pauley entered my office and handed me several pink message slips that had accumulated while I met with the two men. I glanced at the messages and tossed them down on my desk. They could wait.

"I'm going home, Donna," I said. "If you hear from *anyone* who knows *anything* about Elizabeth, please contact me there."

I left the office and walked back to the parking lot beside Ballantine Hall where I had parked my car. The air was already thick with humidity and the sun beaded down directly overhead. The campus stood remarkably still.

Three

W e surged and plunged at 30,000 feet above Lake Erie. Thin clouds swished by at incredible speeds and the luggage compartments rattled from the tossing of unknown contents. Suddenly the jet's engines caught hold again of oxygen and shot us through another air pocket. We leveled off and sunlight unexpectedly streamed through the plane's windows casting a golden hue throughout the fuselage. Reuben smiled at me with a sickish grin.

"Isn't this just god-awful! In my line of work, I fly a couple of times a fortnight, but I'll never get use to turbulence like this."

I shook my head. I truthfully enjoyed the jostling. It took my mind off of all the troubling insecurities that hadn't left me for more than a few seconds the entire day and that were now settling like a large meal in my stomach. Suddenly I was a boy again riding the large roller coaster at Coney Island in Cincinnati with my mother and brother Philip. The three of us, my mother in the middle, had squeezed into the front seat, strapped firmly in by a canvas belt. As we raced past every turn, I remembered the happy screams and the mixed feelings of pain and ecstasy that I felt at having my brother's and mother's weight thrown against me.

This was all part of my personality as an overseas journalist for twenty-five years: the wanderlust, the longing to experience something new and exciting, even if that something new and exciting was merely being jostled on some third-rate national airline. But now I kicked myself for pushing out to find the edge to the point of irrationality. I had simply abandoned my senses, lured by the siren call of a woman I'd loved a long time ago and, if I admitted it, the love of adventure.

It was clearly unpardonable of me to leave Bloomington that evening to go with Nigel Reuben to Cape de Leone. Elizabeth Brownlie was dead. I had no idea what had happened to this beautiful young woman who was like a daughter to me. Moreover, her mother, my old friend, Irene Brownlie, would desperately need to be comforted. And now that I was a responsible teacher instead of a fly-by-night foreign journalist I had a pile of final exams setting on my desk to grade.

But I had to face it. I had to find out if Margaret Mahoney was really alive, because none of this made any sense. I had seen her hung thirty years before and had never received any information to believe she wasn't dead. I did confirm earlier that afternoon, through Bob Zimmer's assistance, that a woman by the name of Margaret Mahoney Reuben had contributed one million pounds (about $1.5 million U.S. dollars) to her alma mater, St. Magdalene Girl's School, a preparatory school in Dublin. Still, how Reuben appeared in my office and the whole timing of the situation made me extremely uneasy.

So it was all a mystery, a conundrum, and I was always a chump for adventure. If I was truly honest with myself, I was returning to this small, inconsequential West African nation with the hope of recapturing the excitement and spiritual understanding that had caused me to go there in the first place nearly forty years before.

The day seemed like several days compressed into one. I'd found out that Elizabeth had died of a broken neck but, beyond that, the police refused to comment. Bob Zimmer confirmed that a suicide note had been found, but it was typed and located in Elizabeth's typewriter. The police refused to share the content with anyone. Neither would the authorities allow me to view Beth's body when I went to the Monroe County hospital where she was being kept in the morgue. Her body had been positively identified by two women students who had rooms next to Beth's—no possibility of mistaken identity.

I had also learned that the police had been unable to locate

Irene Brownlie. I had finally gotten up enough nerve that morning to call Irene's office, but she wasn't there. Irene was the Auditor of Roanoke County, Indiana. She and the county Treasurer, Helen Cox, had left for a four day vacation in northern Michigan the day before and were unreachable. I was successful in contacting Irene's sister and Elizabeth's aunt, Catherine Thompson. I explained to her why I had to leave Bloomington and that I would return within the next two to three days if at all possible.

It was doubtful that Irene would learn of Beth's plight from Michigan. The Upper Peninsula was truly the end of the world and the police wouldn't know where to look.

The authorities told me that unless Irene Brownlie could be located by tomorrow, it was doubtful that the funeral could be held before Friday or Saturday—time for me to get back from my strange odyssey. As for the delay in getting semester grades to the Dean's office, the Dean would just have to wait. Students' final grades were the least of my concerns.

Bob Zimmer had checked Reuben's story, using the contacts he had gained as a Washington, D.C. correspondent several years before. He confirmed that Reuben was the president of the "West African Overseas Trading Company" headquartered in Tangier, Morocco, and that his grandfather and father had been presidents of the company before him. Reuben was also active in West African politics and was a small-time philanthropist of sorts. Most interestingly, his wife had been killed in 1986 during an ambush in Cape de Leone by revolutionary forces that had been fighting against Albert Mubarsoi's government. That was all Zimmer could tell me on such short notice.

So I would go. I knew it all along. Reuben's mission to whisk me to West Africa held an allure that I was embarrassed to admit to myself given the terrible situation I was leaving.

After the flight attendant served us both a bloody Mary, I broke the silence. I wanted to know more about Reuben and, also, how much he knew about me.

Four

"What do you trade?" I asked, looking directly at the man next to me.

The Irishman set down his drink on the small fold out table in front of him. He smiled a little wryly.

"We deal in anything that Europeans are interested in buying: rubber, textiles, diamonds, coffee, art—anything really. When my grandfather started the company in the 1920s, he exported a lot of animal skins and ivory to Europe. But all that is past now. As you probably know, it's now illegal to trade in ivory and most skins are rare to come by due to various animal protection laws."

"But then why do you live in Morocco if most of your business is in West Africa?"

"For the convenience," he replied. "I'm not sure that it eliminates that much travel, but I've been in Tangier for so long that I have no interest in moving now."

He stirred his drink with a celery stick, then popped the end in his mouth and took a bite.

"And you, Professor, were you a journalist even before you went to Cape de Leone in the fifties?"

"I wrote some but I was mostly a farmer," I said, chuckling at how strange it now sounded even to me. "I worked on my grandfather's farm. I now own it. I was twenty-five when I left the farm to go to Cape de Leone. As apparently you already know, I went to be a missionary, not a teacher."

"Yes, the school that you taught at and that Aunt Margaret funded was probably the most important endeavor that she ever undertook. She had greatly hoped that schools of its kind could be established throughout the country. That was extremely important to her."

"All along I assumed that the Jesuits paid for it. We never discussed the financial details."

"No, Aunt Margaret funded it on her own," Reuben answered. "She's also the one that approached Tannen to be in charge of it. The school in Burguna only cost her a few hundred pounds a year to operate, so it was no great expense. Although Aunt Margaret funded it, she never wanted Francis Tannen to think she was over him. But I'm sure it was one of the reasons he didn't take any greater interest in the school than he did."

I closed my eyes to tune Reuben out and then leaned back and momentarily allowed my mind to drift back to these years.

I had taken a ferry up the Tanganeen River from Grand Bassa, Cape de Leone's capital city. Grand Bassa is located on the western edge of the country where the Atlantic Ocean meets and forms its coastline. The ferry, crammed with supplies, traveled upstream to the small village named "Burguna." In 1952 no roads yet connected the village to the outside world. Because I had less than a British pound on me, I had to give the ferry operator my only extra pair of shoes to make up the difference for the cost of the transport.

I had traveled to West Africa to be a Christian missionary to a little known tribe of Creole descent. When I had left the rickety ferry and asked for Father John Stivonovich, my contact, none of the villagers understood me. But a small village boy led me to a Western style house standing on the edge of Burguna. The boy, dressed in rags, knocked on the front door. He ran away before I could give him some hard candy that I had left over from my trip.

The door swung open. A handsome brunette woman appeared in the entrance way. I was shocked as I had not encountered a white person since I had left Grand Bassa and certainly none as attractive as her. I suddenly became very conscious of my unkempt appearance and tried to comb my matted hair with my left hand and wipe the sweat off of my forehead.

"Eugene O'Connor?" she asked. "Oh, what a silly question. Of course, you have to be. Please come in," she said excitedly. "Please do come in. I imagine you must be exhausted."

I immediately noticed her Irish brogue. The lady took the apron that hung around her waist and dried off her hands. "I'm Margaret Mahoney," she said, extending her moist hand.

"How do you know my name, mam?"

"Oh, we'll get to that later, but how about some tea, Eugene?" she asked. "Have you got to liking tea yet? I understand that it is not so popular in your Midwest, but it is all that we have here in abundance. Coffee is so dear."

I nodded and watched my enthusiastic host pour water into a porcelain canister. "The water has to remain in the filter for several minutes, not to steep the tea, but to kill anything that might contaminate it," she said.

Margaret went to a cupboard adjacent to a wood burning stove and pulled out a dish draped with cheesecloth. She lifted the cloth and lowered the dish in front of me. "Would you like a scone, Eugenc?" she asked.

I thanked Margaret and picked up a scone, but she insisted that I take two. "We'll have a proper meal later," she added.

I was confused about her and my new surroundings. I was also nervous about such kindness; overly so, no doubt, because of the ordeal I had been through the previous two weeks. Margaret Mahoney pulled over a chair in front of me and plopped down. She looked all around, got up and went out the front door and came back in again.

"Where are all your bags, Eugene? Are you having them brought from the ferry?" she asked. "I would think they would be here by now. The ferry should have already left for Panguma."

"This is it," I said, embarrassed and pointing to a small knapsack beside me. "Most of my personal things were stolen in Dakar two nights ago when my hotel room was broken into."

I pulled out of the sack a Bible once owned by my mother and a used camera given to me by my Uncle Paul and Aunt

Betty. "I had this camera on me and an extra pair of dress shoes underneath my bed. I had to give my shoes away as part of the fare to take the ferry from Grand Bassa. This Bible was on top of my bed in full view. I guess my thief had already fulfilled his spiritual needs," I said glumly.

"My poor fellow," she said. "I'm so sorry for you. What an awful city, Dakar. Very unsafe. You should never visit there again."

She stood up with arms akimbo. "I have some personal things I can give you," she said, musing, "soap and linens, but clothes?" She stopped in mid-sentence to ponder. "I'll speak with Francis. Perhaps I could alter a pair of his trousers," she said speaking to herself. "Oh, he has gotten so fat lately, and you, you're so thin. It would be quite a task!"

"I don't mean to be a bother," I said. "Perhaps Father Stivonovich might be able to help me."

A large bearded man wearing a Roman collar walked in from the back of the room.

"Francis!" Margaret exclaimed, "You startled me!" Margaret quickly regained her composure, leading the large man by the forearm to me. He looked to be in his early to mid-fifties. His beard was full, unkempt, with strong streaks of gray. She introduced us. He was Father Francis Tannen.

The sturdy, muscular priest shook my hand perfunctorily. His large right hand engulfed mine.

"What brings you to the Mecca of West Africa, Eugene?"

"I've come to work with Father Stivonovich, Father."

Father Tannen laughed rather crazily, I thought, and looked directly at Margaret. "Isn't John something else? He jumps ship but still has the reserves coming." His large black eyes bounced back to me. "I suppose you've come to serve as a missionary to the Tambe?"

"Yes, Father," I said. "Of course, I know I'll need to learn Krio first, but I'm committed to the project."

The priest frowned. "At this point you had better study Arabic," he stated in a surly tone. He looked back at Margaret and smiled. "So you haven't told him yet?"

Margaret hesitated. "Eugene has just arrived, Francis. He has come all the way from the States and he's had a terrible time. All his possessions were stolen in Dakar."

Tannen said nothing but grabbed a scone from the dish and spoke to Margaret as if I wasn't even in the room. "At least he's not as young as that last one. Christ Jesus! John must have been recruiting high school boys!"

Tannen took a large bite from the scone and walked away. He turned his head, shouting over his right shoulder. "How long do you think you'll stay, young man?" The priest bounded to the back door and again threw his head back over his shoulder and laughed. "I'd give you no more than two weeks!"

Margaret's eyes followed the priest out of the door and then she turned to me. "Please don't mind Francis," she said. "He doesn't mean half the things he says."

I sensed that Margaret anticipated my curiosity, but tried to thwart it by announcing that tea was ready. She rushed over to retrieve cups and saucers.

Margaret told me that she was from Dublin and asked me about my ancestry. We both had a second cup of tea and then Margaret led me to a small adjacent room and provided me with a hand basin, a pitcher of water, sweet smelling soap, and a hand towel. She left the small enclosed room. I removed my shirt. I could smell the rank odor of my underarms and the sweat that permeated my garment.

After I had finished my sponge bath, with distaste I put back on my badly soiled shirt. I entered the main room. It was open to the outdoors, where window blinds made of reed were raised inviting early evening breezes to blow freely throughout the thatched house. Birds whistled and crooned and I walked to the edge of the room to look outside. I smelled a sweet aroma, a scent of cinnamon or persimmon.

There was a small thatched building next to us, the only building other than the house we were in larger than a hut. Would this be where I would be working? Perhaps I would be meeting with the Tambe in their huts, I thought. Although I had been brought up in a fundamentalist Christian church, I had come for many reasons, though I wouldn't be telling Margaret Mahoney or anyone else there in the village about this. Rather, I saw this as an opportunity to come to terms with my own faith. And this new place, with this charming woman and natives hungry for spiritual direction, had my mind teeming with possibilities. Father Stivonovich had assured me in his letters that I could quickly learn the language of the Tambe as it was a mixture of English, French, and tribal words. Just as I sat back into my chair, Margaret reappeared through the back entrance.

"I know the trousers are much too large," she said as she held up a pair of khaki pants, "but please try on this shirt. It's the smallest I could find in Francis's closet."

She flung a cotton shirt at me with a laugh. I removed my soiled shirt and slipped my arms into the borrowed garment. "If you tuck it in, I think it will look quite handsome on you, Gene," she said.

Although I swam in the large shirt, Margaret appeared quite happy with her find. She walked backward across the room looking at me until she stepped into a solid object.

"Francis!" she exclaimed, turning around. "I thought you had left."

The priest, having entered through the back door without either of us noticing, growled. "I wanted you to know that I'm having dinner tonight with Chief Faramha. There's no need to prepare anything for me. I'll be out late. I'll meet up with you in the morning."

Father Tannen went to exit when he stopped, turned around and snatched the trousers draped across a chair and threw them down again. He glanced at me, obviously noticing that I had on his shirt. The priest snarled at Margaret. "I would appreciate it if you didn't loan out my possessions." He didn't wait for an explanation but trounced out of the room, slamming the thatched door behind him.

Margaret's face became glum.

"Perhaps I should take off Father Tannen's shirt," I offered.

"Of course not!" Margaret answered. "Francis has more shirts than he can possibly ever wear. He's just being selfish and obstinate."

"I hope Father Tannen didn't taken offense," I said.

"Oh, I'm sure he did!" Margaret retorted. "Francis takes offense with most everything and with most everybody!" She curled her lower lip like a chastised child and then exclaimed. "I'm glad he has gone to be with that old chief. Now we can have supper together. You can tell me all about yourself, Gene! You can tell me about everything! We get so little news here in Burguna."

"But what about Father Stivonovich?" I asked. "Where is he? What did Father Tannen mean about Father Stivonovich *jumping ship?*"

Margaret began to clear the table. She covered the dish of scones with the cheesecloth and placed it back into the rough looking wooden cupboard. She then began humming the first few bars of an Irish ditty. All of a sudden, her humming stopped and she sat down beside me in the chair she had previously pulled up next to mine. Sadness returned to Margaret's face and she sighed deeply.

"Eugene," she said in a soft, gentle voice, "five weeks ago Father Stivonovich left Burguna." Margaret's voice lowered. "John was extremely discouraged about his work with the Tambe and upset with Francis, perhaps with me. Who knows what or who else."

"But where did he go?" I exclaimed.

Margaret clasped her hands together. "We don't know where Father Stivonovich is. One of the villagers told Francis that the night John left, he said he was going to Nigeria." Margaret flailed her arms and began sobbing. "But nobody knows for sure. He just left in the middle of the night—didn't say a word to either Francis or me. He gave away his personal belongings to some villagers and just left."

The more that Margaret explained, the higher pitched her voice became. "Eugene, you've walked into a mess. John could be dead for all we know!" she exclaimed. "There is no easy transport out of Cape de Leone. This is not a forgiving country!"

Margaret's voice turned to anger. "For him to just leave was so inconsiderate and irresponsible. I've been worried sick about him for five weeks and not a word. We keep thinking that he'll return, that he will come to his senses."

I was shocked. I had corresponded regularly with Father Stivonovich for nearly a year in anticipation of coming to Burguna. Now my host had vanished. Margaret took my hand.

"John was so excited last May, Gene, when you wrote to him and said that you had finally decided to come." The corners of her mouth twitched and they began to form a smile. "He started making plans for you to learn Krio. He even had some of the villagers build a hut for you. When John unexpectedly left, I waited a fortnight to write you, thinking that he might return any day. But when he didn't come back, I explained in the letter what had happened, but you obviously didn't receive it."

"But what caused Father Stivonovich to be so upset that he would leave?" I pleaded. "Why now?"

Margaret looked down at the floor. Her expression turned colorless and cold. "Gene, the Tambe have turned from Christ and gone Muslim," she said. "The Chief has forbidden us to hold any Christian services or to even speak about Christ."

> "Gene, the Tambe have turned from Christ and gone Muslim," she said. "The Chief has forbidden us to hold any Christian services or to even speak about Christ."

With those words, Margaret rose and went back to the kitchen. I sat stunned, unable to initiate any sort of conversation. After Margaret had set the table and garnished it with wild African flowers, she invited me to retake my seat.

That evening, during a leisurely but joyless meal, I began to learn the story about Father John Stivonovich, Margaret Mahoney, and Father Francis Tannen, at least as Margaret wished to tell it.

According to Margaret, John Stivonovich had grown up in Poland, but because of the political and social turmoil that beset his native country he immigrated to the United States in the late 1930s. In the U.S., Stivonovich studied at a seminary in New York. He and Margaret, who had left Dublin at about this time, met at the Catholic Worker, a relief house, in New York City. They became close friends. Stivonovich then joined the order of the Society of Jesus (Jesuits) and served as a young teacher at a Jesuit school on the lower East side of Manhattan. Margaret continued to volunteer at the Catholic Worker.

The later years of the great depression placed a great strain on the resources of the charitable organization. "It was not just the poor souls who never had anything that lined up at our soup kitchen," Margaret said.

"We served meals and provided clothing and shelter to people who had lost good jobs, who had dignity. But by coming to our relief house and taking our handouts they thought they had lost it. I saw it in their eyes. I had experienced just as bad of times in my home country, but the Irish people take poverty much better. You Americans are so proud," she observed, "so dependent upon your possessions for your character."

After a few years on Manhattan's lower East side, Stivonovich left New York to take on the priesthood of a parish post in southern Louisiana. He and Margaret corresponded regularly. He described to her in letters, she recalled, how slowly his parishioners talked and how far removed they seemed from the New York poor they both served.

Though she had hoped to visit Father Stivonovich in Louisiana, he left to enter missionary work in West Africa. He had chosen a small village in southeastern Cape de Leone, she said, because he had become acquainted with the Creole people of southern Louisiana. Many of the Creoles had distant ancestral relatives who had returned to West Africa after the abolition of slavery in the United States in the 1860s, settling in the recently formed nation of Liberia. A smaller number of Creole speaking natives located north of Liberia in Cape de Leone. The small West African coastal country had once been claimed by the Portuguese but was then a British protectorate. These Creoles had interestingly assimilated with an indigenous tribe named the "Tambe." They intermarried and lived in a small village in the African bush named "Burguna." They had lived in near isolation there ever since.

That had been six years before. Father Stivonovich had lived in Burguna since that time, that is, up to five weeks ago when he mysteriously disappeared one night after telling only a few of the villagers about his departure.

Father Stivonovich's devotion to the Tambe went beyond his daily prayers that the tribe members would embrace Christ and convert to Christianity. The tribe's own beliefs and form of worship had been an amalgam of several West African spiritual practices, a form of animism, the worship and belief of spirits in plants and animals. Margaret conveyed, often times in near tears, how much energy and devotion Father Stivonovich had poured into the Tambe people. But all of his efforts had obviously ended in failure. Allah had moved in to supersede the God of Abraham.

What I began to learn that night from Margaret told me a great deal about her and the strange and uncertain world I had entered. It was a world where all the country's former institutions and beliefs—political, social, economic, and spiritual—were thrown into turmoil. I had left my small, parochial town in eastern Indiana and had walked into a swirling and bubbling witch's brew. The turmoil had begun with the demise of colonialism after World War II and continued with the sweeping of Islam across this isolated, hostile, and backwater nation called "Cape de Leone."

Margaret explained that the Muslim presence in West Africa

had been sporadic for centuries, dating all the way back to the 1300s. Various tribes had converted to the faith through assimilation or, more likely, through forceful conversion by conquering Muslim tribes from Upper and Middle Niger. In recent decades, a tribe's conversion to another faith had been a "voluntary act" determined solely by the tribal chief.

Father Stivonovich's years of proselytizing in the name of Christ had been overcome by the Tambe's greater commercial contacts through trade with the Muslim world. The Polish Jesuit priest had taught the Tambe love, mercy, tolerance, and restraint in seeking material comforts of this world, while shrewd Muslim traders had brought to the villagers exquisite fineries from the Islamic Sahara.

Chief Faramha made the decision to follow Allah. He was not a bad chief, but simply a very practical man. Trade with the Islamic merchants, Margaret explained, would benefit both his people and himself. Moreover, Chief Faramha had four wives. Christianity meant monogamy, the adoption of which would result in a loss of face and status to the chief. Islamic conversion avoided these problems.

Margaret had talked that evening almost non-stop. She tried to convey information that she had written in the letter that never reached me. We had completed supper—a meal in which ostrich meat, a delicacy, was served—more than two hours before. We were still sitting at the small table covered by a linen table cloth with a fancy floral design. Tall candles on the dinner table provided us with light as melted wax dripped from their stems, forming miniature icicles.

I sensed that what Margaret had told me had been cathartic. Her concerns and worries had been throbbing to be released. Still, I became even more intrigued by Father Francis Tannen. She had said next to nothing about the surly priest and I thought, *What is his role in all of this? Why did Father Tannen not leave as Father Stivonovich had done? What kind of relationship did Margaret and Father Tannen share?*

"But why did Father Tannen have dinner this evening with Chief Faramha?" I finally asked. "Is he trying to convince the Chief that he made a wrong decision when he converted the tribe to Islam?"

Margaret had become lightheaded from all the wine she had drank. "Heavens no!" she exclaimed. "Francis was delighted with the chief's decision. He doesn't now have to maintain the pretense of being a priest." A coy grin emanated from Margaret's lips. "I'm sure that Francis has gone to see Chief Faramha on matters of a more practical nature."

Margaret removed my plate and returned to the table with another opened bottle of red wine. She was no longer in a state of despair, but outright giddy. "You need to have some vino, Gene. Tonight we celebrate your arrival!"

Five

S trangely, it wasn't until Margaret stood over me with the carafe of Sauvignon in her hands that I fully realized how beautiful she was. She had an angular face with high cheek bones, a fair complexion without wrinkles, and eyes full of expression. Her hair was dark brown and she had it pinned up in a bun from which it seemed to be struggling to escape. It was impossible for me to guess how old she was. She could have been thirty-five, forty, perhaps even forty-five. What she went on to say about her life really didn't give me a clue as to her age.

I declined her offer of wine and gently shoved the dinner plate to the center of the table, sitting back in my seat. I asked her about Father Tannen.

Margaret sat back down, poured her tumbler full to the brim, and looked into the glass of red wine. She rolled the stem of her tumbler slowly between her fingers.

"I was already at the Catholic Worker in New York when I met Francis," Margaret said. "Maybe you couldn't tell from his accent, but he's Australian. Francis was raised on a sheep ranch in New South Wales. At the time we met, Francis had already been a priest for several years. He had done his scholastic studies to be a Jesuit at a seminary in California."

Margaret sipped slowly from the tumbler. "I didn't know it before, but Jesuitical studies leading up to ordination takes years of training in theology and philosophy. After his studies, Francis performed some social work in various parishes, but he failed miserably. He'll admit himself that he's not suited to do parish work. As you'll find, he's too high strung, too impatient and intellectual.

"When I first met Francis," Margaret continued, "he was a member of the faculty of the philosophy department at Fordham University. He was teaching a class on the medieval theologian and philosopher Thomas Aquinas. I had been introduced to Aquinas' philosophy as a student in Ireland."

Margaret sat back and rolled her eyes, reminiscencing. "Francis was so handsome, so erudite and witty. None of the women in class could understand why he was a priest." She sighed. "It's just terrible how he has let himself go."

Margaret went on to explain that after only three years of teaching at Fordham, Tannen left to become principal of Ignatius High School in Brooklyn. Before this Margaret had befriended the priest by becoming part of a small circle of devoted students who met regularly with him to discuss ethics. She had also invited him to the Catholic Worker on several occasions and later arranged for him to live in an apartment away from where the other Jesuit faculty members lived. Tannen had detested the priests' cliquishness. He was critical of the Jesuits' high ideal of living together in "spiritual community." In fact, he claimed all the priests did were survive in an insular existence and drink themselves into greater solitude.

"Poor Francis," Margaret said, her voice slightly slurred. "His tenure at Ignatius High School only lasted about as long as his time at Fordham. He told everyone that he had resigned as principal to return to his scholarship, but I know that the school had asked him to leave. This was four years ago. He didn't know what to do. I had written to John Stivonovich about this time. John was then here in Burguna, as a missionary priest to the Tambe. It was his suggestion that Francis start a school in Burguna. He thought that it could serve as a model for other Jesuit schools in West Africa. When I mentioned it to Francis, I was wildly surprised that he liked the idea," Margaret added.

She went on to explain that she had accompanied Father Tannen to Burguna with the understanding that once the school was in operation she would return to the States. But that had been four years before. Since then, nothing had been mentioned about her leaving. Margaret had taken over nearly the complete administration of the school. Francis Tannen was in charge only in name.

All of this was very interesting, but my own career as a missionary had been closed before I even had a chance to begin. I stopped Margaret's story when she paused to take a sip of her wine.

"But what am I to do now?" I asked.

"It's much too soon to try and talk with the Tambe," Margaret replied. "Perhaps Chief Faramha will change his mind, but John didn't think he would. John was convinced that the Muslim leaders in this part of the country won't let that happen. I know that is one reason why John became so discouraged. He thought it could be years before we would have another chance to approach the Tambe."

I didn't know what to say. I couldn't go home. My small town had treated me like Dr. Livingston for my decision to serve in West Africa. How could I possibly return and confess that I had failed to convert even one African soul to the Kingdom of Christ? How would my family and friends in Lisbon believe this incredible story? Besides, all my money, with nearly all my possessions, had been stolen in Senegal.

"Don't be in despair, Gene. You can teach at the school," Margaret proclaimed, as though she had long before reached this conclusion. "We have many more students than the three of us who teach can possibly handle."

"But I have no credentials," I said.

Margaret wrinkled her lips. "Can you read and write and do simple math?"

"Yes, of course."

"Then you can start tomorrow."

Margaret obviously noticed my apprehension. "It will work out, Gene. Maybe this is a different plan than what you expected, but this may well be God's plan for you."

I was still not convinced and my skepticism must have appeared on my face. "You must have faith, Gene," Margaret insisted. "It will work out!"

"Professor O'Connor," Reuben said, nudging me from my reverie, "would you care for coffee?"

The airline attendant stood next to me patiently and smiling. I thought a cup might give me some energy and nodded. The captain announced over the intercom that we would be arriving at the John F. Kennedy International Airport in less than twenty minutes. We were 30,000 feet above northeastern Pennsylvania and at the start of our descent. I was lost as to the time, only knowing that the first leg of our journey had gone by very quickly.

Six

A fter circling New York City several times waiting to land, we finally touched ground at about 8:30 p.m. We taxied to the domestic terminal and obtained our luggage. Reuben and I had to carry it to an adjacent terminal building where all international departures left. Our flight to Paris didn't leave until 11:00 p.m., so we decided to catch a late dinner at a restaurant called the Skyline Club.

We were quickly served. Reuben sighed as he looked over his plate of halibut and parsley potatoes. He lowered his chin onto the palm of his right hand. "Are you anxious about returning to Cape de Leone, Professor?"

"I never planned to return," I replied. "I'm afraid the memories of what Mubarsoi did to the country when I lived there in the fifties are not pleasant."

"What do you think creates a dictator like Albert Mubarsoi?" Reuben asked. "Surely you must have come across dozens of tyrants like him in all the years you served as a foreign correspondent."

It was true, I had reported on coup d'etats and despots from Cuba's Fidel Castro in the early sixties to Pol Pot in Cambodia in the mid-eighties, a span of twenty-five years. Each investigation had given me a greater appreciation for man's primeval ability to destroy life in pursuit of his own goals to dominate.

"I suppose the common factor is the desire to have absolute power over others," I finally said. "That and the fact that evil exists."

"I think it all goes back to childhood," Reuben responded,

obviously having made up his mind long before he ever asked me the question. "Look at Hitler, Stalin, Mao. They all had disturbed childhoods. Freud hit upon it best after all."

I felt argumentative. "How does a disturbed childhood fully explain the evil of these men?" I said. "You can't explain away such depravity by simply attributing it to their upbringing—their toilet training or parental strict discipline. No," I said emphatically. "Evil is more fundamental than this. I think I can partially understand a Hitler or a Stalin, dictators who persecuted anonymous millions because it furthered their own megalomaniac grip on power. But tell me, Mr. Reuben, how do you explain the Nazi doctors who took the Hippocratic oath to preserve life and then destroyed it in the death camps? How do you rationalize the actions of a mother who neglects and abuses her own baby, a child she's brought into the world? That kind of evil I'll never understand!"

On another occasion I would have enjoyed the pseudo-psychological exploration of what creates a Hitler or even a small-time despot such as Albert Mubarsoi, but tonight was not the time. I yawned and stretched before placing my knife and fork on the plate of untouched food. I couldn't eat. I couldn't carry on a conversation. I felt sick to my stomach.

"I'm sorry if I've upset you, Professor," Reuben said.

"I know I'm irritable, Mr. Reuben. I apologize, but I've been yanked from my duties at the university and experienced the unexpected death of my goddaughter and here we are talking about Freud. What I really want to know about is your Aunt Margaret. How did she suddenly just pop up into my life again and I not know about her before now?"

"There's quite a bit to that story and I'm tired, too. We both need to get some rest. Besides, I need to make a telephone call. I'll be back in a few minutes."

I felt like punching Reuben in the face, but there was another side to his refusal to talk to me in detail about Margaret. It pushed me further to the brink of excitement, heightened the mystery.

Was I anxious to be returning to Cape de Leone? Yes, extremely so. There was still a deep feeling of fear emanating from the terror I had experienced before my expulsion thirty years before. And then there was the fear of how I would be received into the country now, even though three decades had passed. And, of course, there was the matter of Elizabeth and Irene Brownlie. I tried to push these thoughts to the back of my mind, but like a child who'd been put in his room to "think things over," the anxious feelings kept coming back. Mixed with these emotions were ones of tremendous warmth and adventure, the kind I had first felt after I had met Margaret and before I almost lost my life.

My first night in Burguna, after I had dinner with Margaret and she had explained about the Tambe converting to Islam, she took me to a small hut that some of the village men had built for me. We each carried a kerosene lantern. During the short walk and in the midst of nearly complete darkness, I remember falling into a large mud hole. My right leg got stuck in muck up past the knee. Margaret laughed herself half-silly as I tugged and grunted.

I had endured so much anxiety and hardship on the trip that the filthy mishap barely phased me. I extricated my leg from the hole and followed Margaret straight to the hut. She continued to laugh, finding everything we did funny. Margaret asked for my trousers to wash for me in the morning and left.

That night I slept on a stuffed mat made out of thatch, the same material that was used for the hut's roof. Protective mosquito netting, hung from short poles, formed a tent around my bed.

The following morning I was awakened by birds that were cawing and clattering in a palm tree outside my small hut. There was a sweet scent of something burning, like incense. A large insect which looked something like a praying mantis crawled across the mud floor. A pair of trousers lay on top of a bamboo chair. They were Father Tannen's pants, the ones that Margaret had showed me the evening before. Remembering the priest's nasty remarks the previous day, I cringed at the thought of wearing them, but they were the only trousers I had to put on.

Emerging from the hut, I observed the beauty of the surroundings and they overwhelmed me. Palm trees, ferns, and vines were extremely green, lush, and thick, truly a tropical forest. The rains of August, September, and October had been extremely plentiful.

I walked about one hundred yards east of my hut along a path that led to a cleared area of tilled fields. Women with small children sat on wooden stools behind small vertical shields made of sticks and large palm leaves. *What were they doing?* Soon large black birds descended onto the fields. The women stood up and threw stones and shouted at the birds to keep them from feeding on the seeded corn. The small children mimicked their mothers.

When I returned to my hut, Margaret stood waiting outside. She greeted me with the same endearing smile and good humor as when she had left me the night before. We greeted each other and I asked, "Why is everyone up so early?"

"To avoid the heat," she said, looking down the path toward the opening to the fields. "It becomes intolerable by mid-day. You'll see." Margaret smiled. "Would you join me for breakfast, Gene?"

After I nodded, Margaret looked down at my legs. "I altered the trousers this morning. I do hope they fit."

"Are you sure it is all right for me to wear them?"

"Don't worry about Francis if that's what you're concerned about," Margaret answered. "I've already spoken with him," she added. "His pants were much too small in the waist for him even before I took them in. Besides, your trousers need a more thorough washing before they're fit to wear again."

We started to walk the short path to Margaret's house. Then suddenly she turned and pointed at a small mud building about fifty feet from my hut. "It's a proper privy by Burguna standards, Gene," she said. "I'll make sure that Samuel Obei, who oversees the house, has a servant boy bring you fresh water each morning. Today you can wash up at my place."

I followed Margaret across the southern edge of the village, being stared at by a few dozen barely dressed villagers. I had suddenly become very conscious of being in full view of so many black-skinned natives, strangers who obviously were as curious about me as I was of them. *My God, what have I gotten myself into?* I wondered.

Breakfast consisted of fried rice patties, dry bread with butter, bean curd, left over ostrich meat from the evening before and, of course, tea. Spiced tea, I discovered, was served with every meal. It was the last vestige of Irish civilization that Margaret refused to deny her guests or herself.

She apologized for not having eggs and sausage, which she was sure I was accustomed to coming from a Midwest farm in the States. I gathered from her remarks that eggs and meat were difficult to obtain and that ostrich meat was a true delicacy reserved for special occasions.

Margaret's hospitality and kindness were already evident. As I became better acquainted with her, I kept searching for a motive behind her generosity and the attention she showered upon me. I believe I finally found it when I fully understood her desire to experience companionship. She longed for intimacy, not physical intimacy but a personal attachment of an emotional kind I hadn't experienced myself until I met her.

At my first morning at school, Margaret began the day by having one of the village women lead the children in singing. The songs were melodic and rich with beat and harmony. She then introduced me.

"Children," she announced. "I want you to greet Mister Eugene O'Connor. From now on, he will assist in your instruction."

The students looked puzzled. Several attempted to say my name and failed miserably. All of them were under the age of twelve. The building simply was not large enough to accommodate a greater number of students, so twelve was the arbitrary cut off age. Margaret spoke to the children in a dialect of Krio that was unique to the tribe, but repeated herself in English.

As the weeks passed, I observed Margaret and the other two teachers, Falaba Cardew and Marabella Farbuto, and assisted wherever I could. Falaba and Marabella appeared to be in their early twenties, but then I found that nearly all West African women look much younger than they really are. Marabella had been raised in Burguna, but she had received additional education in Grand Bassa as a teenage girl. The three women, especially Margaret, were insistent that I begin teaching immediately and not be merely a by-stander. They would translate what I said and then repeat the Krio words back to me so that I might learn the village dialect more quickly.

The students of St. Magdalene numbered approximately 150. They were divided up into three divisions of approximately forty-five to fifty pupils so that each group received at least two hours of instruction daily. The small building could only accommodate fifty students at any one time and these students were divided up into even smaller groups. Margaret would teach language and spelling, while I worked with Marabella on instructing the children in basic math. Falaba taught writing. The facility was extremely meager in terms of what it offered. But the children were eager students and even the worst of conditions are tolerable where the will to learn is great.

To comply with Chief Faramha's orders, we stopped school during the day while prayers to Mecca were offered. The children unrolled their rugs, kneeled, faced east, and prayed to Allah on the command of the muezzin. This was all done in synchronicity with prayers that were offered in the village at large.

Nearly all of the teaching took place in the building that I had originally mistaken as a Christian chapel. But the building was much more, serving as the location for other important village activities: as a makeshift hospital; as a meeting house for local tribal functions, such as when the elders met with Chief Faramha; as a school room where Margaret conducted classes in the evenings for the Tambe women on everything from simple hygiene, to cooking, arts and crafts, and child birth. It was also used daily as a meeting place for the men of the tribe to receive lessons about the Koran in Arabic. Whatever purpose was most pressing got the use of the building because it was the only structure in the entire village other than Margaret's house that was larger than a family's hut.

Every second Monday we vacated the building and taught the children underneath the shade of a small grove of palm trees. On those days a British physician came to Burguna to use the central building. He would treat the villagers for their on-going infections and illnesses. This isolated African community was bereft of even the most basic medicines. The physician's name was Justin Perry, employed by the British government to travel from village to village in southeastern Cape de Leone.

Perry could only see those who were most seriously ill (or at least that is how it seemed patients were selected); the others would be told to come back in two weeks if they were not better. Occasionally he would give them innocuous-looking medicine that appeared to be nothing more than sugar pills. Perry was not, interestingly enough, in competition with the tribal village doctor, someone whom we would call a "witch doctor." Rather, villagers would simply go to both medicine men. The Tambe called Perry *Halemoi*, which means "medicine man" in the language of the Mende, a tribe located nearby.

Perry seemed knowledgeable, but he, like Tannen, was clearly a mysterious character. Why or how he came to Cape de Leone from having done formal training at London's St. Cross Hospital was never quite clear. He was a cordial enough chap, whenever we sat down to talk. But he was also the type of man who expected to get something out of every encounter he had. This aspect of his personality seemed so at odds with his career choice.

Often Perry seemed too willing to accept the villagers' attitude that "God must will it" if they were suddenly struck with illness. The health problems of the Tambe were not inconsequential. They ran the gamut from malaria, yellow fever, cholera and typhoid to tumors, lesions, and more exotic but not-as-yet diagnosed skin rashes. Dysentery, as well, was rampant, especially among the children, whose intestinal tract, like my own, had not yet acquired immunity to the various organisms that always found their way into the drinking water. There was little that could be done to avoid them, except possibly for the malaria. I was sick on several occasions during my first year in Burguna. But it was not until my first brush with a near-death illness that I learned personally about the mysterious Dr. Justin Perry.

Seven

While I waited on Reuben to return from making his telephone call, I sat in the Skyline Club and thought about how my first encountered took place with Dr. Perry. The illness I suffered still brought shivers to me.

At the end of my first week in Burguna, a hot, blistering sun woke me one morning. I gasped for air and the sensation of suffocation overwhelmed me. Mosquito netting, hung from poles over my bed, had fallen on top of me. The netting clung to me like barnacles on a ship's hull. When I tried to swallow, I started to lose my breath again. I spit out what little saliva I had in me. Thick spital caught on the netting and coagulated into globules. I tried to roll from the mattress, but I couldn't free myself from the netting. I panicked when suddenly Samuel Obei, Margaret's main servant, came to the hut's entrance.

"Mr. O'Connor!" Samuel exclaimed. He ran to me and began to unravel the mosquito netting.

"Get Margaret!" I groaned.

Samuel dashed from the hut. I tried to move again, but I had no feeling below my waist. I looked down and saw the matting and my pants soaked with sweat, urine, and excrement.

Margaret rushed in and Samuel followed her. She had her hands cupped, still holding chalk and a black board eraser.

"What's wrong, Gene?" She put the back of her right hand against my forehead. "My God, you're burning up!" Margaret unbuttoned my night shirt and yelled at Samuel to get fresh water.

"I thought something was wrong when you didn't show up for school this morning," she said. She lifted my head up into her lap and supported it with a pillow I had next to the mattress. "I should have sent Samuel for you sooner!"

Margaret could apparently tell that I was having difficulty breathing. She tried to lift the upper half of my body, but I was too heavy. A large figure came into the hut.

"What's wrong with him?"

Margaret moved slightly to the side. It was Father Tannen.

"It may be yellow fever," Margaret replied. She pulled up my eye lids and came within inches of my face. "Francis, Gene's eyes and skin are terribly jaundiced and he's breathing heavy."

"He was all right last evening, wasn't he?" said Tannen. "It's come on him awfully fast for yellow fever." Tannen knelt down. "Open up your mouth, Eugene," he commanded. "Wider!"

Father Tannen took his index and middle fingers of his right hand and probed into my mouth and throat. He removed his hand, wiping thick spittle across his shirt. "Eugene's throat is nearly closed. Help me lift him up."

Samuel ran in with a basin of water and knelt beside the bed. Margaret ripped one of my borrowed shirts in two and took the larger half, dipped it into the water and began to sponge me off.

"We can't give Gene anything to drink," I heard Margaret say. "But look at him! He's so depleted!"

"Samuel," Tannen called. "Dr. Perry is working in Madadi today. Go and bring him back here immediately."

Samuel nodded. Tannen rose, took some paper from the desk and scribbled something on it. He folded and handed the paper to Samuel. "Give this to Dr. Perry. He must come as soon as you reach Madadi. Don't return without him!"

Samuel scurried out of the hut. Margaret sponged me off again. "I must tell Falaba and Marabella I can't teach today," she said.

"No, stay here," replied Tannen. He put his hand on Margaret's left shoulder to keep her from rising. "I'll inform them."

"Tell them not to say anything to the children," Margaret said over her shoulder. "They'll only worry."

Tannen exited and Margaret wiped the perspiration from my face and upper body. I was numb and couldn't feel any aching or cramping; that would come later. The only sensation I had was of intense heat. My skin burned; I felt on fire. Margaret poured water from a pitcher on my forehead. The water drenched and drained down over my shoulders and to my underwear. I had no memory of it at the time, but Margaret had removed my sleeping trousers and I was left in my soaked, smelly under shorts. I couldn't understand what I had done to deserve such humiliation. These were the last thoughts I had before I heard loud voices several hours later.

It was dark now but the numbness still remained in my legs and, to a lesser degree, upper body. Margaret told me later that I had slipped in and out of consciousness all day. Suddenly, I remember hearing voices outside my hut, one of them was Father Tannen's.

"You son-of-a-bitch, where have you been? Why did you refuse to return with Samuel?"

"I'm here, aren't I?" said another man's voice. "I had twenty sick Mende waiting to see me. Many were nearly as ill, no doubt, as your Mr. O'Connor."

"But Samuel gave you the note, didn't he?" asked Tannen. "The man could have died. His throat is almost entirely closed. Margaret has been with him all day just to make sure he didn't stop breathing. What was it—money? You didn't come because you might miss a day of Mende bribes?"

There was more talk, but it was muffled and all I could hear was an angry exchange. The voices stopped and a large man carrying a dark leather bag entered.

"Thank God you're here, Justin," said Margaret. "Gene's temperature has been above a 103 all day long. Could it be yellow fever?"

I started to chill and Margaret, seeing my shivering, quickly covered me with a light blanket. Justin Perry just as quickly yanked the blanket off and began to push around my abdomen, lower groin, and legs.

"Yellow fever doesn't produce paralysis." Perry checked me all over again. "Has he been taking quinine daily?"

"Yes, as far as I know," said Margaret. "We've talked about it when he first came."

"What about boiling his food and water?"

"Yes, of course," Margaret replied. "I mean I've not been with Gene every time he's eaten, but he knows he has to."

Perry stood up. The doctor looked huge and demonic from my vulnerable position. "He's terribly dehydrated. We have to get fluids in him some way, but I'm afraid he'll choke if we try to make him drink anything. I don't have an intravenous unit with me. We'd have to take him back to Grand Bassa to get one. There's no way he would last that long, even if we left first thing in the morning."

"Eugene!" Dr. Perry shouted in my face. "Do you think you could drink some water?"

I nodded out of sheer panic.

Dr. Perry poured water from the pitcher into an opaque ceramic mug. Margaret held my head up. I tried to drink from the mug, but it was no use. As soon as I attempted to swallow, the water came up out of my nose. It was a terrible sensation, like what a drowning person must experience.

Margaret wiped my mouth and perspiring forehead, her right hand and upper body supporting my head and torso. She was trying to keep me upright but she had to be tiring. Dr. Perry stepped away, exiting the hut. Tannen followed him while Margaret started to rock me as if I was a small child.

"If we don't get some fluids in him tonight, I'm afraid his kidneys and heart won't last until morning," I heard Perry say from outside.

"Gene, you must drink something," Margaret said. Her fingers brushed against my forehead and hair again. She lifted the mug and I began to sip, but it was useless. The water exploded out of my nose and my insides felt like they were coming out. Margaret inadvertently dropped the mug on my chest and the water ran down me making me colder. She sponged me off and then she began to rock me in her arms, but I don't remember anything else that happened that night.

Reuben placed his hand on my shoulder.

"Please excuse my delay in getting back with you, Professor. I have a sick wife whom I had to telephone," Reuben said. "I wanted to call to see how she's doing before our departure. It's not yet 6:00 o'clock in the morning at home."

"Is she better, Mr. Reuben?" I asked. I remembered what Bob Zimmer had told me had happened to Reuben's wife. He must have remarried.

"Yes, much better, thank you. I was very concerned about her a couple of days ago before I left for the States."

Reuben smiled and glanced at his watch, announcing that it was time for us to head for our gate.

"Mr. Reuben, I need to call Bloomington first and see if there's any news about my goddaughter."

I excused myself and went to the nearest pay phone. Donna Pauley answered, taking my collect call.

"Donna, I'm just getting ready to leave New York for Paris. Have you heard anything about Elizabeth?"

Donna hesitated and then addressed me by my first name, something she had never done before.

"Gene, the autopsy came back on Elizabeth this evening." Donna's voice started quivering. "The coroner concluded that Elizabeth's neck was broken before she ever fell from the top of Eigenman Hall. In fact, they don't believe she fell at all. They're now treating her case as a homicide."

Donna also reported that Lieutenant Peterson and two investigators from the Indiana State Police Department were looking for me. The two state investigators visited her at her house that evening. They said that they knew I had left the country with Reuben.

"Did you tell them where I was going?"

"No, Professor. I acted dumb, like you leaving with Mr. Reuben was news to me. But I think they could tell I was trying to cover for you. I'm sorry. I didn't know how else to handle it. They started asking personal questions about Elizabeth and you."

"Like what?"

"They wanted to know if you two had ever shown a fondness for each other in the office, things like that."

I suddenly felt nauseated, angry, numb, and dumbfounded all at once. And then, thinking that my heart couldn't sink any lower, I heard the next words from Donna.

"Professor, Irene Brownlie called this evening, just before the police came by. She learned about Elizabeth's death when her friend contacted her office in Lisbon. Irene left northern Michigan this afternoon and she and her friend are driving straight through until they reach Bloomington. They should be here sometime early tomorrow morning."

"How did Irene sound?"

"Pretty much hysterical, Professor. She wouldn't listen to anything I said. She really, really wants to talk with you."

"Donna, did you read her the note I left with you?"

"Yes, of course, but I'm not sure how much of it Irene heard. She was crying most of the time."

"If she calls again tell her I'll be back. Donna, I need to ask one more favor. Please call Bob Zimmer at home. I don't know his number, but you can find it in the telephone directory under his wife's name—Grace. Please get a hold of Bob and ask him to find out anything he can about Nigel Reuben. Tell him to call his national media friends if he has to, but I need to know everything he can possibly get his hands on about this man. Also, can you get me Bob's number so I can call him when I arrive in Paris?"

Donna got me the number and promised to follow through. I hung up with an empty, nauseous feeling at the pit of my stomach. When I returned to the restaurant, Reuben was waiting. He had already paid the check for our dinner, most of which was left uneaten.

As we walked down the modern-looking terminal to board our flight for Paris, my mind drifted back to Burguna, back to that time I had become deathly sick and cared for by Margaret. All of a sudden I began to hear the loud cry of the muezzin, the prayer of the Azan:

"Allahu Akbar!" ("Allah is Most Great!")

The muezzin called still louder.

"Ash-hadu an la ill-Allah" ("I bear witness that there is none worthy of being worshipped except Allah.")

"Allahu Akbar!"

Wakened to my senses by the tribal prayers, I realized that I was in Margaret's bedroom. The sun peeked through the thatched house's east window. Samuel Obei was at my feet, stretched out perpendicular and asleep at the base of the bed. Margaret was asleep as well. She lay next to me, her head resting upon a lace-covered pillow.

As I learned later, the night before, after I had slipped out of consciousness, Tannen and Perry had carried me to Margaret's bedroom. She and Samuel had taken turns watching over me during the night to ensure that I kept breathing. Now both laid asleep, oblivious to my attempted movements and to the morning Islamic prayers chanted in unison in the village center.

I still had little control over my legs, but I could move my arms freely. I breathed deeply, feeling a terrible thirst. I pulled myself up away from the bedding and the smell of my own body.

"So we have another Lazarus!"

Father Tannen's voice startled me. He walked into the bedroom and handed me a large mug, water sloshing from its edges. I took it quickly and drank it all at once.

"Had you given up on me?" I said hoarsely.

The sounds of our voices stirred Margaret awake. She smothered me with a hug and caressed my back and shoulders. "Francis had given you last rites, Gene," she said.

Tannen seemed embarrassed. He winked at me, a truly uncharacteristic gesture.

"Where is Dr. Perry?" I asked. "I'm very grateful to him for treating me. Is he still here in Burguna?"

"Goddamn Perry did nothing for you!" Tannen said. "He gave you up for dead. He's no more a doctor than I am. He's a mercenary. A whoremonger and diamond smuggler. That's all!"

"He at least tried," Margaret said, interrupting Tanner's tirade. "What was he supposed to do, Francis, perform a miracle? Gene's alive, isn't he?"

"No thanks to Perry," the priest responded.

Margaret dismissed Tannen's objections and began to make a fuss over me. Her defense of Perry had obviously angered Tannen and the priest left the room in a huff. She left to make me some coffee and to allow Samuel to help me dress. Sickness had always been a perversely comforting time. As a child, it was one of the few occasions that my mother had ever given all of herself to me. How I relished the indulgences and love pats that came with my coughing, sneezing, and chilling.

After I finished dressing, Margaret reappeared with a tray filled with a glass of goat's milk, some sweet bread that had been sent to her from Ireland, and hot coffee. The coffee had a strong aroma, a smell that was wonderful! It was the first time I had smelled coffee since being in Burguna. Its scarcity was a mystery as it was the major cash crop of several tribes less than a hundred miles from us.

I sipped from the cup slowly, savoring its flavor and every sense around me as though they were all new. The relief of not having a wretched feeling at the pit of my stomach, of tasting the luxurious coffee, helped satiate my tremendous thirst. I thanked Margaret and Samuel, almost weeping. The sun came in and out and a light breeze blew through the open window.

A sound drew my attention to the door. A large man from the village had entered the room. He had teased straight hair and layers of stringed beads and animal teeth strung around his neck which covered an elaborately painted chest. His face had a flatness to it that prompted me to think he looked very much like an American Indian, but, of course, his skin was much darker. Margaret greeted the large man in Krio and they exchanged words. Margaret then smiled warmly and bent down and spoke softly in my left ear.

"Gene, Jarubel Proneeri is the village doctor. He has offered to examine you to see if any evil spirits still occupy your body. Is this all right?"

My apprehension must have been obvious. Margaret added, "Jarubel is highly respected for his medical powers. He won't hurt you."

The witch doctor looked into my eyes and probed my body, just as Justin Perry had done the night before. But instead of using a stethoscope, Jarubel simply put his head flat again my chest and listened to my heartbeat. Once he had performed his diagnosis, he said something to Margaret which I didn't understand, grinned broadly, and then began chanting and dancing in little steps. After he had hopped around for several seconds, he loosened a small pocket-pouch attached to a belt around his waist. From the pouch, he pulled out a small handful of white powder and began to sprinkle it around the room, all while continuing to dance and chant. Then he exited, nodding in a positive way. If the witch doctor had thought I was more gravely ill, he would have performed a more elaborate ceremony, perhaps with other villagers also participating.

Chief Faramha also visited me later that day. The Chief seemed genuinely concerned about my illness. He shook his head and then admonished both Margaret and me to pray to Allah for a full recovery. As I learned later, Chief Faramha hardly ever expressed any emotions, so for him to show such overt concern was a high honor.

Justin Perry had told Margaret the night before that he believed that I had been stricken by bilharzia. Bilharzia is a virus carried by a small snail which is found in African rivers. Perry's diagnosis was that I had drunk contaminated water carrying the extremely small creature. The good news was that, unlike with malaria or yellow fever, the symptoms would not last several months. The bad news—at least for some victims—was that the extremely high temperatures and dehydration caused by bilharzia often killed the disease's host. Perry seemed satisfied that if I could survive the first night and begin to drink fluids again that I would recover fully within a few days.

Nigel Reuben and I had boarded the TWA 747 jet liner at Gate B-17. There were no direct flights available to Cape de Leone from the U.S. We would first travel to Paris in order to change planes to fly on to Grand Bassa early the following day. I was still distracted by the events I was leaving behind. My head swirled and I felt as though I was still in a fog.

We were seated in the first class section, a rarity for me. Reuben acted as though he had never traveled in any lesser comfort.

"Are you tired, Professor?" Reuben asked, breaking the silence between us.

"Exhausted," I answered with a sigh. "What is it, six hours to Paris?"

"At least seven," Reuben said. "Perhaps you can get some sleep."

Unspoken issues hung between us like a giant balloon. We both looked out the airliner window to the left of us and found a silent, black void. New York City's brightly lit skyline was well behind us now. Inside the fuselage, darkness ruled except for a row of dim lights that ran the length of the Boeing 747 above the carry-on luggage compartments. A few passengers had their reading lights on, turning pages of pulp novels to encourage sleep. While I realized that we were traveling several hundred miles an hour eastward, the impenetrable darkness outside made it seem as though we were barely moving and that we were, rather, adrift somewhere timelessly in a black void.

Reuben eased back into his seat. He stirred a scotch and tonic that the flight attendant had brought to him a few minutes before.

"Please tell me about your life, Professor," Reuben said out of nowhere. "Margaret shared with me some about when you two were in Cape de Leone together, but you've traveled and written about so many interesting places in the world since then as a reporter."

I hesitated, but he encouraged me. "I only thought we might pass a little time," he added.

The day's events had been so emotionally taxing that I could hardly recall them all. The day had, in fact, seemed like several days compressed into one. It was only twelve hours before that I had first learned about Elizabeth Brownlie's death. Now I was heading for West Africa with a mysterious stranger whom I had known for even a lesser time, someone who had convinced me that perhaps Margaret Mahoney was still alive. The news of both a death and a resurrection in such a short time was almost more than I could bear. I was as tight as a stretched-out rubber band, but maybe talking would ease the tension.

Roanoke County Courthouse Square, Lisbon, Indiana

Eight

As a foreign correspondent for *The Cincinnati Enquirer* and later *The Chicago Sun-Times*, I had covered events all over the world. My stories had as their subjects everyone from kings, dictators, mercenaries and migrants to religious fundamentalists in the Middle East and communist revolutionaries in Central America and East Asia. Through it all, I had traveled to more than fifty countries from 1960 to 1985. It was obvious to me that Nigel Reuben was at least nominally aware of these experiences when he referred to my life as a reporter. But he urged me to begin at the beginning, so I did.

On January 30, 1927, I was born in my parent's house located at the intersection of Union Street and Railroad Avenue in Lisbon, Indiana, a small town located in the east-central part of the state. We lived across the street from the train station on tracks that cut the town in half.

My older brother Philip had contracted polio and scarlet fever as a toddler. As a result, he was always smaller than the other children his age, walked with a noticeable limp, and had a bad heart, but these inflictions didn't slow him down much. And so our small family of four—my father Patrick, my mother Dorothea (Dorothy), my brother Philip and I—resided during my early childhood years on Railroad Avenue in the little town.

My father worked at the Lisbon Glass Works. A local glass factory, at one time or another it also employed my mother, my maternal grandfather, Hastings Hamilton, and my Uncle Paul Hamilton (my mother's brother). The glass works, which produced beer and ketchup bottles among other things, was an outgrowth of the confluence of natural gas, a ready labor force, and a major railroad line that hauled train cars full of sand. It was by far the largest employer in Lisbon, the center of life in our county. My Grandmother and Grandfather Hamilton were devout members of the Lisbon King of Glory Missionary Church. In many ways it defined them. The church had no denominational affiliation. It was simply started by a group of townspeople who, as they described themselves, "loved the Lord and weren't afraid of telling people about it."

The church's elders ruled with an iron fist. They dictated the appropriate style of dress and form of worship just as resolutely as the strain of Calvinist theology that was to be preached from the pulpit. Men appeared reverently in dark suits; while women, forbidden to wear jewelry or cosmetics, were encouraged to always have their heads covered. The women distinguished themselves by the fragrances of their perfumes. For some ontological reason that only the church's elders knew, God forbade a well-adorned woman, but found delight in a good smelling one.

My grandmother, Rosemary Hamilton, was the church's one great Bible scholar. A small, willowy lady, she spoke out often to correct biblical error espoused by any member of the congregation, even to the point of publicly correcting the minister Reverend Clarence Hogarth. The dopey faced clergyman took her outbursts with great magnanimity.

Rounds of altar calls to facilitate the congregation's forgiveness concluded most church services. It was not uncommon to be nudged by one of the stern elders towards the front altar railings. Somehow they just knew that youthful indiscretions had been committed the previous week that were in need of God's mercy.

If Grandmother Hamilton was the focus of our church life, Grandfather Hamilton was the center of attention in Lisbon itself. Hastings Hamilton was the town gossip and rabble-rouser. He would attend every county council session, school board meeting, and every other kind of community gathering one could think of. He would always have some long-winded opinion he felt compelled to share with the governing body or audience.

If you were not present to catch the exact wording of Hastings' insights, there was nothing to worry about. He would repeat it verbatim the next day on the court house lawn standing in front of what became affectionately known as the "liar's bench." There, at precisely 3:15 p.m., Grandpa Hamilton began his diatribe about the world's problems and the fact, for instance, that the commissioners' recent vote on some local matter just proved his point that the County was being governed by dim-witted and inept fools. The basis of his authority, in his mind at least, rested with the fact that he held the position of being Roanoke County's Republican Party Chairman for the past fifteen years. As a result, he personally knew just about every prominent Republican in the State, including the governor. Because Republicans dominated the county and held most elected positions, grandpa's position was mostly ceremonial. As the party's Grand Pooh-Bah, his main responsibility was to preside over the annual Lincoln Day Dinner (political fund-raiser) held each February. Though basically lazy, he did have redeeming qualities: an uncanny ability to remember names; a love of farming; and, a desire to help residents of the community who had fallen on hard times, which, during the depression, were numerous.

Grandpa Hamilton was a large man with a sloping chest, receding hairline, and a bulging paunch that made his stomach appear greatly out of proportion to his head and shoulders. He walked with a loping gait. The tops of his suspenders would rise with every large stride that propelled him forward. He had a gold front tooth that glistened in the sun when he began to pontificate from the court house bench.

Grandpa had a knack for making pithy statements. When he couldn't get his old truck to start, he would turn to me and say with pure disgust: "You know what 'F-O-R-D' stands for, son? 'Fix or repair daily,' that's what!"

He was to his core a die-hard Republican and relished every opportunity to condemn our country's thirty-second President. "If Roosevelt gets reelected again," I remember my grandfather preaching to a small crowd one hot summer afternoon in 1936, "we won't have a country worth fighting for. Everyone will be in a soup line!"

Hank Powers, Lisbon's popular Democrat mayor stood near the back, ready to differ when grandpa crossed the line.

"It's a far better day, Hastings, than when your Herbert 'Hooverville' Hoover ill served this nation!" Hank yelled. "President Roosevelt has a plan for every unemployed man in America!"

Grandpa stepped forward, hands atop his suspenders, and rejoined loudly. "Yea, Hank, to give him our jobs!"

The crowd roared and applauded, declaring that Hastings had won the round. Hank would smile broadly, shake his head in mock disgust, and go on about his business as mayor. On another occasion years later, grandpa rose from his throne—the court house bench—and just started saying anything to taunt his audience: "Fried rats and stewed cats are good enough for Democrats," causing the Mayor to respond, "Mary had a little lamb; its fleece was white and silky, and every time it raised its tail, it showed its Wendell Willkie." The way grandpa and Hank Powers bantered back and forth, you would have thought they were school boys.

Grandpa Hamilton's most notorious confrontation came, not with Mayor Hank Powers, but with the man who was my paternal grandfather, Michael O'Connor, the local judge. The exchange between the two men became part of the town's folklore; it had occurred several years before I was born. It is also significant to me because it was the incident that brought my parents together.

One week in the early 1920s, a controversial murder trial was going on inside the Circuit Court. The case involved a Mexican migrant who, the prosecutor alleged, burned the house of a local woman, resulting in her death. The trial had been front page news in *The Prophet* for several days. Grandfather Hamilton criticized unmercifully the way the case was being handled by the Honorable Michael O'Connor, a fellow Republican. The two men didn't care for one another despite sharing allegiances to the same political party.

Grandpa Hamilton parked himself under a large elm tree on the court house square and began to rant and rail. His voice was so loud that it could be heard inside the courtroom. Despite admonitions from the bailiff for my Grandpa Hamilton to stop the shouting, Hastings continued. He lambasted Judge O'Connor, the lawyers, FDR, and just about everyone else who had ever worn a judicial robe or held a government position.

Finally my Grandpa O'Connor, Judge of the Roanoke Circuit Court, had had enough. He complained to the bailiff that if the abusive language outside didn't stop immediately, a mistrial would be called. Then, without affording the bailiff a second opportunity to stem the raucous, the Right Honorable Michael J. O'Connor did a most unusual thing. He recessed the trial and proceeded himself in his judicial robe outside to the location of the commotion. There he found Hastings Hamilton righteously condemning the proceedings inside. Next, without any further warning or explanation, he pronounced that Hastings Hamilton was in contempt of court. The indignant judge ordered Hastings arrested on the spot and taken to the county jail. Many a Lisbon citizen has told me that this was the only time they could ever remember when Hastings Hamilton was totally at a loss for words. At the time, both of my parents were working the second shift at the Lisbon Glass Works. My father, Patrick O'Connor, son of the judge, was then twenty-one and operated a lathe. My mother, Dorothy Hamilton, was sixteen and a sophomore in high school. She worked in the packing department after school.

According to my mother, my father came up to her shortly after the incident to apologize for what had happened to her father. This is how my parents first met. Within six months my mother had quit school and the two of them eloped, getting married in Tennessee.

After mother married my father, she never returned to the King of Glory Missionary Church. Until that time my mother had been a faithful churchgoer with her parents since she was a child. She had even been given a Bible from Reverend Hogarth for not missing a day of Sunday school in seven years. That was the Bible that I took with me to Cape de Leone. It was my most prized possession.

Our plane droned on, its engines roaring reassuringly. Reuben interrupted me. "Did you ever think as a young boy that you would travel as you have, Professor?" he asked.

"Never," I replied. "It just didn't occur to me when I was younger that other places mattered. In some ways, Lisbon was its own cosmos. We had our farming, our trading, our schooling, and our social world. But it didn't occur to me until I was at least ten years old that there was a world that was much different from life in Roanoke County. What about your childhood, Mr. Reuben?" I said, trying to get him to open up. "Where were you raised?"

He smiled. "My upbringing was totally different from yours, Professor. While I was born in Dublin, my parents sent me to boarding school at Eton when I was eight. My father was seldom at home because he was constantly traveling back and forth from Africa to Europe due to the demands of his business. And my mother was very busy raising my older sister and being involved with a number of society activities. In many ways I envy you."

"In what ways, Mr. Reuben?"

"Please call me Nigel, Professor," he said.

I nodded. "Tell me what you mean."

My Irish host smiled again and seemed, for the first time, relaxed and willing to share more than mere pleasantries or philosophies. "Well, because I was sent to boarding school at such a young age, I didn't feel as though I ever got to know my parents or my sister. She was six years older than me. She and my parents were wonderful whenever we were together, but it seems that the occasions were few. I think I became closer to my school friends than to my own family. It just sounds as though your life, at least your adolescent years, were entirely different. That's all. Now please continue."

I recalled that on Lisbon's town square sits the Roanoke County Court House, which looks much like a giant wedding cake. A large Civil War memorial stands on the northeast corner of the square, topped with a larger-than-life statute of an infantryman holding a U.S. flag while below him, on stone podiums, are four statutes of soldiers and sailors firing rifles or hoisting sails. My Grandfather Hamilton told Philip and me that Civil War soldiers and their horses were buried beneath the imposing memorial. It was one of his many exaggerations.

The small town of Lisbon, I recollected, had a southern kind of charm to it probably caused by it being only 100 miles north of the Ohio River and settled by Virginians and Carolinians. It was the kind of community where gossiping wasn't a sin but a commandment. "If we don't gossip," Mary Beth Simpson proclaimed to me one Sunday morning after church, "how else, honey child, are we going to know who to pray for?"

> "If we don't gossip," Mary Beth Simpson proclaimed to me one Sunday morning after church, "how else, honey child, are we going to know who to pray for?"

In terms of employment, the glass factory dominated the town. The Lisbon Glass Works never closed down. Its four hot, enormous furnaces operated seven days a week, twenty-four hours a day, spewing out noxious gases and providing sustenance living for more than half of the townspeople. There were three daily eight-hour shifts and the employees rotated shifts every two weeks except those employees with at least twenty-five years of seniority. They could remain on the same eight-hour shift indefinitely. This is what my Grandpa Hamilton did.

Three times a day a loud whistle blew from compressed air from one of the factory's generators. Minutes after the 7:00 a.m., 3:00 p.m., and 11:00 p.m. shifts, a major, if temporary, traffic jam appeared in downtown Lisbon. After my mother and father married, they always worked different shifts from the other at the Glass Works. I think it was meant to be that way to keep them from killing one another. I remember one particular week when mother and father had an argument. Fighting between them had become a blood sport. At the time, I was eight years old and in second grade. After the last heated exchange, mother, Philip and I left home for several days to stay with Grandpa and Grandma Hamilton on their farm east of Lisbon. We finally returned home on a Sunday evening to find my father drunk.

We had been home no longer than a couple of hours when our Uncle Paul, my mother's brother, came to the door. Mother was preparing dinner. Uncle Paul also drank to excess, which meant he and father had something in common other than the fact that they worked at the glass factory together.

"Is it a bad time?" Uncle Paul asked as he opened the screened porch door. Philip and I stood on the porch anxious to see him. He rubbed our heads, looked through the porch to mother in the kitchen and repeated himself. "Is it a bad time, sis?"

Mother looked over her shoulder. She had just finished slicing the last of several potatoes into a frying pan. She smiled and seemed pleased to have company. "Come on in, Mutt," she said. "We just returned home. Spent a few days at Ma and Pa's."

"Mutt" was Uncle Paul's nickname. He smiled. "Yea, Ma told me you had gone for a *visit*." Paul looked around and didn't see Dad. "Is everything okay, Dorothy?" he whispered to mom.

In one motion mother tossed her head back, rolled her eyes, and raised her shoulders. Father sat in the living room listening to the radio and drinking cheap whiskey. She explained that dad was in no mood to be bothered. Uncle Paul grabbed a beer out of the ice box, opened it, and mother and he began to talk about Uncle Paul's wife, Betty. Whereas Uncle Paul was thin and wiry,

Aunt Betty was the largest, most obese woman I had ever seen. Rumor was that Aunt Betty had actually worked as the "fat lady" in a traveling circus before she met Uncle Paul. She and Paul were complete opposites, but their marriage, as I look back upon it now, was heavenly in comparison with mother's and father's.

Suddenly dad appeared in the kitchen. "My dear old Mutt," he announced in a slurred voice. Father could barely stand and, in fact, gripped a chair with his left hand to steady himself. "Have you been on vacation? Haven't seen you at work in a couple weeks. Thought maybe you had quit or something, gone out to make your fortune," dad added with a laugh.

"Howdy, Patrick," Uncle Paul replied, pulling the beer from his lips. "Nope, nothing special. Just took a week off to help Betty around the house. We're trying to paint it while the weather's good. Don't want to wait until July when the humidity gets so bad. Damn paint leaves blotches when the humidity is like it is in summer."

Father's eyes were glazed. "You know, Mutt, Dorothy took a vacation last week, too. Took a vacation from me. Took the boys and left, she did. Now, that wasn't a very Christian thing for a wife to do, was it, Mutt? Take a vacation away from her husband."

Uncle Paul remained silent. His eyes darted between mother and father, then to Philip and me. Mother urged father to go back where he had been, saying she would bring him dinner.

Father turned on mother. "Goddammit, I don't want to go into no goddamn living room," he said. "You come home after bein' gone almost a week and you and the boys don't want to be around me. Goddammit, I'll stay in here! I'll just stay here and visit with Mutt!"

I could tell that mother was starting to panic. She didn't want to have a fight in front of Uncle Paul. She moved over to the sink. Father followed her. Paul stood up quickly to intervene, when all of a sudden mother turned around and pushed dad gently away from her.

"Maybe you ought to go, Mutt," mother said, directing the conversation back to Uncle Paul.

Uncle Paul's eyes darted again between Mom and Dad. "You sure, Dorothy?" he asked.

Mother feigned a smile. "It's all right, Mutt. I'll give you a call tomorrow."

Mother waved at Uncle Paul to leave. He went to the screen door, opened it, and the latch and screen door banged against the frame.

Within a minute after Mutt's departure, whining pleas came from the living room where dad had returned.

"Come on in here, Dorothea," father yelled. "Come and have a drink with me. Bring a glass, honey. The boys can eat by themselves."

Mother continued to scoop the fried potatoes onto our plates and then the peas and gravy.

"Dorothea, come and have a drink!" father grumbled. "You ain't no Nazarene anymore, honey! Rosemary ain't watching over you, child. Come have a drink!"

"Dorothea!" dad screamed. Mother hated to be called by her given name. She continued to ignore his pleas and placed the steaming plates of food in front of us.

Suddenly dad reappeared in the kitchen. Mother was sitting at the small dining room table with us trying to eat. Dad put his hand on mother's shoulder. "Goddammit, Dorothy, have a drink with me!" he said, twisting her left arm. Mother's plate fell on the floor and the potatoes, peas, and gravy splattered on the dingy linoleum.

Mother ordered us to our bedroom. We ran to the room, slammed the door shut and heard horrible noises, screaming, lamps falling, and a body slammed, causing the pictures of Philip and me in our bedroom to jump off the wall. Philip cracked the door and we peered outside from a slit no more than six inches wide.

"You don't give me no respect, Dorothy!" father yelled, his hands over his eyes. "You treat me like some piddling-ass stranger!" Just then mother threw a dish at father, striking the living room wall behind him. He staggered towards mom.

"You've turned the boys against me," father moaned. "I don't get no attention from you or the boys, Dorothy. A Goddamn stinkin' pole cat ain't treated as bad as me. Oh, Dorothy! Oh, Dorothy!" father's arms reached out to mother as though to embrace her, but her flailing hands struck his shoulders and head, forcing him to retreat.

"Leave me alone, Patrick!" mother screamed. "For Christ's sake, you're drunk! Just leave me alone!"

But father wouldn't stop. He kept walking towards her and she kept swinging her arms and hitting him in the shoulders and face. Though the aggressor, he was the recipient of most of the blows. He looked pitiful, defenseless, emasculated, feeble. Suddenly father toppled from his feet and we heard the sound of a big thud. He had fallen on his back. He remained on the floor motionless, briefly stunned.

Just as he stood, mother pushed dad away again and he staggered, appearing to fall only to catch himself. He looked up at her in disbelief.

"Go to bed, Patrick!" she pleaded in a strained voice. "Please, please go to bed!"

Nine

P hilip closed the door to our room and we ran to our beds afraid that we might be caught watching the melee by mother. We kept the light off, quivering under our blankets like small rabbits huddled under thick foliage, afraid that their scent might be smelled by the neighborhood cat.

After several minutes of silence, Philip slid quietly out of bed, said nothing, and disappeared from our room. He was not gone long. When he returned, he turned on the small lamp on the night stand between our twin beds. He held a plate of potatoes, gravy, and peas with two forks. He whispered.

"All we got, Genie. Mom's plate and mine's all over the floor. Mom told us to stay in here, to leave her and dad alone."

Philip sat beside me on my bed and placed the plate of food on top of my lap. We both began to eat off of the one plate. The potatoes, gravy and peas were cold, but it didn't matter.

Philip could see that I was shaking. "It'll be all right, Genie," he whispered, as we took turns stabbing and eating the cold potatoes and peas. "Mom's crying now, but she told me to tell you not to worry. She'll see us in the morning."

We finished eating everything off of the plate. Philip made sure I had the most. I was still shaking. He placed the dirty plate on the night stand and told me to go to sleep, but I still shivered.

"We don't have to brush our teeth tonight," he announced to try and cheer me up.

Philip then got up and tried to tuck me in as mother would do. He told me again that everything would be all right in the morning, but I knew that it wouldn't be. During each of our parents' fights the violence only became worse. It couldn't go on like this for much longer. One of them was going to kill the other if it did.

The next day, Monday, father began the 7:00 a.m. to 3:00 p.m. shift at the glass factory. We waited until he had gone to work before we left our room. Nothing was said about the night before.

After a fairly normal day at school, Philip and I walked home together. Despite his lame left leg, he could keep up pretty well. We were both surprised to find mother in the house as she had normally left for work by now. Piles of clothes, linens, and personal things were spread around the living room. She looked tired and distracted.

"Honey," she said, "we're going to go again and spend a few days with grandpa and grandma. Hurry now and get your toys. I have your clothes here already." Mother placed her hand on a pile of my pants, shirts, and underwear. She was folding Philip's clothes as well. Philip pulled at me to indicate that this was serious and not to be giving mother any trouble.

Soon after Grandpa Hamilton screeched up in his truck in front of our house. He told us we had to leave immediately. Dad had found out that we were leaving him and he had been drinking at Maynard's tavern all afternoon.

Grandpa finally saw Philip and me. "Get your things, boys!" he shouted. He then turned back to mother. "Dorothy, we've got to go! Pick up what you can and leave the rest for later. Patrick could be here any minute."

Mother panicked. She grabbed one pile of clothing only to throw it down and pick up another. Grandpa snatched a basket full of linens and scurried as fast as his loping legs would allow him out to the truck. In five short minutes, we had managed to get most of our clothes and personal items into the truck's rusted flatbed. The weather had suddenly turned cooler. The wind had picked up and dark clouds started to roll in from the southwest.

"That's enough, boys!" grandpa yelled, holding another basket full of clothes. "We got to go, Dorothy," he screamed back at mother. Grandpa loved her more than anything on earth.

We ran and got into the cab of the truck. Mother followed us with her dresses draped partially over her arms, the hems of the garments dragging against the ground. She had her Bible underneath her left arm and tripped as she stepped into the cab. Just then a terrible thought came to my mind.

"We gotta take Ring!" I screamed. Grandpa scooted from the truck and ordered both Philip and me out. We all three started yelling Ring's name. Finally Ring came running and he ran into my arms.

"Get back in, boys," Grandpa commanded. "I'll put Ring in the back. Come on, get in!"

Philip and I squeezed in next to mother. Grandpa lifted Ring and placed him in the flat bed next to some blankets. Ring stood panting and barking in the back of the truck. Suddenly it started to rain.

We had gone no farther than half a block when we saw dad driving hurriedly from the opposite direction in his green Oldsmobile. I started to wave, but Philip pulled my arm down. As the Oldsmobile passed by, dad looked at us with a face of terror, disbelief, ghastly horror. The rain came down harder. Mother looked straight ahead and grandpa accelerated the truck.

We traveled south on Union Street to Washington Avenue and then turned right and followed the Greenville Pike out of town. I sensed that we all wondered whether dad would follow us, but none of us said a word. The wipers squeaked against the wind shield. We bounced in the Ford down the bumpy tar road when suddenly the truck hit a shallow puddle, soaking the cab, Ring, and all of our possessions in the truck's bed. We kept going straight out into the country, finally turning down the long gravel lane that led to grandpa's and grandma's farm house.

When we got out of the truck, we all waited, waited in the deluge to see dad's Oldsmobile come down the lane after us. The rain kept pouring. Our hearts raced excitedly. But father never came.

Ten

"**S**o what happened after your mother, brother, and you left, Professor?" Reuben asked. I was surprised that he wanted so much detail, but perhaps Reuben saw how willing I was to confide such painful memories. The cabin on the plane was dark and quiet, and all we could hear was the monotone roar of jet engines. I placed a pillow behind my head, covered my lap with a small blue blanket and continued my story.

The school year was nearing the end when we left to go to my grandparents' farm that windy, rainy Monday afternoon in May 1935. Soon we were freed from our daily imprisonment for summer vacation. In the fall, we began classes at a new elementary in the country.

Mother quit her job at the Lisbon Glass Works. She said she needed to be with us more, to help out grandpa and grandma around the house and on the farm. Philip told me that he didn't think that was the reason at all. Mother just didn't want to be working at the same factory as dad; she didn't want to take the chance of meeting him on the job. This was during the height (or should I say depth) of the Great Depression. For anyone to give up a job voluntarily was seen as an act of lunacy.

The farm that Grandpa and Grandma Hamilton owned was only eighty acres. In 1919, grandpa used every dollar they had to purchase the farm they would name "Blessed Acres." From then on Hastings Hamilton put on airs that he was a big-time farmer, a "man of the land," a member of the "landed gentry" of Roanoke County. The fact was that Hastings Hamilton barely knew which end of a horse to hitch a plow to or how to start a tractor. If there is such a thing as a born farmer, he was the exact opposite of that. The rows of his corn curved more than a baby's bottom because he would always be looking behind him when he planted, gloating over what a fantastic job he was doing.

What made matters worse is that only forty acres of the farm were tillable, and those acres were some of the scruffiest ground in all of soil-rich Roanoke County. One of the saving graces about Blessed Acres was that the back forty acres were covered completely with woods. Philip and I loved to play in the thick forest; everything seemed so strange and exotic, so full of possibilities with the discovery of a bee-hive, a fox's den, or the work of a beaver damming the small stream that meandered through the back of the farm.

Mother was a great help to Grandma Hamilton by planting a garden and taking on most of the chores around the house. This was especially true because grandma was sick most of the time. Rosemary Hamilton was seldom out of bed except to attend church, and she continually complained of one mysterious ailment after another. Yet, she would never go to a doctor. Grandma Hamilton repeatedly proclaimed that God would heal her when He was ready and that "prayer and fasting" were the best medicines.

If being the son of Patrick O'Connor had been a great disappointment, being the grandson of Hastings Hamilton had been a boom to my ego. Many a Lisbon merchant would ask, "Aren't you Hastings Hamilton's grandson" and I would beam proudly as I pronounced that I was. Grandpa was clearly the most well known man in our small town, a large minnow in a dinky little pond. In the evenings, he would deliver food to poor widows, occasionally take off work during the day to drive a person who didn't have a car to a doctor's appointment, and generally thought that the welfare of the community was his personal responsibility—all of this because of his position as Chairman of the County's Republican Party.

The first year living with Grandpa and Grandma Hamilton

was a glorious one. No more worries about whether we'd wake up and find mother crying with a black eye, or dad on a drunken binge that would keep him home for days at a time from the Glass Works. On the farm, Philip and I had a few chores—to feed the chickens and sheep (we had several of each) and to milk the one cow that grandpa kept for fresh milk. When we went to town on Friday or Saturday nights, I eagerly looked for dad in the crowds that milled around and window-shopped along Lisbon's broad sidewalks. But I never saw him and his name was never mentioned in the house again. It was as though Patrick O'Connor had ceased to exist.

By late October Grandpa Hamilton had become ill. The doctors reported that he had a bad heart. He would have to work fewer hours at the glass factory or risk another attack. He was only fifty-seven. But worst of all, to reduce stress his primary doctor recommended that granddad resign as Chairman of the Roanoke County Republican Party. What the doctors didn't understand is that Hastings Hamilton wouldn't give up the position while there was still a pulse left in his body.

Through it all, Hastings remained in good spirits. After only a few days of rest, the doctors allowed him to return to work three days a week, but he was to come straight home afterwards. No more attending town board meetings and getting himself upset over things he couldn't control.

In early November, mother returned to work to help with the household finances, but the only job she could find was as an operator at the local telephone company. The position paid less than half what she had made at the Glass Works and, even worse, forced her to work the night shift. The irony was—because we lived in the country—we didn't have a telephone.

We got through a particularly harsh winter. Spring finally came and the rites of that season along with it: the blooming of white peonies, the berthing of baby lambs, and the planting of new curved rows of corn by grandpa. More important to granddad, the doctors had released him to return to work full time and, with that, to resume his afternoon vigils on the court house bench and his activism on behalf of Roanoke County's residents.

For me, those were the happiest times I can remember. I think this was true for Philip as well. But for mother, it was otherwise. My father was regularly sending her letters begging her for us to come home to him.

I remember one day in particular that she received one of father's letters, because that was the day Uncle Paul had come to help granddad shear the winter wool from the twenty or so sheep we kept on the farm. Philip and I were holding the sheep until Uncle Paul and granddad were ready for them. Uncle Paul had nicked several of the farm animals, leaving them bleeding. He was obviously shearing them too closely.

Grandpa finally erupted when one sheep jumped up with red all over its body. "Lordy, Mutt, we just need the sheep sheared. Don't want a sacrifice!"

"Sorry, Pa," said Uncle Paul, continuing to be challenged by the large scissors and wiggling ruminant animals.

Suddenly we noticed two men approaching us from the west with shotguns in their hands. They were on top of us almost before we knew it.

Grandpa glared briefly at the two men, as if he was sizing them up. "Howdy, Buck. Howdy, Ted," grandpa replied. "Looks like you've been hunting."

The older man that grandpa had addressed as Buck spoke first.

"We've got a problem, Hastings. I've talked to you about it before."

Mother came out of the house just at this time with a laundry basket full of wet clothes. She started to walk toward the clothes line, then she saw us and came our direction. Uncle Paul released the sheep he was holding, and it ran off to be with the others in the small herd. It looked funny as only one side of its body had been sheared.

"Howdy, Buck, Ted," mother said to the men. "What's the problem?"

Both farmers removed their hats and Buck spoke first. "Just about to tell your Pa, Dorothy, we had some sheep killed this morning. Same pack of dogs that we saw before did it. Four or five running together like wolves."

"I saw 'em, Hastings," Ted said. "Your dog was one of them. They came early this morning and killed two of our sheep. This is the third time."

Mother seemed confused. "You mean Ring?"

"That's right, Dorothy," said Ted. "The black one with a brown circle around his neck. He has some German Shepherd in him. He was one of them. I seen him, I did!" he said emphatically, anticipating our denial.

"It couldn't be Ring!" I yelled.

"Shush, Gene," mother said, dropping the laundry basket.

"Hastings, you know the law," Buck said. "I can't do anything if he's on your property, but the moment I see your dog on mine and if he's running my sheep, I'm going to shoot him, you understand?"

The two men nodded their heads and then walked away back across the field and into the small woods that separated our two properties. Buck Sterling was the older man. Ted was his son. They were big cattle and sheep farmers just west of us.

"We all know Ring is gone for days at a time," mother said. "Had Buck given you the description of Ring before?"

Grandpa nodded sheepishly.

"Then you had to know it was Ring. We have to tie him up. There ain't no choice, Pa, you know that."

"But Ring's a roaming dog, mommy," I said.

"He won't do it any more," Philip added. "We promise. We'll keep a watch on Ring."

No sooner had the words left Philip's mouth than we all spotted Ring and three other dogs running towards us from the north, along our long gravel lane that connected to the Greenville Pike.

"Get the sheep in the pen, Mutt!" grandpa yelled.

Uncle Paul quickly herded the sheep into the small fenced area next to the barn. Mother stepped in front of all of us. She turned to me. "Call for Ring, Eugene."

"Ring!" I yelled. "Come here boy. Come here Ring!"

He came running towards us and the other dogs followed closely behind. When I called his name again, Ring left the pack and came up to me. He allowed me to take him by his collar and pet him. Mother quickly looked at Ring and then suddenly, unexpectedly charged at the other dogs, scaring them away.

"You hold Ring, Eugene," mother said, returning to us. "Don't let go of him! You hear?"

Mother ran into the house. We couldn't figure out why she left. Then all of a sudden she came out of the back door with grandpa's rifle. Mother stretched out her right arm with the rifle in her hand towards grandpa and Uncle Paul.

"Which one of you is going to do it?" she asked in a deep, emotional voice. "Because if you're not willing to tie him up, there's no other option."

All of us—grandpa, Uncle Paul, Philip and me—were frozen and stunned. I couldn't understand what mother meant at the time. She stood defiantly and continued to hold out the gun to Uncle Paul and granddad, but neither moved or said anything. Ring began to bark.

"Let me have him, Eugene," mother finally screamed. She grabbed Ring by the collar and yanked him out of my hands. She moved so quickly that I couldn't comprehend what was happening. Ring wouldn't go with mother, so she drug him across the barn lot, his hind legs stirring up dust.

"No, mommy!" I screamed.

But before the echo of my voice had stopped, she had pulled Ring around the back of the barn. And then we all heard a terrible sounding bang and a yelp!

Mother reappeared from behind the barn alone, only with the gun in her right hand.

"Don't you boys go back there, you hear me!" she spouted. Mother threw down the gun and spit on the ground next to it. She glared at Uncle Paul and grandpa. "Since neither of you were man enough to do what you should have, the least you can do is bury him," she said. "I'm going in and helping ma with dinner."

Eleven

I didn't hate mom for what she did, because I realized that if she hadn't received father's letter that morning—the one that begged her to come back to him—then she might not have shot Ring. It was one of those unintended consequences that changes lives forever. But even though I knew it wasn't her fault, I couldn't forgive mother for what she had done.

But the rest of our lives went on that summer much as the summer before. Each morning grandpa rose, loped to the west picture window and gaped with a sense of awe over what he considered to be his "magnificent crop." His chest would swell with the pride of an Olympian farmer, and he would daily talk about his forty acres on the court house bench as if he was personally responsible for feeding half the population of Roanoke County. In fact, his forty acres of sorry looking corn amounted to a field of stubby stalks infiltrated heavily by ragweed.

Grandmother's modus operandi changed little as well. On most days, she continued to lie in bed reading her Bible, praying over her poor health, and fretting about the world's problems. Sundays were special, as she would rise to attend the King of Glory Missionary Church and bolster her reputation as the congregation's one true Bible scholar.

Philip and I fed and watered the animals, played in the woods, and listened to grandma's Bible stories in late afternoon before dinner. Life on the farm was still an adventure, as we investigated every nook and cranny in search of squirrels, groundhogs, and muskrats. We stood in wonder at the slow transformation of a worm into a cocoon into a butterfly.

Mother still worked at the telephone company. Her position there enabled her to become a great source of gossip as she listened, against company policy of course, to the conversations of Lisbon callers. She refused to go to Church anymore, however, often saying that she was too tired or had too many chores around the house to do.

I didn't go into all this detail with Reuben about my early life, but I did think about it on our trip across the Atlantic. And I realize now that I have forgotten to share the most curious anomaly about my grandparents' farm.

Blessed Acres lay due east of Lisbon's town limits precisely five miles. The train tracks that I grew up next to on Railroad Avenue continued eastward to the point that they cut grandma and grandpa's farm precisely in half: they owned forty acres north of the tracks (the section Grandpa farmed) and forty acres south of the tracks (the woods).

Philip and I shared the back upstairs bedroom in the old farmhouse. Our room looked out over the train tracks which were about 200 feet south of the house. Literally dozens of trains passed by each day, as the New York Central Railroad (the double set of tracks) was a major east-west transportation link through the Midwest. At nights I would lie in bed and listen to the trains that rumbled through our back yard.

The familiar sounds of the trains helped ease the transition of moving to grandpa and grandma's farm. But another sound, a more distant one, was even more comforting. Each day at 7:00 a.m., 3:00 p.m. and 11:00 p.m., I would stop whatever I was doing, as if a Muslim obeying the daily ritual of prayers, to listen to the whistle blows at the Lisbon Glass Works. If I was really quiet and nothing else was making a sound, I could faintly hear the horn.

I knew exactly what shift dad was on. I kept a calendar underneath my bed of every shift rotation he had every two weeks. At nights, if he was on the 3:00 to 11:00 p.m. shift, I would stay awake just so I could hear the sound of the whistle.

When I had a hard time getting up the next morning, mother would accuse Philip and me of staying up at night and talking to each other. But we weren't. Philip could testify to that.

But I didn't go to sleep until I heard the whistle at 11:00 p.m. Night after night I would fabricate a different scenario of dad's whereabouts when I heard the whistle: one night he might be talking to Claude Welch at Claude's machine; another night he might stop at the canteen to buy a cup of coffee and talk to Nelly Stump, the canteen's manager; another night he might be thinking about Philip and me and how we were getting along. The cycle of my life at the farm revolved around the whistle that blew at the end of every eight hour shift at the Glass Works. It helped in a small way ameliorate the longing for love and acceptance that plagued all my early life and finally helped send me to Africa.

One evening all of us had just finished listening to "The Shadow" on mother's old RCA radio. I had become enthralled with this mysterious voice that "possessed the power to cloud men's minds!" "Oh, who knows what evil lurks in the hearts of men! Only the Shadow knows!"

Immediately after the broadcast came on the voice of Franklin Delano Roosevelt. He was delivering one of his famous "Fireside Chats:"

> My fellow Americans, it has been several months since I have talked with you concerning the problems of government. Since January, those of us in whom you have vested responsibility have been engaged in the fulfillment of plans and policies which had been widely discussed in previous months. . .

Grandfather Hamilton was reading *The Prophet*. He suddenly dropped the newspaper and moved his head closer to the radio. "Is that the President, Genie?" he asked.

"Yea, grandpa. President Roosevelt is talking to us directly from the White House. Do you want it louder?"

"Heavens no, child! Turn it off quickly before we hear any more!"

I turned the radio off and grandpa clutched his heart and fell to the floor as if he had had another attack. He rolled around for several seconds, moving his hands up to cover his ears. "Oh, Genie!" he cried. "What an awful thing for an old man to be exposed to. How could you do that to a die-hard Republican, Genie? Oh, mother," he said to grandma, "I've been tainted, tainted by the great evil spirit in the White House. Would you pray for me Sister Hamilton to remove this evil spirit from within me?"

Grandma dismissed grandpa's attempt at humor by simply ignoring him. When he didn't get the rise out of her that he had hoped for, grandpa returned to me. "Genie, I need 'The Shadow' to rescue me from this deep infirmity! Do you know 'The Shadow,' my boy?"

"I am The Shadow, grandpa," I proclaimed. "I will come to your rescue." I immediately fell into his arms and we wrestled on the hardwood floor in the living room. Philip watched us and laughed before mother got up and put her right foot between grandpa and me to separate us.

"Pa, you're in no condition to be acting like that," mother said, berating him. "Come on, Eugene. Get up! You and Philip have got to go to bed. Come on now!"

How I loved to wrestle with grandpa. It happened so seldom. He unclutched me and the evening was over. The Shadow would have to wait until another night to rescue grandpa from the great evil spirit in the White House.

Nigel Reuben laughed when I told him this last story. He tilted his seat backward and placed his feet without his shoes underneath the seat in front of him.

"It sounds like growing up on your grandparents' farm was nearly idyllic," Reuben said.

"It was, Nigel," I replied soberly and then gulped, "until the very next day."

"What happened then to change it, professor?"

I looked straight ahead and took the last sip from my mixed drink, realizing that I had cracked open the closet door and was about to give the stranger a glimpse of my other childhood portrait. I recalled that the evening I had just told Reuben about was the last time that all five of us—grandpa, grandma, mother, Philip, and me—were together. I became choked and my eyes watered. I finally answered with no emotion. "My mother and brother were killed."

The story was front page news in the October 5, 1937, edition of *The Prophet:*

FREAK FARM ACCIDENT CLAIMS LIVES OF MOTHER, SON

Dorothea Mary O'Connor, 33, and son, Philip Paul, 12, were killed yesterday evening in a freak farm accident at Mrs. O'Connor's parents's home. Mrs. O'Connor and son are the daughter and grandson, respectively, of Roanoke County Republican Chairman Hastings and Rosemary Hamilton. It is reported that Mrs. O'Connor and son had been working in a barn when corn silage stored in a wooden silo broke through the loft of the barn, completely covering them. Police authorities said that the two suffocated before Mr. Hamilton and Mrs. O'Connor's other son, Eugene, could rescue the two from the silage.

The brief account went on to state who the next of kin were and that services were pending at the Lisbon King of Glory Missionary Church. I could have quoted the obituaries verbatim to Reuben, but I chose to spare him the morbid recitation. Still, I couldn't get over how the reporting of mother's and Philip's deaths seemed so sterile—just two young lives taken, buried in an avalanche of corn. Below the news report of mother and Philip's accident read the headline, in still larger print: "**FRANKLIN JACOBS SELLS PRIZE SOW TO KANSAS FARMER FOR RECORD $8,500.**"

I have little recollection of what took place during the two days between the accident and the funeral. The days and nights seem all a blur. I do recall that grandma secluded herself in her bedroom and prayed and fasted. Grandpa tried to cook us meals on the wood burning stove but scorched everything. And neighbors brought dishes of fried chicken, casseroles, canned vegetables, and pies, but they all remained untouched. None of us could eat. Grandpa was a ghost—white, aloof, a specter of the person he had been prior to the accident. I don't think he had bothered to bath or shave for two days, and the scorched and spoiled food in the kitchen and our bodies and clothes themselves all smelled like death and decay.

The viewing and funeral took place in the sanctuary of the King of Glory Missionary Church. The autumn sun pierced through the beautiful stain glass window of Christ praying in the Garden of Gethsemane. Flowers surrounded both caskets. Vases and baskets of roses, azaleas, and violets overflowed with the sweet scents that I had long associated with perfumes worn by the large bosom women of the church.

Reverend Hogarth eulogized the two people I loved most on earth and then stepped down from the pulpit and walked over to Philip's casket. Philip lay in the velvet covered coffin in his boy scout uniform. He looked so small in the large casket. Reverend Hogarth touched Philip's lifeless arm on the sleeve in a tender gesture that moved me more than all he had said from the pulpit.

He then escorted mother and Philip with words into heaven, but beyond these sketchy remembrances, I can't recollect much that was said during the lengthy sermon. I sat between Grandpa and Grandma Hamilton, the tears coming down my cheeks so fast that I had gone through two handkerchiefs before the service ended.

When the funeral concluded, the caskets were closed and rolled out on short carts to a hearse waiting out front. We were about to leave the sanctuary when father walked up to me. Uncle Paul stood beside me and father put his hand on my shoulder.

"Hi, son," he said. "How are you getting along?" I couldn't speak. Dad didn't say anything to Uncle Paul, just nodded. "I miss you, son," he said, turning back to me.

"I miss you, too, dad," I said between sobs.

Curiously father then reached for my left hand, put something folded in it, and closed my hand over the folded paper. "I'll be seeing you, son," he said moving away.

Father's action had so surprised me that when I opened my hand, the paper dropped from it. It was a folded five dollar bill. Father didn't see that I had dropped the money unintentionally, but Uncle Paul apparently saw what happened and called out to father.

"Hey, Patrick," Uncle Paul said, reaching down and picking up the money. "You dropped something." He handed dad the five dollar bill and dad embarrassedly took it. Nothing was said. Father looked over at me, shook his head and then walked out of the church, following the others who were leaving to get into their cars.

"Hastings," I heard a deep voice say softly. The large man who was a stranger to me reached out his hand to both grandpa and Uncle Paul. "You know how much I thought of Dorothy," he said.

"We know, Randall," said grandpa, tearing up. "She and Philip were such a good daughter and grandson. I'm afraid we can't get over the shock, Randall," grandfather said. He then broke down. It was the first and only time I saw grandpa cry. "Oh, Randall, Randall, what a terrible thing to happen. What a terrible thing." The large man put his right hand on grandpa's shoulder and tried to comfort him. Grandpa finally regained composure.

Next, the stranger, who must have been at least six feet three inches tall, crouched down such that he and I were at eye level.

"Eugene," he said, placing his hand on my shoulder. "You don't know me, but my name is Randall Shore. I went to school with your mom. We were good friends, special friends," he added.

"You had a wonderful mother, Eugene."

The large man named Shore rubbed my shoulder and stood up. "Eugene, I have a farm on the edge of town where I raise thoroughbreds. Do you like to ride horses?"

I was numb. I couldn't understand why he would ask me such a question and I couldn't think of anything to say. I just stood there. I wanted to leave to go where they had taken mother and Philip. Mr. Shore finally smiled at me and turned back to grandpa and Uncle Paul. He shook their hands and left us in the sanctuary alone.

As we left the church, the sky was a beautiful azure color and the air was brisk. Orange, red, and yellow leaves blew all around the cars that formed the funeral procession, and the sun cast long shadows along the winding road that took us to the cemetery and eventually home.

Twelve

A couple days after mother's and Philip's funeral, I still couldn't sleep and everything I ate I threw up within minutes. I stayed in my room so grandpa and grandma wouldn't fuss over me. They said nothing about me returning to school, and although I opened my text books it was useless to try and study.

On the second day after the funeral, I received a letter from my teacher. I opened and read it quickly.

October 8, 1937

Dear Eugene,

I wanted to write to share the condolences of your entire class and myself over the passing of your mother and brother. Many of your classmates— Tommy Hampshire, Melissa Thompson, Homer Cantron, and many others—have asked about you. They want me to convey their deep sympathy.

Whenever you feel up to it, we would like to have you back in class. I realize it may be too soon, but we are still reading *The Call of the Wild* and I know how much you enjoy the novel. Please know that we miss you and pray that God is with you and your grandparents during your time of healing.

Your friend and teacher,

Signed, Evelyn Wilkins

Mrs. Wilkins' letter cheered me up. I put it down momentarily. I would read it again, several times in fact, but I wanted to open a second envelope that grandpa had slipped under my door. It was addressed:

Eugene O'Connor, Esq.
c/o Hastings Hamilton
Greenville Pike
Lisbon, Indiana

When I opened it, I simply found a handwritten note and a five dollar bill. The note read, "Hope to see you soon," but it was not signed. I immediately thought of father. I knew then he was thinking about me. How glad I was that he realized that what Uncle Paul had said and done at the church wasn't my doing. I was so pleased to receive the note. I took Mrs. Wilkins' letter, the five dollar bill and note from father, and placed them both under Philip's pillow on his bed. I didn't say anything to grandma or grandpa. From time to time during the day, after feeding the animals and doing the other chores, I would slip back into my bedroom like a thief and stealthily extract both envelopes from beneath Philip's pillow. I read their contents over and over.

That evening was the first time I ate an entire meal in five days. After I went to bed, I stayed awake until I heard the whistle from the Glass Works announcing the end of the 11:00 p.m. shift. I don't remember anything else until I woke the next morning.

I glanced at Reuben and realized I had been talking almost non-stop for an hour. It was only then that it occurred to me that I was monopolizing the conversation. His eyelids drooped and he didn't ask me to continue. I stopped and waited for him to say something, but his eyes slowly closed and he fell asleep. My mind started to drift back to how the events of that day first began. Elizabeth's death haunted me, making me sick to my stomach. She had picked up some papers to grade the previous Friday afternoon, helping me mark a couple dozen end-of-term themes.

"Gene," she said, having dropped the reference to me as "uncle" when she became my student assistant. "Some of the faculty and grad students are going to go to Nick's later on. Join us for a drink. We'd love for you to come along."

Elizabeth stood in my office doorway, her head cocked at an angle, her auburn hair flowing down over her shoulders. She looked the age of an undergraduate and not a twenty-seven-year-old professional woman. She smiled, knowing that smile had gotten her almost anything she had ever wanted from me. "Come on. Don't be a stick-in-the-mud," she added.

"Not tonight, Beth," I said, begging off. "It's been a long week. I just want to have a quiet dinner and get through some of these exams."

Beth frowned in a pouty way, but I knew it wasn't serious.

"Another time, okay?" I said.

She came up to me and gave me a big hug. She wasn't shy in showing affection. I liked that about her. Beth was confident, ebullient. Whatever she would end up doing, she would be successful.

"When you're old and gray, don't cry to me that I didn't want you around," she announced.

I pushed her away playfully and smiled, "I'm already old and gray and you wouldn't want me around for long."

Beth laughed and turned to leave. I saw Julie Emery, a fellow journalism professor, pass outside my doorway. "And whatever you do, Beth, don't associate with the likes of Emery or Coldren," I said loudly. "They'll only turn you into a cynic!"

Beth laughed. Julie Emery tucked her head in the doorway. "I heard that, O'Connor," she said. "And to think I used to like you!"

Beth bounded out of my office one way and Julie Emery the other, and that was it, the last time I saw Beth alive. And now here I was hurling away at several hundred miles an hour to a third world country and she was lying in the Monroe County morgue. What had gotten into me to think that I could just leave?

I had to call as soon as I could back to Bloomington to see if there was any new information. We were still a few hours out of Paris and I was extremely anxious to have the second leg of our journey completed.

I tried to change my thoughts and started to think about what it would be like to see Margaret Mahoney again. I simply couldn't comprehend how she could still be alive when I had seen her myself at the end of a noose shortly before I had been beaten by Mubarsoi's guards and deported. *What had happened? Was that not Margaret I saw? Had I assumed she was dead all these years when she was alive and living in Spain or Cape de Leone? Was my memory playing tricks with me?*

Although it had been thirty years ago, the events of those last days in Cape de Leone seemed indelibly imprinted in my mind. But maybe I had been mistaken? It was an eerie feeling. The thought of Margaret brought back a flood of memories of my early time in Burguna.

Feeling glad to be up and around, I looked on with some bewilderment as I scoured the village. In the early morning heat, Burguna rocked with activity. Hundreds of villagers moved to the commands of three Islamic technicians charged with directing the activity.

Lightly clothed Tambe men and women walked in a semi-regimented file behind one another. Each balanced several pounds of a mud-clay material. The women carried the slabs in a sling that draped over their right shoulders and in front of them. The men carried the slabs on top of their shoulders on slightly curved but pliable baskets made of thatch. When both the men and women reached the center of the village, they dumped the slabs on to large piles. Here several boys doused the growing piles with water to keep the clay-based mixture from drying out.

"Move the pulley out of the way, you dumb ass," screamed one of the Islamic commanders in Krio to a young Tambe man.

The young man was positioned on top of frail scaffolding. He strained to hold up probably more than eighty pounds of clay over his head, glancing painfully at the supervisor as if he had been whipped. The villager grabbed the pulley to try and brace himself, but it was no use. The weight of the clay was obviously too great. It tumbled from atop his shoulder, and the worker fell, too, bringing down part of the scaffolding in a crash. He barely escaped disaster.

The Islamic commander ran to the scene of the catastrophe and began to berate the worker unmercifully. Tribal members stopped to look on, but the other two Islamic supervisors quickly directed them back to their work, herding them like cattle.

The base of the mosque was already up. The outlines of the walls were beginning to take form. Scaffolding already appeared that suggested the shape and height of one of the two large minarets that would be erected last. The size of the mosque would dwarf the small building that had been used as a Christian chapel and school.

I was extremely impressed with the well organized manner by which the three Muslim supervisors from Tripoli directed hundreds of Tambe into constructive activities. The Tambe, to my observation of them over nearly eight months, were essentially a contented, not overly energetic or ambitious people. It was astonishing to see them work together in such an efficient way. The plan was to complete construction of the mosque before the rainy season came in September. Left to their own devices, it would have taken the Tambe years to complete what they had otherwise done to this point in a few weeks.

"It doesn't look like your services as a Christian missionary will be needed any time soon, Mr. O'Connor." I turned around quickly, startled by the voice. It was Justin Perry. He stood with his large arms folded across his barrel-like chest, beads of sweat popping out all over his face and khaki shirt. The sarcasm was matched by a smirk on his face.

"Perhaps if we had been half as organized, we'd still be in business," I said.

"You know, these men work as a team," Perry went on. "They go from village to village and oversee the construction of mosques. They built one in Japuta this past spring. Before that, they were in French Guinea for three years."

So that was the way they proselytized, I thought to myself. The calculated measures behind the spread of Islam across West Africa that took place in the 1940s and 1950s was through cooperation of economic, political, and religious interests. The Muslim traders and religious leaders worked arm and arm to corner the market, an early form of franchising. Not only were they able to gain millions of converts, but, probably foremost to their thinking, millions of trading partners and military alliances. Compared to this organized effort were Christian missionaries who were spread thin in countries such as French Guinea, Ivory Coast, Nigeria, Liberia, and Cape de Leone. They had come with the thought of converting individual souls by prayer and appealing to tribal members' faith and spirituality. How utopian-thinking of us all!

Justin Perry took a few steps away from me. "Mr. Mahomet Ali-Said," yelled Perry to a thin, middle-aged Arab man fifty feet away. The man was dressed in a flowing white robe and satin headdress. "Are you pleased with the progress, your Excellency?"

Mr. Ali-Said was the main Islamic advisor to Chief Faramha. In the local language, he was known as a "marabout"—a holy man who acts as a cross between a priest and an adviser for local people. His robe was as white as the snow he had never seen. He had also traveled from Tripoli about a month before to assist in the village's assimilation to Islam.

"When one submits to the will of God," Ali-Said replied, "all things are possible." He smiled at Perry. "Yes, I am well pleased, Dr. Perry."

"Is Allah proud that such a grand mosque is being built to worship him while the villagers go hungry and suffer from disease, your Excellency?"

In fact, Perry had exaggerated. While many Tambe suffered from a multitude of diseases, few, if any, went hungry.

"Allah never desires that his people suffer," responded Ali-Said.

"Then perhaps one turret would be sufficient, your Excellency?" Perry suggested. "The money for the second turret could be spared and left in the hands of the villagers."

"That, of course, is for Chief Faramha and the village elders to decide, Dr. Perry. As you know I am only here to help advise the council on legal and spiritual matters."

"Ah, but you help interpret what Allah desires, do you not, your Excellency?"

Ali-Said seemed to tire of Perry's rejoinders. "I am not a prophet myself, Dr. Perry. I'm only a man who has been asked to spread the prophecy of Allah as revealed through Mohammed. That is sufficient."

Perry exerted a big laugh and made a gesture as though he was toasting Ali-Said. I couldn't figure out what the exchange was all about between Justin Perry and Ali-Said, but it led me to understand more about their characters.

If Reuben had asked me that night how I could possibly have stayed seven years in Cape de Leone, I would have lied and given some bogus explanation. But the real reason was Margaret. I fell in love with her within a few weeks. But it did not take me long to figure out that she was completely devoted to Father Francis Tannen. I would eventually accept that our relationships formed a strange little triangle of unrequited love.

After my recovery from the near-fatal illness and as the mosque went up, life went on. Margaret's and my work at the school filled all of our time during the day, but the evenings were essentially our own. Daylight generally ended in Burguna around 8:00 p.m. Because we were so close to the equator, the sun's rising and setting didn't vary more than a few minutes from one season to another. The sunsets, also, were not nearly as lengthy as those in Indiana.

Margaret and I spent most evenings together. We would go for walks in Burguna and stop and chat with many of the villagers. During these leisurely jaunts, I got to know a great deal about her. But whenever Tannen was in the village, Margaret would not stray far from her house and seemed hesitant to engage in any lengthy conversations. She was very tight lipped about her relationship with Tannen. It seemed clear that they didn't live together in any common law arrangement as man and wife. Tannen was too much of a consecrated Jesuit, it seemed, to compromise his vows for the sake of love or sex. Yet, there was definitely an attraction between them, a strange, bizarre kind of allurement that involved their hearts and minds. Their affinity for one another seemed so bizarre because they were entirely different in terms of demeanor and personality.

Tannen was erudite but brooding and bombastic. He appeared to often be engaged in a tormented mind game in which some sort of twisted logic, known only to him, would dictate the outcome. Margaret, to the contrary, was lighthearted, although she was evidently quite intelligent and capable of serious discussion of her own. She countered Tannen's moody ways with a levity that kept the situation tolerable whenever the Jesuit priest was around. Further, Margaret was truly devoted to her vision of seeing primary schools established throughout the country and she believed that, through Tannen, there might be a way of accomplishing this ambition. Her motives in serving the priest were not totally selfless, it seemed to me.

Tannen lived in a large room that was attached to Margaret's house, a room filled with bookshelves stuffed well beyond their shelf space. He slept on a canvas cot. Margaret did his cooking (he generally refused to allow anyone else to prepare his meals), and she also saw that his clothes were washed and made presentable. She hired one of the Tambe women to do the latter. On occasion when I was out late, I would see Tannen's gas lantern lit and the priest reading well past midnight. He had a prodigious memory and seemed to relish sharing his esoteric tidbits of knowledge. This was the only way we truly interacted.

One day I slipped into his room and looked at the covers of

his books. He had dozens of volumes on military history and strategy, but also books on primitive African society and western philosophy and ethics. At the time, he was reading Aristotle's *Politics*. The book was upside down on his reading chair with the pages spread flat against the seat.

Tannen had almost nothing to do with the school. He was chief administrator of St. Magdalene's in name only. He would be gone for days at a time traveling. This was when Margaret and I would spend our evenings together. Early on, I had inquired as to where Father Tannen had traveled to, but Margaret was always rather vague in telling me where he had gone or the purpose for his absence. She initially told me that Tannen was traveling from village to village to meet with other tribal chiefs. "Francis is testing the waters, Gene," Margaret once said, "to see if it is possible to establish other schools modeled after St. Magdalene."

But she didn't mention this any more after our first few conversations and I eventually just stopped asking, recognizing that she was uncomfortable in talking about Tannen and even more so about his frequent departures. I just accepted them and was grateful because it enabled me to spend more time with her.

Margaret's assessment of Francis was that he was brilliant (which he was). To say that Francis Tannen is a scholar is like saying that the 1927 New York Yankees was a great baseball team or that water solidifies in freezing temperatures. He almost always had a book in hand. He was also a master of languages. Margaret claimed that Francis spoke some seven or eight European tongues and had picked up a smattering of West African languages as well during the short time he had been in Cape de Leone. He was clearly fluent in Krio. To Margaret, somehow Tannen's intellect and scholarly interests made up for all his social and moral deficiencies. It was this blind acceptance of him that I could never quite understand about her.

"Francis is writing a history of the ideas of Saint Thomas Aquinas," Margaret told me one evening. "I'm certain the history will be a great contribution to the understanding of the influences of Aristotelian thought on Christianity."

I looked at her rather blankly for the next ten minutes while she explained the influence of Aquinas on Christendom. I tried to act interested. But all I could think of was how beautiful she looked in her brightly-colored European cut dress, so strikingly different from the faded, smock-like garments worn by the Tambe women. The drift of conversation between us concealed the glowing admiration and libidinal longings that I felt for her. During the months I'd known Margaret, it seemed that she had started to dress more daring or wear her perfume stronger. Something was definitely different about her, but I couldn't quite identify it. I started to notice more the outlined shape of her breasts beneath her blouses and the few strands of her brunette hair that weren't perfectly combed across her forehead. Her silky hair was long, but she almost always wore it up. It made her look prim and secretarial. I sensed that her pinned up hair hid a kind of kinetic energy that if unleashed would flow, and her along with it, into sensual abandonment. The mere thought of it stirred me to the very depths of my stomach and I was crazy about her through a combination of love and lust.

"Gene," she said that evening, suddenly ending her discussion about Aquinas, "you look at me with such yearning. Haven't you ever had a sweetheart before?"

Margaret's question jarred me from my state of arousal. I had tried to conceal my longing for her, but obviously it hadn't worked. "Yes, I've had a sweetheart. Her name is Irene Sommers," I said, in a matter of fact way that surprised even me. "We've known each other since grade school."

"And where is she now, Gene?"

"Back in my home town."

"Then why are you here and not with Irene?"

My heart shriveled at Margaret's question. Why was she questioning me now about this? What did I bring on by looking at her so lustily? I did the best that I could to frame a plausible answer. "I've come to serve the Tambe as a missionary, of course,"

I said. "Isn't that a good enough reason?"

"But what does Irene think?" asked Margaret.

That I couldn't answer. Irene and I had seen each other for several years back in Lisbon, but it seemed like nothing serious could come of it. Irene was a lovely women; she had a simple charm and a warm personality, but there was something that kept us apart, something that wouldn't allow us to connect.

"I'm sorry, I didn't mean to intrude," she said. "Please tell me more about your family, Gene. I know so little about them."

The West African air, thick with moisture that was worse than Indiana humidity in August, began to squeeze in on me, causing distress. I had intentionally said little about Lisbon or my family to Margaret to try and avoid just this conversation. The memories were too disturbing, still too fresh to want to revisit them.

"The few letters I receive," I said with a short gasp. "They come mostly from members of my home church."

"And your family, Gene? Tell me more. You've been so. . ." Margaret paused and smiled before completing her thought, "secretive about them."

I instantaneously broke out into a sweat. The limpid soggy heat opened the pores of my skin and the perspiration poured from my underarms and chest. I tried to control my reaction but it seemed like the more I dwelt on it, the more I perspired. A dozen mops couldn't have kept me dry.

"My grandmother writes occasionally," I sputtered, wiping my perspiring forehead. "She's a strong, Bible-reading Christian even though she's a little odd."

"And your parents?" asked Margaret.

"I have only seen my father once since I was eight," I said. "I suppose he knows I'm here—meaning here in Africa," I added, explaining, "I doubt that he has the faintest idea where Cape de Leone is."

"He must be proud of you though, Gene."

Margaret immediately sensed that she had said something wrong, as if her comment, intended as a compliment, sounded disingenuous. There was an awkward silence between us. I cleared my throat and decided to plunge in.

"My mother and brother Philip were killed in an accident when I was ten," I blurted out.

"Oh, Gene," Margaret exclaimed, "I'm so sorry. I didn't intend to bring up such painful memories."

What Margaret intended really didn't matter now. And in some perverse way I was pleased that she had inquired into my past, because I had longed to share myself beyond some superficial accounting. But what started out as confession to lay bare my sins resulted in something quite unexpected. Instead of being for the purpose of expiation, our conversation took on an intimacy that only increased the powerful emotional feelings I had for Margaret. That evening we talked until midnight, and each evening we met thereafter we immediately lapsed into that kind of chatter that is normally reserved for lovers. But we weren't lovers, at least not in any sort of way beyond the suggestion of words. But, oh, the words were a powerful aphrodisiac, and I burned with passion every time we conversed. And one thing was now abundantly clear to me: I had fallen madly in love with Margaret Mahoney.

Thirteen

"I just can't understand, Nigel, why Margaret didn't contact me before," I said to him after he had woken. "If she knew I was alive, then what prevented her from locating me? It wouldn't have been that difficult."

"I believe she was afraid to contact you. You've explained to me how shell-shocked you were after going through the civil war. The same was true for Margaret, but even more so. She was completely devastated. Horrors of that kind aren't easily erased. In fact, she became a recluse. She didn't even communicate with her own family."

"That I can understand," I exclaimed, "but I still don't understand why she didn't try to contact me? She cared for me deeply. I know this as certain as I know we're on this plane together."

"I don't have all the answers, Professor. Just trust me that you'll have a much better understanding once we get to Grand Bassa."

"But—"

Reuben stopped me cold. "Think back to what you went through, Professor. Then think about what hardships Margaret suffered because she decided to follow Tannen. If you do, then I believe you'll realize just how ravaged Margaret was, even though she physically survived."

I laid my head back against the headrest of my seat and pondered what Reuben said. I remembered how it took me about two years of living in Cape de Leone before I began to have even a partial understanding of the complexity of West African society and the brutality that rocked the nation.

Cape de Leone is a small country about the size of South

Carolina, bounded to the west by the Atlantic Ocean, to the north and northeast by French Guinea and to the south and southeast by Liberia. In the 1950s, it had a population of about three million, but no one knew for sure how many people lived in the country because a census hadn't been performed since 1940 when the British were still in power. Moreover, because there were several nomadic tribes that lived in the eastern part of the country, it was doubtful that all of the natives were counted. Cape de Leone, to a large extent, was representative of West Africa as a whole. It was an extremely poor nation, but essentially self-sustaining. The various tribal members seemed generally happy despite the heartaches they suffered. For instance, due to disease, lack of medical care, and a shortage of nutritious food, infant mortality was high and the life span of those who did survive childhood averaged only about forty years of age.

The country was divided into three large provinces. There were more than fifteen major ethnic groups spread throughout Cape de Leone and a few dozen tribal villages within each ethnic group. The country was approximately sixty percent Islam, thirty percent Animist, and just ten percent Christian. Less than a quarter of the people were literate. Outside of Grand Bassa, the nation's capital, almost all work was agricultural in nature except for some diamond mining in the northeast region.

Politically, Cape de Leone was in a continual state of confusion. It was unclear who, if any one, was in charge prior to the take over by Albert Mubarsoi in the 1950s. The area that now comprised the country had been occupied by European forces since the 1700s (first the Dutch, then the Portuguese, who named it, and later the British). In 1896 England proclaimed Cape de Leone a "protectorate." This meant that the country was not a "colony" with all the rights and obligations that goes along with that designation. This was a wise course, because it would have been nearly impossible to impose British law and customs on the various tribesmen who were completely unfamiliar with European legal and social customs.

Until the early 1950s, the bureaucrats of "Whitehall" (England's location for its civil service in London) ruled this insular and poverty-stricken nation through efficient ministers and foreign civil service officers. These officers were selected for positions in Grand Bassa after having been passed over for more prestigious appointments to African diplomatic posts such as Cairo, Praetoria, Addis Ababa, and Khartoom. Nonetheless, through these ministers England effectively governed the country for more than fifty years. The arrangement was quite agreeable to most of the Leoneons who lived outside of Grand Bassa. The British officers did not involve themselves in internal tribal matters. They focused their energy and resources on national issues, leaving the tribal chiefs to exercise their own local autonomy and authority.

Francis Tanner had been the source of this information. From time to time we would get a newspaper from Grand Bassa or even the *Times* of London, but Tanner knew more than what could be found in a hundred newspapers. His knowledge was encyclopedic. He explained to me how after World War II everything had changed in West Africa. The cry against European colonialism swept across the region, as it did across most of sub-Sahara Africa. The prevailing views by native nationalist leaders were that colonialism equated with paternalism and stifled native initiative. Beyond that, colonialism was simply viewed as an unjust, humiliating, and evil system. It was repugnant to the growing sense of nationalism that spread wildly throughout Africa in the 1950s and 1960s. One by one, nation after nation in West Africa followed Cape de Leone's lead in declaring independence: Ghana in 1957 from England; Mali in 1958 from France; Nigeria from England in 1960 as well as most of the rest of West Africa's countries from France in 1960, including Mauritania, Senegal, Cote d'Ivoire (Ivory Coast), Togo, and Upper Volta (now Burkino Faso). Later The Gambia claimed independence from England in 1965 and Guinea-Bissau from Portugal in 1974.

To England's credit, it didn't allow its political and military ties to be cut with the nation all at once. Its ministers recognized that chaos would erupt if a responsible government was not put in place before English civil servants departed. In 1950 England had drafted a plan that intended to transfer power to a democratically elected native executive ruler and parliament. The approach appeared workable in concept; in practice the plan utterly failed.

When I had arrived in Burguna in November 1952, I had no idea how unstable it was. From 1950 to that date, the tiny nation had already had three different tribal chiefs serve as President. Each President's tenure was remarkably brief, rife with corruption and absent of any accomplishment. The main preoccupation of each leader had been simply to retain power. Gaining presidential office was simple in comparison to retaining it. Rather than be democratically elected, as the Brits had proposed, each of the presidents had been removed by a successor through a bloodless coup and retired back to his native village. There the former Leonean President presided once again over his tribe and became a local hero for life.

Despite England's objections to such a rapid and unruly usurpation of power, it had publicly committed itself to allowing the people of Cape de Leone to determine their own destiny. England simply didn't have the resources to address the problem. It had kept a skeleton force of troops and a few dozen advisors in Grand Bassa, but Whitehall was essentially out of the political loop at this point. It readily admitted that it had bungled any hopes to put in place an orderly and democratically elected government.

"Since the war, Churchill, Eden, and Parliament have had too many domestic problems to concern themselves about without worrying about West African politics," Tanner said one afternoon in about 1954. "The British Empire is dead! England will be lucky to control its own fate, let alone a small African nation three thousand miles away."

I had no idea that the man who spoke these words would someday have much to say about the fate of my host country.

As I told Reuben about my initial encounter with politics in Cape de Leone, his eyes brightened. He sat up in his seat and drained his Bloody Mary with one large gulp.

"Did you have any idea you would be in the center of Tannen's civil war?" Reuben asked.

"Never," I replied. "I had no knowledge that Tannen was planning anything. He kept his personal agenda so secret that I don't think Margaret even knew half of his plot. The first moment I had an inkling of his extreme interest in the country's political life was when Justin Perry reported on Albert Mubarsoi's successful coup in 1955. I remember that Tannen just peppered Perry with question after question, digging for all the information he could pull out of him."

It was a sweltering evening in October 1955 and there had just been a downpour when we gathered in Margaret's house. She had invited Tannen and me to taste a Moselle wine she had intended to save for a special occasion. For some reason, on a lark, she decided to uncork the bottle. We had no more than sat down, when the ubiquitous Dr. Perry popped his large head through the open window.

"Mind if I join you?" he asked.

"Justin," Margaret exclaimed, "we'd be delighted. Please come in."

Perry had just finished his rounds of tending to the sick Tambe. His shirt was soaked. Margaret placed a chair for him farthest away from Tannen. When Perry entered the thatched house and sat down, she poured his glass first.

"Have anything stronger, Margaret?" Perry asked. He wiped his brow with the back of his forearm.

Margaret, seeming somewhat embarrassed, responded. "I'm afraid, Justin, I haven't had any hard liquor for months, but Francis has some whis—" Margaret suddenly looked at Tannen and noticed a scowl starting to form on his face. She continued without missing a beat. "I'm afraid this is all I have now, Justin. I've ordered some scotch. Next time, okay?"

Perry smiled and then gestured to indicate that the wine was fine. She poured his tumbler full. Before she had finished pouring for the rest of us, Perry guzzled his first glass as if it was beer and held the tumbler forward for a refill.

"What do you know about Mubarsoi's coup, Justin?" Tannen asked out of nowhere. "Any chance he won't survive?"

Perry had visited a couple weeks before and had warned us that the government headed by former Paramount Chief Makimbi Bangura was extremely weak and ripe for take over. Perry rocked on the back legs of his crudely made bamboo chair.

"General Mubarsoi's the first president, I think, that can retain power," he responded. "No, I'll make a stronger prediction. Mubarsoi will retain power and there's nobody in Grand Bassa that thinks he touchable. The whole city is scared to death of him. Worse of all are the British diplomats. They don't know what to make of him." Perry took another large swallow of the Moselle. "He'll do anything to retain the office. The way he dealt with Bangura proves that."

"What happened to Bangura?" Margaret asked.

"Mubarsoi killed him and ate his heart!" Tannen said, reporting the sickening news in an absurd, theatrical, envious tone of voice.

"You're joking, aren't you?" Margaret responded.

"The hell I am!" said Tannen. "Three days ago Mubarsoi held a press conference in the reception hall of the capitol building. He invited the entire press corp and literally ate Bangura's heart in front of them while he dictated his plans to maintain control of the country."

Margaret looked at Perry in puzzlement, aghast.

"It's true, Margaret," confirmed Perry. "It's an old tribal tradition to eat the chief's heart of the tribe you've just conquered. It was on the front page of the largest newspaper in

Grand Bassa. Mubarsoi sat eating Bangura's heart while he answered questions from the local press."

Margaret's face became ashen. I listened for the next hour while Perry recounted Mubarsoi's rise to power. Being on the southeastern edge of Cape de Leone, news about what happened in Grand Bassa, located on the country's western coastline, came slowly. The information that we did receive by word of mouth often seemed apocryphal, larger than life, while the reports we listened to over the BBC appeared just the opposite, being presented in a low-key, sanitized manner. Perry seemed intimately associated with the details.

"Where did Mubarsoi come from?" asked Tannen. "I hadn't heard his name until he was made a general by Mayamba last year."

"He grew up in a tribe called the Kholifa in the northern province. It's near the diamond mines," said Perry. "Mubarsoi joined the West African Frontier Force at the age of sixteen. He was the first Black from Cape de Leone to receive an appointment to Sandhurst, the same military institution that educated Winston Churchill. Quite a feat!"

Mubarsoi's meteoric rise seemed to be nothing less than remarkable. From simply being a son of a farmer in the Kholifa tribe, Mubarsoi had reached the top of political leadership through a very unorthodox path. He was now President of Cape de Leone at the age of thirty-eight, and his position there, at least by recent standards, seemed secure.

Perry explained that when the British were still in full control, prior to 1950, the traditional path to leadership in Cape de Leone's politics was through the civil service. Still, London's Whitehall had a patronizing view about the natives' ability to self-govern. The British considered the locals capable of processing paperwork and filling bureaucratic positions, but questioned the Leoneons' proficiency to lead the country politically. The successive coup d'etats since Whitehall relinquished control of the government showed they were right.

But Mubarsoi proved the exception on all fronts.

Perry answered question after question that Tannen threw at him. On Mubarsoi's return to Cape de Leone from the Royal Military College at Sandhurst, he had quickly moved up the ranks of military leadership. Finally, Bo Mayamba, the country's Prime Minister, had promoted Mubarsoi to General and Commander-in-Chief of the armed forces eighteen months before.

Mubarsoi had a long way to go to reform a poorly trained and compensated military. Cape de Leone's political elite viewed the military with contempt, but still regarded the institution as a necessary evil to maintain order in a society too often threatened by mob riot. The armed forces had little respect before Mubarsoi took control of them. The government also feared the military because if it ever realized its true potential, a takeover of the government was very likely. The country's armed forces were provided with outdated armaments and largely used for ceremonial occasions: trotting out to the national airport to greet the Prime Minister from a trip abroad; appearing in regiment to be reviewed by some visiting African head of state; standing guard at Parliamentary garden parties. In recent years, its one true accomplishment was to deliver mail when the postal union went on strike for six weeks in 1953. For this, an editorial in Grand Bassa's *Daily News* lavishly praised the military for executing this "critical task" with "great efficiency and aplomb."[1] But in reality, the military was a sign that the country was nothing but a banana republic. But this was all before Mubarsoi!

"If Mubarsoi has all this education and experience, why would he resort to such savagery as executing the previous President and eating his heart?" I asked Perry. "What does he gain from that except looking like a thug and a heathen?"

Perry glanced at Tannen and then back at me.

"First," the doctor responded, "he strikes fear in every paramount chief in the country. Bangura was seen as weak and

---

1 See generally, Joe A.D. Alle, *A New History of Sierra Leone*, (Gordonsville, VA: Palgrave MacMillan), 1990, pp. 236-239

ineffective, but he was loved for his efforts to bring peace and order. For Mubarsoi to take Bangura out like he did forces every chief to acknowledge that he means business. It's an outdated custom, of course, but in tribal cultural memory it will make every chief think hard before attempting another coup."

"Just as important," Tannen interrupted, "Mubarsoi distances himself from the British."

Indeed, as I was to learn, Mubarsoi's willingness to use destruction and intimidation made him into almost a god to the Leoneon people. He would be a force not easily toppled in this one-party state where he had become President, Commander-in-Chief, and also head of the Cape de Leone People's Party.

Reuben listened intently as I shared my story about Mubarsoi's early achievements and brutality. He seemed eager to talk about them.

"I knew about Mubarsoi executing Bangura and eating his heart," he said. "Those acts are still talked about frequently in many circles. But I wasn't aware, Professor, how important it was that Mubarsoi be seen to distance himself from the British government. It's ironic because he's constantly seeking British economic aid today."

"It's probably a reflection of how bad the times have become in the country," I said. "You've been there off and on, Nigel. Don't you agree?"

"Absolutely. Unemployment in Grand Bassa is nearly fifty percent and it's even worse out in the provinces. It's made life unbearable for most citizens. That's why the natives supporting Josiah Kimba's party have little reason to stop their attempts to overthrow the government. Times have become even more desperate, if that's possible. But it's also made Mubarsoi even more determined to keep a lid on any opposition. The Leoneon military has become extremely brutal in stamping out any support for Kimba. I don't believe the upcoming election will be anything but a sham. Mubarsoi isn't going to allow any opposition movement to appear to have any large scale support. It's an extremely volatile situation right now. I'm afraid some kind of full blown civil war is going to erupt very soon if something isn't resolved.

"But please continue," Reuben added. "Tell me how you became so personally involved in the efforts to overthrow Mubarsoi by the CPP."

The airline attendant had brought Reuben a second drink. The edginess that he had earlier displayed was now gone and he seemed totally relaxed. But before I could explain to Reuben how I became involved with the Christian Peoples Party, I had to sort out first the relationships that had developed with Tannen and Margaret. My commitment to the CPP was inseparable from my involvement with the two of them. Thank goodness Reuben was a patient listener.

Fourteen

Margaret came to my hut one evening after supper. That evening, in April 1958, she announced she was leaving to return to Ireland.

"You can't go!" I exclaimed. "I can't function without you. None of us can."

"Gene, I'm not leaving for good," Margaret explained. "I'm going back to visit my mother in Dublin. I'll return by July. Don't worry. Marabella, Falaba, and you can continue teaching. Surely you can operate the school without me for a few weeks."

"But you're positive you're coming back?" I insisted.

"Gene, you can trust me. You know that."

Margaret hugged me and then whispered that she was leaving the next day. I wondered why she hadn't told me before, but the reason was irrelevant now. When I got up early the next morning to see her off, she had already left. Samuel Obei accompanied Margaret to Lelahue by ferry. From there, she would travel on to Grand Bassa on her own.

The next evening, I noticed a light on in her house. It was a kerosene lamp and it made me curious. I walked in and noticed on Margaret's dining room table several books, most of them opened: *Von Kriege* (On War) by Carl Clausewitz, which was in German; Aristotle's *Politics*, and, *The History of the Crusades*. There were several other books on African warfare and spirituality. Finally I noticed a worn *Encyclopaedia Britannica* with a bookmark in it. I opened it and saw an entry underlined in pencil. It was a short passage:

Margaret of Angouleme also called Margaret of Navarre (born April 11, 1492—died. Dec. 21, 1549), queen consort of Henry II of Navarre, who, as patron of Humanists and Reformers, and as an author in her own right, was one of the most outstanding figures of the French Renaissance. Margaret extended her protection both to men of artistic and scholarly genius and to advocates of doctrinal and disciplinary reform within the Church. Francois Rabelais, Clement Marot, Bonaventure Des Periers, and Etienne Dolet were all in her circle. Her personal religious inclinations tended toward a sort of mystical pietism, but she was also influenced by the Humanist Jacques Lefevre, who saw St. Paul's Epistles as a primary source of Christian doctrine.

The most important of Margaret's own literary works is the Heptameron. These stories, illustrating the triumphs of virtue, honour, and quick-wittedness and the ruination caused by vice and hypocrisy, contain a strong element of satire directed against licentious and grasping monks and clerics.

"Ah, caught you in the act!" came a deep voice from the doorway.

"Francis," I said, startled. I laughed nervously, thinking he was joking. "You scared me."

"You know Margaret is gone, don't you?"

"Yes, yes," I said, stuttering to think what to say. "I didn't intend to be nosy. I was just curious about the lamp burning."

"You shouldn't be in the house when Margaret isn't here," he replied in a surly voice. He then obviously noticed the encyclopedia in front of me and his tone became more friendly, but also slightly satirical. "Have you taken a sudden interest in reading, Eugene? I don't often see you with a book, but then I'm not around you as much as Margaret is."

What did he mean? "There isn't much to read," I said aloud.

"The children's literature is so simple."

"I imagine you must find that fascinating then?" Tannen said.

There was a lull. Tannen moved toward me. He had a glass in his left hand and a whiskey bottle in his right. He kicked a chair from out underneath the table and it fell on its side. He sat on the table, his heavy body causing it to bow under his great weight. His black shirt and white, Roman collar were soaked with perspiration.

"Tell me, Eugene," Tannen said with a smirk I had come to know. "Are they all as stupid as you where you're from or is Burguna just blessed with being host to one of America's most feeble minds?"

"I'm sorry about coming in uninvited," I said, standing up to leave. "I simply wondered if anything was wrong."

"Oh, no, I quite enjoy companionship with stupid people. It's just an education for me to realize that there are so many of you. I've forgotten after being in this intellectual haven for so long, enjoying all these cerebral discussions I've had with the Tambe about Freud, Einstein, Planck, Darwin."

Tannen took a drink from the bottle, seeming to forget he held a glass full of whiskey. "I bet you find the Tambe fascinating, don't you, Eugene? You speak their lingo, don't you?" He laughed. "Have you ever screwed one of their women, Eugene? Why, I bet a Tambe woman would gladly allow you to come onto her. Just think of it, you could talk dirty to her about the sweet passions of cow-milking. Wouldn't that be something?"

Suddenly Tannen hurled the whiskey bottle past my left ear and it thumped loudly against the thatch wall. "I think I've had enough intellectualizing for one night, Eugene! If you don't mind, I much prefer to be alone. Why don't you go out and screw a few Tambe women now? When Margaret returns, you need to have something to confess to her about. She'd be terribly disappointed if you didn't have some deep, disturbing secrets to confide."

Tannen slammed the glass down on the table and the whiskey flew out. I started walking backwards towards the front door.

"Before you leave, Eugene," Tannen called out to me, "please tell me, just which one of you plays the priest and which the penitent? I've never quite figured that out. Or do you two just take turns pouring out your souls to one another? I know that Margaret's a great one for confession." Tannen started to take a giant gulp from his whiskey glass, obviously forgetting that it was now empty. He then laughed. "What has she confided to you about me, Eugene? What sins am I guilty of? Haughtiness? Arrogance? Debauchery? Surely she must have told you of many!"

I stood in the doorway and Tannen yelled after me. "Tell me to my face, Eugene! Be felicitous to this curious aging priest! Why, you possess the eyes, ears and heart of the great saint, Margaret Mahoney!"

The last thing I saw before I fled Margaret's house was Tannen staggering to the chair I had momentarily occupied. Once seated, he lifted the encyclopedia and slammed it down. The whiskey glass toppled from the table, struck the hardwood floor, and broke into a hundred pieces. My heart raced as I ran back to my hut. For the next hour I kept watch, afraid that the intoxicated priest might come after me.

After I told Reuben about this strange, revealing encounter with Tannen, I noticed that he began yawning. We had been in the air for almost four hours out of New York and I had talked almost non-stop. With the exchange of a few words we both lay our heads back against the head rests. I finally fell asleep for about forty-five minutes, but not before ruminating about that horrid exchange with Tannen.

It hadn't occurred to me before that night that Tannen might somehow be jealous of me. But the throwing of the whiskey bottle and the hateful diatribe showed the priest's own dependence on Margaret. Their souls were bound with some sort of mutually forged chains. For her part, Margaret never strayed far from her house whenever Tannen was in the village; dinner invitations and conversations beyond our school day stopped when he was present. Margaret had become even more guarded in discussing anything about Francis's frequent absences.

It occurred to me that perhaps Margaret was trying to protect me from the priest. I didn't know, but Tannen's outburst that evening in 1958 did confirm in my own mind the disdain he held for me, a young interloper from the U.S. As I thought about it, I started to understand why he might feel the way he did.

Margaret had already told me that I had stayed longer than any of the previous four "recruits" that Father Stivonovich had brought to Burguna in the several years preceding my arrival. This greatly angered Tannen, especially since Stivonovich himself had vanished from the village, not to be seen or heard from again after five years. More importantly, I was a perceived threat to Tannen because of the friendship that Margaret and I had established. Interestingly, that friendship had developed mostly due to the priest's frequent absences from Burguna.

After our ugly wrangle that sultry night, I intentionally avoided going anywhere near where Tannen might see me. The unfortunate fact was that St. Magdalene School was right next to Margaret's house. It was well known that Francis slept late in the mornings, so I felt safe from encountering him before our mid-day break. But there was a much greater chance of running into the priest in the evenings if I was out. Burguna was, after all, a village of less than 700 natives.

A couple of days after Tannen's wild, drunken outburst, I returned to my hut after teaching. A paper sack sat on my desk. It had a note attached to it:

> Gene,
>
> Sorry about the other night. Too much booze, not enough snooze. Hope to make it up to you. Thought you might enjoy some reading material from two of my favorite authors. Might find getting through the ideas a little heavy sloshing, but it should be well worth your time if you're in for an intellectual challenge. Cheers!
>
> Signed, Francis

I opened up the sack and found two books: *Folklore and Myth in the African Mind* by Antoine Bushey and *An Introduction to Aristotelian Thought* by Francis J. Tannen, S.J. No sooner had I opened Tannen's book than I heard a whistle. It was the author himself.

"Well, what do you think of the gifts?" he asked as he popped his large head through the open door of my hut. "Will you be an apostle or a critic of their ideas?"

I quickly thumbed through the pages of his thick book, an outright tome. I was amazed at the small print and detail for an "introductory" text.

"Neither one until I read them," I said. "Give me at least thirty minutes."

Tannen laughed heartily. "If you don't understand everything the first time, don't worry. You're not expected to. It's pretty weighty material." He pulled at his beard. "How about dinner tomorrow evening? We can discuss them then."

My heart cringed at the thought of a meal with the surly priest, but I didn't dare decline the offer. "Sure," I said. "Where? What time?"

"Be at the house," Tannen answered. "I'll have Marabella fix something for us. Come at eight o'clock."

I soon realized that if Francis Tannen was serious about discussing the books, I had to read as much of them as possible that evening. After a quick and simple meal of rice and African vegetables, I picked up Tannen's book again. The first few pages were fairly easy reading. Tannen discussed Aristotle's significance in Western thought and his importance in devising a classification system in order to systematically discuss ideas that governed man and nature. I was able to follow Tannen's discussion of Aristotle's logic until the third chapter, at which time the discussion and vocabulary became much more difficult. Finally, I became completely lost.

I next moved onto *Folklore and Myth in the African Mind*. The book was divided into various chapters, a chapter each on a particular tribe. I flipped to the table of contents and identified a short chapter about the Tambe. I found Bushey's description of their beliefs to be what I'd observed myself. He had obviously done his homework. I was just about to go to bed when I picked up Tannen's book again and read the back flap of the dust jacket. It showed a picture of a much younger looking Francis Tannen. A brief biography was below the picture.

> Francis J. Tannen is a Catholic priest and a member of The Society of Jesus (Jesuits). Born and raised in New South Wales, Australia, he obtained his undergraduate degree with honours in classical philosophy from the University of Adelaide and his Ph.D. from Trinity College, Dublin, Ireland, where he wrote his doctoral thesis on the medieval theologian Saint Thomas Aquinas. . . .

Neither Margaret or Tannen had ever mentioned that he had studied in Dublin. It made me curious: why had it never come up in any of our conversations? I went to bed dreading the thought of having supper the following evening.

As Bushey discussed in his chapter on the Tambe, the tribal members were essentially a kind, pliant, and gentle people— desiring to please and seldom complaining. The men who remained in the village tended to be older, lacked ambition and any interest in hard work. On the other hand the villagers were slow to rile, accommodating, and above all else were extremely superstitious. They only desired to be allowed to continue their tribal traditions as part of their conversion to Islam. In the African mind one can embrace a new religion while still holding fast to the beliefs of another faith. Thus, despite pledging allegiance to the one and only God, Allah, the Tambe still saw spirits and many gods acting in almost every aspect of their lives: if the weather changed for the worse, the gods were angry; inanimate objects such as trees, wood carvings, and sculptures were viewed as "fetishes," worshipped for their inherent magical powers. When a white panther wandered into Burguna one evening, the villagers were convinced that the beautiful animal was actually a spy from a neighboring tribe snooping about to report back about the Tambe's activities. This "ju-ju mentality" governed nearly every aspect of the tribe's daily life.

The villagers' bodies were adorned with lucky rings, bangles, necklaces, anklets and other trinkets that were supposed to protect the bearer from evil and bring good fortune and fertility. The Tambe held to these superstitions while at the same time religiously obeying the strict commands of Islam. Five times a day they unrolled their prayer mats and followed the calls of the Muezzin; they observed the special festivals and religious holidays such as "Muharram," the Islamic new year; the "Id al Kabir," commemorating Abraham's sacrifice, and; of course, "Ramadan," the month of fasting.

We were in Ramadan at present. I knew that was why Tannen had invited me to dine with him so late the following evening. Although Margaret, Tannen, and I did not participate in any of the Islamic forms of worship, we were very careful to respect the Muslim teachings and practices that the Tambe were now required to follow. Tannen had ingratiated himself with Chief Farahma through great deference on this point. In particular, he had gained favor with the chief by advising him about how he could navigate the difficult task of appeasing the Islamic "supervisors" while at the same time remaining within the good graces of the tribe's elders, who were reluctant to give up any of the Tambe's spiritual and cultural traditions. Tannen was the consummate politician and diplomat. Even though Margaret had said little about the role that Francis played as an advisor to Chief Farahma, it was obvious that he had skills in tribal diplomacy.

The following night I arrived at Margaret's house, where Marabella had prepared dinner. Nearly all food, for some unknown reason in West Africa, was referred to as *chop* accompanied by what the natives referred to as *gadgets*. Marabella had prepared a glorified native dish called palm-oil chop, which was chicken stewed in palm oil. It had a golden red color, about the same hue and consistency as engine oil. Served with the stewed chicken were peppers and rice and all sorts of side-dishes (*gadgets*), consisting of fried onions, raw onions, chopped-up coconut, and fried bananas. Tannen provided the wine. During the course of dinner, our conversation started off with the political issue of the day.

"Do you think the paramount chiefs will have any success in repealing the hut tax?" I asked Tannen. I had heard Francis speak about the tax before in conversations he had with Justin Perry and I knew he had strong feelings.

"You ask an interesting question," Tannen responded. "I doubt that there is much they can do about it given the stronghold that Mubarsoi has over Parliament. But if his promises about using the revenue to improve roads, sanitation, and education go unfulfilled, then he will run into trouble."

Since Mubarsoi had taken power, several political and legal changes had occurred that had created hostility between the self-anointed leader and the nation's 150 or so paramount chiefs. Traditionally, the President of the country did little more than preside over the capital city and its immediate environs. There was no money to expand authority to the provinces over which the tribal chiefs maintained control. That was the reason that the chiefs really didn't care much who was President, because their authority had remained essentially intact regardless of who officiated in Grand Bassa.

But Mubarsoi was trying to change all that. Within a few short months of his successful coup in October 1955, Mubarsoi had levied what had become known as a "hut tax." The assessed taxation amounted to twenty shillings (then about five U.S. dollars) to anyone who owned a hut of three rooms or more and ten shillings to anyone who owned a hut with fewer than three rooms. Both the paramount chiefs and villagers strongly opposed the tax. They believed that taxation on their huts implied a kind of rent, which, in their minds, denied them ownership rights. To make the chiefs even more upset, Mubarsoi had passed laws extending the rights of the central government over civil and criminal cases and passed new land regulations. For example, foreign companies mining minerals now had to pay a mining fee directly to the central government. This also took revenue away from the provincial and tribal governments.

In exchange for this shift of power from the tribes to the national government, Mubarsoi had promised much: the building of new roads; the construction of a new railroad line that would cut through the center of the country; the development of a sanitation system in Grand Bassa; and, the offering of educational opportunities that had hitherto been unavailable to almost all children of the country.

If Mubarsoi's attempts at consolidating and expanding his power were met with strong opposition by the paramount chiefs, his personal appeal to the natives was wildly favorable. The various villagers wanted a strong leader; they craved for a national figure who wouldn't back down from the chiefs. They revered and worshipped Mubarsoi as if he were a god! And Mubarsoi regarded himself as a god, a demon, a ruler born for the times! He manipulated the press in a shrewd, sophisticated way reminiscent of modern Twentieth Century world leaders such as Hitler, Mao, and Stalin. He was the first Leoneon leader to leave Grand Bassa to campaign for his reforms in the provinces. He staged speaking appearances with thousands of admiring supporters; he promised orphanages, hospitals, and schools to the grand applause of children, the elderly, and administrators. He maintained his support for a better educated, trained, and paid military. He had a mesmerizing persona and a confidence in his abilities that was unique among African leaders. Mubarsoi was ahead of his time in the march against colonialism which culminated in the independence of one African nation after another in the 1950s and 1960s.

Tannen was absolutely obsessed by Mubarsoi. We spent almost the entire evening discussing the leader's personal traits and his chances of remaining a long-time political and military power in West Africa. Still, there were a number of other issues and ideas that Tannen obviously derived great pleasure in talking about. His facile mind was amazing, and I realized after that night that Margaret was right: Francis Tannen was brilliant beyond words! As he expounded for two hours about one topic after another—law, economics, politics, science, African cultures, military strategy, religion—I could only find myself asking one simple question: *what was a remarkable man like this doing in this god-forsaken country?*

Fifteen

The British had ruled Cape de Leone for more than a half century before I arrived in 1952. During most of those years, the tribes in the interior part of the country were left alone, but occasionally the British government's provincial governor would visit a village to conduct a survey of its activities and to hear any complaints.

A few years before I arrived, the Tambe had been plagued by a nearby tribe named the Koshsue, who were notorious thieves.[2] They didn't farm or hunt but mostly lived off what they could pilfer from other tribes. They had raided the village of Burguna a couple of times, plundering from the Tambe all of the animals and personal property they could snatch in a quick sweep. Strangely, they never hurt anyone, but the raids were impossible to predict.

The Tambe finally complained to the provincial governor. The "PC," as he was called, met with the chieftain of the thieving tribe and informed him that such treachery was devastating the Tambe and disgracing the Koshsue's reputation.

The Koshsue chieftain listened carefully to the PC. He said that the words of the great wise counselor had caused him to see the errors of his ways. That owing to the PC's convincing arguments, the Koshsue would forego piracy and become self-sufficient and model citizens. The PC was extremely pleased with himself. Upon his departure, he reported this good news back to Chief Faramha. The very next night, the Koshsue raided Burguna and stole everything that wasn't tied down.

I always remembered this story whenever I was approached

---

2 Adapted, *Tales from the Dark Continent*, ed. Charles Allen (New York: St. Martin's Press, 1979), p. 92.

to solve any problem that the Tambe presented to me. I never wanted to arbitrate a dispute where I couldn't possibly understand the rules and variables, but one minor incident stuck in my mind where I did just that.

There had been a tradition among tribes in the area that before the rains came to pray for them and to pay homage to the local rainmaker.[3] But this year no one from the Tambe followed the tradition. Marabella Farbuto and Falaba Cardew informed the elders that this was old-fashioned thinking and that the rainmaker had no more power to make it rain than he did to make the Tambe wealthy.

But no rains had come for several months and the tribe was very concerned. One of the elders finally went to the rainmaker, but the rainmaker rebuffed the elder. Joseph Obei came to me soon after and pleaded for me to intervene. "The rainmaker will listen to you, Mr. O'Connor. Please, we need your help."

So against my better judgment, off I went to find this hermit. He lived on the foothill of a small mountain. I found him in a hut.

"Why should I help the Tambe when they refuse to believe in my magic?" said the rainmaker.

I gave several reasons, none of which seemed to move him. Finally, I humbled myself. "If you won't do it for them, then please help me. My adopted village has come to me for help and I cannot accomplish this without you."

He smiled. "For you I will do it."

And so the rainmaker prayed, and I spent the evening watching him prepare for and execute a simple ceremony. We drank cognac together from a bottle I had taken from Margaret's stock of liquor, and I listened to him ramble about the importance of honoring the rain gods. By the end of the evening we were both very drunk and slapping each other on the back as if old friends. I returned to Burguna the next day with a splitting

3 *Ibid.*, pp. 88-89.

headache but pleased that I could report to the village that the hermit had performed his magic. A couple of evenings later I was sitting in my hut reading when I suddenly heard raindrops pelt the thatch roof. The gods had answered.

This all took place during the few weeks Margaret was gone. Time without her seemed like an eternity. I had forgotten how much I had depended upon her for companionship. If we were not talking together about our lives over dinner, we would discuss the nightly BBC news broadcast or tutor Tambe children who wanted extra help with their fractions or spelling. Three mornings a week—Tuesdays, Thursdays, and Sundays—we would rise at 5:30 a.m. and share devotions together. I always enjoyed those special, private times most. It was then that I saw a deeper, spiritual side to Margaret. I had the opportunity to hear her beautiful prayers that the villagers would one day have the opportunity again to receive the saving message of Jesus Christ. I was also examining my own spiritual beliefs at the time. Margaret knew this because I had confided in her. She possessed a quiet acceptance of adversity which had a calming affect on me; whereas I felt my own life was marred by the belief that life was God's puzzle whose challenge it was for each of us to figure out. The longer Margaret was absent, the more I lapsed back into this thinking and the more I became anxious that I had reached no decisions about my future or my faith. I longed for her return and the reassurances she would bring with her.

As for Francis Tannen, he continued to be absent from Burguna for weeks at a time. Occasionally he would reappear, but for no more than a day or two. His brief returns seemed to be for nothing more than to obtain fresh clothes and to collect some different books that he always took with him whenever he traveled. He made no pretense of interest in the school. I also noticed that Tannen had stopped wearing his roman collar. It had been more than two years since I'd observed him performing any clerical functions, such as hearing confession or giving last rites. I had never seen Father Tannen celebrate communion. Margaret and I shared our own private devotions and prayers, but Francis never worshipped with us.

Samuel Obei helped out at the school and was the head domestic for Margaret and Tannen. While Margaret was gone, Samuel saw that Tannen's meals were prepared during the few days the priest was back in Burguna. Samuel also had a Tambe woman wash Tannen's clothes. It would be beneath any Tambe man, let alone someone of Samuel's status in the tribe, to wash clothes himself.

By necessity husbands and wives lived apart much of the time. Most of the young men left Burguna at about the age of sixteen to find work in the diamond mines in northeastern Cape de Leone, about 125 miles north of Burguna. They would return once or twice a year, wealthier than they were when they had left, take a wife, father a child, and go back to the mines with a newly acquired status. Although mining was hard work and dangerous, its compensation was far above subsistence farming, which was pretty much all that was left for the men to do who didn't leave Burguna.

One evening before Margaret returned, I sat in my hut reading another book that Tannen had loaned me. It was about West African folklore, written by an early American missionary who believed that the stories should be recorded. I suddenly heard a call from outside.

"Mind if I come in?"

Justin Perry stood at the opening of my hut. He held his doctor's bag, still having a stethoscope hanging around his neck. He looked exhausted. Beads of sweat rolled down his forehead and temples.

"I can't find anyone home, Gene," he announced. "Is Margaret back yet?"

"No, but she should be here any day," I answered. "I received a letter from her a few days ago. She wrote, saying she'd return by this week. Anything new with you, Justin? We reserved St. Magdalene for you two weeks ago. We wondered what happened when you didn't show."

"I had to miss a round. Sorry I didn't let you know in advance. There was an outbreak of malaria in the Pampana Province. I've had a terrible time. The quinine's not working worth a damn. I think the malaria there is a new strain. It's resistant to any medicine I have. We lost a lot of children."

The last time Perry had been in the village was right after Margaret had left on her trip back to Ireland. I noticed that he looked heavier and that his hair was also thinner than I had remembered. He was nearly bald except for a few strands that tasseled his forehead and that he combed back to cover as much of his large, shiny skull as possible.

"Can I get you some tea?" I asked.

"You don't have any whiskey or port, do you?"

"I can check over at Margaret's," I said, "but basil tea is the strongest thing I have to offer."

Perry smiled. "Needn't bother. I can't stay long. Have to leave for Negbema in a little while unless I spend the night."

He removed his stethoscope and placed it in his doctor's bag. Perry next plopped down in the only other chair in the small hut and wiped his sweating brow with the back of his left forearm. He looked ghastly.

"Have you seen much of Tannen lately?" Perry asked.

"He's gone almost all the time," I replied. "Only here long enough to get a supply of fresh things and then he's off again. Won't say a thing about where he's been or where's he going."

Perry nodded and sighed.

"Have you thought about how much longer you're going to stay, Gene? I mean, you've been here past five years, haven't you? Don't you have any plans, any desire to return home?" He wiped more sweat off of his face. "Now might be a good time to leave. You've stuck it out longer than any before you."

Perry's question struck me in the face. Had I thought about leaving and returning to Lisbon? Only a hundred thousand times, but the thought of leaving Margaret kept me from considering it seriously.

"But the Tambe need me," I responded, concealing the true reason for staying.

"Whether they need you or not, I can't say," Perry replied. "But I know they'd soon see you go." Then he added, "Look here, my friend"—when Perry said "my friend" you knew he meant something serious—"it's not just you. The Tambe would prefer we all go, the whole bloody lot of us. From the very moment we set foot in this village, we've been intruders. Don't you remember the first week you were here and how sick you became?"

"What does that have to do with anything?" I asked.

"Did you really think you were near death from bilharzia?" Perry replied. "Hell, no, there isn't bilharzia a hundred miles from here. I had to give some bogus excuse. In my mind you were poisoned, Gene. My best bet is that you were poisoned from velatoma. It's an extract from a native plant found here in the forest. It wouldn't surprise me if both Margaret and Francis knew, but they wouldn't admit it. The Tambe didn't want to kill you. You obviously had a greater reaction than they expected. All they wanted to do was scare you. Make you so sick that you wouldn't want to stay."

"I can't believe it," I said, shocked. "Who's they you keep talking about?

"Chief Faramha and the elders. They'd just converted the village to Islam and got rid of John Stivonovich. The last thing they wanted was another enthusiastic young man professing to be the new Christian missionary!"

"But we've done some good. The school and Margaret—"

"They want Margaret gone, too. All of us."

I stared at him, my mouth wide open.

"How naïve are you, Gene? The Tambe will be here long after we're gone and they'll be little different than when we first came."

Perry continued. "Maybe we've given them a little medicine to save their babies from dying from malaria and typhoid. Maybe we taught a few school lessons to their young and secretly saved a few souls to the higher glory of God. Hell, I don't know about any of that. But I do know that for the most part, we're doing it to satisfy our own vanity, because the moment we're gone, you'll be hard pressed to see where we made one iota of difference. You're not going to change the African mind in a year, a decade or a century. You'll destroy it first before you change it any."

For a moment I could have sworn it was Tannen speaking. With that kind of attitude, why had Perry himself bothered to stay?

"I'm telling you for your own good, Gene," Perry said rising from the chair. "This part of the country is in trouble. Tannen is up to something. You'd better leave now while you still can. You'll never see the day when you can serve openly as a Christian missionary. Hell, if you truly want to do missions work in Africa you'd be better off going to Kenya or Rhodesia. At least there you wouldn't have to fight the Muslims."

> "Hell, if you truly want to do missions work in Africa you'd be better off going to Kenya or Rhodesia. At least there you wouldn't have to fight the Muslims."

Perry nodded his head to say goodbye. "I'll see you in a fortnight, Gene. Give Margaret my regards." He stopped and turned around before he left. "And give what I just told you some serious thought. Margaret won't disagree with me if she's honest."

Nigel Reuben couldn't sleep anymore, so I told him of Perry's warning to me as I continued my tale. We were only an hour away from Paris.

"But why didn't you leave as Justin Perry recommended, Professor? What kept you from returning to Indiana?"

"I did go back to Indiana, Nigel, although not for the reason Justin Perry gave. I went back only about two months after Margaret returned from Ireland. I returned for my grandfather's funeral."

"But how can that be?" he asked. "You were in Cape de Leone during the entire civil war. You couldn't have been in both places."

"You're right, Nigel. I had gone back to Indiana, but then I returned to Cape de Leone shortly after I learned that the war had broken out and that Margaret might be in danger."

"I'm confused," Reuben said.

"I'm not surprised. You see there is much more that you don't know."

One thing that Reuben still didn't understand is what took me to Cape de Leone to begin with. Until he learned this, the rest of my story made little sense.

After the death of mother and Philip, I just assumed that I would go back and live with my father. But after several weeks, I still hadn't heard from dad except for the short note that I thought he had sent to me along with the money. I was perplexed, and then slowly and painfully I realized that father didn't want me back.

I was afraid my life would be limited to the farm with Grandpa and Grandma Hamilton. Our daily routines didn't change much, except that both grandpa and grandma became more tied to the home place. For grandma, that was difficult to do, because even before the accident she seldom left Blessed Acres except to attend church on Sunday mornings and occasionally Wednesday evening prayer services. But for Grandfather Hamilton, it was different. He took mother and Philip's deaths even harder. He seemed to lose much of the buoyant, spirited nature that made him so well known and liked by the townsfolk. While he still could be found on the court house bench every day after work, he didn't participate any more in the rabble-rousing that had made him Lisbon's most popular town-crier. I could tell that there was a sorrow in grandpa, a deep sorrow that mother's and Philip's deaths had brought about.

But there was more than just the deaths—there was also the

shadow, the dark shadow that hovered over all. Time would never take away that shadow, I felt. We had a brutally cold winter that year and grandpa insisted that I do all the hard, arduous outdoor work of feeding the animals, milking our one cow, cleaning out the barn, and the other hundred chores that go along with running a small farm. Normally grandpa and Uncle Paul helped, but not during these months. Grandpa and grandma said very little to me, but if the chores weren't performed exactly on time or how they thought they should be, I caught hell. We now seldom went to town, except occasionally on Saturdays. And grandpa refused to allow me to listen to the radio anymore, claiming that I always ran the battery down too much so that the "machine" (grandpa's reference to his old Ford truck) wouldn't start. The only thing left in the evenings was to read and, of course, in the winter months it got dark by 5:00 p.m. At best I could read after dinner for an hour by light from a kerosene lantern.

In the late winter of 1938, several months after mother and Philip were killed, one Saturday afternoon grandpa decided to go into town. He needed to buy some fencing and see about a loan to plant the coming year's crops. I hadn't been to Lisbon since before Christmas, so I joined grandpa on the trip.

"You stay out here, Eugene, while I see if I can talk to someone," grandpa said once we got inside The Roanoke County Bank.

While waiting on grandpa, I noticed the large mural against the bank's west wall. I had seen it before, but I hadn't paid much attention to the details. From a closer look, I could see that it was a visual history of Roanoke County with written headings explaining the mural: portraits of important men, local pioneers who founded the county in the early 1800s, Civil War veterans, and Delaware Indians.

"So you decided to bring along this good-looking young man with you, Hastings," I heard a voice say from behind me.

Grandpa stood next to a large man who was dressed sharply in a blue, double breasted suit. They had just come out of the back offices. I vaguely recognized him.

"Eugene, do you remember me?" the large man asked. "I'm Randall Shore."

Grandpa could tell I was having trouble recalling the stranger. "Remember Mr. Shore, Eugene? He's vice-president of the bank, son."

I nodded. "Howdy, Mr. Shore."

Grandpa and Mr. Shore spoke about a farm loan that grandpa was negotiating. Mr. Shore then surprised us both by offering tickets to that night's basketball sectional championship game. Lisbon was host to the first round of the Indiana State High School basketball tournament and a few thousand visitors were in town for Saturday's contests.

"Thank you, Randy," grandpa answered. "But we need to get back home. Ma is waiting for us and Eugene has some chores to do this evening. Thanks for the offer, though."

I felt crushed. I loved basketball with a passion. I knew grandpa wouldn't accept the offer, especially since the shadow had fallen, the shadow that wouldn't go away. Mr. Shore nodded to grandpa, accepting his explanation, but I think he could see my disappointment.

"Are you ever going to visit me at my horse farm, Eugene?" he asked, trying to cheer me up.

"Hope to," I answered. "If I can ever get all the chores done at home."

Mr. Shore asked that I visit him when I had time and then he said, "Eugene, did you ever get the note and money I sent you?"

I at first didn't understand what he meant, but then slowly it sank in. I stood flabbergasted.

"You mean you're the one who sent me the five dollar bill after mom's and Philip's funeral?" I asked in astonishment.

The large man looked at me puzzled, perplexed. "Yes, Eugene, didn't you get my note? I'm sorry. I mean I hope it was all right. I saw where your Uncle Paul gave the bill back to your father. I thought you should have the money."

Grandpa looked befuddled. He didn't have a clue what Shore

was talking about. "You sent Eugene some money, Randall?" grandpa asked.

Shore nodded haltingly. "It was only a five dollar bill, Hastings. It was nothing."

"And you didn't thank him, Eugene?" grandpa said, turning to me. I couldn't respond as I was dumbfounded. "Well, thank him now, Eugene! Thank Mr. Shore," grandpa commanded. "Thank him now, son!"

But I was in shock. My mind became blank and all I could think of was fleeing. I ran out through the revolving door of the bank and down the sidewalk towards Hubert Walker's Drug store. The sun had gone in and a heavy snow came down pelting the sidewalk with thick, wet flakes. I ran into Walker's and down the center aisle to the back of the store where the toiletries were located. Close fitting show cases filled with perfumes and fancy soaps formed an oval with no outlet. There was no where to hide, no spot from which I couldn't be seen. The drug-store was packed with customers, strangers from out of town who had wandered into the store after the morning round of basketball games.

Suddenly, in front of all the strangers, tears rolled down my face and I started to bawl. Everyone was staring at me, but I couldn't stop. The tears ran down my cheeks and into my mouth. I covered my face to try and hide from the curious on-lookers. I was eleven-years-old and I knew I was much too old to cry.

Grandpa found me and drove us back home, refusing to say anything. When we returned to Blessed Acres, he ordered me to do the chores and announced that I could forget about having dinner that evening. Once I came in from outside, I went to my room and took the envelope that I'd received after mother's and Philip's funeral from underneath Philip's pillow. I pulled out the note from the envelope: "Hope to see you soon," it said. Then I stuffed my hand deeper into the envelope and there in the left hand corner I found a small business card. I couldn't believe that I had overlooked it all this time! The card read:

Randall Shore, Vice-President
THE ROANOKE COUNTY BANK
224 W. Washington Street
Lisbon, Indiana
(Phone) Blue 228
"You Can Count On Us to Fulfill Your Dreams!"

I threw the envelope down and fell back on my bed in tears. I couldn't help but remember that moment. It was the loneliest time of my life, more solitary even than the night after mother's and Philip's deaths. How I wanted to sleep, but I couldn't. When I heard the company whistle at 11:00 p.m. announcing the end of second shift at the Glass Works, I thought that the world had forgotten about me. I never stayed up again to listen to the company whistle. I did everything in my power to avoid it.

Over the course of the next several years, life was much the same. I would always come straight home after the end of the school day because I had chores to do and the school bus was the only way home. Uncle Paul helped me when the work on the farm was beyond grandpa's aging body. Mutt was a good man. He was also naïve, capable of the most illogical logic I had ever heard, and never failed to produce laughter, usually at his own expense. Uncle Paul had a tremendous aversion to employment at the Glass Works. He spent most of his waking hours trying to figure out a scheme to make his fortune so that he would never have to go back again to that "hotter than hell hole," as he called it. Had Mutt any business sense or luck, he may have realized his dream, but he was woefully short of both.

His most recent venture was to purchase a laundromat in Lisbon, one of the first of its kind in Indiana. For the first six months, Uncle Paul and Aunt Betty ran the business themselves successfully. But after that Mutt hired a woman to manage the laundry in their absence and trusted her with signature authority to conduct business on his behalf. One Monday morning, after a heated argument with Uncle Paul, the woman employee went to The Roanoke County Bank with the purported intention of depositing that previous Saturday's profits. Instead, she withdrew everything Mutt and Aunt Betty had accumulated over six months, hauled away five carton loads of soap, a dozen customer's clothes, and left Lisbon never to be seen again. She had literally "cleaned out" Uncle Paul, who had no insurance and no other choice but to sell the laundry or go completely bust.

Now Mutt had to work overtime at the Glass Works just to pay off the debts he had incurred to purchase the laundromat, a business, I might add, for which he had paid an exorbitant price. But that was Uncle Paul's luck. "Murphy's law" could have just as easily been named "Mutt's law" for all Uncle Paul's bad fortune. Sadly, he too often dealt with his farcical life by drinking himself into oblivion.

I felt that in some bizarre way that Uncle Paul's luck had rubbed off on me. At the age of sixteen, I rebelled against everything that was familiar. As I reviewed the world that I knew, it made little sense. Honesty, integrity, hard work, and other virtues that I had been taught seemed to always be rewarded with hardship and suffering; while deceit, subterfuge, hypocrisy, and boasting seemed to always be the recipient of unwarranted benevolence. It was part of the shadow which now relentlessly pursued me. It affected everything and made it bad. Peppered with a dose of adolescent pimples and having become a gangling high school sophomore, I had reached the conclusion that God didn't exist. Or if He did conceivably exist, that He cared so little about us, mere mortals, as to not give one twit about whether we are happy. For how else could I explain my own pitiful predicament?

My mother and bother were dead; my father wouldn't acknowledge my existence; my grandparents could barely tolerate me, and; my world revolved around some hellish life on a small, struggling Indiana farm in the middle of nowhere. It was verbalizing this grand conclusion that sent shock waves through our farm house one Sunday morning in 1943. While the country was involved in a terrible world war, I could think of nothing but my own trifling situation as I lay in bed, angry and in near tears.

Grandpa called me to come down to leave for church that Sunday morning. I threw open my door and, with only my sleeping bottoms on, ran to the edge of the stairwell railing. "I'm not going!" I screamed. "I'm not going to church any more and be around all you hypocrites."

The look that gradually came over grandfather's face was ghastly, as if he had been shot and was just now realizing it.

"Hypocrites are we?" he said. "Just where did you come up with that idea, young man? Why, you're fortunate to be around such God-fearing people. Who do you want to associate with, Eugene, liars and scoundrels? Some of your hooligan friends?"

"They're not liars and scoundrels, grandpa, but the members of the Church are. All they want to do is control other peoples' lives and make you feel bad because you're not as good as them. They're no more Christian than the sheep in the pasture!"

I ran into my room and locked the door behind me, but grandpa knocked it down. He chased me out of my bedroom, out of the house, and through the back yard. A passenger train charged down the tracks towards our property and I believed that I could beat it to get into the back woods. The horn of the large diesel locomotive sounded loudly. I scampered the last one hundred feet as fast as I possibly could and lunged across the tracks, the train barely missing me! I grabbed my left leg in pain and looked back to find grandpa. The train's cars roared past one by one. It seemed like an eternity before the caboose rolled by.

"Grandpa!" I screamed.

I couldn't see him. There was nothing to be seen on the other side of the tracks. I looked down at the tracks themselves and found nothing. Then slowly I saw his large frame rise from a shallow gully that dipped to the north of the tracks. His beautiful, blue vested suit was covered with dust and dirt and the left leg of his trousers was torn nearly off. He limped across the tracks toward me holding his left shoulder. A trickle of blood seeped from the corner of his mouth.

"Are you hurt?" he asked.

"Ain't nothing," I answered angrily as I lifted and rubbed my left heal.

Before I could get out 'what about you?,' grandpa swung his right hand and struck me in the left jaw. I fell to the ground, my jaw hurting twice as much as my left leg.

"Do you want to kill yourself?" grandpa said.

I got up slowly from the ground and guarded my face, afraid he might strike me again.

"Would it matter to you, old man?"

Grandpa's cheeks became flushed and he took a half-step back, almost as if he was going to fall. When I saw that he wasn't going to, I spewed out the most spiteful, vexatious, contemptible thing that I could think to say to him. I screamed it with every ounce of energy I had.

"Hastings Hamilton, you know what you are? You're a goddamn lousy farmer!"

Grandpa held his left shoulder again. He started to dust himself off and then tore the left leg of his trousers off that dangled from his upper thigh. He looked back at me.

"So that's what you think of me, uh?" he said. "That's how you feel about your old granddad who has raised you like his own son because your own good-for-nothing father won't have anything to do with you?"

"I'm not going to church anymore, grandpa!" I said. "I ain't going because there ain't no God!"

Grandpa took his suit jacket off and flung it over his left shoulder. He was in pain. Sweat poured from his face.

"If there ain't no God, Eugene, then there ain't no Sabbath," grandpa said softly, not angrily. "If you're not going to church, then I expect you to work. You understand me? You can start by hoeing the garden for weeds, and the small shed needs whitewashed. I expect those chores done before your grandma and me gets back from taking communion to the shut-ins this afternoon."

Grandpa stood resolute. I could tell he wasn't going to back down. "If you don't like it, Eugene, you can always leave," he added. Grandpa turned to walk away and then looked back at me. He bit his lower lip as if to try and stop the pain and then spat on the ground. "I won't stop you, son."

"Blessed Acres," rural Roanoke County, Indiana

Sixteen

randpa knew that I had no where else to go. My only possible option was to live with Uncle Paul and Aunt Betty, but they had such a small house on Franklin Street that I simply couldn't impose on them. I had no money to offer and another mouth to feed would be difficult, especially since one of the existing mouths was Aunt Betty's. World War II was raging and supplies and food were scarce.

I swallowed my pride and stayed at Blessed Acres. I continued my routinely monotonous chores, living a life devoid of any joy and experiencing nominal contact with the outside world. I did, however, continue to attend William H. Taft High School, that is until I turned eighteen-years-old on January 30, 1945. At the time, there was a peculiar law that said that if a young man turned eighteen and was still in school, he either had to enlist in the military or quit school. Ironically, I was eligible for a deferment because farmers weren't subject to the draft. The local board informed my principal that I still had to quit school or else join the military.

Hastings Hamilton made sure that I didn't enlist. He didn't want to lose my services on the farm. Besides grandpa didn't believe in conscription. On this issue, he was a true libertarian.

Although I was forced to quit school before the end of my senior year, I was still allowed to graduate with the senior class in the spring of 1945. Grandpa and grandma attended the ceremony as did Uncle Paul and Aunt Betty. The way they carried on about me (grandpa stood and hooted when I received my diploma while Uncle Paul yelled, "That a boy, Gene!"), you would have thought that I had been named a Rhodes Scholar. But my diploma didn't gain me instant access to employment. After the spring planting, I submitted my application to work at the glass factory. But by this time many of the local men were already returning home to Lisbon from the War. The personnel director told me that the plant had an obligation to rehire these men before they could consider new hires. So while I waited for an opening at the Glass Works, I went to work at Gibson's Filling Station pumping gas and doing minor mechanical work. I enjoyed the work and the opportunity to see people every day. In my off hours and on weekends, I still farmed. Grandpa relied upon me more and more to see that the crops were planted and fertilized in the spring, weeded in the summer, and harvested in the fall. By this point, farming had become second nature. Due to the use of better fertilizer and proper planting, I had been able to increase the yield per acre by about one-third. This didn't go unnoticed by Hastings Hamilton, who began boasting on the court house lawn and at the 4-H Fairgrounds that Blessed Acres was now one of the most productive farms in all of Roanoke County. In his old age, grandpa had become a member of the "landed gentry," the status he had so long aspired to.

At this time something else happened that changed my life dramatically. It was the opportunity that would lead me to choose writing as a profession. I had taken typing in high school for no other reason than it was easier than other elective courses. Apparently Jake Colliers, publisher of *The Prophet*, had heard about my nominal typing skills. He also knew that I loved basketball, because in high school I always attended the Friday and Saturday night games. In November 1945, six months after I had graduated, Colliers was desperate for a sports writer to cover rural county school games. He came to Gibson's Filling Station one afternoon and begged me to cover my alma mater, the William H. Taft High School "Presidents" in their opening game against the Ridgeville "Cossacks." The Cossacks were ranked number one in the county in a pre-season poll. In exchange for a 350 word typed summary of the game, he promised me free admission, $5.00, and all the popcorn I could eat. All I had to do is have the article to the sports editor at *The Prophet*'s office by 2:00 a.m. Saturday morning.

I gladly took the assignment and from that humble beginning, I reported on about thirty games for the newspaper during the 1945-46 season. I spent every Friday and Saturday night till early March in one packed, smelly, and boisterous Roanoke County gymnasium after another.

Jake Colliers said that I had a knack for describing the action of the games and correctly quoting the coaches. After the season was over, he asked if I wanted to try and do some human feature writing. He was always looking for articles about local people. So I took on this additional assignment, earning $10.00 a story, to write one feature article a week on a resident of Roanoke County. Over the next two years, my Wednesday feature stories in *The Prophet* covered everything from a story about Maude Nichols who, at the age of eighty-five, learned to play the bag-pipes to Roland Chittick's 800 pound sow that captured the Grand-Champion prize at the Indiana State Fair. Each week was something different, and I was always amazed that I could find a new story to write about. In addition to my writing, I continued to farm for grandpa and work at Gibson's Filling Station. I also tried to save some money so that I might one day have a place of my own.

In November 1946, another memorable event happened. I had gone to work at Gibson's one Saturday morning. Rosemary Siebert drove up beside one of the gas pumps in her beautiful 1945 Chevrolet sedan. New cars were scarce shortly after the War years, so to see a modern model like Rosemary's Chevrolet was a rare sight.

Rosemary and I talked about the latest movie in town and the start of this year's basketball season, and then she asked me if I knew Irene Sommers. I said that I did and that I liked Irene a lot.

"Why don't you ask her out?" Rosemary asked.

Now I wasn't such a hick that I didn't know that Rosemary

wouldn't have done that if Irene hadn't suggested it. Wonder of wonders! Back inside the filling station, I charged up my courage and called Irene to ask if she'd join me in attending that night's Huntsville Redmen versus Spartensburg Tom Cats basketball game. Irene said yes and we made a date for 5:30 p.m.

After I picked up Irene in my grandfather's old Ford truck, it occurred to me that I had not mentioned anything about dinner. I apologized several times, but Irene didn't seem in the least bit disappointed.

"It's all right, Eugene," Irene said. "We can get something at the game."

"We can have all the popcorn we can eat free," I told Irene, trying to impress her. "It's part of my deal with the paper."

Irene, being the sweet soul that she is, acted impressed.

"We can get a hot dog, too," I added as an afterthought.

"That would be great, Eugene," Irene said.

The game that night was held in a cracker box gym. There were bleachers on only one side of the court and at the south end, where they were stacked on top of a theatre stage. I knew the contest would be well attended, because it was the first game of the season. The two schools, located on the southern edge of the county, had been perennial rivals. Even though we arrived thirty minutes before the start of the junior varsity game, the gymnasium was packed and Irene and I had to sit at the top of the bleachers on the stage.

We sat in the section for the visiting team. In a rage most of the night, the Huntsville fans kept standing up and screaming, forcing Irene and me to stand as well. The officiating during the varsity game was terrible and the aggressive play of both teams resulted in dozens of fouls. The game became a free-throw shooting contest. In the last five minutes, the teams marched from one end of the court to the other, exchanging foul shots. At the rate they were going, neither team would have any players left because they would all be fouled out.

Finally, with only fifteen seconds left in the game, Huntsville was down by only one point. Fortunately for the "Redmen," they had the ball out of bounds on the Spartensburg end of the court. The team had a dandy, quick guard by the name of Bobby Lawson. Lawson came across mid-court with the ball, passed it to a forward, and then cut to the basket. He got the ball back and made a fake, then went up for a shot from ten-feet. It looked liked Lawson had been hit on his shooting arm by one of Spartensburg's players, but nothing was called. The ball careened out of the field goal, where it was tapped to the top of the free-throw line. By the time a Redmen teammate retrieved it, the game-ending horn had sounded! The visiting team had lost by one point and the Huntsville fans were booing in anger!

"Disgusting!" said a Huntsville fan. "Absolutely disgusting! Our boys played their hearts out just to have the game taken away by those zebra shirts!"

Irene patiently listened to several more minutes of grumbling and insults while I checked my score book and tallied up the points, fouls, and rebounds for each player. By the time I had finished my rounds of visiting both locker rooms, it was 10:30 p.m. I found Irene sitting on the bleachers talking to a young boy. She looked up and smiled. I helped her on with her coat and we drove to her home out in the country, a farm house about the same distance north of Lisbon as Blessed Acres is east. "I had a wonderful time," Irene said. "I mean it!"

We said good night and she waved at me from her front door as I drove away in grandpa's old Ford truck. She didn't mention that I had forgotten to get her a hotdog.

I shifted the truck into third gear, forced my right foot down on the accelerator, and sped towards Lisbon and the newspaper office. I wanted to make the story something special because the contest was the opening game of the season and I knew that Irene would read about it in the next morning's issue of *The Prophet*.

I had known Irene Sommers ever since childhood when she lived with her parents east of us in an area known as the "Island." It was even a poorer section of town than near the train depot where we first lived.

Irene and I went to elementary school together up to the second grade. At that time, Irene's father worked for the New York Central railroad. When Irene was about eight, her father was killed in a train accident when he fell between two railroad cars while walking on top of a freighter traveling east to Ohio. Mother took Philip and me to the Catholic Church to pay our respects. The family received next to nothing from the railroad in the way of compensation for Mr. Sommers' death. As a result, Irene's mother was forced to let their small white shingled house go back to the bank. Irene and her mother moved in with Irene's grandparents on a farm on Tompkin Road north of town. Irene started going to a different elementary school. But even then, we occasionally saw each other in Lisbon at the library or while attending a mutual friend's birthday party. That is how I knew Irene Sommers, the woman who has been one of my closest friends since childhood and the one-time sweetheart I told Margaret about.

By the spring of 1947, I had saved enough money to purchase a car for $650.00 and I continued to work at Gibson's Filling Station. One morning in August I had a radiator of a Buick torn apart and Junior was showing me how to plug a leak. All of a sudden I looked up and saw a shiny, new Lincoln roll into the station. I knew immediately who it was. I ran out to the pumps, eager to service the vehicle. It was Randall Shore and he invited me to come to his office at The Roanoke County Bank after work. I arrived at about 4:00 p.m. and was taken by the receptionist to a cherry paneled conference room in the center of the bank.

"Eugene, I'm glad you could come and be with us," Randall Shore said, welcoming me. He shook my hand warmly and then immediately turned me to several men sitting around a long walnut conference table. They were older men, conservatively dressed in expensive business suits.

"Eugene, I'd like to introduce you to the other directors of the bank."

At this point, each of the men stood up and Shore escorted me around the table and introduced me, telling me each director's name. By the time I had shaken hands with the last man, however, I had completely forgotten each director's name except for Max Bauman. I recognized Bauman because he was a farmer, had been involved in Republican politics, and was a good friend of my grandfather Hamilton. I felt very uncomfortable with the men. My clothes were stained and sweaty smelling.

We exchanged pleasantries about the corn crop and grandpa's failing health before Mr. Shore interrupted by clearing his throat and pulling at his shirt collar.

"Eugene, I'm sure you're wondering why I asked you to join us this afternoon. We've had something come up here at the bank that we wanted to share with you, hoping you might be interested."

The other directors were now focused on me and I had suddenly become extremely self-conscious. I tried to concentrate totally on Shore.

"You're probably too young to remember Carl Pennington, Eugene, but Mr. Pennington was President and a director of The Roanoke County Bank for nearly forty years. I succeeded him as President about three years ago. Your grandfather Hamilton knew Carl well." Shore glanced around at the other directors and continued. "Anyway, Mr. Pennington was also a trustee of Hanover College in Hanover, Indiana."

I looked at Mr. Shore expectantly. *What was this all about?*

"The purpose of my telling you this is that Mr. Pennington never had any children of his own. He passed away this past April and his wife died a few years ago. In his will he left a sizeable amount of money in a trust for the purpose of sending deserving high school graduates from the county to Hanover. It was a very generous amount. It should cover the cost of schooling for at least one student each year."

"Eugene, have you ever thought of going to college?" one of the board members asked.

I was a bit stunned by the question. "I'm afraid I never have," I answered.

"We've been impressed with your articles in *The Prophet*," said another director. "You have some excellent writing abilities, young man."

"Eugene," Shore continued. "We know this is already August, but the trust funds just came available. School starts at Hanover in only about three weeks, but we wanted to call you in to see if you might be interested in matriculating. I'm sure admission won't be any problem. The college is aware of the scholarship that Mr. Pennington has set up."

"It's a great opportunity to better yourself," said another man. "Wish I was forty years younger to take advantage of it myself."

Sorting through the exchange, I finally pulled myself together. "You mean the scholarship pays for everything? Tuition? Books? A place to stay?"

"Everything," Shore replied. "We'll even see that you have some spending money so that you can come back and forth to home two or three times a year."

I didn't know how to answer and sat there in silence. Another director spoke.

"I think we agreed that a student has to maintain a B grade average, Randall. Eugene needs to know that. After the freshman year, the scholarship is renewable annually so long as the student remains in good-standing and has at least a B average."

Shore nodded and turned back to me. "Eugene, do you understand the conditions?"

I nodded.

The bank president glanced around one last time at all the directors before returning to me. "Can you let us know by next Monday if you're interested?"

"Yes, sure, of course!" I said all at once, tripping over my words.

"Good," said Shore. "We appreciate you coming in today on such short notice, Eugene. We hope it's been worthwhile."

I left the room after shaking each of the directors' hands again. I walked down the long corridor towards the lobby with an incredible spring in my legs. The receptionist, Shirley Spaulding, wished me a good day as I left, winking at me when I went by her desk.

That evening, after dinner, I spoke to grandpa about the scholarship offer. He immediately dismissed the idea.

"You can't afford to go to college, Eugene. You got to be rich, know someone," grandpa responded.

"But I just told you, grandpa, that Randall Shore said that everything would be paid for. Tuition, a place to stay, books. Everything!"

"But how is college going to help you?"

"I don't know for sure," I answered. "Maybe it will make me a better writer."

"There ain't no money in writing, Eugene. How much have you made for all the hours you've worked at the newspaper? Just pennies, I bet! That's all you'll ever make!"

"It's an honor to be asked to go to college," I said. "There's not many in the whole county who've been to college."

"Yea, the school teachers who have, you see what they're making. Heavens, Eugene, they're poorer than we are. Ain't no money in writing and ain't no money in teaching. You'd be better off farming and letting me get you on at the glass works."

I thought grandpa would be pleased that his grandson had a chance to attend college. He had seemed so proud when I graduated from high school.

"And if you go, who's going to plant and harvest the crops, Eugene?" grandpa exclaimed. "Who's going to take care of the livestock? You need to let me get you on at the glass factory, son! When you start making some decent money, you'll forget all about this college business."

Who was going to farm Blessed Acres if I left for college?

Mutt couldn't be counted on to show up for Sunday dinner, let alone with running the farm. Grandpa knew that. Hastings Hamilton also knew that he was in no physical shape to handle the farm himself. His aging body had become arthritic and swollen from an ever worsening condition of gout and diabetes. His ankles and lower legs were terribly bloated from standing on his feet all day at the glass factory. He'd come home each evening and soak his feet in Epsom salts just to get a small amount of relief from the pain. Yes, Hastings Hamilton knew! He knew I was his only hope for him to retain his standing as a "gentleman farmer" of Roanoke County.

When I went to see Irene the next night, I tried to explain to her granddad's objections, but she wouldn't hear any of it.

"You can't live your life for your grandfather, Eugene," she said. "This is a tremendous opportunity. Every high school graduate near the top of his class in the county would give his eyeteeth to have a full scholarship to Hanover. You have to take advantage of this opportunity, Eugene!" Irene took my hand and kissed it. "As much as I'd hate to see you leave, you have to go! When will you have another chance like this?"

Seventeen

Within three weeks I had matriculated at Hanover College in southeastern Indiana, a picturesque campus that overlooks the Ohio River. Suddenly life changed, because as soon as it was announced that I had won the Carl C. Pennington Memorial Scholarship the citizens of Lisbon—who didn't know any better—began to treat me differently. But I grimaced at the thought of my former high school classmates reading the front page headline in *The Prophet*: **"Eugene F. O'Connor, Local Farmer, Reporter, is Selected First Carl C. Pennington Memorial Scholar."**

SCHOLAR?!? I could just imagine their guffaws as they recalled the struggles I had with simple algebra and my English theme papers that were plastered with enough red markings on them that you'd thought they were hemorrhaging blood. So what if I had less than a sterling high school career? This was a new chance, a new opportunity to prove myself! I would have four years to do it in! It's not like I had to discover a new quantum theory of physics during my freshman year!

But the problem was that the expectations didn't stop in Roanoke County. They continued on, exponentially so, at Hanover! How did I know before I accepted the scholarship that Carl C. Pennington, a great student-athlete and former chairman of the college's board of trustees, was esteemed only slightly less than God on the small Presbyterian campus?

Sadly, with great aplomb I soon quashed everyone's high expectations as demonstrated by my first semester grades: Introduction to Biology (C minus); Introduction to Calculus (D); Western Civilization I (C minus); Introduction to Music (C minus).

The only first semester course I received a B grade in was English. That was only because I could put together a decent paragraph. My experience as a reporter for *The Prophet* was little help when it came to mastering the rudiments of writing expected in college English papers. The newspaper's publisher, Jake Colliers, simply wanted articles that the half-literate citizens of Roanoke County could read and understand. He wasn't looking for "no Goddamn William Faulkner!" (as Jake so eloquently reminded me). My second semester grades were much the same.

Because of my poor performance, I was placed on academic probation at the end of my freshman year. I blamed my first year's struggles on everything from having inept high school teachers to having to spend one week in the fall of 1947 and one week in the spring of 1948 harvesting and planting crops at Blessed Acres. But the reality was that I just didn't grasp the material. Still, the trustees of the Carl C. Pennington Trust gave me a second chance by not imposing the grade requirement that I had originally been told I had to maintain in order to keep the scholarship.

My second year efforts at Hanover were just as great, but my performance didn't change. In early May 1949 I remember emerging from each exam room, not with a sense of exhilaration, but with a foreboding feeling of defeat. The drive back to Lisbon in mid-May had been one of the longest, most joyless that I can remember.

At Blessed Acres I threw myself into farming to try and escape from the sickening feeling that overwhelmed me: mucking out a barn that didn't need cleaned; hoeing weeds that hadn't yet surfaced between corn rows that hadn't yet sprouted; plowing and discing fields that grandpa and I had earlier agreed should lay fallow. No physical activity could be punishing enough to make me forget the dismay I felt over my pathetic academic performance of the previous week.

When my grade card came at the end of May, I was already expecting the worst, and the envelope didn't contain any surprises:

Chemistry: D+

World History: C

Higher Geometry: D+

Introduction to Psychology: C+

Nineteenth Century British Novel: B+

Only two days later came the much anticipated letter that I had dreaded even more than the grade card itself. The letter was short and to the point:

22 May, 1949

Dear Eugene:

The Administrators of the Carl C. Pennington Memorial Education Trust regret to inform you that your scholarship to Hanover College will not be renewed for a third academic year. As you recall, a condition of the scholarship is that the recipient maintain at least a B grade average in all subjects. This, of course, you have not been able to do. Again, we regret this action, but the terms of the Trust require this decision.

We wish you the best of luck in your future endeavors.

Very Truly Yours,

Randall Shore

President

The Roanoke County Bank

P.S. Eugene, we know that you tried your best. Please come and see me at the bank when you have the opportunity.

The letter from Shore revoking my scholarship was anti-climactic. Still, that failure was another in the chain of events that propelled me towards Africa and Margaret.

My thoughts now returned to the present. Our pilot announced that we were an hour away from the Charles de Gaulle International Airport in Paris. I looked over at Reuben, who had just awakened from a short nap.

"Professor," he said, stretching, "before we land, I have a small request to make of you." He took his brief case from underneath the seat in front of him, twirled numbers near the handle to release the lock, and opened it. He glanced around rather suspiciously and then pulled out a false bottom from the brief case. He turned to me. "May I have your passport?"

The casualness of his request stunned me. I slowly reached inside my left suit jacket pocket. "I'm not normally inclined to hand over my passport, Mr. Reuben," I said, retrieving it in my right hand. "Especially when we're traveling to a country such as Cape de Leone."

"Oh, I understand, Professor. But I'm prepared to give you something in exchange, something even better." Reuben pulled from the false bottom another passport and a couple pieces of paper stapled together. He first handed me the passport. I opened it up and saw my picture. For a quick second I thought Reuben had merely a duplicate of mine. But then I looked at it closer. The picture was of me, but the name underneath the photo was of another person, a "Donald T. Engels."

"Who is this man?" I exclaimed. "I don't know a Donald Engels."

"He's you, Professor," Reuben answered. "Or rather you're him. You see, I'm afraid I need to ask you to assume Mr. Engels' identity from now on. It's all right there on this paper. Everything that you need to know, I hope, in case any questions come up about your past and why you're traveling to Cape de Leone. I would be greatly obliged if you would read it closely. I'll be glad to answer any questions after you have read it."

I quickly looked over the paper. It was in resume form.

Donald T. Engels
1721 Canalonia Drive
Garfield Heights, Ohio 44125

Personal:
Birth date: January 30, 1927
Birth place:
Sandusky, Ohio
Family:
Wife: Marilyn (59); Children: Joseph (33),
Ronald (31) & Melissa (27)

Education:
College of Wooster, Wooster, Ohio (B.A., 1949)
The Ohio State University, Columbus, Ohio
(M.B.A., 1951)

The resume contained other information, including details about a family business named "Engels Kitchen Ware," small business awards that Engels had received, and some personal information, including hobbies and memberships in clubs.

"I kept the birth dates the same, Professor," Reuben interjected. "The less to memorize the better, I thought."

I laid the paper down and glanced again at the duplicate passport. I recognized the picture of me as one taken the previous fall for the faculty directory in the Journalism Department. I looked up at Reuben. I was not happy.

"I don't like the thought of passing myself off as this man from Ohio," I said to Reuben. "I don't get the point. What's the need in all of this?"

"First of all, Professor, don't worry about Mr. Engels. He won't mind because he doesn't exist. He's a phantom, an apparition. Once you leave Cape de Leone, you resume being yourself. You're just playing a little make believe."

"What's the point?" I asked. "Why do I need to conceal my identity to see Margaret?"

"Professor, there may be persons who are not exactly pleased to have you back in the country. The year 1959 may seem like a distant time to you, but memories in Cape de Leone go back a long way, especially for some persons in power. For your own safety, I think—"

"Who are these persons in power, Mr. Reuben?"

"Albert Mubarsoi is one, Professor."

My ire was rising. Danger wasn't part of the deal.

"But I won't be seeing Mubarsoi, will I? You've assured me some safety. I'm not here for any political or military reason. I don't see the need to hide my identity."

"Under normal circumstances, neither would I, Professor. But I think it's better to be cautious than sorry."

I wasn't sure what Reuben meant, but his request concerned me. "I just don't like the idea of being this other person, Mr. Reuben. Why didn't you tell me this before we left Indiana?"

"Professor, I apologize. I simply didn't want to upset you any more than you already were at the time. You've had so much placed upon you in the last twenty-four hours. What with your goddaughter's death and me showing up on your door unannounced. I simply didn't want to put any more stress on you. Trust me, this is for your own protection."

I wasn't satisfied with Reuben's answer, but what was I to do now? Say no? If Reuben knew some reason why my own identity should be concealed, perhaps I should go along with his plan. But I clearly didn't like the secret way he sprung a fraudulent passport on me. Besides, that in itself was a crime. This whole thing was getting murkier.

"Why would the president of an Ohio appliance company go to Cape de Leone?" I asked.

"To sell toasters, of course," Reuben answered and grinned. "Read the second page, Professor."

I flipped the first page over.

Purpose for visit: Donald T. Engels learned while traveling in Europe last summer that West Africans have a love of baked and toasted breads. He has contacted an Arab businessman, Askia Muhammad, in Grand Bassa, Republic of Cape de Leone, who is willing to serve as the national distributor of Engels Kitchen Ware. Engels is now visiting Mr. Muhammad for the first time to discuss sales of the company's new toaster and other company products. Mr. Muhammad is located at Kings Street, Grand Bassa.

"Who is this Askia Muhammad?" I asked.

"He's a friend of mine."

"I suppose that's not his real name either?" I retorted.

Reuben smiled. "You're too suspicious, Professor."

Reuben could see that I still wasn't happy with his vague and incomplete answers. He looked at me and then laughed. "Please see this as a game, Professor O'Connor. A game of impostors. Don't take it so seriously. Look here," he pulled out a flyer and a brochure from his brief case. "This is your excellent product. Be proud to bring the opportunity to thousands of Leoneons to have toast in the morning with their tea."

I looked at the literature and, sure enough, they contained information about different assortment of toasters with suggested list prices in American dollars. The headings of the brochure and flyer were printed in dark bold letters: "**ENGELS KITCHEN WARE—When Quality Counts!**"

I slowly started to hand him my passport when suddenly I snatched the fake one out of his hand and pocketed it and my own in my right front breast pocket.

"Mr. Reuben, I'll run a few of my own risks, if it's all the same to you," I announced.

Reuben's empty left hand remained held in the air and his shocked face slowly turned to one of disappointment. My action must have been interpreted by Reuben as if I didn't trust him, which, quite frankly, I didn't. But this I did know: I had come this far and was willing, for the chance to see Margaret, to buy into his game of impostors, for now at least. But perhaps I had overreacted; I wasn't sure. I tried to bring a smile to Reuben.

"Thank goodness the kids are through college, married and on their own," I said with a feigned sigh of relief. "Melissa's pregnant, you know."

Reuben looked at me puzzled. He finally caught my attempt at humor. He nodded, exclaiming, "My heartiest congratulations, Mr. Engels! You'll make a splendid grandfather!"

Eighteen

The sun had been up for nearly an hour as we sped toward Paris and the completion of the first leg of our journey to West Africa. Light streamed through a handful of the windows. The in-flight movie that had been showing, *Terms of Endearment*, ended just a few minutes before. Few passengers had bothered to watch it, preferring to read or just sleep. Reuben pulled out a copy of the previous day's *Guardian* and started to read the financial section. He appeared a little more at ease now, and I was glad that I had joked with him as it seemed to lessen the tension that had started to build between us. I laid my head back against the head rest and closed my eyes. But just then Reuben put aside the paper and asked me to continue my story of how I got to Cape de Leone in 1952. I was pleased to have a willing listener and continued the tale of how I left Lisbon and finally ended up entering into the world of Margaret Mahoney, Francis Tannen, and life in West Africa.

Randall Shore's letter to me in May 1949 had sealed my fate about continuing my education at Hanover College. Tuition, room, board, and books were only about $1,200.00 per year, but it was $1,200.00 more than I had. I refused to approach granddad for financial help because I didn't want to humble myself to ask nor experience the humiliation of his almost certain denial. He had opposed me going to Hanover from the very beginning. Now he would be happy.

I returned to my former life at Blessed Acres and began again the daily routine of taking care of the chores on the farm. Junior Gibson hired me back at the filling station, but I refused to write for *The Prophet*, even after Jake Colliers flattered me by offering a substantial raise. I had suffered enough indignity by returning to Lisbon without my coveted college degree to have my name publicized again in the newspaper as a local reporter. I desired total obscurity.

If there was any consolation in my return to Roanoke County it was the reception I received from Irene Sommers. Irene, still a secretary at the Lisbon Electric Company, welcomed me back joyfully into her life and we dated frequently for the better part of the next two years.

The winter of 1949-1950 was especially brutal, with temperatures hovering as low as twenty below zero for a week in late January. The snow got so high that it completely covered the rear tires on granddad's old Ford tractor. Getting in and out of the farm house down the long lane was impossible; fortunately, we had plenty of food from the canning of fruits and vegetables that I had helped Aunt Betty do the summer before. There was little to do but feed the small amount of livestock that we had and read. My two years at Hanover had turned me into a voracious reader, and I regularly visited the local Lisbon Carnegie library.

Granddad's gout and arthritis kept him from farming, so the spring planting now fell entirely on me. By late May, all of the crops were in the fields. In the evenings we listened to the nightly news on the radio. For a time, reports of the United States' interest in the conflict in Korea dominated the news. I remember the headline in *The Prophet*: "**President Truman calls on U.N. to aid South Koreans!**" Only a couple of weeks later I received the letter that I had expected ever since I learned of our involvement in that north Asian country. The letter commanded me to appear at the Lisbon National Guard Armory on July 14th to receive my physical and to prepare to report to Fort Benjamin Harrison in Indianapolis. There I would receive training with the intention of being shipped to Korea.

"There's no way you're going, Eugene!" grandpa announced loudly after I plopped the letter in his lap and he had read it.

"You're needed here on the farm. It's not our war and there's no sense you getting shot at to please some Democrat like Truman." Grandpa reread the notice and then exclaimed again in an even more boisterous tone. "Lordy, let the President send his own son if he thinks it's so important that we defend that far off little country!"

"President Truman doesn't have a son, grandpa," I said.

"Well, no difference," he bellowed. "He's not having you!"

"I may have no choice but to go," I responded. "The military isn't going to let me out just because you don't like it."

Hastings Hamilton didn't like my response, I could tell. He sat in his rocking chair with his arms folded atop his large stomach and rocked back and forth, angry, plotting, a discontented old man with gout.

After I took my physical examination at the Lisbon National Guard Armory, I immediately resigned myself that I would be heading to training camp in two days and eventually shipped to this unknown country called Korea. I went to see Irene and to tell her. We were both in tears when I left her house. But the next day, the day before I was to leave, a most extraordinary event happened. Grandpa drove his old Ford truck into Gibson's Service Station, pounding on the horn and waving at me excitedly.

"It's done, Eugene!" he screamed from the truck as I came running out of the station. "I got it done!"

"What are you talking about?" I asked.

"Your deferment!" he yelled. "John Campbell from the draft board agreed to give you a deferment. John and I are old friends. We worked together at the glass works several years ago. I helped him get his position of commander of the National Guard unit when it came open here in town. He owed me a favor. It's done, Eugene!" grandpa repeated gleefully. "Just think, son, you don't have to go!"

I stood in utter disbelief, not sure how to respond. "But I didn't ask you to go to John Campbell," I finally said.

I stood arguing with grandpa, outraged at his meddling. Grandpa's eyes suddenly became moist and piercing. His face turned stone-like and cold. He revved up the engine and shifted the truck into first gear. He yelled above the screech of the transmission, spital coming from his crusty mouth. "You're totally ungrateful, Eugene. Just add that to your other sins, you selfless miscreant!"

The truck sped away, leaving me speechless. The whole conversation between us upset me terribly, and all I could think of that afternoon was grandpa's use of the word "miscreant." Where in the world did he come up with that? Surely he hadn't read it in *The Prophet*. I finally surmised that he must have heard it during one of Reverend Hogarth's sermons. Perhaps I was ungrateful, perhaps even a rake, rogue, scoundrel, but "miscreant?" Hastings Hamilton had really outdone himself this time! But I also knew that if I didn't go to war when I was drafted that I'd also be known by other names in Lisbon: "Coward!" "Yellow Belly!" "Unpatriotic!"

I didn't go back to the farm house that evening until very late, well after grandpa and grandma had gone to bed. I didn't know what to do: whether to pack and prepare to leave for Fort Benjamin Harrison the following morning or to go about my life just as before, knowing what grandpa had done for me.

Tossing in bed, I couldn't sleep that night. Finally, at 4:00 a.m. I got up and packed. I fed the animals and then drove down the long lane just as a tinge of sunlight peeked out from the east. I traveled into Lisbon and parked a half block north of the train station where I stayed in my car.

Soon after a steady stream of automobiles pulled up at the station and several men, many my friends, got out of their vehicles with their families. Wives and girlfriends hung onto the men, sobbing. One man obviously had his children with him as three small figures clung to their father's legs. There was crying, whaling, hugging, and kissing.

Finally, the train slowly pulled up to the edge of the platform from the east. The men lifted their duffel bags over their shoulders and gave their loved ones one last kiss goodbye. And then quietly, solemnly the men boarded the train and disappeared, as though disappearing from existence. The wives, girlfriends, and children lingered briefly, commiserating with one another before getting back into their vehicles and driving away.

I watched this episode of parting unfold totally unattached, as though a landscape artist looking at a pastoral scene for just the right moment to capture his still-life painting. I couldn't understand why I didn't go with the men. I started the engine and began to leave when I recognized another vehicle pull up and park in back of the train station. A woman got out and ran to the platform. She looked down the tracks, then ran into the station and emerged again, checking her wristwatch several times. All of a sudden she burst into crying. And then I knew for certain that it was Irene. I could see how terribly upset she was. The tears poured from her and she paced back and forth on the platform several times before returning to her car and driving away.

When I returned to Blessed Acres that morning, I parked my rusty Oldsmobile in the barn lot, beneath the large weeping willow tree. I didn't go inside the farm house. Instead I walked across the train tracks, the very tracks that thirty minutes before carried the train that transported the soon-to-be soldiers onto the first leg of their journey to patriotic duty.

I went back into the "other world" as Philip and I called it, back to the forty acre woods. I walked between the large maple and walnut trees, around the brush and thickets of sage and mulberry bushes. I stayed there until late morning just walking around, remembering how Philip and I would play by the small stream that meandered through the back of Blessed Acres.

When I emerged from the woods in late morning, grandpa had already gone to work and grandma was in the house sewing. She said nothing about the unusual fact of me being home at this time of the day. Rather, she asked me if I wanted any breakfast, which I refused. And then she motioned towards the kitchen table.

"Something came for you in the mail this morning, Eugene." I saw a letter on the table top and quickly recognized the return address. I slit the envelope open with a paring knife and pulled out the folded piece of paper. It simply read:

> July 15, 1950
> TO: Eugene F. O'Connor
> 4D (Deferred)
> Signed: Jonathan T. Campbell, Captain
> United States Military Reserves, Lisbon, Indiana

Reuben interrupted my story to ask what staying home from Korea had to do with my decision to go to West Africa as a missionary.

"By the autumn of 1950," I replied, "something like 400 men from Roanoke County had gone to fight in Korea. I was one of the few younger men who still lived and worked in Lisbon. By the spring of 1951, five soldiers from the county had been killed in Korea, including two good friends. In the back of my mind, I think I experienced tremendous guilt at having accepted the deferment.

"Shortly after I received the deferral I started to attend the King of Glory Missionary Church again. In some ways it is mysterious even to me why I did it, but I kept having this feeling that my mother wanted me to be closer to God, to reach out and find him. Perhaps I attended again out of guilt, partially to please my grandparents; I don't know exactly myself. But I do remember that it made my grandparents extremely happy to see me worshiping in church again. I also began for the first time in my life to pray to God for direction and purpose, because I didn't feel as though I had either."

The airline captain's voice came over the speaker. He announced that we were beginning our descent to Charles de Gaulle International Airport. We had been in the air nearly seven hours with little sleep. I hurried along to answer this part of Reuben's query before we arrived in Paris.

In December 1951, I had driven into town to return some books at the public library. I specifically remember that before I left the library, I checked out Joseph Conrad's *Heart of Darkness*. I had read the novella in a cursory fashion at Hanover, but I wanted to read it again to better understand it. On my way out of the library, I noticed a small display table filled with books, journals, and magazines. I scanned several of them and then I saw an issue of the Catholic publication called *Our Sunday Visitor*. I had first seen it at the college library at Hanover. I picked up the newspaper and noticed what I thought to be a bookmark stuck between some pages. I opened the paper to that spot and saw an advertisement. It read:

"IS GOD CALLING YOU TO SERVE IN OVERSEAS MISSIONS?"

If you think that God may be calling you to spread the saving message of Christ to an underdeveloped world, contact the Society of Jesus (Jesuits) of West Africa. We may have the answer to that Calling! Write to:

Father John Stivonovich, S.J.

c/o Victoria Station

Grand Bassa, Cape de Leone, West Africa

Perhaps I would have thought nothing more about the advertisement, except that when I glanced at the back of what I thought was the bookmark I saw the scribbled writing of Romans 10: 13-17. And then when I turned the clipped bookmark over, I realized it was not a bookmark at all, but a business card. It read:

Randall Shore, President

THE ROANOKE COUNTY BANK

224 West Washington Street

Lisbon, Indiana (Telephone) Blue-228

"You Can Count On Us to Fulfill Your Dreams."

As I drove back to Blessed Acres that night, I kept thinking: why does this man, Randall Shore, keep entering my life? What is he or God trying to tell me? I had never stopped to see Shore after I received his letter informing me that my scholarship at Hanover had been discontinued. Was his business card a sign that I couldn't remove myself from him even if I wanted to? When I returned home, I read and reread Romans 10: 13-17. I can quote the scripture verbatim to this very day.

For whosoever shall call upon the name of the Lord shall be saved.

How then shall they call on him in whom they have not believed? And how shall they believe in him of whom they have not heard? And how shall they hear without a preacher?

And how shall they preach, except they be sent? As it is written, How beautiful are the feet of them that preach the gospel of peace, and bring glad tidings of good things. . . !

So then faith cometh by hearing, and hearing by the word of God.

And all I could think about that night was: is this what God has in store for me? Is this the answer to my prayers? Had I, in my own self-absorption and inability to connect with God, failed to see the opportunity of reaching out to help others find their own relationship with Him?

I wrote to Father John Stivonovich and requested information about missions work in Cape de Leone. I intentionally didn't mention my education or occupation, as I thought the priest would be apt to question why a man with two years of college would be a farmer and a service station attendant. To my surprise, an encouraging response came back in about six weeks.

And that was the start of my correspondence with Father Stivonovich. It continued on for the next six months, until in May 1952, I finally committed to going to Cape de Leone to serve as a missionary. I told my grandparents of this decision in September, withholding from them that the organization I would be serving under was Catholic. From that time to the day I boarded the train bound for Africa they treated me with the utmost respect and deference. It was as though I had undergone a complete metamorphosis in their eyes, from being their hopelessly ungrateful and vexed grandson to God's own chosen apostle.

But the response from Irene Sommers was entirely different. While Irene had been very supportive of me attending college, she was just as adamantly opposed to my decision to serve in overseas missions. She couldn't understand this calling that I spoke about in such ephemeral terms.

"Eugene," Irene said when I told her of my decision, "I've never heard you talk this way before. How did God speak to you so that you know that this is what you want? I don't understand? Are you sure this is the direction that you're led to pursue? It has come all of a sudden. Why now? And why Africa?"

But the decision had been made and I intended to see it through. I had arranged to leave after the harvest, so that grandpa wouldn't have to hire someone to combine and store the corn and soybeans we had planted that year on Blessed Acres.

On the morning of November 2, 1952, I got up, having packed the night before. I had managed to pack all that I was informed I would need by Father Stivonovich into two large suitcases. Over the past several weeks, I had received a number of gifts from well-wishers, but there simply wasn't room to take anything but the bare necessities. I remember as I rose that morning, I heard the faint sound of the whistle from the glass works. I hadn't heard it in years. Then there was a knock on the door.

"Eugene," granddad said, "is it all right for me to come in, son?"

"Sure, grandpa. I'm dressed," I answered, putting on the last of my suspenders. He limped into the room. He now used a cane.

"I'm sorry about sleeping in," I said before he had a chance to say anything. "I'm not sure how it happened, but I'll feed the sheep and chickens. Won't take me but a few minutes."

"Na," he said, "don't worry, son. I've already done it. We got to make sure you're all ready to go." Granddad then slowly scratched the tip of his nose, seeming to prolong the activity to give him additional time to think what next to say. "Have you got everything ready?" he finally asked.

"I think I'm all packed," I said.

"Good," he said slowly, with deep emotion. "Real good."

Granddad next hobbled back out of my bedroom without saying anything. I wondered why he left, but just at that time he came hobbling back in holding a garment bag.

"Your grandma and I got something for you, son," he said. He pulled up the garment bag and removed from it a beautiful suit. It was dark gray with a bow tie tied around the neck of the suit.

"Your grandma and me thought you should have something special to wear when you leave," he said. "You won't mind wearing this today, will you?"

He handed me the suit and I examined it closely. "It's beautiful, grandpa."

"I'll take your things down while you change, Eugene." Granddad grabbed the larger of my two suitcases and lumbered out of the room and down the staircase. I changed quickly and followed him, carrying the other suitcase. When I got to the kitchen, I could see that grandma had the breakfast table set. She looked up at me from the wood burning stove. A plate of buckwheat pancakes and bacon, my favorite breakfast food, was setting on the warmer.

"You look mighty handsome, Mister O'Connor," she said.

After I finished eating breakfast, grandma handed me a book and said, "I want you to have this, Eugene."

It was mother's Bible, the one that had been given to her for attending Sunday school for seven years straight.

"You sure you want me to take ma's Bible?" I asked. "I know how much this means to you."

"If your mother knew what you're leaving to go do, son,

she'd want you to have it. You make sure and read it every day, you hear. Don't worry if you don't understand everything at once. It takes time."

I thanked grandma and went to kiss her good-bye, but she announced that she was going with us to town. We traveled into Lisbon and grandpa drove to the back of the train station. A crowd parted to allow the truck through. When I got out, the crowd roared loudly and started clapping. As I looked at the faces of the people, I realized that I recognized almost every one there. I was momentarily stunned, failing to comprehend what was happening.

"Godspeed be with you, Gene!" a voice yelled from my right.

"We're proud of you, Eugene!" hollered Mary McKnight, a member of my church, from my left. "Go do God's work, young man!"

My head kept moving from one side of the crowd to the other as I attempted to follow where the yells of praise were coming from. Screams came from a dozen other well-wishers as grandpa and I maneuvered between all the people to get to the station. Once we reached the top of the platform, a man came towards me holding a scroll. It was Lisbon's mayor Hank Powers. He reached for my right hand and pumped it several times. Then music blared from behind by the Lisbon Community Band. It played a rousing rendition of "Onward Christian Soldiers." The crowd started cheering louder and suddenly two young boys hoisted a large banner, producing a loud, euphoric "Hurrah" from the crowd:

"TO CHRIST BE THE GLORY!!!"
Eugene O'Connor, Lisbon's Missionary to Africa!
November 2, 1952

Just at the point where I thought nothing more could possibly happen, Hank Powers quelled the commotion and read from a scroll at the top of his voice. He announced that the community was sending me off to face certain danger, but that God would protect me so that I could fulfill my quest to take

Christ's redemptive love to the heathen continent of Africa. And then the mayor announced that by his authority he was naming the day "Eugene Fitzpatrick O'Connor Day" in honor of me.

The crowd roared again and the two young boys hoisted the banner even higher, causing everyone to applaud and scream! Hank Powers handed me the scroll he had just read and a photographer from *The Prophet* took a picture of Hank and me. The band resumed playing a spirited version of "Onward Christian Soldiers." And then, almost as if on cue, the sleek passenger train rolled in from the west exactly on time. The train coasted into the station, docking at the platform. Uncle Paul helped me on with my luggage and a couple of other passengers also climbed on, seeming to enjoy vicariously the excitement that was directed at me.

Grandpa, grandma and Uncle Paul gave me a hug and Aunt Betty, not knowing her own strength, squeezed the air out of me in a fleeting embrace. The conductor hollered "All Aboard" and I stepped on to the train.

As I looked out through the door's opening at the still cheering, boisterous crowd, I suddenly saw Randall Shore waving at me. When he saw that he had caught my eye, he yelled, "Godspeed, Gene! Do God's work!" I smiled and waved at him and he smiled back, happy that we had made eye contact.

And then I glanced in back of Shore and saw Irene Sommers. Irene hadn't visited or called me in over two weeks before this morning, but she now stood several feet behind Shore. She looked sad and wistful. How dreadfully I wished I had known she was there and had given her a last hug and kiss!

But it was too late now! The train pulled away from the platform! The throng of well-wishers cheered and the band played noisily. As the train picked up speed, I stuck my head out of the open door and waved again and again back at the jubilant crowd. Tears dripped from my own cheeks as the faces of Lisbon's truly finest citizens grew smaller.

Nineteen

As the Boeing 747 jumbo jetliner touched down in Paris, I felt a sense of relief at having concluded my story of how I ended up in Cape de Leone. Reuben and I disembarked, traveled through customs, where I presented my passport as Donald Engels, the entrepreneur toaster salesman. We walked to the terminal to obtain our baggage. I felt groggy and disoriented, the results of having flown through seven time zones and not having slept for more than a couple of hours in a day and a half. The local time was 1:00 p.m. and there was a hubbub of activity running through the terminal.

Our flight to Grand Bassa didn't leave until 3:30 p.m. After we checked our bags at the West African Airways counter, Reuben and I sauntered to the middle of the terminal. I sighed from exhaustion.

"I'm getting too old for this international travel," I said. "I'd need to be thirty again to get any enjoyment out of this."

Reuben sighed as well. "I now remember why I don't go to the States more often, Professor. That's one wide pond!"

We smiled at one another and then, without speaking, started walking down the terminal towards where there was greater activity. Despite concluding that neither of us were hungry, we drifted into a small cafe and ordered coffee. I also ate a croissant. The small bit of caffeine and food revived me.

"Nigel," I said, feeling more awake, "now you must tell me about Margaret. What was she doing in Spain? I'm shocked that I didn't know about her being alive and her whereabouts during this time. You owe it to me. I've waited—"

"Professor," Reuben said, stopping me, "after Albert

Mubarsoi expelled Margaret from Cape de Leone, she lived in exile in south central Spain."

"Yes, you mentioned this when we first met," I said. "But why Spain?"

"More precisely, Professor, in a convent in south central Spain. The convent belonged to a small Catholic order located near Córdoba." Reuben looked up from his cup. "Professor, Margaret never left the convent. She was not allowed to leave until 1979."

"Why not?"

"It's a long story, but the short of it is that Mubarsoi had established a friendship with Spain's dictator Ferdinan Franco that went back to 1959. You know the old saying, 'politics makes strange bedfellows'. Well, Mubarsoi and Franco had become friends when Franco provided Mubarsoi with arms during the civil war you helped fight. When Mubarsoi spared Margaret's life, he deported her to the convent with Franco's approval that she was never to leave."

"And what forced her to remain there?" I asked. "Was she imprisoned?

"Yes, she was physically restrained until Franco died, but then she chose to stay because she didn't want to risk the consequences if she left," Reuben answered.

"What do you mean 'risk the consequences'?"

Reuben sat still, stirred his coffee and said nothing.

"Well, what happened to her then? Did she join the Order?" I asked. "Can you at least tell me that?"

Reuben looked up. "Aunt Margaret was still married to my uncle, Derrick Reuben. They never divorced. I thought you at least knew that."

I nodded. Yes, I was aware that Margaret had been married to Derrick Reuben, a very successful Irish businessman and one-time politician. But Reuben had been dead for more than a decade. It had always been difficult for me to accept that Margaret belonged to any man, any man other than Francis Tannen, that is. However, once I had accepted the possibility that she was alive, Reuben's explanation that Margaret had ended up in a convent didn't surprise me.

"Well, tell me the rest. I want to know."

"I can't," Reuben replied sharply. "You have to trust that you'll learn everything you want once we get to Cape de Leone."

"I don't understand your stone-walling, Nigel? If you know then why don't you tell me?"

Reuben lifted his head and stared straight into my eyes. "Margaret didn't contact you for your own protection, not because she didn't want to. That's all I'm at liberty to say. When we arrive in Cape de Leone every possible question you have will be answered by others, not by me."

Reuben stood up, telling me that he had to make a telephone call back to his office. When he returned, he had no more than sat down when I heard the following announcement over the intercom. "West African Airways is paging a Monsieur Nigel Reuben to the customer service counter." The announcement was repeated in French and English.

"Please excuse me," Reuben said, getting up. "I'll be back as soon as I can."

Reuben stood and exited our small table. I followed him out of the cafe with my eyes and, oddly, he seemed to know exactly where to go to find the customer service counter. He carried his attaché case with him, never letting go of it. As I observed him, Reuben seemed to have everything in order: all the details of our trip; the answers to all my questions, if he would only tell me; a confidence that was not only noticeable, but striking. He now looked as neatly dressed and groomed as the first moment I met him, while I felt as though I had been to hell and back, with my suit cleaned and blessed by the Devil.

Reuben suddenly appeared again, speaking quickly. "Professor, there has been a change in our plans. I apologize but our flight to Grand Bassa has been delayed. It will be necessary for us to charter a flight."

"Charter a private plane from Paris to Grand Bassa?" I exclaimed.

"Yes, immediately," Reuben responded.

"But that will cost a fortune! How long can the delay possibly be?"

"They say it will only be a couple of hours, but I don't trust the airline. It's never been known for punctuality. Two hours could easily turn into five. We don't have time to wait."

"But how are you going to charter a plane just like that? You're talking about a two thousand mile flight."

Reuben smiled. "I already have one, Professor. It will be at Gate 55 in twenty minutes. Do you want anything to eat or drink? There won't be any food service or toilet on the plane."

All the feelings of not trusting Reuben rushed through me again. I couldn't dismiss the coincidence of him leaving to make a telephone call and then, as soon as he returned, there being an announcement for him to come to the customer service desk of the West African Airlines. Why would only he be notified of the delay? Why hadn't there been a general announcement? For that matter, why would there be any announcement at all? Flights run late all the time. Things weren't adding up.

"Excuse me, Nigel, but I'm going to the restroom," I said, thinking of an excuse to get away. "I'll be back in just a few minutes."

I started to walk out of the cafe. "Professor O'Connor," Reuben called after me. "There's a men's room here. Just ask the maitre' d."

I smiled and shook my head, mumbling to Reuben that I needed to stretch my legs. As soon as I reached the point where I believed Reuben couldn't see me, I sprinted as fast as sixty-two-year-old legs could take me to the nearest pay telephone. I retrieved the envelope from my breast pocket and called Bob Zimmer collect. Zimmer didn't sound the least bit tired but relieved, quickly quizzing me.

"Gene, did Donna Pauley tell you anything about the results of the autopsy performed on Elizabeth?"

"Donna said the police are now treating Elizabeth's death as a homicide. Is that true? Do they have any leads?"

"Yes," Zimmer said. "They have a main lead and you're not going to like who it is."

"Someone I know?"

"It's you!"

I went breathless as if I'd been hit in the chest by a thrown basketball.

"Gene, I hate to have to tell you, but the investigator's office has reason to believe that Elizabeth and you were having an affair, that Elizabeth wanted to call it off but you wouldn't let her. They believe she threatened to tell her mother about it if you didn't leave her alone. One theory is that you killed her and tried to make it look like a suicide."

"But that's ludicrous."

"Yes, of course, but the evidence they've come up with is almost totally against you."

"Like what?"

"Apparently whoever entered Elizabeth's dormitory room late Sunday night had a key or she let them in voluntarily. There's no evidence of forced entry."

"But how does that implicate me? Elizabeth could have let in any friend, not just me."

"But they found your fingerprints in Elizabeth's room. Also, the police got a search warrant for your house last evening. They found a bottle of chloroform. It's odorless and colorless. The authorities believe it could have been used on Elizabeth as an anesthetic to make her unconscious. There's no evidence of any struggle in her room, so the police are thinking that maybe you used it to subdue her."

"I wouldn't know what chloroform is if you put it right in front of me," I replied. "Bob, it had to be planted in my house. Isn't there anyone at the dorm who saw something? Eigenman Hall has hundreds of students. Surely someone saw something if there was fowl play involved."

"No one has come forward yet. But there's also evidence that doesn't support you as the subject."

"Like what?"

"The suicide note, for one. It was typed and full of misspellings. That was the first clue that Elizabeth or you probably didn't write it. After all, you're both teachers of writing, unless you—"

"Unless what, Bob?"

"Unless you intentionally misspelled the note to make it look like someone else did it."

"Surely you don't believe that!"

"Of course not, but the investigators have cause to."

"Anything else that exonerates me?"

"Yea, the fact that the campus radio station and the newspaper's own news bureau received calls about Elizabeth's death yesterday morning that didn't come from the police or lead investigator. Why would you draw attention to her death or have someone else do it for you? That doesn't make any sense. Honestly, Gene, I don't think the police would be looking at you as the sole suspect if it wasn't for you leaving the country yesterday evening. That didn't look good at all, especially when you left with this stranger immediately after being interviewed about Elizabeth's death. That was a big mistake!"

"Well, I can't change that now."

"No, but you can get back here immediately and get this cleared up," Zimmer said. "Several Indianapolis television stations are here and the rumors are going crazy. It wouldn't surprise me if your name isn't mentioned by the press today as the prime suspect. I imagine the university's information office is livid with you. I've even heard that the prosecutor is thinking of bringing together a grand jury investigation. This isn't good, Gene. By the way, where are you?"

"Paris right now, but I'm getting ready to fly on to Cape de Leone. I'll be back as soon as I can, but I can't return yet. It would take me several minutes to explain why, but just trust me. Please do what you can for me there. I promise that I'll be back as soon as I can, hopefully within the next couple of days."

"Is there anything specific I can do?"

"Yes, Bob, I need to know everything you can get your hands on about Nigel Reuben."

"Donna Pauley has already called me this morning about that, Gene, but I haven't had time to make any phone calls. I may know something later this morning."

"Please do whatever it takes, Bob. This situation is getting stranger by the minute. Much of what I've been able to pull out of Reuben sounds familiar, but it just doesn't add up. Also, I need to know whether a Donald T. Engels exists in Garfield Heights, Ohio."

"A who, Gene?"

"Please write this down, Bob! A Donald T. Engels. The last name is spelled E-N-G-E-L-S. He may be some kind of businessman. I'm just not sure. That's why I want you to check and see if such a person exists in the Garfield Heights or Cleveland, Ohio, areas. If this Engels guy exists, then I want as much information on him that you can find as well."

"What does Donald Engels have to do with anything?"

"Reuben has asked me to assume his identity when we get to Cape de Leone. But Reuben also said that Engels doesn't exist, that he's a fictitious person. I just need to find out if Reuben is telling me the truth. The first place to start is to see if Donald T. Engels is a real person. Reuben gave me an address for him in Garfield Heights, Ohio. This fictitious guy is supposed to operate a business that producers kitchen appliances—toasters, coffee makers, things like that."

"Gene, this doesn't sound good. I think you should bale out now. Don't take the chance. The possibility of seeing this long-time friend of yours isn't worth getting yourself killed over."

"There's enough to his story to make me think he may be telling me the truth, just not the whole truth. I'm going to see it through, Bob, at least until I learn more so I can make an informed decision."

"Do you have a number where you can be contacted?"

"No, I'm leaving now to go to Cape de Leone! I'll call you as soon as I reach Grand Bassa and can get to a telephone. It may be late this afternoon or early evening, but please let Grace and your office know where you can be reached at all times, okay? I owe you a big steak dinner when I get back." I paused to catch my breath. "Bob, I'm counting on you, buddy."

"Gene, call as soon as you can. I'll try to have some news to report. Please take care of yourself."

I hung up the receiver and turned around right into Reuben.

"Why didn't you tell me you needed to use the telephone, Professor?" Reuben asked. "I would have gladly given you a number that you could have used to call any where you needed."

"It just occurred to me, Nigel," I said, thinking quickly, "that I should check on things back in Bloomington before we leave the airport. I didn't know how long it might be before we will be near a telephone again."

"Yes, I see," said Reuben. "Have they found out any more about your goddaughter?

"Nothing yet," I answered. "I'll need to call when we get to Grand Bassa."

"Yes, of course," Reuben said. "That can be arranged. Now we need to go to our gate quickly. Our plane is waiting."

We started walking back towards the direction we originally came from, passed the small cafe where we had stopped for coffee. I looked up at one of the departure screen terminals and found the flight number that we had originally planned to take on West African Airlines to Grand Bassa. It still read: "3:30 p.m.— On Time."

When we got to the end of the terminal, I finally saw gate 55. It was the last gate, tucked away next to an exit sign. No one was there except two large burly men, each wearing leisure suits that were popular in the 1970s. One sported a stubby beard, with an ear ring in his left ear.

"I want to introduce you to a couple of gentlemen who will

be accompanying us, Professor," Reuben said as we approached the large men.

"Professor O'Connor, this is Mr. Thombi Jones and Mr. Karim Smith."

I shook hands with both men. They were both muscular, bruising types who looked like they could be defensive linemen for the Green Bay Packers. No sooner had we exchanged greetings, than both men, without any prompting, moved to our right carrying our luggage. They opened the gate door. Reuben motioned for me to follow them. When we passed through the door, there was a stairway down to the tarmac. I looked out from the top of the stairs and I noticed a small twin engine jet liner, a Lear Jet-35, about 150 feet from us.

"We're not going in that, are we?" I exclaimed.

"Yes," Reuben answered with a chuckle. "All the way to Cape de Leone. We have a very experienced pilot."

I suppose I could be forgiven for sending him a doubting glance. I really wished I could hit him.

"Professor," Reuben said, slapping me on the shoulder, "relax. Enjoy the moment. Don't worry—you're in safe hands."

But all I could think about was, *What have I gotten myself into? Why did I ever agree to leave with this stranger? Will I ever see Margaret Mahoney?*

Twenty

As we flew over the Mediterranean Ocean, the thought of seeing Margaret again intensified every memory I had about her. She was the glue that held everything together in Burguna: she educated the children at St. Magdalene School; she helped bring Tambe babies into the world as a midwife; she taught the women of the village classes on hygiene, sewing, and how to deal with a child's "gippy tummy" (diarrhea), high fever, or bleeding cut. But Margaret had assumed these positions of village responsibility only after spending a great deal of time with the Tambe. "An African won't trust you until he knows you," I remember Margaret telling me one night after I had been in Burguna for only a few weeks.

The first task of any outsider to an African village is to become accepted. "I had to be very careful not to offend the Tambe when I first came," Margaret said. "I knew if they thought I was trying to wipe out all the ways they did things, all their customs, then they wouldn't be willing to have me stay."

Still, Margaret brought innovation to the tribe. Female education didn't exist in the village prior to Margaret's and Tannen's establishment of St. Magdalene School. Young girls only had educational opportunities if they were fortunate enough to attend mission schools in and around Grand Bassa—never if they lived in an isolated, distant village such as Burguna.

Prior to the village's conversion to Islam, Margaret also assisted Fathers Stivonovich and Tannen with religious services by handing out rosaries and conducting prayer circles for the women. She shared with me several times that it was this spiritual dimension that she missed most since the tribe had converted to

Islam; she yearned for the opportunity to share the teachings of Christ with the villagers. And through this sharing, she craved to experience the mystery of Christ's love herself. Because of Margaret's central role in the life of the village, I wasn't convinced by Justin Perry's conjecture that the Tambe would prefer that even she leave.

The longer I stayed the more I realized the respect that Margaret had achieved exceeded the boundaries of tiny Burguna. Shortly after she returned from visiting Ireland, she was called upon by a nearby village to assume yet another important role[4] One day, about noon, a young man from the Moyshoni tribe had traveled by foot to Burguna searching for this "white, Christian missionary woman," as he described her in his native tongue. He spoke Kawaili, the native language of the Moyshoni tribe. As he shared with Joseph Obei, who knew some Kawaili, there had been a serious disturbance in his tribe. The chief couldn't preside over the disturbance because he had gone to a meeting of paramount chiefs in a village west of Burguna about three walking days away. I knew this because Chief Faramha had also gone to this regional meeting of chieftains, accompanied by Francis Tannen.

This ordeal that the young Moyshoni man spoke of apparently involved a domestic quarrel between a husband and a wife. The elders in his village said that the dispute, the nature of which wasn't made precisely clear by the stranger, had to be decided immediately. They wanted to form a council, selected from the elders themselves, to serve as judge and jury. But the women of the tribe greatly opposed this scheme. They claimed that since the tribal chief was not present that a neutral third party should preside. A number of women had heard of this "white, Christian missionary woman" in nearby Burguna and demanded that she be approached to preside over the dispute.

When Margaret was presented with the proposal, she simply

---

4 Adapted from Emily Hawn, "I Say This," *The New Yorker*, July 31, 1995, pp. 35–39.

asked Joseph Obei, "Is it safe to go?"

"Yes, madama," Joseph said. "The Moyshoni are a peaceful tribe. They mean no ill will towards us. I trust that the man is not trying to trick you."

And that is all Margaret needed to know. Within an hour, she had packed a small case of personal items and asked if I wanted to go along. The opportunity to experience some diversion from the routine of teaching at the school seemed quite appealing, so I quickly said yes. Joseph Obei would accompany us and serve as our interpreter. Menilek Obei, a much younger cousin of Joseph's who the British would call "small boy" (meaning the second steward, responsible for managing our personal items) helped transport our few supplies. And so the five of us—Margaret, Joseph and Menilek Obei, the young Moyshoni man, and I—set out for our adventure to the Moyshoni village of Kampupu.

There were no roads through the jungle between Burguna and Kampupu. We traversed over overgrown pathways that were more or less animal tracks. After about six hours of arduous walking, we arrived at Kampupu without incident in the early evening. When we arrived, approximately fifty women with their children came out to the edge of the village to greet us, clapping their hands and ululating very loudly. It was a West African tribe's way to greet guests.

Margaret was obviously accustomed to the tradition as she smiled broadly and gently patted the place over her heart with her right hand and gestured for me to do likewise. This, as I learned, was the polite way to acknowledge a village's welcome. The crowd of well-wishers followed behind as we entered into the center part of the village. There we found a scene that was little different than what one would find in Burguna: Moyshoni women, many with babies tied to their backs, scrubbing clothing, grinding meal in large wooden kettles, or working on small tracts of land; children watching over animals or playing in the village with sticks and wood-carved balls.

Since it was late, we assumed that whatever work had to be

done would not begin until the following morning. We were unusually tired, not being used to traveling for so long a time without resting. But as soon as we unloaded our gear, a group of the village's elders and their wives congregated. According to the local rules of etiquette, we were approached by the village headman, or capita, as he was called.

"Greetings, madama," the capita said, bowing to Margaret. The capita then bowed to the rest of us who formed Margaret's retinue. He next told her how much the village appreciated her coming so far to help settle the dispute. Then he turned to me but addressed Margaret.

"Is this your master?" the capita asked in Kawaili. Joseph explained "master" in Kawaili meant 'husband.'

By Margaret's facial reaction, it was obvious she was irritated by the question, but answered graciously. "Joseph, please tell his Honor that I have no master but Jesus Christ, Son of the Living God."

Joseph translated and the capita nodded and then immediately followed up with the question, "Then who is this man?" referring to me.

"He is my brother in Christ," Margaret said without hesitation, "Monsieur O'Connor."

Margaret's answer embarrassed the capita, but before he had an opportunity to apologize, amazing things started to happen. Local men carried out a table and set it down in front of where we were talking. Then several adolescent boys carried a large chair and placed it behind the table. It was a grand chair, complete with ornately decorated arms and legs. To our surprise, the village was getting ready for a *baraza*, a calling together of the elders—all male, of course. But much to the elders' surprise, a similar number of women began to form a line opposite them. The two groups started to talk among themselves. It didn't seem to occur to either group that their visiting party was completely exhausted, in need of food and rest.

The capita politely pulled out the chair from the table and gestured for Margaret to take her duly appointed judgment seat.

As soon as she did, both groups started speaking at once. The capita raised his voice, quieting the riotous commotion, and then pointed to the spokesman of the elders. The group of women grumbled and pouted when they didn't have the opportunity to begin first. Joseph stood to Margaret's left, prepared to translate. It was only then that the capita spoke to Margaret about the substance of the disagreement.

The entire brouhaha amounted to this: a man, the plaintiff in this dispute, had married a young tribal woman three weeks before. As was the custom of the tribe, he had properly paid for his wife (a husband's dowry) by way of a gift of animals, but she had now deserted him. The husband demanded that either his wife return to him or else that the dowry he had given to the woman's father be returned. The strangeness of the situation was that the father was on the side of the husband.

"And why does she not choose to live with you?" Margaret asked the plaintiff-husband. He shrugged his shoulders, explaining in his native language that he knew of no just reason.

"And what do you say?" Margaret next asked the woman who was the wife's mother, the spokeswoman of the women's group.

"This man," the mother began, "is cruel, carries on with many other women of the tribe, and smells. My daughter should not have to put up with him."

"What do you say to this?" Margaret said, directing her question back to the husband.

"This is not true," he declared. "She (referring to his wife) is a wild one and will not serve me. A man cannot have his own wife disobey him. It is against our custom and the custom of our forefathers."

To this point, the elders all stood in agreement, stamping their feet against the ground. The women, on the contrary, hissed and clapped their hands, showing their repugnance.

"What does this wife of yours refuse to do?" Margaret asked the husband.

To which he answered, "She refuses to cook for me, tend to

my animals, and sleep with me."

Margaret next listened to the mother's rejoinder as to why her daughter, the wife, was completely justified in not being compliant. Margaret patiently listened to one side and then the other, all the time having to wait while Joseph Obei translated the nuances of the marital dispute. The villagers loved the arguing, as it seemed to be a much relished form of entertainment. But finally, after about fifteen minutes of disputation, Margaret stood forcefully, causing the argument to come to an abrupt halt.

"Bring out the woman!" Margaret said. "I want to hear her reason why she won't go back to her husband."

The women defenders pulled the young bride from the back of the group. She appeared to dislike the attention. What all of us saw was a young girl who couldn't have been more than fourteen-years-old. She was spindly looking but had a lovely, albeit defiant, face. Glancing at Margaret's expression, I could see that she immediately had great empathy for the girl, but tried to give the impression of impartiality.

"Why did you run away from your husband?" Margaret asked. "What has he done so terrible that you won't honor your marriage vows."

"I don't like him," the young woman replied. "I was not consulted when my father arranged the marriage. I did not want it. Besides, he is mean to me, spends his time lying with other women, and smells like a goat."

The women laughed loudly and made unintelligible comments in derision of the husband. But by the reaction on the elders' faces, it was evident that they didn't think the young bride's answer was a good reason for her to bolt. Margaret surmised the elders' response and sought a compromise.

"But why can't you," Margaret asked, pointing to the father of the bride, "simply give back the dowry to this man and let your daughter have her freedom?"

The father stepped forward. "I have already butchered the chickens and other animals for my family," he said, "and besides, this is not my daughter's decision to make."

"And if I order you to go back to your husband," Margaret said to the young bride, "will you go?"

"No," said the Moyshoni woman, "I will kill myself first!"

Margaret turned to the husband. "What good is this woman to you? If I order her to return, she will only do harm to herself. Isn't this true?"

"Yes," the husband admitted, "but I still want her back or I want compensation for my animals," he declared.

Margaret stood up and started to announce that she needed time to deliberate. But then another village woman stepped forward from the crowd of women.

"Madama!" she announced in her native Kawaili, "I will serve this man as his wife."

Chatter filled the air. Margaret sat back down in the judgment seat and the capita held his arms high again to quiet the crowd.

"Who is this woman?" Margaret asked.

"She is my older daughter," said the mother of the defiant bride.

"She's ugly!" screamed the husband.

The remark caused the woman who stood forward to cast down her face. Margaret gave a menacing stare at the husband. Indeed, the woman who now stood in front of Margaret was rotund and had a face that was large and piggish in appearance.

"You have no husband?" asked Margaret.

"No, madama," she answered.

"And you are this girl's older sister?" Margaret asked the large woman, pointing to the young bride.

"Yes, madama."

Margaret's eyes glistened, reflecting light that emanated from torches that illuminated the village.

"Would you agree to prepare this man's meals, tend to his animals, sleep with him, and serve him as he wishes?" asked Margaret.

The large sister's stoic face changed into a warm smile. "Yes, madama," she answered. "I would do all these things."

"Then what do you say to this?" Margaret asked, turning to the husband.

He started to object, at which time Margaret cut him off.

"But you said that this is what you want from your present wife, isn't that right?"

"Yes, Madama, yes it was."

"And there is no objection from either the father or the mother of these two women?" Margaret turned first to the father, whose face lit up like a candle, nodding his head with great excitement. The mother was less inclined to grant her approval. Finally she nodded after receiving the cold stares of both daughters.

Margaret held her right hand high to signal a cessation in the proceedings. She then briefly met with Joseph Obei and the capita. After the three consulted among themselves, Margaret stepped back in front of her judgment seat and raised a large spear that had been handed to her by the capita.

"By the power invested in me by the great Moyshoni tribe, in the absence of Chieftain Ghawini Mubolo, I hereby declare the marriage of this man and woman," Margaret pointed to the plaintiff-husband and the defiant bride, "null and void." Joseph translated the declaration to the capita, who in turn announced it loudly to the two gatherings.

"I further pronounce," Margaret declared and then paused momentarily. At this time, Joseph Obei walked out to the larger, older daughter and guided her towards the husband, while the capita did the same in moving the somewhat bewildered looking husband towards the large, piggish looking woman. Margaret continued, repeating, "I further pronounce that no further dowry is due the father, and this man and this woman are hereby united in holy matrimony as husband and wife."

After the capita's translation, the elders and the village women alike erupted into applause and a pounding of feet, while the large, older sister gave her new husband a big embrace and kiss. I noticed that the younger, comely sister slipped into the crowd of well-wishers in obscurity. The compromise seemed to appease everyone, and if the plaintiff-husband did object, he was clearly not going to be able to voice it yet this night.

This incidence bounced into my memory when Reuben reminded me about Margaret being married. Margaret did not easily admit to having a husband. Her reply to the Moyshoni capita ("Joseph, please tell his Honor that I have no master but Jesus Christ, Son of the Living God.") was appropriate to her. Margaret valued her freedom greatly. I knew her well enough to know that the thought of her being under the authority of any man, even Francis Tannen, was anathema to her. On reflection, what further amazed me was how shrewdly one woman (Margaret) who refused to acknowledge a husband was able to assist another in getting rid of one.

We returned to Burguna the next day. Margaret never mentioned again the sleight-of-hand maneuvering in Kampupu. In fact, it was about this time that I noticed that Margaret became more sullen and distracted from carrying out the daily tasks that she customarily bore. She focused more on reading, prayer and seclusion. Ever since she had returned from Ireland, she wanted to be left alone, which was just the opposite of her normally gregarious and endearing disposition. It was as though she was going through some kind of pain, some anguish, which she was trying to get rid of by distancing herself from normal contact with the world.

One morning something happened that added to Margaret's worries. She had received a telegram addressed to me. It had been transported to the village by ferry, brought from the Western Union station in Grand Bassa. Margaret called me out of class, asking Falaba Cardew to take over for me. I sensed in her voice something was wrong.

"Gene, I wanted to get this to you immediately," Margaret said, handing me the telegram.

I read it quickly. I then had to read it again in order for the message to sink in:

> Eugene O'Connor   28 Sept. 1958
> Burguna, Cape de Leone, West Africa:
> Both grandparents very ill. Need you to return to
> Lisbon. Please wire when you receive this.
> Love. Aunt Betty

I looked up at Margaret. Small tears drained from her eyes, moistening her white cheeks. She had obviously read the telegram and realized its significance.

"Is there anything I can do?" Margaret asked.

"I need some time to think," I said, "but I need to get back to the students."

"Don't bother with that, Gene," Margaret said. "Falaba can take over your classes today. Why don't you go take a walk up Mount Dugaga? It's a beautiful day. I can prepare a lunch for you."

"No, I will be able to think better after school," I answered. "I will walk to the top of Mount Dugaga then, but will you join me? I have missed you greatly. You were gone for too long."

Margaret nodded, and I went back to school and resumed teaching arithmetic to the children. They were such bright students, but what if Margaret and I weren't here? Would the children have any formal education at all? I couldn't see how.

That evening I changed into hiking boots and asked Margaret again to accompany me up the trail to the top of Mount Dugaga. She suggested that I go alone, but added that she would join me at the top of the small mountain within the hour. Eastern Cape de Leone generally is a rainy, lush region. But there had been little rain this year and the grass lands, the veld, to the northwest of Burguna were scorched and brown-looking. This is the area that contained a large hill that the natives had named "Mount Dugaga," meaning "land of splendor." In terms of height the large hill was certainly nothing spectacular, but sloped upward off of the grassy plains approximately 1,500 feet above the rest of the terrain. Mount Dugaga could be easily trekked up in forty-five minutes.

I had been to the top of the small mountain for only about fifteen minutes when I sighted Margaret. She had her hiking gear on and her hair pinned back, looking even more stunning than usual. I could tell she had fixed herself up, wearing brown leather boots, tight fitting khaki slacks, and a European cut blouse.

"You mustn't have started long after me!" I yelled down to Margaret, sitting on my back side, resting my upper body on my arms bent behind me.

"I've made good time," Margaret replied, calling up and smiling. "I got a second wind!" She took what few remaining steps were necessary to reach the top and then stood, turned slowly, and surveyed the land below us. There was forest and rougher terrain to the east and grasslands to the west. "Isn't it just beautiful up here, Gene?" she said. "I had forgotten how lovely this is."

"Yes," I said, "It's beautiful. I can see why the Tambe have their burial ground here."

Margaret twirled her body one more time, looking down from the hill top. She then walked over and sat down next to me. Margaret next pointed with her left hand to a flower that grew beside a large rock.

"Look, Gene," Margaret said. "An African violet. It's remarkable that one would be found so high, away from its normal environment in the jungle."

The lovely flower was attached to a small vine. Its delicate petals were perfect in shape, its pure purple color in total contrast to the green frosty leaves and stem that supported it.

"Just think, Gene, if we hadn't walked up here this evening, it's very possible no one would have ever seen it. Wouldn't that be a shame? Something so beautiful and special never to be experienced?"

Margaret jumped up and went to the flower.

"What are you doing?" I exclaimed.

"I'm picking it," she answered. "I know that I could leave it, but the violet will only wither. I want to keep it. It will always remind me of you."

Margaret plucked the flower and a few inches of its stem. She secured it to her blouse by running the short stem through her top button hole. The sun had just about met the horizon and we both knew we had less than an hour more of light.

"Gene," Margaret said in a serious voice, returning to my side. "What are you going to do?"

"I don't want to leave, Margaret," I answered. "I'm needed here."

"But you may be needed more back at your home," she said. "It's been nearly six years since they've seen you. Don't you think you owe it to your family to return?"

I looked at Margaret who sat on her backside, arms folded across her knees. She looked supple and beautiful, but also unusually vulnerable.

"What's holding you back, Gene?" Margaret asked.

"For one thing the money to get home," I said.

"You know that isn't a problem," she said. "There are funds for you to return. I've told you that before. You've more than exceeded any expectations and you're entitled to payment. You simply refuse compensation any time I raise the issue."

I didn't know how to take Margaret's reply. Did she want me to leave? From the tone of her voice, I couldn't tell.

"Do you want me to go?" I blurted. "Is there something I don't know?"

"Possibly," Margaret said, "Francis has designs that may put us all in danger. I can't tell you everything. I don't know all myself. But I do know that Francis has plans to convert the Tambe and several other tribes to Christianity, and it has little to do with any spiritual beliefs he has."

"But why are you suddenly concerned about my safety now? You didn't seem to mind me being poisoned when I first came?" I said, lashing out and hurt that she wasn't trying to convince me to stay.

"How do you know about that?" Margaret asked.

"Justin Perry told me," I replied. "He said Francis and you knew all along."

"But I didn't know about it right away, Gene. You have to believe me. When I did learn, I had Francis go directly to Chief Faramha and demand that you not be bothered again. It was the best way to handle it."

"But you still didn't say anything to me!" I said. "You could have warned me! Couldn't you?"

"Yes," Margaret said slowly, sadly, "yes, I could have."

"Then why didn't you?"

"Because I didn't want you to leave, Gene. John Stivonovich had just deserted us. The village had just converted to Islam. I'm sorry, but I couldn't have handled it if you had left, too."

"I should have gone years ago," I replied. "Trying to help the tribe is like trying to wear down rock with water."

"But eventually pebbles do grow smooth, Gene. Things change—slowly. The Tambe's needs here are so great. And if you truly feel that way, why didn't you leave long before now?"

"You know why." I took Margaret's hand, longing to hold it and her, but Margaret unclasped my hand gently.

"You didn't stay just for me, did you?"

"No," I admitted, "not just for you, but you and the children. They draw you into their circle. It's a strong pull. I don't know how to say it. My heart just melts when I see the children learning their fractions and spelling and knowing that there is a possibility that their lives will be changed because of the school, because we're here."

"I agree with you, Gene, but it sounds so contradictory to what you just said. What you have to realize is that things are changing around us in all sorts of ways."

"So now it's different?" I asked.

"Yes," Margaret answered, "Yes, it's different because neither of us have any control over Francis or the powers in the capital city—Mubarsoi's government. I don't know what's going to happen, but I am afraid for you. I'm afraid for all of us."

By this time the sun had dipped below the horizon and we both knew that we had to get down the small mountain or risk danger by trying to walk down in darkness. We started out and by the time we reached Burguna, it was late. After embracing me, Margaret went to her house and I returned to my hut. Tannen was gone again to another meeting of the tribal chiefs.

Shortly after I rose the next morning, Samuel Obei came to my hut and informed me that Margaret had prepared breakfast and arranged for Falaba to teach for me that day. After breakfast, Margaret announced that she thought today was the time for me to go. A ferry would be arriving in the afternoon and I could be back in Grand Bassa by tomorrow.

"Gene," she said, handing me an envelope, "there's more than enough in here to get you home and then some. Please take it. I am terribly sorry that you must leave."

After that, Margaret ran from the kitchen into her bedroom. I started to follow her when Samuel, who had witnessed everything from the edge of the kitchen, stood up and came over to me. "Not now, Mr. O'Connor," Samuel said. "Now is not a good time."

Samuel escorted me back to my hut, informing me that the ferry heading west on the Tanganeen River would be stopping by Burguna in a few hours. He suggested that I should heed Margaret's advice and prepare to go.

"The children will want to see you before you leave, Mr. O'Connor. Please stop and see Falaba, Marabella, and the children," Joseph said.

I knew that Joseph was saying what Margaret wanted said. I felt at this point that the decision about my departure had become a fait accompli. I returned to my hut and began packing the few possessions I had accumulated in the six years I had lived in Burguna. Shortly after midday, in the blazing heat, Chief Faramha came to my hut and bid me good-bye. There were many other well-wishers, as well, from the tribe.

By early afternoon, Samuel had returned and asked that I

accompany him to the school. As we approached the small building that I had taught in since 1952, curiously I saw none of the children outside playing as was typical. When I opened the door, however, young voices screamed at me in Krio, "Surprise, Mister O'Connor, Surprise!" Falaba and Marabella had nearly all of the school children present, not just the ones in the afternoon class. Others came from around the back of the building, those who couldn't fit inside. Dozens of children came up to me and gave me a hug and wished me well. It took me nearly an hour to say good-bye to all of them. It was nearly as emotional for me as the send-off I had received from Lisbon six years before. Then when I was about to say good-bye to the last child, Marabella yelled, "Children, please come to order."

Marabella pulled out a small pitch-pipe and blew into it softly. Then she started singing and the children, with faces intent, followed closely:

Jesus loves me, this I know
For the Bible tells me so,
Little ones to Him belong,
They are weak, but He is strong.

Yes, Jesus loves me.
Yes, Jesus loves me.
Yes, Jesus loves me.
The Bible tells me so.

The children then sang out to me in unison, "Good-bye, Mister O'Connor, we love you!"

Joseph pulled me from the small building, telling me that I must hurry as the ferry to Grand Bassa would be arriving soon. I waved one last time to the children and returned to my hut to retrieve my two bags. When I entered the hut, Margaret stood near the opening. Joseph remained outside, allowing us to speak in private.

"You knew I wouldn't let you go without saying good-bye,

didn't you?" Margaret asked.

"I had prayed that this morning wasn't the last time I would see you."

Margaret came over and put her arms around me and hugged me closely.

"Did you hear what the children just did?" I whispered to her.

"You mean singing to you?"

"Yes, but they sang *Jesus Loves Me*, Margaret," I exclaimed, "I don't want you or Marabella or Falaba to get in trouble."

"We talked to the children ahead of time, Gene. They know they're not to say anything to their parents about it. It's our little secret."

Margaret then put her arms around my shoulders again. "I love you, Eugene O'Connor! Always remember this wherever you go."

I embraced and kissed Margaret on her left cheek. She held me close for several seconds and then, without saying anything more, she unclasped me and ran from the hut back to her house. I picked up my two bags and walked to the dock on the river's edge. When I looked back, I prayed that Margaret might peer out the window and wave to me one last time. But I saw no movement and I realized then that it was time for me to go. The ferry finally came and I started the long, solemn journey back to Grand Bassa and eventually to home.

Twenty One

G randpa coughed and sputtered and I could tell he was having a difficult time breathing. He had been unconscious for the past two weeks, including the five days I had been back in Lisbon. Uncle Paul, Aunt Betty, and I took turns being with grandpa at the hospital, while the other two stayed with grandma back at Blessed Acres. She was nearly as ill as grandpa, but she refused to go to the hospital, claiming that God had sustained her for seventy-eight years without the intervention of doctors or modern medicine. He would do it again.

Hastings Hamilton couldn't afford to be so spiritually certain. His bad heart had finally done him in. According to the doctors at the Roanoke County Hospital, it was pumping so inefficiently that he was likely to suffer another heart attack or possibly a stroke due to oxygen deprivation to his brain. He was filling up with fluid and the lungs in his bloated body gasped for air, causing him to emit a rasping, wheezing sound that could be heard down the long hallway.

A night nurse came into his room. She smiled and glanced at her watch. "It's nearly midnight, Mr. O'Connor. Can I get you something? A cot? I can set it up near your grandfather's bed."

"No," I said. "I need to get out and stretch my legs for a while. Perhaps later, thank you, but not now."

The nurse walked around me, went over to grandpa's bed and checked his pulse. She looked back at me and shook her head. Her face took on a dour expression. "Too slow," she said. "Much too slow."

I left the hospital and drove around Lisbon for a couple of

hours, which is a difficult task given that one can drive from one end of the town to the other in less than five minutes. But I did it. I drove down nearly every side street and through most alleys. I drove past the elementary school I had attended, past the high school, and the local soda shop that had just closed. I could see someone cleaning up inside. I stopped a few minutes at the dilapidated laundromat that Uncle Paul had briefly owned and my father's house on Railroad Avenue. I then drove out past the Limberlost Cemetery where mother and Philip were buried. The large iron gate that encased the entrance was now closed and locked. Even though it was dark, somehow the cemetery didn't seem so scary to me as it did when I was a child. Then the entire area around the large graveyard, including the houses and the Buick car dealership right beside it, took on an eerie quality.

When I could think of no where else to drive in Lisbon, I drove out to Irene Sommers' place. There were no lights on and no activity. Sage, Irene's old collie, slept on the side porch. As I drove away, Sage woke and crawled off of the porch barking.

When I finally returned to the hospital, it was about 3:00 a.m. As soon as I walked into the foyer, the nurse who I had talked to earlier ran up to me and exclaimed, "He's conscious, Mr. O'Connor. Your grandfather came to about an hour ago. I told him you would be right back."

I ran up the two flights of stairs and into grandpa's room. His eyes were closed and he looked little different from when I had left him. But slowly his eye lids opened and he started to squint, as if looking into direct sunlight.

"Who's there?" grandpa asked.

"It's me, grandpa," I said, "Eugene."

"Genie!" he said excitedly, with an amazingly strong voice.

"Yes, grandpa, it's me. I've come back from Africa to be with you."

"Ah, Genie," he said, "it's good to have you back."

Grandpa tried to move his left arm, but it fell back to the side of his bed after he had been able to raise it only a few inches.

"Where's your mother, Genie? Where's Dorothy?"

I was startled. "Grandpa, mother's not here. She's not with us anymore," I said.

Several seconds passed by in which he said nothing and made no motion. And then I could tell by grandpa's reaction that something had clicked in his weakened mind and he started to weep. I felt awful, too. Grandpa was sharp enough to know why.

"I'm so sorry, Genie," he said, opening his eyes partially with tears starting to form. "I'm sorry, son. I didn't mean it. I didn't mean to say anything. Please forgive me, Genie."

"It's okay, grandpa," I replied. "I know you didn't. You forgave me and I've never forgotten that we all need to forgive. I love you, grandpa."

I couldn't tell if he heard me or not, but he didn't respond if he did. I sat there for the next half hour speaking to him every few minutes and hoping he might regain consciousness. But he never did. About two hours later Aunt Betty came and took my place, allowing me to go back to Blessed Acres. I didn't say anything to her about me being gone that night, but I did tell her about grandpa talking. I had encouraged her to speak to him to try and get him to respond.

Hastings Horatio Hamilton died of a cerebral hemorrhage later that day, October 25, 1958, at about three o'clock in the afternoon. I regretted deeply not being at his bedside when it happened, but I believe that it wouldn't have made any difference, not to Hastings Hamilton anyway. The man who was known throughout Roanoke County for his wit and oratory had said what little he needed to say to me in the form of an apology and I had heard it. The shadow now seemed to retreat, to flicker a bit.

Harlem Fraze, the owner of Fraze Funeral Home, recommended that grandpa's funeral be held at the Lisbon High School gymnasium. As Harlem explained, he had received so many inquiries about grandpa's death that he was convinced that neither his modest sized mortuary nor the King of Glory Missionary Church could hold all who desired to attend the funeral service.

After a long evening of viewing, with lines extending outside the gymnasium door, grandpa's funeral was held on the morning of October 28th. Reverend Clarence Hogarth conducted the service, returning to Lisbon from Florida where he and his wife had retired after serving a short-time pastorate in Sarasota. Approximately 300 people sat in chairs covering the gymnasium floor. U.S. Congressman Dan Jarvis and our state senator to the Indiana General Assembly, Bertram Townsend, gave short eulogies. The latter briefly read a letter from the Governor praising Hastings Hamilton for his many years of service to our community. All of this reminded me that grandpa was probably the best known politician in east central Indiana despite never having held elective office.

Many farm families came as well representing different generations who had been touched by grandpa's long-time work with the Roanoke County 4-H. The farmers wore their work clothes, not as a sign of disrespect, but just the opposite. Clad in their overalls, farm hats, boots, and red handkerchiefs tied around their necks, they came to pay homage to a man who they considered was one of their own. In his death, Hastings Hamilton had realized his ultimate dream—to be accepted into the loyal brotherhood of Roanoke County farmers—a membership into the agrarian fraternity he had longed for his entire life.

After the hour-long service, hundreds of people piled into their cars in back of the hearse to be part of the funeral procession. But behind the automobiles was even a more impressive sight—perhaps as many as seventy-five tractors were parked in rows that the farmers had driven to town to attend the service.

And then perhaps the most remarkable sight I have ever seen occurred right in front of my eyes. As pall bearers, we were lined up three to a side to walk with the carriage to the Limberlost

Cemetery. After we had taken our positions, Hank Powers, retired mayor of Lisbon, stepped from the crowd to the front of the carriage-hearse. He held a staff in his right hand. Every one in town knew that Hank was suffering from bone cancer. He looked near death himself. But the former mayor positioned himself in front of the entire procession, dressed in a dark gray suit that hung loosely around his infirmed body. And then slowly another figure emerged from the crowd, a teenager no older than sixteen. A snare drum was strapped around his neck. The young drummer stood behind and slightly to the left of Hank.

After a moment of complete silence, the young drummer began to play softly. And then we moved forward in unison. The funeral procession started going west on Franklin Street before turning south on Main Street to travel seven blocks to the cemetery and grandpa's final resting place.

For three days after grandpa's funeral, I stayed at Blessed Acres and didn't go into town. Aunt Betty was now Grandma Hamilton's permanent caretaker. Grandma's health seemed to be deteriorating daily and there was nothing we could do to help her: she refused to take any medicine, be seen by a doctor or be taken to the hospital. Blessed Acres had also deteriorated greatly since I had left the farm six years before. Perhaps as many as one hundred dead trees had fallen in the woods and remained uncleared. The house was badly in need of paint and minor repairs. The barn had a hole in the roof the size of a large watermelon. The hole allowed rain to drain into the hay loft, causing much of the hay stored there to mildew and rot. I climbed to the top and examined the rafters. They were slowly rotting, too. The whole east end of the barn was in jeopardy of toppling unless measures were taken soon to repair and shore up the roof. And then there was twenty-five acres of corn that still had to be harvested.

After working on the roof for two days, I decided to take on the harvesting of the corn. The touch of the combine wheel felt good and satisfying. The next day I borrowed Jake Meadow's flat bed truck and hauled about three tons to the grain elevator. When I arrived, I thought I recognized the attendant who agreed to weigh the grain, but I wasn't sure. He finally called out to me.

"Gene O'Conner!" he exclaimed. "Is that you? It's been so long."

"It's great to see you, Homer!" I said, shaking his hand. "It must be ten years since I saw you last."

"At least seven or eight, Gene," he replied. "You've been in Africa the past several years, haven't you?"

I nodded.

"When you didn't show up for our ten year reunion, we all talked about you, Gene. I bet your ears were burning all the way in Africa."

I laughed and Homer Cantron laughed, too. He had an over bite which became more pronounced when he laughed. Homer hadn't changed much at all. He was a farm boy through and through. I doubt that he ever thought about another occupation. Homer pulled the flaps down over his ears and sniffled as though he was fighting off a cold. His smile turned to a sad frown.

"Sure sorry to hear about your grandpa, Gene. I didn't know you were back or I would have gone to the viewing."

"No worries, Homer," I said. "But thanks for your sympathy. I've never seen such an outpouring as I did for grandpa's funeral."

"Your granddad was sure a character, Gene," Homer said, grinning. "He's the only man I've ever seen that could get old man Godfrey to up the price on a truck load of corn. Why, Hastings brought in some of the sorriest looking grain I'd ever se—"

Homer suddenly stopped, catching himself in mid-sentence. He peered over the side of Jake's flat bed truck and saw its contents and smiled.

"It's okay, Homer," I said. "I know grandpa's reputation. Growing things wasn't one of his strong suits." Homer looked embarrassed, causing me to want to change the subject. "Where's Calvin? He still owns the elevator, doesn't he?" I asked.

"Sure does," Homer replied, "but he's gone till next Monday.

His daughter is getting hitched this weekend down in Dearborn County. Calvin's already left for the wedding."

We made small talk for another few minutes and then Homer drove the truck to the scales to have it weighed. When he returned, Homer asked if I had heard about the fighting going on the country where I lived in West Africa. I couldn't fathom that Homer had heard something about Cape de Leone over an Indiana radio station. He must have been mistaken. I quizzed Homer more about what he had actually heard, but he couldn't tell me anything beyond what little he had already shared.

The next morning I drove into town and went to the public library. I scoured *The Indianapolis Star* and *The Chicago Tribune* for any mention of Cape de Leone but, again, found nothing. Finally I thumbed through the pages of the *New York Times*, where I found a small headline on one of the back pages. I read the brief article several times. It sounded like any fighting that had gone on had been restricted to Grand Bassa, but, of course, it was impossible for me to know for sure. I returned to Blessed Acres that afternoon and immediately composed a letter to Margaret.

After I posted the letter in town, I realized that it was time for me to pick up Irene Sommers for dinner. Irene had stopped me after grandpa's funeral and asked if we could get together that evening. It was great to see her. We drove to Muncie and had dinner and then we drove back to her place north of Lisbon. We parked in the barn lot, where I left the car running so that the heater would keep us warm. Looking through the windshield at the sky, I noticed a sliver shape of moon, distant and small.

"Irene, do you remember our first date?" I asked.

"Yes. It was a high school basketball game. I still have the program—the Huntsville Redmen vs. the Spartensburg Tom Cats—and the article you wrote about the game," Irene said.

"Not a very romantic first date, was it?" I asked, chuckling.

"I was so excited when you called me, Gene. It wouldn't have mattered what we did. I would have gone with you to watch crocuses grow."

We both laughed and then Irene took my hand and pressed it tightly.

"I was so surprised when I learned that you had returned," Irene continued. "You had written nothing about it in your last letter. Do you think you'll stay, Gene?"

I looked up at the sky again through the windshield. There were no outside lights on to diminish the view. It was a clear, crisp November night and the stars twinkled with such brilliance; they seemed to beckon me in a strange sort of way.

And then suddenly a past childhood memory flashed into my mind. It came to me as quickly and vividly as the stars appeared in Irene's barn lot. Philip and I had been playing "hide and seek" at Blessed Acres one evening, the first autumn after we had moved back with mother to my grandparent's farm. I was only about eight and I had stolen away in the middle of the corn field to the west of the farm house, satisfied with my secretive hiding place. I waited with such anticipation to hear Philip's voice calling out that he had given up, that I had won, and to produce myself. But after what seemed to be an infinitesimal period of time, I still heard nothing and started to look up. It was dusk and getting dark. I kept wondering—why doesn't Philip call out to me? Has he simply given up? And then I decided to come out on my own. But after several minutes of walking between the thicket of stalks, I realized I had gone the wrong way. The sun had gone down and I was so small that I couldn't see up over the corn to find the horizon. And then it suddenly occurred to me that I was lost, lost in a forty acre corn field! I started to panic.

All of a sudden I began crying uncontrollably. The tears poured out of me until I felt that I had watered half of the corn field myself. And I continued to cry for several minutes, until all I could think to do was to pray to God to deliver me from this darkened maze!

Then miraculously something told me to look up! I suddenly gazed at the night's sky and the stars began to form and glitter with such brilliance. The more I studied them, the more I seemed to detect some pattern, a pattern that pointed to a particular direction. I started following it, almost hypnotically. I didn't panic any longer but only followed the cluster of stars until all at once I stepped out of the corn field to freedom and onto the Greenville Pike!

From there I ran down our long lane to the farm house. Grandpa, grandma, mother, and Philip had been searching for me in the back woods, thinking I had gotten lost there. They were so happy to see me! Grandma dropped to her knees and prayed openly to God, praising the Almighty that I had been delivered. Philip jumped on top of me out of joy, and mother cried and smothered me with kisses and hugs.

"Gene. Do you think you'll stay?"

I looked again at the twinkling sky. I realized it was the same sky that I had gazed at in wonder more than twenty years before, the same sky that now covered the nation of Cape de Leone and Margaret's small house in Burguna. But I couldn't detect a pattern this time, no direction. The sky was simply plastered with glittering lights, lights that seemed to speak out to me but in a foreign language I couldn't understand.

"I don't know, Irene," I finally answered. "I don't know what my plans are. I've been back such a short time and so much has happened, what with Grandpa Hamilton's death and funeral."

"Of course," Irene replied. "I understand. You'll need to think what's best for you, for you and your family."

There was an awkward pause.

"Gene," Irene said, letting go of my hand, "I have something important to tell you. I'm going to be married. I was going to write you. Honestly I was. I had no idea you were coming back now."

"But to whom?"

"To Merlin Brownlie, Gene. On Christmas Day. I don't know if you know him, but Merlin runs the International Harvester dealership west of town."

"Merlin Brownlie!" I screamed. "Not Merlin, Irene! Jesus Christ, please don't tell me it's Merlin!"

"Shush, Gene," Irene said, "you shouldn't speak that way being a missionary and all."

"But, Irene, you simply can't be serious! I've known Merlin Brownlie since I was a kid helping grandpa on the farm. Everyone in Roanoke County knows he's a drunk!"

"And he's promised me that his drinking days are all behind him, Gene. Merlin's a good man. He treats me nice."

"But he's an old man, Irene. Heavens, Merlin must be twenty-five, thirty years older than us."

"Twenty-seven to be exact," Irene said. "But what difference does age matter? He's financially secure; he has a good job; he's never been married."

"That's because no woman would have him, Irene. Think about it, will you? Merlin's in his late fifties and he's never been married. Doesn't that tell you something? Are you sure you're not rushing into this?" I said in desperation. "Think about it! Please think about it!"

"I'm thirty-one years old," Irene cried. "I don't want to end up an old maid with no future. I wasn't going to wait around on you, if that's what you're getting at by all your objections."

It had never occurred to me that Irene would marry. But why not? She was attractive, extremely kind and congenial. Irene was now sobbing and hiccuping uncontrollably. I reached for her hand but she recoiled and pushed me away.

"Why did you have to come back now, Gene? Why now after I had finally gotten you out of my mind. Do you know how many nights I stayed awake after I received one of your letters? They were enough to keep me dreaming about you. Who else could understand you like I do? Who else, Gene, could love you like I could?"

Irene opened the passenger door. "Good-night," she said. "Thank you for dinner. I'm sorry the evening had to end this way."

I remember waking up the next morning after a restless night of sleep. I had a terrible headache and all I could think of was

Irene's last words to me: *"Who else could understand you like I do? Who else, Gene, could love you like I could?"*

When I walked into the kitchen, I found a slip of paper on the kitchen table that contained the following note:

> Eugene, breakfast is on the warmer. Had to go to town to run some errands. Mother is still sleeping. Hope you won't mind looking after her till I return.
> Love, Aunt Betty.

I checked on grandma in her room. She was now awake, but her eyes were closed. She lay in her bed mumbling Bible verses she had memorized and said every morning as part of her devotions. I returned to the kitchen and ate the plate of eggs, bacon, and toast that Aunt Betty had prepared. When I was about done, I heard grandma's shrill voice call out from her room.

"Betty!" she hollowed, "Betty! It's time for breakfast, darling! I'm hungry now!"

Grandma was essentially bedridden, although it was possible for her to get up to go to the bathroom, which was nothing more than using a chamber pot slid beneath her antique bed. I walked into her bedroom and grandma's face peered from underneath her covers. She still wore her sleeping bonnet.

"Grandma," I said, "Aunt Betty has gone to town. She should be back in a little while. Do you want me to fix you something for breakfast?"

"No, Eugene," grandma said sourly, "I want Betty. She never told me she was leaving the house. I want you to get Betty now!"

My head started to pound. "You were probably sleeping when Betty left and she didn't want to wake you. She'll be back in a little while. I'll fix you some poached eggs, toast, whatever you want."

"You don't know how to fix anything, Eugene," grandma said in a dismissive tone. "I don't know why Betty can't be here when I need her. I pay her good money to look after me."

"You do nothing of the sort, grandma," I said. "You give her some spending money and that's all. Betty answers to your every beck and call. I wouldn't do half of the things she does for you."

"That's because you're selfish, Eugene," grandma said, raising her body from beneath the bed covers. "You never think of anyone but yourself. Never have." Grandma started to whimper. "If you'd been here looking after the farm instead of off in Africa, Hastings would be alive today." She started crying. "He had his last attack when he tried to farm again last month. He got up on that old tractor to harvest the corn. Hastings had no business on a tractor! No business being in the fields! But he had no one he could depend on. He said the corn was wet and going to spoil if it wasn't harvested right away. And then he had that attack in the field. Paul found him there by the tractor barely breathing." Grandma broke down completely and wailed. "Where were you, Eugene? Where were you when your grandpa needed you? No, you wouldn't do half the things Betty does!"

My head was pounding harder and I couldn't contain myself any longer. "You're the one all wet, Grandma! You're the one that's selfish—can only think about your needs! You have no human emotions! You'd rather live in your idea of Heaven than in the real world that might demand something of you."

I wouldn't let grandma respond but continued. "I worked on this Goddamn farm for half of my life without even a thank you from grandpa and you! I got up at 5:00 o'clock every morning of every day just so you could stay in your bed and say your prayers, grandma! I hauled tons of sheep shit so you and grandpa wouldn't have to soil yourselves, so he could remain a gentleman farmer without getting his hands dirty! Don't tell me now, grandma, about how selfish I am! Hell, I spent half my life on this plantation, a slave to grandpa and you! 'Yes, mam,' 'no, mam,' 'How would you like the garden planted, mam?' 'How would you like the house cleaned, mam?' 'Can I do more laundry for you, mam, while you stay in your room and read your Bible, mam?' 'Can I milk the cows, gather the eggs, shovel the sheep shit out of the barn, Sister Hamilton, so you can continue your prayer vigil?'"

I went into the kitchen, my heart and head pounding. All that she had said was too much for me to take, especially after dealing with Irene's outburst the night before. I couldn't contain my anger and immediately returned to her bedroom. Grandma still shivered under the covers, afraid to leave the only protection between her nest and the world.

"Let me tell you something else, Sister Hamilton," I said. "I'm going to finish fixing the barn roof today. You understand? And then tomorrow I'm leaving and I'm never coming back. You hear? You'll never see me again because I'm never going to step foot back onto this farm. I've had it, and I want a check for fifteen hundred dollars given to me by tomorrow morning. Grandpa and you never gave me a dime for the years I slaved away at this place and I have earned it! You hear me, Sister? I know you have that much in the bank because I just deposited forty-five hundred dollars from the corn I sold two days ago and grandpa's funeral expenses have all been paid."

I stormed out of grandma's bedroom and out of the house to the barn. The next morning I packed my bags. I had said my good-byes to Uncle Paul and Aunt Betty the night before. They both begged me to stay, but my mind was made up. James Killion, a childhood friend, agreed to pick me up at the end of the lane at 7:00 a.m. and take me to the train station.

As I prepared to walk out the back door, I glanced around the farm house, convinced that this was the last time I would ever step foot onto Blessed Acres. I walked into the kitchen and on the kitchen table I found the check for fifteen hundred dollars that I had demanded from grandma. Beside the check was a hand written note:

> "Eugene, may God forgive you for your sins. I don't think that I can."
> Signed, Grandma Hamilton

Twenty Two

"You're crazy, mon!" the boatman said in broken English, sounding Jamaican. He was responding to my demands to be taken up the Tanganeen River all the way to Burguna. "You want to be killed or something, mon?" he said, shaking his head. "Well, go ahead and die if you want, but I want to live. This is all the farther I'm taking you. I told you that when we left Kawawi!"

"How much more would it take?" I pleaded. "A hundred and fifty leones?" I fanned the national currency in front of him like a seductress attempting to charm her lover into one more act of lunacy.

The boatman kept shaking his head. "No, mon. You don't have enough leones in all the world to get me to take you to Burguna. It's death there."

"Here," I pleaded, "here is three hundred!" I stuck the money in front of his drawn face. "How can you turn this down, mon?" I asked, trying to speak the boatman's lingo. "That must be a month's wages for you!"

The boatman shook his head. "No, mon," he said. He unmoored his boat from the rickety pier that jutted out into the muddy and slow moving river. He pulled from my hands fifty leones, the equivalent of about ten U.S. dollars.

"This is it, mon. I take what we agreed to and you leave my boat." He next flung my two cloth bags onto the dock. "I got to go, mon! Goodbye, goodbye!" he repeated, pulling at my arm to leave his vessel.

I had no other option but to leap onto the pier. The river's shoreline was several feet below normal due to the drought. I watched the ferry gradually turn and float downstream. The boatman would return to Kawawi, a distance of about a half-day's travel time. I realized I was still another three to four hours away from Burguna by boat and a good seven to nine hours away by land, that is if I could even get there through the thicket that grew along the river.

That morning I had spent several hours in Kawawi trying to find a ferry that would take me to Burguna. The best I could do was to persuade this boatman to transport me to Jampula, a tiny village fifteen miles short of Burguna. Nearly all ferry activity had stopped along the Tanganeen River because of sporadic acts of piracy. Troops and renegade tribes were arbitrarily stopping the ferries and plundering everything from their owners, sometimes taking their lives.

When I had reached Grand Bassa the day before, I was amazed at the capital city's deterioration that had occurred during the short six weeks I had been gone: stores were closed, many of them from being looted; buses and trains didn't run because drivers feared for their safety; soldiers dressed in deep green khaki uniforms stalked the streets, carrying large guns, yet seemingly under no one's authority; even the city's clocks didn't run on time, reflecting the fact that electrical power throughout Grand Bassa had been shut down repeatedly. Nothing seemed to work.

I started walking toward the village with my two bags. I had to climb a steep incline to get to Jampula, it being built on a high hill overlooking the Tanganeen River. I saw only a couple of natives in the entire village. I spoke to the first one I met, hoping he might understand my rusty Krio. He was squat and elderly and gawked at me as one might expect considering I was probably the first white man he had seen in years.

"I need to speak to your chief," I explained to the Jampulan. He obviously didn't understand me, but he grabbed one of my bags and led the way towards the center of the village. As I surveyed the mud huts, I noticed how Spartan everything looked. There was a strange, eerie feeling about the village, but I couldn't put my finger on why I felt this way. The elderly man took me to a hut and stepped inside, addressing someone in his native language. Another man, younger but with most of his teeth missing, emerged.

"Do you speak Krio?" I asked.

His eyes lit up and he made a gesture with his hand. "Yes, a little," he replied, and then said, "Why are you here? Are you not afraid?"

"Afraid of all the fighting?"

"Yes, of course."

"I came by ferry," I said. "From Kawawi."

He nodded his head, acting surprised.

"I need to get to Burguna," I added. "Do you have a guide I can hire to get me the rest of the way there?"

"Burguna?" he asked. "There is no one here that can take you to Burguna!"

"Why not?"

"Everyone has gone," he said. "They have all fled. Gone to Ivory Coast."

"Because of all the fighting?"

"Yes, of course," he answered forcefully.

"But why have you stayed?"

The toothless Jampulan tugged at me by the arm. He pulled me back to the edge of his hut and pointed at a mat inside. I could see a human form on the mat, an old woman moaning, but she didn't move.

"My mother is dying," he said matter-of-factly. "She cannot travel. My wives and children have fled with the rest of the village. I will follow after them after my mother dies."

"I am sorry about your mother," I said.

He shrugged his shoulders as if to say my condolences meant nothing to him.

"And your chief? Where is he?"

"He is gone with the tribe. They all left. Took everything with them," he answered. "It is not safe to stay."

"But I must get to Burguna," I repeated. "I have friends who are waiting for me there."

"No you don't," said the man.

"What do you mean?"

"The village was destroyed three days ago," said the man. He took his hands and wrung them like a butcher wringing the neck of a chicken.

The breath went out of me. "Explain yourself," I demanded. "What happened in Burguna?"

"Soldiers came," he said. "Soldiers came and destroyed the village. Killed everyone. Killed everything. It's why my people fled to Ivory Coast. Afraid that same soldiers will come here and destroy Jampula."

"But how do you know this?" I exclaimed. "If everyone was killed, then who told you?"

"Some escaped from Burguna. They came here but now they're gone with our tribe. They went to Ivory Coast, too. Left two days ago."

My sense of urgency to get to Burguna only increased by what the toothless villager told me. He looked long and hard at me. "It will be dark soon. If you are not afraid, stay here until morning and leave then. I will give you directions."

I decided to spend the night. As anxious as I was to travel on, I knew there was a very good chance of getting lost. I needed to travel in day light to better my chances of finding my way. I stayed in one of the deserted huts next to the man and his dying mother. He brought me some vegetables he had prepared for his dinner, along with some strips of burnt chicken. I had not eaten since before leaving Kawawi that morning and the food, although poorly prepared, was satisfying.

I was able to sleep very little that night, but morning finally came. The toothless villager arrived at my borrowed hut. He held a small bowl of corn meal and a piece of bark from a teak tree. On the bark were scribblings. He pointed the way to Burguna, using the crude map he had drawn as a reference point. I was vaguely familiar with the area and believed I could find my way if I could only stay on the right paths. There were no roads between the two villages.

"Whatever you do," said the toothless man, "avoid going along the river. That is where the troops are likely to be camped."

I consolidated my most valuable belongings, including my compass, binoculars, and mother's Bible, into one of my cloth bags. I gave the other bag, which contained mostly clothes, to the man. He seemed deeply appreciative. "I am certain she will die today," he said of his mother as we walked to the edge of the village.

We parted and within four hours of leaving Jampula, I had traveled more than half way to Burguna. The paths were dry, allowing me to make good time. Even better, I hadn't encountered anyone, seeing only a few monkeys playing up in some trees overhead and a warthog that was as interested in getting away from me as I was of him. The surroundings were beginning to look more familiar, and I was convinced that I could now find my way to Burguna without difficulty.

Suddenly I saw a group of tribesmen walking towards me. I scrambled into a thicket of vines and bushes and prayed that the natives didn't see me. They walked by carrying machetes, talking to each other in a tribal language I didn't recognize.

I returned to the path and within three hours neared Burguna. I sensed something strange, not unlike the eerie tranquility I experienced in Jampula. It was early afternoon and the temperature had risen to well above 90 degrees Fahrenheit. I removed my wrinkled cotton shirt and went bare chested. As long as the sun was out, the mosquitoes wouldn't bother me.

Burguna is surrounded by a jungle except for a clearing to the east where the villagers plant their vegetable gardens. To the south of Burguna, about seventy-five yards, runs the Tanganeen River. Its banks are about ten feet lower than the ground on which the village is built. When I walked into Burguna, all of a sudden a flock of birds—vultures and large black birds—flew up from the ground. I smelled something horrendous—putrid meat, raw sewage—something extremely rotting. My stomach churned.

Coming to the edge of the village, I noticed that the huts were knocked down and thatch roofs burned. A wisp of smoke rose from smoldering thatch on a couple of the toppled huts. The putrid, rotting smell worsened. Only two buildings were standing—Margaret's house and the Islamic mosque. Everything else was razed including St. Magdalene's chapel where Margaret and I had taught school for six years. Several small mounds rose from the center of the village, the area where the birds had flown up from. As I got closer, I noticed the piles were of bodies, dismembered and laying on top of one another. Arms, legs, torsos, and heads were strewn about everywhere. Many of the bodies were stripped of any clothing, naked and laying on top of one another, covered with blood and swarms of flies. The stench was ubiquitous, inescapable.

Nausea overcame me and I ran into Margaret's house. I covered my face with a towel I found on top of her night stand to attempt to block the smell, but it helped little. I fell onto her bed gasping for fresh air and then I heard a voice calling me.

"Mr. O'Connor! We must leave! Please, Mr. O'Connor!"

I looked up from the bed and recognized the familiar face. "Joseph!" I exclaimed. "Where did you come from?"

"Mr. O'Connor, we can't stay! Please come with me! We must leave. We must leave now!"

Joseph Obei pulled me from the bed. He also grabbed my cloth bag and tugged at my arms, my hands holding the towel over my face. We scampered from the house, and the terrible heat and smell overcame me. It was like I had been thrown into a fiery furnace at a rendering plant.

Joseph helped me walk past the demolished St. Magdalene's school house and into a thicket southeast of the village. We continued to walk away from Burguna. After several hundred feet, I was able to regain my bearing and the awful smell had dissipated to the point that it no longer overwhelmed me. We had said nothing to one another when finally I pulled at the back of his shirt.

"Where's Margaret?" I asked. "What happened to Margaret?"

Joseph kept walking quickly as if he didn't hear me. I followed closely, trying to keep up with him. "Joseph!"

He turned back to me and put his fingers to his mouth, "Shush, Mr. O'Connor," he whispered. "Do you want to be heard?"

We walked about thirty yards more into a dense thicket of trees, vines, and bushes. Joseph suddenly stopped, looked up and scoured the jungle quickly, and then took me by the arm. He pulled me off of the path and into a small cliff-like area that was covered by gargantuan fronds. I looked out and couldn't believe it.

"Margaret," I exclaimed. "Oh, Margaret!" A large smile covered her face and she ran towards me.

"Gene!" she cried, embracing me. "Gene, you've come back!" She kissed me all over my face and forehead as the tears poured down her cheeks. "I can't believe it!" Margaret said. "I can't believe you've come back! Just when I questioned everything, you've returned! You've returned to us! Oh, Gene!"

Margaret's embrace continued and then her hands touched my temples and ears as though she was confirming that I wasn't simply an apparition. It was only when Margaret let go of me that I noticed several Tambe villagers behind her, huddled together. Most of the villagers were small children, some of whom I had taught at St. Magdalene's. But there were also a couple of mothers who held babies tightly to their breasts.

"Where is everyone else?" I asked.

Margaret glanced over at the pitiful-looking women and children and then turned back to me.

"We don't know," she answered. "Joseph and I have been taking turns going back to the village to try and find others who may have escaped. We've found a few children since Monday and brought them back here. We believe that other children may still be in the forest surrounding Burguna, but they're too frightened to come out. We're afraid ourselves to go searching much during the day because there may still be troops around."

"Then everyone else in the village was killed?"

"About two hundred men were away when it happened. They've been fighting near Grand Bassa," Margaret answered. Her face became ashen. "But everyone else—the elders, women and children—were all in the village when the troops came." Margaret sighed. "Oh, Gene, it was so terrible, so awful what happened!" She looked up at me. "There was nothing we could do. The troops ransacked the village so quickly. We had little time to escape. The soldiers took their machetes and simply started hacking everyone. We had no warning!"

"But I saw some tribesmen with machetes just a couple of hours ago on the path from Jampula," I said. "When did this happen to you?"

"Sunday night," Margaret replied, adding, "but it was military troops who came. Men dressed in uniforms. The tribesmen you saw must be from another village."

"How did you and Joseph get away?"

"We just ran out of the house. The troops were on top of us so quickly, we just ran. We didn't have time to get anything, to save any of the children or warn any of the families." Margaret continued to tell about the slaughter of three nights before, when she suddenly stopped, gasped for breath and said, "Gene, Marabella and Falaba are dead!"

"How do you know that?" I asked.

"Because I saw their bodies. I went back to look for them Monday morning and found them both bludgeoned to death in their huts." Margaret buried her face in my chest and then looked up at me. "Worst of all, there's been no way that Joseph or I could go back to bury the bodies. We can't take the chance of being seen in case there are still troops around. And now," Margaret blurted, "the bodies are decaying and bloating in this heat, we're afraid to go back, afraid of all the disease. Oh, Gene, it's so terrible! The animals are coming at night and carrying the bodies into the forests and eating them! It's just terrible!"

Margaret was not herself. I placed my arms around her, shielding her from the children and the two young mothers who were huddled together underneath the cliff, trembling and bewildered.

"Where's Francis?" I asked. "Was he back when all of this happened?"

"Oh, no," Margaret answered. "He's been away from Burguna for almost as long as you've been gone. The last I knew, Francis was near Grand Bassa. He's advising the paramount chiefs who went there to try and overthrow Mubarsoi's government."

"And you've not heard from him since he's left?" I asked.

"Yes, he wrote two weeks ago. That's the last time I've had any communication from him."

"Then he doesn't know what's happened here?"

Margaret pulled at her hair. "I don't know, Gene. We sent a boy to Topego with a message. I heard they have a short wave radio in the village. We hope that someone will get word to the paramount chiefs about what's happened. But we've no way of knowing whether the boy will be successful. He's not returned." Margaret paused, reflecting upon what she had just said. "But how would anyone find us if they did come?" she asked rhetorically. "That's another reason why Joseph and I keep taking turns returning to the village in case there's anyone who's come after us."

"Well, the massacre is known in Jampula," I said. "I just came from there this morning. Almost the entire village has fled to the Ivory Coast. They were afraid that Mubarsoi's troops would come and do the same thing to them that happened here in Burguna. Apparently a few Tambe escaped and got as far as Jampula and warned their chief." I put my arm around Margaret's shoulder to comfort her again. "Surely word will get back to Grand Bassa. Surely someone will learn of this and come to help," I repeated, as much to try and convince myself as Margaret.

Margaret nodded, but her eyes told me that she really didn't believe what I was telling her. She turned to the children and two mothers and spoke softly, reassuringly in Krio. "Everything will be all right," she said. "Gene says others know what's gone on here. Help will come." But the beleaguered souls looked at us with terror in their eyes, and I could tell that they didn't believe either.

As I stood there thinking of the horrors that Margaret, Joseph, and the few surviving villagers had experienced during the past three days, all I could think of was—*What kind of monster is this Mubarsoi? What kind of thug masquerading as a national leader could authorize such savagery against his own people?*

Twenty Three

or two days we searched the forest trying to find any other survivors of the massacre. We only came across three small children, about five, seven, and eight years of age. They were a brother and two sisters. Somehow on the night of the attack they had fled their hut and escaped the flailing machetes of the troops. They were in terrible shape: bruised, bloodied, full of ticks and burrs, and emaciated in appearance. With the three, the total number of children in our small group numbered fourteen. There were also the two young mothers, both of whom were nursing babies. The other, smaller children were so hungry that they repeatedly tried to climb onto the women's laps and suckle from their deflated, milk-drawn breasts.

We had eaten what few vegetables we had found in Margaret's house. I caught a small boa, a harmless West African snake. I skinned and skewed it, and the children took turns picking off the moist meat from the stick. But it was too little food for too many mouths. While the variety of vegetation is great in the forest around Burguna, very little of it is edible. Foraging for something to eat was an on-going problem. We knew there was very little chance that there were other survivors and that we had to find help, but the prospect of traveling with the children, several of whom would have to be carried, was daunting. As for the bodies, nothing could be done but for them to remain in the village and decompose. Jackals, hyenas, and tiger cats came in the night and had a feeding frenzy. We heard the awful sounding struggles of the carnivorous animals as they fought between themselves for the privilege of carrying away a human limb or torso to the wild.

The next morning, Margaret and I decided that we had no other choice but to leave our small camp-site and to seek help. We gathered up the children and started back towards the village. We walked to the north so that we were out of sight and smell of the bodies. We could no longer worry about being intercepted by opposition troops. We prayed for a miracle.

We had gone no more than a couple of miles when Joseph, who walked about fifty yards in front of us, motioned for us to get off of the path and lie down. He had obviously sighted something. Some of the children started crying.

Over a small ridge a group of soldiers advanced. They walked in single file, their eyes scouring the path we were on. Several of the children began crying louder. Apparently Joseph knew that we would soon be seen or heard. He jumped out in front of the soldiers, making himself readily seen. The troops quickly surrounded him, pointing guns with long bandits at his chest. They talked for several minutes, and then Joseph suddenly motioned for us to come forward.

"Stay here," I whispered to Margaret. "This may be a trick. If I motion, you run with the children and spread out into the bush."

I walked up to where the soldiers had surrounded Joseph.

"They're here for us, Mr. O'Connor!" Joseph said, smiling as I approached. "The troops are here to rescue us!"

"Who sent you?" I demanded.

"President Jeremiah Bantu and Secretary Francis Tannen," said the lead soldier.

"Francis Tannen?" I asked. "You mean the Catholic priest who is from Burguna?"

"Yes, sir," replied the officer. "Reverend Tannen is now Secretary of Internal Affairs."

"You mean Father Tannen is part of the new government? That President Mubarsoi has been overthrown?"

"Not exactly, sir," said the officer. "There is still fighting going on in Grand Bassa. Mubarsoi is still positioned in the capitol, but we do not believe his government to be any longer the legitimate power."

"What brought you here?"

The young black officer, who looked to be in his early twenties, pulled from his breast pocket a piece of paper and then looked back up. "We have orders to return Margaret Mahoney and Joseph Obei to our base camp near Grand Bassa. Who are you?

"Eugene O'Connor," I answered. "I am with Miss Mahoney and Mr. Obei. I've lived in Burguna for the past six years with them."

The officer looked skeptical.

"It's true, your honor," added Joseph. "Mr. O'Connor is with us. He's a friend, a good friend."

The young officer seemed more satisfied. I extended my hand to him. "May I see your orders, officer?"

The young man handed me a formal-looking piece of paper which read:

> By the authority of the Christian Peoples Party of Cape de Leone, Major-General Charles de Gaulle is hereby ordered to retrieve and produce Margaret Mary Mahoney and Joseph Obei of the Province of Dugaga, Village of Burguna, to military headquarters, Grand Bassa, Cape de Leone. Dated 17 Nov., 1958.
>
> Signed:
>
> Jeremiah Bantu Francis Tannen
> President Secretary of Internal Affairs
> *Christian Peoples Party of the Sovereign Nation of Cape de Leone*

In Cape de Leone, much like most West African nations, every government document—from a simple traveling visa to a major international treaty—is floridly designed on embossed letterhead and planted with a colorful seal. To see such an official-looking document really meant little, but with Francis Tannen's name on it—well, that was quite another matter. And from another perspective, what difference did it make? Five adults and fourteen children who had been starving for several days weren't about to attempt an escape from a band of soldiers, especially when those troops possibly offered us sanctuary.

I surveyed the young faces of the soldiers and then returned the document to the officer. "You're who—General de Gaulle?"

"Yes, sir," he answered. "I am in charge of this company of men."

"I don't recognize any of your soldiers, General. Are any from the village of Burguna?"

"None," the officer replied.

"Where are the men from Burguna?" I asked. "It's my understanding that about 200 went to fight with the paramount chiefs against Mubarsoi's forces."

"I believe, sir, they are all still at our base camp outside Grand Bassa."

I glanced again at the troops and then into the young face of the officer. "We have several small children with us, General, and two young mothers. Are you prepared to take them back with you?"

"Sir, we only have orders to return Miss Mahoney and Mr. Obei. We have no authority to transport any children or other villagers. Neither do we have room."

"Room where?"

"In our two trucks, sir. They're parked a few miles north and west of here. It's as far as we could drive into the jungle."

A thought entered my mind. "Are you carrying your own petrol?"

"Yes," said the officer. "Since the outbreak of the war, there are no outlets for the sale of petrol except on the black market. We have our own. Why do you ask?"

"First," I answered, "I believe I speak for Miss Mahoney and Mr. Obei. They won't go back with you voluntarily unless you also take the children and the two women." Joseph nodded vigorously in front of the general to show support for my statement.

"Second, two miles back are over four hundred rotting

corpses that something needs to be done about. There is no way they can all be buried. But with several gallon of petrol, we can burn the bodies and properly dispose of them the best we can."

The young officer's eyes opened wide. He took a deep breath. "I have no authority to accede to either of your demands, sir." He pulled the order again out of his top left vest pocket and started to present it to me.

"I know what your order says," I replied. "I'm telling you that the three of us will not return with you voluntarily unless you also do as I ask. Are you prepared to answer to your superior if you don't bring back Miss Mahoney and Mr. Obei?"

The young officer started to appear nervous. He glanced back of him to see the reaction of his men. Some were starting to fidget. The young general didn't want to appear to have his authority challenged, and I realized then that I had made a major mistake by being so forceful in my demands.

"Major General de Gaulle," I addressed him, standing at attention. "Secretary Tannen was top advisor to Chief Faramha of the village of Burguna before he assumed his ministerial position with your government. He was also the administrator of the St. Magdalene School of Burguna, where Miss Mahoney and I taught. She, Mr. Obei, and I are very good friends of Secretary Tannen. We will praise you and your men for fulfilling what we believe would be his own desires if he were present."

My act of subservience seemed to no longer challenge his authority. The young officer quickly turned around to his troops.

"I need you men," he said, pointing to four soldiers, "to return to the trucks and for each of you to bring a five gallon container of petrol. Do you understand me?"

The four soldiers nodded their heads.

"General, when your men return, they need to carry the containers on to Burguna. If they follow this path east, they will run into the village."

"Did you hear the man?" the young general asked his selected soldiers.

They nodded, saluted their commanding officer, and then started back from where they came.

"General de Gaulle," I said. "We need the rest of your men to return with me to Burguna to prepare the bodies for burning. The children can remain here until we return. They are tired and weak."

The young officer nodded his head and ordered the remainder of his men to follow. We walked back to where Margaret and the others were waiting along side the path. I explained to Margaret our plan.

"Joseph," Margaret said, turning to him, "will you remain with the children while I return with Gene and the troupes?"

"Yes, madama."

"They need to remain off of the path," I reminded Joseph. I then turned to the general. "Can you spare one of your men to also stay with Mr. Obei and the children?"

General de Gaulle looked at me with an expression of annoyance, but conceded. We walked back to the village and the appearance that came over the troops' faces when they came upon the rotting corpses was one of horror and disbelief. The stench was even more sickening than I had remembered. All of the troops covered their faces with handkerchiefs or pulled up their shirts over their noses and mouths. They walked around the bodies as if in a stupor, aghast at the carnage and smell.

After three hours of carrying decayed arms, legs, and torsos to the middle of the village, we stopped when the four soldiers returned with the containers of gasoline. We doused the bodies with the fuel and then lit the pile with matches. Margaret buried her face in my chest. She was in shock, I believe. It was a mistake for her to return, and I deeply regretted not having the foresight to know what the experience would do to her. Suddenly I felt a hand tugging on my right shoulder. A soldier turned Margaret and me around so that our backs faced the blaze.

"A picture," he said in broken English. He held an old American camera, one that you look through from the top to focus, and said, "General de Gaulle wants picture."

Without having the will to object, Margaret and I stood in front of the stack of burning bodies—flames stretching more than twenty feet high—and allowed the soldier to snap several pictures of us with the corpses in the background. The air began to be filled with small flakes of ash and the stench of rotting human carcasses already seemed to lessen. I looked at the young general named Charles de Gaulle as he gazed at the flames. An expression of total anger came over his face.

The two military trucks were jammed and overloaded with exhausted soldiers and children. The vehicles' springs bowed from all the weight. We had hungry and restless young boys and girls who hung partially out of the cabs' broken side windows. Soldiers, still traumatized from assisting in the burning of the corpses, rode on the trucks' hoods. Margaret, Joseph, and I were packed in the bed of one of the trucks holding the smaller children. We traveled like this across most of the breadth of Cape de Leone, a distance of about 150 miles. It took an entire day to arrive at the make-shift campsite outside Grand Bassa. Along the way I learned some interesting things from our young Major-General Charles de Gaulle.

More than a month before fifteen paramount chiefs had formed a council to establish a government to replace Mubarsoi. The ring leader had been none other than Francis Tannen. Tannen had pretended to be simply an adviser to the paramount chiefs, but he was, in reality, the lead instigator behind the opposition movement. The council had made certain demands on Mubarsoi. It contended that the President either meet the demands or else resign. Some of the more important ones were that Mubarsoi should eliminate the hut-tax and relinquish all control the central government now asserted over what had been traditionally tribal affairs. But the most contentious demand was that Mubarsoi stop supporting the conversion of villages to Islam. He had done so, so the council claimed, by allowing Muslim traders and theologians to have free access to the various tribes. The council contended that on the issue of religion Mubarsoi should remain neutral and not promote Islam over any other faith. At this point, the spreading of Christianity in any way was strictly forbidden by national law. On top of all this, the council contended that Mubarsoi was expropriating funds for his own private use and building up a large fortune for himself in overseas banks.

Mubarsoi made several arguments against complying with any of the council's demands: first, the council itself was made up of only about one-tenth of all the paramount chiefs in the country. He contended it had little authority to assert that it was speaking for even a majority of the tribal leaders; second, the hut-tax and other taxes were necessary in order to modernize Cape de Leone. They were not unduly burdensome considering the benefits that all provinces would receive one day; and third, that while it was true that Christianity was outlawed, this was done by an act of the Cape de Leonean Parliament. He, Mubarsoi, had only signed the legislation into law. Finally, Mubarsoi strongly refuted that he was exploiting the nation's treasury for his own personal gain. He claimed that there was no evidence that would show he had done anything improper.

When Mubarsoi refused to concede to any of the council's demands, the council called for his resignation and formed its own government. It claimed this new government, named the "Christian Peoples Party of Cape de Leone," better represented the interests of the people. Most of the fifteen paramount chiefs that formed the nucleus of the council represented the few villages in the country that still embraced Christianity. The exception was Chief Faramha who Tannen had convinced to join the council despite his village's (Burguna) own conversion to Islam. Most of the paramount chiefs who made up the council were able to draft men from their tribes to join the new political/military alliance. At the same time, the council had taken over an old British military base on the south edge of Grand Bassa. It was from this base that they launched the attack against Mubarsoi's forces on the night of October 30th. They were unable to take possession of the capitol building and several troops on both sides were killed during the fighting. The leader of Parliament, a Mubarsoi crony, denounced the attack the next day and dissolved Parliament. He claimed that no official business could be conducted while such chaos reigned.

"The members of Parliament are all scared for their lives, Mr. O'Conner," said the young general to me during our long trek west. "That is the reason Parliament dissolved. The members were afraid we would overthrow them and make them hostages," he added, smiling broadly.

Mubarsoi immediately called for martial law, suspending the operation of civil government. He further placed the Cape de Leone military, in which he was Chief, in charge of running the country. This had all taken place during the six weeks I had been gone.

At the campsite the troops that surrounded us, like the soldiers who came to our rescue in Burguna, tended to be young, idealistic, and adventure-seeking. They knew little about what they were fighting for, but they liked wearing khaki uniforms, brandishing outdated British rifles, and assuming a role in a revolutionary movement. Only a few years before these same rebel soldiers had been village boys responsible for shepherding the communal goats or, more recently, working long hours in the diamond mines in the northern region.

In their actions, the soldiers imitated military heroes in history. Their desire to be one with such heroes caused several to even assume their heroes' names. Thus, a young man from the western village of Dughur (with the given name of Momeebi O'bod) became Charles de Gaulle when he was promoted to Major-General. Over the course of the next several weeks, I met other young black revolutionary officers of the CPP: "George S. Patton"; "Bernard ('Monty') Montgomery"; "Douglas MacArthur"; and even "George Washington." Tannen applauded these young officers' assumption of pseudonyms. It furthered the revolutionary spirit of their struggle.

Once we had arrived at the campsite, Margaret and I were separated. We had a chance to clean up and then we came together for a meal in a makeshift "mess hall." It was a joy to see the children eat something more substantial than a piece of rotting fruit or a crusty rice-cake. We had just finished our dinner when a young soldier came to our table and asked to escort Margaret to headquarters.

Margaret glanced at me and then back to the soldier. "Can Mr. O'Connor come, too?"

"I was ordered to bring only you, madam," the officer said.

"Who gave the order?" I asked.

"Secretary Tannen, sir," he replied.

"Gene, I will go and see what Francis wants," Margaret said. "I'll make sure and call for you."

Margaret left with the young officer. I remained with the two mothers and children until they had finished eating. A soldier then took them to where they would spend the night. A doctor would examine them in the morning. I drifted off to sleep on a cot. Several minutes later the same officer who escorted Margaret came back and took me to the office where Margaret and Tannen were waiting.

"It's good to see you, Gene," Francis Tannen said as we shook hands.

"It's good to be alive, Francis," I replied. I turned to my left and saw Margaret sitting comfortably in a chair facing the desk. She held a glass of red wine. Margaret smiled and winked at me.

"I apologize for how late it is, Gene," Tannen said. "It was a surprise for me to learn that you're back in the country. But since you're here, I wanted to see you before I go. I'm leaving early in the morning."

"It would have been a shame to miss you, Francis," I said, hoping I didn't sound insincere, which I was. "You're on the move so much, it could be a while before our paths cross again."

"Yes, exactly," said Tannen. "That's why it's necessary to talk with both Margaret and you here tonight even though I've learned you've been through a terrible ordeal these past few days."

I said nothing, choosing to let Tannen explain his motive behind the meeting.

"I first want to thank you, Gene," the priest continued. "Margaret says that you saved her life and the lives of several small children. You're a hero!"

"I did nothing extraordinary," I replied. "Margaret protected the children. They wouldn't be here without her."

"Well, let's just say, then, that we have two mutual admiration societies and you two are the presidents of each other's respective clubs," Tannen said with a laugh. "Truly, Gene, the things that Margaret talked about. Oh, my God, how ghastly. I'm surprised anyone survived such a nightmare."

"I'm surprised the village was left unprotected," I replied. Thinking my comment might be perceived as too critical of my host, I added. "But then who could have known that Mubarsoi would act so ruthlessly."

"Damn right!" Tannen replied. "Even with knowledge of how Mubarsoi achieved power, who would have thought he'd undertake such a savage act against innocent villagers."

Tannen sat back down in his chair, placed his elbows on the table and his hands underneath his chin so that they propped up his large head. He had trimmed his beard close to his face, sculptured it to make him look younger and more cunning, I thought. He also appeared to have lost a considerable amount of weight. The priest looked healthy and fit.

"I'm afraid it's only going to get worse," Tannen continued. "All Hell may break lose unless we can convince a larger number of paramount chiefs to support our cause. Margaret and I have just been talking about it."

"Gene," Margaret interjected, "Francis believes this is an excellent time to bring Christianity to the whole nation."

"The timing is right," added Tannen. "If we attempt to do it piecemeal—village by village—it could take years to convert the entire country."

"But Mubarsoi seems to be gaining control, not losing it," I replied. Tannen stared with a curious look on his face, as if he was studying me. "Well, that's what I've heard," I added. "Is there something I don't know? I mean, Parliament has disbanded. Who's to prevent Mubarsoi from simply continuing military rule?"

"We are!" replied Tannen. "Mubarsoi is only in power because he's had the tacit consent from the paramount chiefs. No, quite the opposite, Gene. I think Parliament's dissolution hurts Mubarsoi. He's now ruling solely by military force. He can no longer argue that he's been given the authority to rule by Parliament."

I wasn't convinced by Tannen's logic, but I wasn't going to argue with him. The priest opened his middle desk drawer and pulled out a large manila envelope. He opened the envelope, removed some pictures, and passed them on to me.

"I can't conceive anything more damaging to Mubarsoi than these," Tannen said.

I glanced at the pictures. I immediately recognized that they were taken of Margaret and me in front of the stack of burning bodies in Burguna the day before.

"My God!" I said. I examined the pictures more closely. Margaret and I had forlorn, doomed expressions on our faces, with rings under our eyes. I sported a heavy beard from not having shaved for several days.

"I don't think that the chiefs can continue supporting Mubarsoi long when this gets out," Tannen said. "To have instigated such an atrocity against his own people—the chiefs won't stand for it!"

"Gene," Margaret said with a tone of urgency. "Francis wants you and me to help. We can play a role in bringing Mubarsoi down and seeing that a more responsible, compassionate government is put in place."

"And one that returns power to the chiefs. Remember that Margaret," Tannen added. "Gene," the priest said, "this is an excellent time to reveal to the tribal leaders just what kind of tyrant Mubarsoi is. Few chiefs have had any contact with him to know how maniacal he is. If news of the massacre doesn't get communicated, he'll just gain a greater foothold on power. He's become a dictator. He's already ruled nearly four years without even a mention of an election. Who's to say how long he might be in power unless something is done. Now is the time!"

"But we also want to spread our faith. Right, Francis?" Margaret said. "That's why we came here to begin with. That and to establish schools for the children."

"Yes, of course," Tannen replied with little enthusiasm.

"But how can I help?" I asked. "I don't see how I could possibly be of any use."

Twenty Four

T he heavyset chieftain sat attentive until Margaret's homily had been translated by the appointed tribesman. The chieftain then stood up, surrounded by a dozen elders who remained seated, and pounded his gargantuan right foot against the ground.

"Your God is not a God of love!" he exclaimed. "All we have known is famine, disease, and drought since your Christian party has been fighting to gain control of the country! We are not safe in our own village. Half of my tribe has fled. Many have died in raids. How can you say your God is merciful, loving, and wants what is best for us?"

"But your Excellency," Margaret said in response, "my God is all those things and more. It is we humans, who because of our disobedience to Him, have caused the strife that you speak of. Please, your Excellency, understand that this world that you and I know, this world that has brought so much pain, so much grief, is not the world that I speak of. It is not the eternal world that my God promises."

By the chieftain's expression, it was evident that Margaret's rejoinder had no affect on him whatsoever. The elders sat mute-like, shaken to the core by their chief's outburst. Several awkward seconds passed, and then Margaret did a most unusual thing. She stepped towards the chief and knelt directly in front of him. He looked down at her half out of suspicion, half still in anger. Margaret next took the hem of her long dress and began to wipe the dust and perspiration off of the chief's thick, swollen-looking ankles and large feet.

Suddenly the chief exploded, apparently believing Margaret

was mocking him by what she intended as an act of humility. "Get gone, woman," he screamed, kicking Margaret in the face. Margaret staggered as she tried to stand, her eye lids shut tight from the blow. Blood trickled from the left corner of her mouth and rolled down her lower chin. I could tell the chief's outburst, his rejection of everything Margaret had talked about for thirty minutes, hurt her more than the fact she had been physically struck by him, but she was clearly in pain.

Suddenly the chief exploded, apparently believing Margaret was mocking him by what she intended as an act of humility. "Get gone, woman," he screamed, kicking Margaret in the face.

I rushed over to help Margaret to her feet. The chief wadded up the newspaper clipping we had given to him and threw it at her. Margaret reached down, retrieved the wadded up paper and then turned to the tribal translator. "Please ask your Excellency, kind sir, to forgive me if I have offended him. This was not my intention. May my God bless him and the Juba abundantly."

After the translator conveyed these few words, the chief said nothing, but stalked brusquely through the council of elders, indicating the baraza was over. The elders stood, disbanded, and formed smaller groups, talking among themselves. Margaret and I were joined by Joseph Obei. One of the elder's wives came to Margaret with a cup of water and a small rag. "Madama," she said excitedly, "please let me help you." The woman began wiping the blood off of Margaret's chin and pressed the moist rag against her swelling lower lip.

After the charged exchange with the chief, I assumed it would now be impossible to be given a place to sleep for the night. But the woman who aided Margaret asked that we follow her. She led us to a hut on the outskirts of the village, a hut that had been deserted by one of the fleeing families that the chief had mentioned. "You stay here," said the woman. "I will bring you food and water. You are good people."

The rejection by the Juba tribe chieftain was not unlike others we had encountered during the five months we had gone from village to village spreading the news of the massacre at Burguna and seeking the conversion of tribes to Christianity. But it was clearly the most volatile. During the first couple of months, we were met with almost uniform compassion as we shared the story of Mubarsoi's brutality. The various tribes and elders seemed genuinely interested and horrified by our account of what had happened. We would show the clipping from the front page of the *Daily-Times*, the one containing the picture of Margaret and me standing in front of the burning pile of bodies. After this, Margaret would share about how the Christian God, meaning Jesus, didn't believe in violence, but taught that through repentance and humility, God would forgive us and allow everyone to live peaceably with one another. But after several months of civil war, months in which some villages had been completely wiped out while other tribes had fled for their lives, our message, nigh our very presence, was becoming less and less welcomed.

As soon as the picture and story about the massacre at Burguna was published, Mubarsoi denied any responsibility for the atrocity. He stated that the entire account, reported in great detail in the *Daily-Times* from interviews that we gave, had been fabricated by us to make his government look bad. But his denials didn't stop the outrage that the picture, the article, and the personal testimony by Margaret and me had fueled. One by one, tribal leader after tribal leader denounced the massacre and Mubarsoi. The ten paramount chiefs in Parliament all resigned. Eight of them pledged their allegiance to the Christian Peoples Party. This brought the number of paramount chiefs who supported the new party to roughly sixty. Mubarsoi immediately shut down the *Daily-Times*, claiming that the newspaper had become a front, a propaganda tool for the "communist" Christian Peoples Party.

Despite our initial success, our attempts to persuade the remaining paramount chiefs to support the new CPP met with marginal results. The first hurdle was simply the logistics in reaching them. Outside of Grand Bassa, hardly any roads existed and no means of communications such as what we take for granted today. Margaret and I, given a driver, traveled by truck along what stretches of land were navigable by that means. But after that we simply had to walk and this was extremely dangerous. Not only was the terrain rugged in many areas, but simply carrying enough supplies to get from village to village was a difficult task. On top of all of this, troops loyal to Mubarsoi, called "Peoples Defense Forces" (P.D.F.), were always touring. An encounter with one of their squads would mean certain death.

Despite this, we decided against traveling with soldiers from our own Christian Peoples Party because of the fear that this would generate when we appeared at a village unannounced. The villages had no knowledge that we were coming. We simply showed up, asked to speak with the chief and his elders, and shared our story. Contrary to what Tannen had told Margaret and me, if the entire country was going to be Christianized, it would be village by village. There was no central or even regional body that held sway over the villages. The only common factor was the tribes. Some tribes lived all in one village, like the Tambe in Burguna, while a few tribes lived in different villages.

The success we had in proselytizing was as varied as the tribes we met with. Some chieftains were extremely moved by the story that Margaret and I shared about the massacre at Burguna as well as about Christ's redemptive love. Others, on the other hand, weren't receptive at all.

"We have had Christian missionaries here before," said one chief. "We have heard your story, but it is Allah that we follow. Allah and none other."

But then there was a middle ground. "We are grateful for what you have taught us, Madama," one chief said after we had stayed in his small village for two days preaching. "But why can't we worship both Allah and Christ?"

"Because only through the sole belief in Christ is one saved for eternal life," replied Margaret.

The chief simply shook his head, confused no doubt because just a couple years before Islamic leaders had drilled into his mind that only through following the Koran's Shari 'ah (roughly meaning "the path leading to water") is a convert guaranteed everlasting life. Even when a particular tribe embraced Christianity, we were not sure that the villagers were really committed to their new faith. Somehow they undertook the symbolic acts of baptism and communion much like when they routinely knelt down on their prayer mats five times a day and prayed to Allah. It was ritual, it was expected, but did it amount to conversion?

We left the Juba village of Mobutoo the following day after it was clear that the chief and elder council had little interest in our testimony or our God. The next village was several miles east, about five miles west of Cape de Leone's border with southern Guinea. We knew from earlier reports that there had been fighting in this region. Guinean officials were forcing the refugees back into Cape de Leone, because western Guinea had become flooded with unwanted emigres. Makeshift refugee camps had sprung up in several locations. It created a terrible problem on both sides of the border.

As we reached the edge of the small village of Longula, I noticed an eerie stillness. The lone sound was of a baby crying. Margaret glanced at me and then we both instinctually, almost in unison, stopped and listened together. The crying child was all we could hear. We walked much more slowly and stooped down so as to be hidden by some ferns that surrounded what otherwise appeared to be the opening to the village.

Several bodies lay on the ground. Most huts had been burned, smoke still smoldering from their thatch roofs. Suddenly a young African woman came stumbling out, as though drunk, from one of the huts. She wailed uncontrollably and was badly hurt. She hobbled, falling to the ground, unable to walk any further. Margaret stood up to go to the woman's rescue, when I grabbed her left arm and pulled her down behind some ferns.

"Wait!" I said. "This could be a trick. Maybe someone saw us coming."

Margaret paused while the native woman wriggled in the dirt next to a dead body. She began screaming and moaning.

"I have to go," she said. Margaret jumped up and ran to the woman and I followed. When we reached her, the native looked up at us with terror in her eyes. Margaret brushed the woman's forehead and then we both quickly examined her. The woman stretched out her arms to Margaret. She had a terrible cut down the left side of her face from which she was bleeding profusely. Also, her legs were cut badly, the back of her hamstrings having been sliced by what must have been a machete. All I knew to do was to try and move her back into the hut from which she had stumbled out. Margaret went to retrieve medical supplies we had in our backpacks left at the village's edge.

As I carried the woman to the hut, the front of my shirt became soaked in blood from her open wounds. I backed into the hut, trying to avoid brushing the woman's legs against the narrow opening. I laid her down on the hut's mud floor and then turned around and looked up, becoming frightened beyond explanation.

"Who are you?" said a bushy haired white man with a straggly beard. He looked middle-aged. He spoke English with an accent and sat in one of the corners of the hut. He cradled a tiny, naked baby, adding a surreal, dream-like sense to the surprise.

"My God! You scared me half to death!" I replied.

"I'm sorry," said the stranger. He lifted the baby to get a better hold of it. "Where did you come from?" he asked. "Don't you know that troops were just here raiding the village? Can't you see what you've walked into?"

"No," I replied. "We had no idea. We knew there was fighting in the area, but we had no knowledge—"

The badly wounded African woman screamed out again in pain and anguish. I put my hand on her forehead and stroked it gently as Margaret had done, trying to console her. There was nothing else I could do; she was bleeding to death right in front of us and I saw the terror reappear in her eyes.

Margaret came to the edge of the hut with a canvas bag that held what few medical supplies we carried. She peered in, looked up and became startled. She looked right passed me and the wailing woman and starred at the stranger. She dropped to her knees. "John," she said. "I can't believe it's you! Where have you been? My Lord, John, I thought you'd vanished from the face of the earth!"

"Hello, Margaret," the stranger replied. "No, not the face of the earth. Just from Cape de Leone. I've come back to help in the refugee camps."

"Oh, John," Margaret exclaimed. "I can't believe it's you." Margaret started to move closer, but she would have had to cross over both me and the wailing woman to reach the man. Margaret then pulled out a supply of gauze and bandages. She first blotted blood from the woman's face and then began to wrap the woman's bleeding legs. I tried to help.

"You are wasting your time," said the man. "She's going to die. Don't waste your bandages."

Margaret looked at the man as if she refused to believe his prognosis. But after several more seconds, seconds in which blood flowed even more freely from the woman's nearly severed calves, Margaret leaned back on her own heals and gave up.

"Let me exchange places with you," said the man to me. We quickly moved around each other in the hut's cramped quarters. The man who Margaret referred to as John kneeled near the dying woman and placed on top of her abdomen the baby. We watched the woman hold the child on top of her stomach. Her face, distorted-looking from pain, suddenly took on a visage of calmness.

John then sat on his haunches and laid his right hand on the woman's forehead. He began administering last rites to the woman. She looked up at him with frightened eyes. Then suddenly her breathing became heavier. Before he finished, the woman's grasp of the baby became less secure and Margaret slid her hands underneath the baby's bottom to support it on top of the woman. Finally, the woman's hands fell lifelessly from the baby to the ground and she died.

The man said a brief prayer and fell back, his shoulders resting against the hut's interior wall. He appeared exhausted, drained, depleted.

Margaret looked up at the man, holding the baby and caressing its tiny back. "How did this happen, John?"

He didn't look at Margaret but focused his eyes on the dead woman. He seemed lifeless, like her, as he answered.

"All I know is the Banju were turned away from one of the refugee camps across the border. The Guinean officials simply refused to allow them to stay. They beat them, told them there wasn't room for them. Some of the stronger tribal members moved on to the interior of Guinea, but about half, mostly the women with children and the elderly, came back here to the village. That was obviously their big mistake."

"But how did you get here?"

"I was working at the refugee camp when the Banju were turned away two days ago. After they left Tuesday, I waited a day and then followed them here to see if I could help."

"Were you here when the government troops came through and destroyed the village?" I asked.

"Government troops?" he sneered. "No, it wasn't P.D.F. soldiers! It was a gang of teenage thugs from the Christian Peoples Party that did this!"

"That can't be," said Margaret.

"But it was," said John in his strong accent. "That's what I was told by a couple of villagers. A gang of twenty hoodlums, none any older than eighteen, ransacked the village and bludgeoned the Banju to death. Several of the women were raped before they were killed. Surely you've seen the carnage outside!" he screamed at us, showing the first sign of any real emotion. "The women who spoke to me said they played dead until the gang left. Otherwise they'd been killed to. They've since fled. I got here only about an hour ago myself. I heard the baby crying and came to this hut and found this woman. She was hysterical. I couldn't get her calmed down. That was just before you came."

I looked at the man who seemed to still be in a zombie state. His hands were folded across his lap. I noticed the large cross-shaped necklace that hung around his neck. He continued to stare at the dead woman, whose eyes were still open. He closed them.

"Father Stivonovich, I'm Eugene O'Connor," I said extending my hand. "I'm sorry we've never had the chance to meet before."

The priest looked at me blankly and made no effort to shake my hand. "I was hoping you wouldn't know who I was," he said. "I guess I'm the one responsible for you being here. I suppose you wish now I'd never answered your letters, don't you, son?"

"No," I said, "I chose to come. You didn't force me. In a way, I have found my world."

My reply generated no response from Father Stivonovich. He just sat there without showing any emotion. "Who could have guessed that it would turn out like this?" he said mindlessly.

After a period of silence, in which the only sound came from the baby, Stivonovich stood up. He had to stoop, because the hut's ceiling could not accommodate a person nearly six feet tall.

"We need to bury the bodies," he announced.

It would be impossible for us to dig enough individual graves. The ground was hard and dusty from several months of drought. However, we found an old pick and shovel and started digging a large hole. It was nearly dusk when we finished burying the bodies, some of which had to lie above ground level because we couldn't dig the mass grave deep enough. We covered these the best we could with a layer of dirt in hopes that animals wouldn't dig them up later.

The westerly sun cast shadows across the desolate village. Suddenly I saw a figure emerge from the forest. It was an African boy no more than twelve or thirteen. He moved toward us hesitantly, unsure of himself.

"Father?" he called out.

"Yes, Yappi?" the priest replied, acknowledging the boy by name.

"I've come to get you, Father."

"Who sent you, Yappi?"

"Monsieur Tarabi, Father. He heard about the fighting, the deaths," the boy responded while pointing to the large mound covering the bodies. "He is afraid for you. He wants you to come back to the camp."

"Now, Yappi?"

"Yes, Father. Yet this evening. I have been given orders."

Father Stivonovich stepped back from the mound and grabbed his shirt that he had tossed to the ground. "Then I will go."

"Now?" I exclaimed.

"Yes, there is nothing more for me to do here," the priest replied, kicking dirt on top of the mound of bodies.

"Well, let me at least get Margaret," I said. She had remained inside the hut caring for the baby while we worked.

"No," said Father Stivonovich firmly, "I have nothing more to say to her. I'm sorry that I must leave this way, but this is how I feel."

The priest buttoned his shirt, shook my hand and stepped away. Suddenly he looked back at me, scowling. "I'll probably be struck down for saying this, but I don't care. Whatever you do, Eugene, don't trust Francis Tannen! No matter how much he flatters you, cajoles you, takes you under his wing, just remember he's as devious as the Devil. He's been a misfit with the Jesuits ever since he joined the order. I'll never forgive myself for suggesting that he and Margaret come to Cape de Leone. He drove me away from Burguna with all of his lies and conniving.

Tannen is responsible for all of this," the priest said, pointing his right hand at the mass grave.

Father Stivonovich started to walk away with the young boy when Margaret emerged from the hut holding the baby.

"John," she called out. "You're not leaving are you?"

"I have to, Margaret," Stivonovich replied. "The refugee camp across the boarder has sent this young fellow after me. We need to leave now. It will be dark very soon."

"But can't you at least stay the night?" Margaret begged. "We need to talk. You need something to eat, don't you?" Just then the baby squirmed in her arms, distracting Margaret momentarily and causing her to turn her back to us to readjust her hold of the infant. Father Stivonovich turned to me quickly, "Remember what I said about Tannen! You can tell him I told you so. I don't care!"

By this time Margaret, with the baby adjusted in her arms, stepped towards us, but the priest started moving away quickly. "God's mercy be with you, Margaret," he yelled back before stepping into the forest with the young African guide and disappearing.

"John!" she called after him, but he didn't return. Margaret's face turned gray and lifeless. She held the baby tighter and kept looking at the spot in the forest where the priest had disappeared.

The next morning we walked west, leaving behind the destroyed village of Longula and the mound of buried bodies. But in addition to hauling the supplies we had brought with us, we now had the small child, a little girl, to carry as well. Margaret and I took turns carrying the baby. She had wrapped the child in some cloth she had found in the hut. The baby cried nearly continuously and Margaret thought it had colic. It must have been no more than three or four months old.

We were scheduled to meet Joseph Obei that afternoon in a village west and south of us. We decided not to stay in the village, however. The risk was too great given what we had learned about all the fighting. We met Joseph and he traveled with us. Periodically we came across a stream of peasant villagers who were fleeing to Guinea. They carried all their possessions in their arms or on their heads. Many walked next to goats and cattle and carried flimsy wooden cages containing three or four straggly looking chickens—a lifetime accumulation for some. From these refugees we learned where troops from both the government and rebel forces had last been seen.

We traveled for two days, carrying the baby girl who had long ago used up the bottle of goat's milk we had been given by one of the fleeing villagers. We finally arrived on the outskirts again of Grand Bassa. We had planned to meet Tannen in an old dilapidated warehouse in a suburb northwest of the city. The makeshift camp that the Christian Peoples Party forces had occupied previously had been abandoned three months earlier. Tannen had feared a reprisal by Mubarsoi's forces. The number of CPP soldiers probably now exceeded the government's, but the P.D.F. troops were clearly better armed.

When we arrived at the warehouse, a young officer assisted us. He saw that we were given our first decent meal in days and the opportunity for our first warm bath in over two months. I had long ago gotten over smelling the stench of my own body. Margaret reluctantly handed over the baby. The little girl had become quite attached to her, but she now seemed to be very sick. We believed she had a reaction to the goat's milk. The child had a bad case of diarrhea and Margaret worried that it was suffering from dehydration.

"Is Secretary Tannen here?" Margaret asked after we had a chance to clean up and report to the officer in charge.

"No, madam," the officer responded. "We are unsure when he will arrive."

Margaret nodded with disappointment on her face. The young officer that first assisted us walked up to me next.

"Mr. O'Connor, we have been waiting for you. I have a letter. It came more than a month ago."

He handed me the envelope and I immediately recognized the delicate cursive handwriting. It was Aunt Betty's. It was addressed to me at Victoria Station in Grand Bassa. I was amazed it had reached me and that it hadn't been lost or intercepted. When I opened the envelope, I found that the letter inside had actually been written by Uncle Paul who had, at best, a child's handwriting ability.

Jan. 30, 1959

Dear Gene,

I got some bad news. Ma passed away yesterday. She died peaceful in her sleep. The funeral is in two days at the church and Rev. Hogarth is coming back from Florida—like he did for Pa's funeral—to conduct the service. We knew there would be no way to get a hold of you to get back in time.

Ma had her will changed after you went back to Africa. She left you the farm and house. It's probably for the best. You worked hard on it for years. No hard feelings, Gene. Carl Thompson said he'll farm it till you let him know differently. He's willing to do it for halves.

The weather has been a bear, making it hard to get around in all the snow. Can't wait till Spring. Take care of yourself, Gene. Hope you celebrated your birthday today. Let us hear from you.

Paul

P.S. Irene Sommers got married to Merlin Brownlie on Christmas day. Betty went to the wedding and said it was real nice. We know how you always liked Irene.

Twenty Five

"You now see how I came into owning the family farm, Nigel," I said after I told him about Uncle Paul's letter. "While I had vowed never to set foot again on Blessed Acres, my grandma's decision to leave it to me changed everything."

It was early evening and Reuben and I were now inside a small airport terminal outside of the capital city of Nouakchott, Mauritania. The country is about 1200 miles south from the northern tip of Africa along the western coastline. The pilot had landed the Lear jet because he believed he heard something wrong with one of the engines, something that was causing it to work harder than normal. He was now checking it out and having the plane refueled.

I took the opportunity to find a pay telephone away from Reuben. After several frustrating minutes of working though a long-distance operator, I finally got Bob Zimmer on the other end.

"We have a layover in Mauritania while an engine's being worked on," I told him. "It's nearly six in the evening here. I'm not sure what I've got myself into, Bob. It's a strange situation, but I'm going to see it through, wherever it leads. Can you tell me anything new about Elizabeth? What the police have found out?"

"Gene, the forensics expert is now sure Elizabeth didn't die from a fall from her room."

"How does he know that?"

"A severe blow to her head caused her death. If she had fallen, there would have been more injuries to her body. Also, there's another obvious clue. When Elizabeth was found early

Monday morning, the clothes she was wearing were dry. There was a downpour early Monday morning that lasted until around 4:00 a.m. If she had jumped or been pushed from her window earlier, her clothes would have been soaked. The coroner's pretty certain that she was killed several hours earlier and taken back to her dormitory to try and make it look like a suicide or a botched murder. Whoever did it wanted her to be found."

"But why would anyone want to kill Elizabeth and then frame me? It doesn't make sense, Bob. I can't imagine that Elizabeth has an enemy in the world."

"What about Reuben? Could he have anything to do with it?" Zimmer asked.

"Good question, but I can't imagine why he would be involved."

"There's something else that's come up that's very interesting. Gene, did you know that *The Indianapolis Star* was going to publish an article that Elizabeth had written about a drug cartel from Chicago trying to move into Indianapolis?"

"When?"

"It was supposed to run a week from Sunday, but the editor, James Campion, told me the news department is questioning now whether to run it. He told me that he doubted you knew. He said that Elizabeth was going to surprise you and show you the article when it was actually published. Why would Elizabeth be writing an article about a drug cartel?"

"Because she was doing research on drug trafficking for her dissertation. She was analyzing newspaper articles that had been run in Detroit and Chicago about drug activity prior to prosecution. For her dissertation, she was going to show how the media can influence what does and doesn't get prosecuted. I was the one that suggested the topic to her based on an article I had read in the *Los Angeles Times*. Bob, I think that's it! We need to find out if this cartel knew that Elizabeth was writing the story about it."

"I don't have the resources to take this on by myself, Gene.

And besides, you're still the main suspect. Whoever did it, did a good job of implicating you, and, of course, you leaving the state so mysteriously hasn't helped. Your name is going to be dragged through the mud in the next few days."

"I promise I'll be back by the end of the week. In the meantime, please see what you can find out about this cartel. Go to Jim Daily in the prosecutor's office and see if you can't get him to start the investigation. It's a lead that has to be followed."

Bob agreed to do it. He also told me that he had checked everywhere about the existence of a Donald E. Engels and could find nothing about him or his supposed company in Ohio. Then he went on to tell me what he had found out about Reuben. "It's just like I told you earlier, Gene, he's president of an import-export business based out of Tangier, Morocco. Apparently he's been quite busy with politics in Cape de Leone, trying to oust the present regime. He's had to go undercover. No one has seen him in weeks. A friend of mine at the State Department even told me that some think he's dead. Reuben's been the brains behind the attempt to overthrow Albert Mubarsoi. Seems he and his wife got in the middle of an ambush in the country-side in Cape de Leone a couple of years ago and she was killed in the attack. She died and he barely survived, but he has some terrible looking scars from being in a fire. Gene, you don't want to be seen in Cape de Leone with this guy, whatever you do. He's enemy number one!"

"Do you know if he's remarried, Bob? He has mentioned a wife to me a couple of times."

"Not unless it's happened recently," said Zimmer. "Oh, Gene, by coincidence I learned that Reuben's mother lived in Cape de Leone in the late forties and into the fifties. She's the one you had me check to see if she had given the large gift to that girl's school in Ireland."

"You mean Reuben's aunt, don't you?"

"No," Zimmer responded. "Mahoney was his mother's maiden name. I doubled check. I was told she was a very dynamic, beautiful woman. She and Reuben's father never divorced, but they were separated most of their lives."

Suddenly Reuben came walking towards me. I quickly said goodbye to Bob Zimmer and hung up as Reuben approached. He said the left engine had a partial fuel line clog but that it had been easily fixed. We quickly boarded and I looked at him with real suspicion as we took off. What in the world was all this about? Margaret his mother? Reuben her son? There were no scars on his face.

"How much farther to Grand Bassa?" I asked coldly as we took off from the runway in Mauritania.

"Another two hours," Reuben answered. He then sat back in his seat and surveyed the country we were quickly ascending upward from. The other two—Thombi Smith and Karim Jones—talked between themselves in low voices. "Did you learned anything more about your goddaughter?"

"Nothing," I said, turning my head away. Reuben apparently could tell I had no interest in discussing Beth's situation. He changed the subject.

"Did you have any idea, Professor, how much of a threat you were to Mubarsoi during the Civil War you've been describing? I mean, the CPP nearly had him overthrown."

"Margaret and I were too busy traveling to various villages to see the bigger picture. At least I was. Perhaps Margaret saw it differently, but I think it was much later if she ever did."

"Do you know that you're still thought of as a revolutionary hero?" Reuben asked.

"Revolutionary hero?" I laughed bitterly. "No, I don't think so."

"It's true," Reuben remarked. "At least by a small, influential circle of people in Cape de Leone who either lived through the times or have studied them closely,"

I eyed him. Obviously he meant his comment seriously. Reuben proceeded to open his brief case. He pulled out a book, *The Oxford Modern History of Western Africa*. "Have you ever seen this before?" Reuben asked, handing me the tome.

"No," I said.

Reuben retrieved it from me, flipped the pages to where he had a bookmark placed, and then handed it back again. The chapter heading was "Islamic Republic of Cape de Leone," page 239, and several paragraphs were underlined in deep blue ink:

> . . . The most serious threat to Albert Mubarsoi's dictatorship came early during his rule by an uprising of nearly one-half of the paramount chiefs in 1958-59. A bloody civil war resulted, responsible for the deaths of an estimated 600,000 natives, the fleeing of more than 1,500,000 villagers from the country (about one-half the nation's population at the time), and the destruction of much of village life.

The summary went on to explain that the major non-military leaders of the opposition movement were Dr. Jeremiah Bantu, from the Kopula tribe, Francis Tannen, a Jesuit priest originally from Australia, and two foreign Christian missionaries by the names of Margaret Mahoney Reuben and Eugene O'Conner. It gave a brief description about each of us, stating that Bantu and Tannen were killed towards the end of the war.

I glanced at Reuben. "So, you've convinced me I'm a penny-anti hero," I said, anxious to read on. "Where did you come across this?"

"Oh, there are other accounts of the civil war, Professor," said Reuben. "I just thought you might find this one particularly interesting since you're mentioned in it."

I read on. The facts were essentially correct, but the author of the history hadn't conveyed the true horror that I still remember so vividly. Somehow the human elements—that of individual suffering and the total disregard for life—had become lost in all the recording of dates and events. But the summary also gave me hope, because it said nothing about what had happened to

Margaret or me. Perhaps she was still alive after all, whoever she was mother of!

Cape de Leone in the late 1950s was like most sub-Saharan African countries in that "national politics" essentially entailed what happened in the capital city. Only here could the most important of the nation's buildings and institutions be found: the presidential palace; Parliament House; the armed forces; broadcasting and newspaper services; and the like. Political and military power was further consolidated in Grand Bassa by virtue of the fact that the bureaucrats and officers who comprised the civilian and military leadership, the so-called "elites," lived only in the capital city or in a nearby suburb. By deploying a few heavily armed troops and capturing the right mixture of ministers, parliamentarians, and generals, a coup could be accomplished without much problem and on a moment's notice. This is why four coups had been successful within three years of Cape de Leone obtaining independence from England in 1950.

Mubarsoi had been shrewd enough to know this. He had gained control by exploiting this centralization of power himself. But it was also another reason why he now ruled with a "reign of terror." If a tribal chief wanted to overthrow Mubarsoi, he had better be successful, for otherwise he faced certain execution. And this was true for any revolutionary soldiers who joined in the coup effort. The attempt in late October of 1958 proved this. Approximately fifty troops loyal to the uprising paramount chiefs were hung and left on view for several days outside the capital building.

Tannen's ambitious plan to overthrow Mubarsoi, plotted in the mid-1950s and first executed in 1958, gathered adherents and attention like pins to a magnet. In March of 1959, the evening after Margaret and I arrived at the warehouse carrying the small child we had found in the village of Longula, we were approached by one of the African senior officers of the compound. He was accompanied by an aide and spoke with a hint of a British accent. Secretary Tannen wanted to see us. It was about 7:00 o'clock in the evening when we were led down a flight of stairs and blindfolded. We sped away in what seemed to be a very small car and traveled for about five minutes. Suddenly we stopped, were pulled from the tight-fitting vehicle, and led by the same men up an elevator. It clanked at each floor, then stopped and dropped down about a foot before it opened. The senior officer and his aide loosened the blindfolds.

"We will be here for you when you finish Mr. O'Connor, Madam," said the officer.

Margaret and I popped through the elevator door, a bit dazed and disoriented. There before us were a group of men, sitting in chairs around a semi-circle in a barren room shadow-illuminated by one light bulb hung from a twisted wire. Tannen was one of them. He stood quickly, excused himself from the others, and greeted us. Then he said, "I want you to meet some senior officials from the British Consulate." Tannen led us to the center of the large room.

"Carlton Ellis," said Tannen, "I would like you to meet Margaret Mahoney and Eugene O'Connor."

The man stood up dressed in a rumpled, tailored-looking suit and shook our hands.

"George Kirkland," said Tannen, "Margaret Mahoney and Eugene O'Connor."

The second man also shook our hands and greeted us warmly. An elderly African man with short cropped and graying hair, a slightly wrinkled face, and white capped teeth rose now.

"Jeremiah," Tannen said to the distinguished-looking man in a dark suit, "You've already met Margaret and Eugene, haven't you?"

"I've had the pleasure of meeting this beautiful young lady before," he said as he reached over, took her right hand and kissed it gently, "it's so good to see you again, Margaret." He then turned to me. "But I've not had the opportunity to become acquainted with this young man. Eugene, I'm so glad that we can finally meet," he said shaking my hand firmly. "I'm Jeremiah Bantu. I've heard a lot about the good work you're doing."

Jeremiah Bantu was the President of the Christian Peoples Party. He radiated gentility and aristocracy. Tannen had two chairs for us. Once we finished greeting the strangers, Tannen turned us sideways and I did a double-take.

"Justin," I exclaimed. "I didn't expect you here."

Margaret turned to her right as well and saw Dr. Perry. She embraced Perry, and he greeted me by shaking my hand in a nervous, uncharacteristic way. Tannen then asked us to all sit and the discussion resumed.

"As I mentioned, gentlemen," Tannen said, "I wanted Margaret and Eugene here so you could meet them personally. They've been some of our front people. Have done a great job as I said."

"How many villages have you visited?" asked the man named Kirkland.

Margaret glanced at me apparently expecting me to respond. "Nearly seventy, I suppose," I said stuttering. "Haven't really kept track."

"Excellent," said Kirkland. "And most of them have been receptive, have they?"

"Of converting to Christianity?"

"No," Kirkland said, "Of supporting the CPP."

"Well, yes," I answered hesitantly. "But by no means has there been a uniform response. Some are more willing than others."

"That's to be expected," Ellis remarked. "But how many can we count on for troops?"

Tannen interrupted. "I believe we can rely upon thirty-five to forty villages, especially those belonging to the larger tribes like the Fula, Moyamba, and Soso."

"Is that so?" said Kirkland shaking his head, obviously impressed. "Well, you've done good work, President Bantu, Secretary Tannen." Ellis glanced quickly at Kirkland. "Aren't you surprised, George?"

"Yes," Kirkland said, "that's quite an impressive number. How many men would that be? More than twenty thousand?"

"More like twenty-five," said Tannen confidently.

I looked squarely at Margaret to see her reaction, but her face remained stoic, emotionless. Both of the British officials sat quietly, nodding their heads.

There was a brief silence when suddenly Jeremiah Bantu scooted his chair closer into the semi-circle. "Gentlemen," Bantu said addressing Kirkland and Ellis, "we understand that you may be in a position to help us."

"Yes," said Kirkland, "there is interest among some of our associates."

"Good," Bantu replied. "We're trying to calculate how much support we might receive from these colleagues of yours."

"Before we discuss this, Mr. President, it needs to be made clear that we're not talking about any involvement on the part of the British government. Our representation here this evening has nothing to do with our official capacities. You understand this?" he said directing his inquiry towards both Bantu and Tannen.

"Of course," said Tannen, "we understand."

"Because none of these discussions can ever be shared beyond this room," added Ellis, looking directly at Margaret and me. "Whitehall would have our heads if it learned we are somehow involved in your takeover plot."

"Yes, we understand that the business interests you represent are totally separate from your government," Bantu replied. "But once we're successful we are looking to your government to announce its support of our regime. We'll need that, gentlemen. We're expecting it."

There was an awkward pause, then Tannen interjected impatiently. "How many guns, how many trucks and light artillery can we expect?"

"You need numbers tonight, Mr. Secretary?" asked Ellis.

"Yes," Tannen exclaimed, "we're now in a position to take on Mubarsoi here in Grand Bassa. We have the manpower to strike. I just told you that, but what we need now are guns, ammunition, trucks, artillery. Our troops aren't content to simply conduct village raids. We are ready to take control. That's why we need a commitment, a time-frame."

"Well, I'm not sure we're in a position to be that exact this evening, Mr. Secretary," said Ellis. "What do you think, George?" Ellis asked, turning to his colleague. "Do you have a feel for any numbers?"

"I don't know," Kirkland replied. "Perhaps we can come up with 1,500 to 2,000 rifles by the first of May. Maybe forty trucks, 150 mortars. We'll have to check before we can commit."

Tannen glanced coldly at Perry and then said in a stern tone, "Gentlemen, we've been led to believe you could come up with four times that much."

I could tell that Tannen's blunt response caught Kirkland and Ellis off guard. Kirkland's rather gray demeanor quickly changed, becoming animated.

"But that's why we wanted to make clear from the very beginning, Mr. Secretary, that you understand that we have only private backers," responded Kirkland. "We're not talking about the British government's treasury supporting your coup. Two thousand guns, forty trucks, plus artillery—you're talking upwards of nearly a million pounds right there. That's a huge investment."

"Mr. Kirkland, Mr. Ellis," replied Tannen, "if you can't do any better than that, you might as well tell your friends that they'll never carry out another carat of diamond from the northern mines. You and I both know what tremendous reserves are there—the best in West Africa! We need at least four times what you've just offered to defeat Mubarsoi. Anything less and your friends, Mr. Stewart from Cobb and Mr. Clarkson from DeBeers, might as well kiss good-bye any chance of ever having a presence in Cape de Leone. They've been eliminated from the country for the past six years, their mines nationalized; you'd think they know we're the only chance of them regaining concessions during their life times."

Both Kirkland and Ellis cringed when Tannen mentioned the names of Stewart, Cobb, Clarkson, and DeBeers. Justin Perry also squirmed in his chair when the names were mentioned, but he still said nothing.

"We'll see what can be done, Mr. President, Secretary Tannen," Kirkland finally responded. He and Ellis rose.

"We need an answer within the week," replied Tannen.

Both of the men nodded. Everyone shook hands and the British officials left, being escorted down the elevator by the same senior officer who had brought Margaret and me up. No sooner had the elevator door closed than Perry turned to Tannen.

"You agreed you wouldn't mention names. What are you trying to do, Francis, sabotage the deal before it's even struck?"

"If that's the deal, then it's not worth having," Tannen replied. "You said they would come up with at least 10,000 rifles, 150 trucks. What gives?"

"You're too impatient, Francis," Perry responded. "I believe they will, but not all at once. If you want their support then you need to give them something in exchange other than a promise. You control the Koinadogo mine. Why didn't you offer them that?"

Margaret and I continued exchanging glances. This was all new to us.

"It's too unstable," Tannen blurted. "DeBeers isn't going to subject its workers to possible raids and shootings."

"But I'm still going in? Right, Francis?" Perry replied in a panic. "You've given me one week for my men to be able to go in and drill. What we mine, we keep! That's the deal!"

"But you didn't keep your end of the promise!" Tannen shouted.

"I promised you a meeting with Kirkland and Ellis!" Perry retorted just as angrily. "You knew in advance you might not get all you wanted."

Tannen glanced at Jeremiah Bantu, who had a puzzled expression on his face. "We'll talk about it later, Justin," Tannen replied. "Now's not the time."

Tannen looked at Margaret and me. "It's late. I think you

should both go. We need to discuss some matters here."

"Will I see you later, Francis?" asked Margaret.

"Yes, I'll call for you. Probably tomorrow morning."

Margaret and I shook hands again with Jeremiah Bantu and Perry, and Tannen escorted us to the elevator. Margaret embraced Tannen before she allowed the guard to place the blindfold on her. Then the guard tied the blindfold around my face, and Margaret and I were led back into the elevator and taken down to the ground floor.

We got into a small car and traveled no more than a mile or two when the young guard driving said, "I need to talk with you about the baby you brought into headquarters, madam?"

Margaret gasped. "Something's not wrong with her, is it?"

"No, madam. She is getting stronger. She's not crying so much and she is eating better."

"Thank goodness," said Margaret.

"But we have a problem, madam."

"What's wrong?"

"We don't know what to call her," replied the young driver.

"Madam, you should name her," said the senior officer with the slight British accent from the front passenger seat. "Since you found her, you should name her."

"How about Margaret?" I said as we made a sharp turn.

Margaret cleared her throat. "No," she said firmly. The baby needs an African name. Yes—and two Christian names." There was a momentary pause. "What about Falaba-Marabella?"

"Falaba-Marabella?" asked the young guard.

"That's a lovely name," said the senior officer. "We will report that to the nurse who is taking care of the child. I like that very much," said the senior officer in an agreeable voice.

"And she needs to be christened as soon as possible," Margaret added. "I'll talk with Francis and see when Falaba-Marabella can be baptized."

"Lovely," said the senior officer.

We soon arrived back at the large, dilapidated warehouse that served as the CPP's temporary headquarters. Margaret spent the rest of the night caring for the small child she had just named. I got off a letter to Uncle Paul and Aunt Betty, telling them that I was all right and to convey my best to Irene on her wedding. I wasn't yet in a frame of mind to write her directly.

The next morning I got up late from bed. Margaret came into my room and announced that she had already met with Francis, Falaba-Marabella had been christened, and Tannen had already left. He never stayed at the same place more than one night at a time. Before Tannen left, he asked if Margaret and I would be willing to travel to Mendala, a province in the southern part of the country. There were several tribes there that he believed might be receptive to our teachings: the Limbie, Lokano, Yalunkee, and Mandingo. They were all part of the Mande language group. Also, it was an area of the country where support for the CPP and Christianity had been weakest.

We remained that day at the makeshift headquarters and left early the following morning accompanied by African soldiers. We drove south along the western coastline. We had to cut inland sooner than expected because government troops occupied check-points along the main coastal route. There were few roads and the ones that did exist tended to be monitored heavily with half-naked soldiers, sporting self-made turbans that flowed down over their shoulders, sunning themselves on top of old, dilapidated jeeps. The ground was now crusty from lack of rain and the grass was singed and beaten down. The burning African sun blistered and scorched the land. We were repeatedly stopping to pour water into the trucks' radiators to keep them from overheating.

We passed by monstrous ant hills, the height of a large elephant's shoulders, but there were few wild animals to be seen except a few carcasses that had been picked over, victims of the terrible drought. Margaret sat between me and the young African driver who drove shirtless, his bare chest streaming with sweat. She pressed against me tightly and our bodies melted together from all the heat and perspiration. Were we lost?

I had dozed off when suddenly a deafening explosion jarred me awake. The truck in front of us was ablaze, and the men in the bed of the truck were scampering to get out. Gun shots rang out and two soldiers in the front truck were mowed down while attempting to flee the truck's bed. The truck we were in skidded to a stop, only about twenty feet from behind the lead, burning truck. All of the soldiers started yelling in their native languages. Gunfire erupted from the left side. I dragged Margaret out of the front seat opposite the shooting. We scampered towards some rocks, shielded from the gunfire by the truck, and ran up a large hill. The noise and shooting continued behind us. We climbed about a third of the way up the hillside before turning around. Several bodies were sprawled on the ground surrounding the two trucks. The lead truck burned uncontrollably, emitting black smoke from the cab. Apparently some kind of bomb or mortar had hit the truck's gas tank, causing the terrible explosion. Just in back of the second truck, the one we were riding in, we saw government troops with rifles lining up six of our soldiers. The government troops raised their rifles and fired. The executed soldiers, our colleagues, fell limp to the ground.

"Oh, my God!" Margaret screamed. I covered her mouth with my hand and pulled her down with me behind a large rock. Neither of us looked up for a short time. My heart beat wildly!

When I did look up, several government soldiers were milling around the trucks. They appeared to be counting the number of CPP soldiers that were dead. Then, amazingly, the government troops started to walk our direction. Three of them split off from the others and walked up the foot of the hillside, taking the same path that Margaret and I had traversed just minutes before. Margaret and I huddled as close to the large rock as we could, embracing the stone and lying flat against the hot, sandy soil. The government soldiers came closer then passed us by. They talked to each other in their native language, being no more than a few feet from us. Then remarkably the movement of their legs and the sound of their voices started to fade.

We didn't move for several minutes before peeking over the rock. We saw the bodies of the dead CPP soldiers strewn about the disabled trucks. The sun was going down and it was early evening.

Margaret and I stayed in place for nearly an hour more, whispering to one another but not moving from behind the large boulder. Finally we stood and then sat on the rocky ledge that now served as a lookout point. The night air was still, warm, and moist. We were stranded. Margaret finally laid her head against my shoulder.

"Why is it during times like this that God seems to be farthest away," I muttered.

Margaret looked up at me with a stoic face. "This can't go on, Gene. Too much pain, too much suffering, too much killing. Either Francis and the Party must win control soon or we must give up and leave."

"How is it going to change, Margaret? The war has gone on for six months with no signs of ending. The bloodbath has just started."

"Francis may be forced out," said Margaret. "He told me this morning that the Jesuit Council from Rome has written him. It told him he must either resign his position with the CPP or give up his orders with the Jesuits. He can't do both."

"Heavens, I don't see that ultimatum as a deterrent," I said firmly. "Francis has essentially renounced the priesthood already. Why would he give up his leadership in the Party for something he doesn't value?"

"I think being a Jesuit is still very important to him, Gene," Margaret said. "More so than you might understand."

I shrugged. "Francis Tannen can commit hara-kiri for all I care, because I view him much like I view God Himself—we're all pawns to be used for his purposes, his glory, but he doesn't care one twit for what happens to us."

"Gene, surely you can't believe that about God?"

"That's exactly how I feel, Margaret," I said, not backing down. "I didn't think that God was with me as a child and I don't think God is with us now. Except as a child I thought it was all my own fault. Now I see it entirely differently."

"I knew you came to Cape de Leone without a clear sense of calling, Gene, but I've seen a tremendous change in you. As you became caught up in the work, the teaching, your faith has deepened. You've gone with me as a missionary to nearly a hundred villages, seeking souls for Christ."

I looked down at the truth—smoke smoldering from a bombed truck and more than a dozen CPP soldiers lying slaughtered on the ground.

"Half of me did, Margaret. The other half keeps shouting, 'Do You love me, Lord? I can't feel it! I preach Your words, but for all I know, You might not even exist!'"

"But how can you feel this way, Gene?"

"Guilt," I answered. "At least part of it is that."

It was time for the shadow—the real one, not Lamont Cranston—to come to the surface.

"It's how my mother and brother died, Margaret."

"But you said that was an accident. You told me how it happened years ago. It couldn't have been avoided."

"There was more that I didn't tell you," I said.

And so for the next several minutes, half way up a craggy mountain in West Africa, in near pitch darkness, I spewed out my heart to Margaret.

"The evening that my mother and brother were killed, we were in the barn loading a large flatbed wagon with corn to take to the grain elevator the next day. I was standing on top of one of the front wagon wheels. Grandpa was sitting on the tractor seat. He could never drive a tractor worth a darn, and he was having trouble backing the wagon up so that it was underneath the chute where the corn was being stored."

"'Get down off of the wheel, Genie,'" grandpa yelled at me. "'I can't back up until you're completely off.'"

"'But the 'Shadow' knows what lurks behind the hearts of men, granddad!'" I yelled to him over the noise of the tractor engine. I teetered on top of the wheel and began play-acting from the night before when we had listened to the 'Shadow' on radio.

"'I don't care what the Shadow knows, son, get down!'" grandpa commanded.

Then I started to slip from the top of the wheel. Suddenly I grabbed onto a long rope that extended down near the wagon to gain my balance. The rope was tied to a chute. The chute was connected to a trap door located in the loft of the barn. In the loft, grandpa had built a makeshift silo for storing grain. The trap door opened by way of a strong spring, and as long as the rope was pulled taunt, the corn flowed out rapidly through the chute. Mother and Philip were standing just fifteen feet away, underneath the chute. They were trying to direct grandpa where to park the wagon. When I fell with the rope in my hand, the chute opened and the corn rained down on them, covering them quickly up to their waists."

"But it was an accident!" Margaret insisted.

"And then grandpa yelled to me," I said, dismissing Margaret's excuse, "'Let go of the rope, Genie!'" he pleaded, "'For God's sake, let go of the rope!'"

"It took me several seconds to react—I guess it was the shock of it all. The mechanism got stuck and the corn cascaded down on mother and Philip. I saw the looks of horror on their faces as they tried to escape, but the grain had covered them to their shoulders, immobilizing and drowning them in a shower. I just kept hanging on to the rope. And then the floor boards holding the corn in storage broke completely, the loft of the barn giving way and dumping tons of corn over both mother and Philip. They disappeared from total view, as if magically."

Margaret tried to put her arms around me, but I pushed her away.

"By the time grandpa and I dug through the silage to find

mother and Philip, they were dead, suffocated. It was so terrible, Margaret! And for months afterwards I simply kept asking myself, 'Why did I do it? What caused me to hold on to the rope, when if I had only let go they might still be alive today?' And I could never find an answer. I searched and searched in my mind for why I did it.

"And all this time, I'm saying, 'Where is God? Why has this happened to me? What did any of us do to deserve this?' It was not that I felt that God didn't exist or that He had deserted me, because I never felt that He had been with me to begin with. But at other times, I thought that God had to exist. Even as a boy I thought that there has to be a Grand Designer. You can't grow up on a Midwest farm and think that all that nature has to offer— the planting and harvesting of crops, the sun rising and setting, the birthing of baby lambs and calves, the passing of seasons— Oh, Margaret, the seasons are just beautiful in Roanoke County—but you can't think that this just happened! There has to be a plan, and for there to be a plan, there has to be a Planner. But although I could think this through rationally, I never felt God's presence. And I couldn't understand why! Can't you see how infuriating it was, Margaret?

"Grandma would give her lengthy testimony during church service about how God had touched her life, how God had come to her in a vision, how God had healed her and forgiven her sins. But for me, I felt none of this! I felt no divine presence! I didn't feel forgiven! I didn't feel loved! And I couldn't understand why!"

Margaret reached over with her right arm and placed it around my shoulder. Tears streamed down my face.

"Despite it all, Gene," she said, "you're here now, aren't you? If God wasn't in your life, how could you be here so far away from home, going from village to village praising His name and preaching Christ's message of love and redemption? Do you think that this just happened? Do you think you just answered that advertisement from John Stivonovich because of your own desires? Your own life is the source for your conviction that God does exist and that He has a plan for you."

I'm not sure that I comprehended all that she said to me, and I may well have looked unconvinced because of what she said next.

"Gene, I have never told anyone what I am about to say to you now. But I am convinced that God is with you—whatever happens to us next, whether we survive this terrible night or not—because I have known myself the kind of despair you've just described."

I must have looked surprised as I thought that I knew most everything about Margaret's life.

"When I was a child, my parents raised me on a small peat farm in the northwest part of Ireland near a village called Willenda. I wasn't raised in Dublin like I told you."

Her voice was soft, blended with the sound of crickets on the parched grassland. "When I was growing up we lived in poverty, but still my mother kept giving birth to more and more babies. I was the oldest that survived, but three more babies died in child birth after me and four more died of childhood diseases. And yet the babies kept coming. I couldn't understand and kept asking myself—'why are father and mother having more and more children when so many babies have died and they can't feed the ones they have now?' Mother gave birth to fifteen children altogether, only six of whom survived into adulthood.

"Because I was the oldest and mother was often sick and nursing the younger ones, it became my responsibility to take care of our small home. Father was gone for weeks at a time to work in the coal mines and I was the only child old enough to help mother. Because I had to take care of the house and my younger brothers and sisters, I didn't have the opportunity to go to school. I barely knew how to read and write.

"But then our local priest came to our house one summer day and talked to mother. He told her that a Catholic girl's school in Dublin invited our parish to send a student to attend at no cost. The priest asked my parents if I could be that student. Despite father's initial objection, I found myself, within days, attending this boarding school in Dublin. It is named St. Magdalene Preparatory School for Girls."

"So that's where our school in Burguna got its name?" I said. Strangely it had never occurred to me before to ask Margaret that simple question.

Margaret nodded and continued. "I was so poorly prepared for St. Magdalene. But an elderly nun who was a teacher at the school—Sister Mary McLaughlin—took me under her wing. She didn't let me feel sorry for myself. She tutored me at nights, and after only two years I was doing almost as well as the girls who had been studying at St. Magdalene nearly all of their lives. After four years, Gene, I finally graduated from St. Magdalene, it being considered one of the best preparatory girl's schools in Great Britain. I became employed as a secretary at Trinity College, Dublin. I was secretary to the senior tutor.

"It was there that I met my husband-to-be, Derrick Reuben. I realize I've never told you that I'm married, but I'm doing it now to let you know that I have experienced despair, just as you are now."

Margaret went on to tell me how she had fallen in love with Reuben, whose father was an important man in Irish commerce and a senior minister in the government's cabinet. As I watched the moon rise through clouds, Margaret partially covered her face with her hands and spoke in a whisper.

"Gene, my life soon turned into a lie, a complete, continuous lie! I told Derrick and his parents that my father and mother were dead and I only had a rich aunt living, who was an invalid at an institution in Cork. Amazingly, they believed my story. If anything, my story made me more wanted by Derrick and his parents, and they adopted me as their own daughter.

"When Derrick and I got married, I had woman attendants who I barely knew stand up for me as bridesmaids. I was too afraid that my own girl friends, who knew too well about my former life, might reveal something to Derrick and his family and ruin everything. The worst of it all, I couldn't even tell my own parents and siblings that I was marrying into one of the wealthiest, most respected families in all of Ireland. I had essentially dropped out of sight in terms of the Mahoneys.

"And then here comes the despair, Eugene," Margaret said, forewarning me. "It was only three months into our marriage when I became pregnant."

"But why was that so terrible?" I asked.

"It wasn't, but what happened next was. I gave birth to a beautiful baby boy, Stephen Douglas. But when he was only a year old, he developed pneumonia, ran a high fever, and died in my arms one night after several days of sickness. Derrick was traveling on business at the time.

"Immediately Derrick wanted to have another child, but not me. I was still in too much depression. And all the childhood memories came back to me of the babies that mother had who died. Because of these memories, I fled from Derrick whenever he tried to come near me. This was bad enough, but then his father, now the Secretary of the Exchequer, learned that I wasn't from a respectable family from Cork after all. Rather, he learned that my father was alive and a miner in one of the coal mines in which he owned an interest. Can you believe the coincidence? Derrick's father was a part-owner in a coal mine where my father, Carey Mahoney, made a miserable, subsistence living.

"And from then on Derrick's family would have nothing to do with me. Derrick also began to treat me differently. He no longer took me out, but began socializing by himself with his old friends. Then there were rumors of affairs, that Derrick had some mistresses. Our marriage fell apart at the seams."

"But when did you meet Francis?" I asked. "After all this?"

"No, I had actually met Francis before this time, about six months after I began serving as secretary to the senior tutor and before I married Derrick. Francis was beginning work on his doctorate. He was already a Jesuit by then and he taught some in the department of philosophy. He was so learned, so unbelievably bright. He took to me and shared his learning. In some ways Francis was my salvation, but then he left, too, to go to New York and teach at Fordham University. All was gone like flowers in November.

"I swore that God had abandoned me. I went back to Derrick and begged him for a divorce. But, of course, that was asking for nearly the impossible. In Ireland divorce is illegal and Derrick refused to go to another country to obtain one. He said a divorce would ruin him in the future politically, and that it would be viewed as scandalous if the prominent son of the Secretary of the Exchequer left his wife. And so I was stuck!"

Margaret went on to explain how desperate she became, so desperate that she decided to take her husband's gun, drive back to her childhood home, and commit suicide.

"Gene, I had driven only a few times in my entire life and didn't know my way very well to my home village. Anyway, the sun was shining, the glow of autumn colors was brilliant, and I was lost in myself and in this unknown countryside in a way that I had never been lost before.

"And this last part that I am about to tell you, Gene, is why I have disclosed to you all the sordid details of my past, a past that no one knows fully, even Francis. Because what happened next is the most amazing thing that I've ever experienced!

"I was driving along this lovely, Irish country road where rock fences lined the narrow berm. I was in absolute despair when I drove slowly around a curve in the road, still trying to find some landmark, some sign that was recognizable to me. Then I looked to my left at this open field of recently mowed hay and there He was! God Himself! I know you think I'm crazy or that it was an illusion, but I promise you that God was there in that field. His presence overcame me to the point that I was afraid of crashing the automobile and I slowed down to a mere crawl. And then I looked to my right, in another open field and there was God again! And in each and every field along that lovely country road I felt His presence. It occurred for perhaps as long as a minute. And He kept saying to me, not in words but in an indescribable language through telepathy, "*It will be all right, Margaret. You are safe now. You have nothing more to fear, nothing more to worry about. You have experienced the worst, for not even death can separate us now. You are with Me and I have a plan for you!*"

"I stopped the car and cried uncontrollably for several minutes. And when I finally regained control of my senses, Gene, I realized then what I had just experienced, and it is this: God is always with us just as he is with us at this very moment. He surrounds us, in our best of times and in our worst; in our times of frenzied activity and during our times of deepest solitude. It is we that don't recognize His presence that causes us to feel so alone, so abandoned, so much a victim of the world's wickedness.

"Don't you see why it is that during times of great upheaval we most often experience God like I did? It is only then that we are most vulnerable and therefore most receptive to experiencing His presence."

Margaret continued, but with a more buoyant face. "Gene, how did I end up here in Cape de Leone with Francis and you? My story is just as improbable as yours, perhaps even more so. Do you still think that it was just some accident, after what we have learned about each other here tonight, that we are in this desperate situation together?"

"But how did you end up here, Margaret?" I asked, breaking up her story. "How did you go from almost killing yourself in Ireland and being married to your husband to being here?"

Margaret laid her head back against the large rock which hid us. She sighed and explained that after she decided not to commit suicide that she left Dublin to follow after Tannen to New York and to reestablish a life for herself there. She had money that her husband had given her. Further, her husband's family owned an import-export business in West Africa, which included owning interests in diamond mines in northern Cape de Leone. Because of her knowledge, albeit limited, about the country, it was she who had suggested to Father John Stivonovich to leave and to go to West Africa after he had expressed an interest in pursuing missions work. It was only two years later, after Tannen had been dismissed as principal of the Jesuit high school in New York, that Tannen and she followed Stivonovich at the Polish priest's invitation.

Margaret's story had moved me so emotionally that it took me several minutes to collect my thoughts and to return to the reality that confronted us. We were both exhausted and parched. The pangs of hunger come and go, but the gut-wrenching feeling of thirst never leaves. We had to do something. In this arid part of Cape de Leone, which was bone dry from over a year of drought, we would certainly die in a couple of days if we remained with the slight hope of someone rescuing us.

I told Margaret of my plan to return to the undamaged truck in hopes of finding water. But before I could leave, she grabbed me by the neck and hugged me closely, pulling me down to her kneeling position. As I stood up from her embrace, my right hand caressed her hair gently. I couldn't comprehend how any man could leave her for another woman.

I started down the small mountain and quickly realized we were farther up than I had initially thought. There was still some moonlight. I tripped and stumbled over several stubby bushes that hugged the slopping terrain. By the time I reached the bottom, I saw several of our troops lay dead surrounding the two trucks. Their bodies were already bloating from the heat. In the back of the second truck, there were a couple of canteens and a large ten gallon metal container. I shook the canteens and they were empty, but when I tipped the container slightly, I heard water sloshing inside. Quickly I unscrewed the top of the container and scooped out water with my dirty hands. It was very warm and it had a salty taste to it, but I drank and drank until I couldn't hold any more. Then I started to pour some water into one of the empty canteens to take back to Margaret, when suddenly I was hit in the head by something from behind.

I next remember lying prostrate beside the second truck, surrounded by government soldiers. The sun was now nearly up. One young soldier beat me with the butt of his rifle. Two other soldiers stopped him. They argued with each other, and then they grabbed me by my shirt collar and dragged me behind a formation of large rocks, the area that they had first shot at us from the day before.

Next an African man in civilian clothes was pushed out from behind a rock by two other soldiers. After a second look, I recognized him as our interpreter, Thomas Mbonampeka. We had met only the day before when we set out on our journey to the Mendala Province. Thomas had blood dried down his left temple and his shirt was badly torn. The first soldier who had beat me with the butt of his rifle spoke first. Thomas then translated. They wanted to know where "the woman" was and I denied her existence. An angry conversation ensued.

"They saw you two run up the mountain yesterday after the attack," Mbonampeka said. "The leader told me to tell you that the missionary traitor Eugene O'Connor should know better than to think that he can escape from the P.D.F."

After more demands for knowledge about Margaret, more denials on my part, and more beatings, two soldiers lifted me and threw me into the back of our military truck. Thomas was dragged to the truck and two soldiers threw him into the bed beside me. Three soldiers piled into the cab. The truck was started and we turned around, going back the direction we had come from the day before. One soldier snarled back a comment to Thomas.

"What did he just say?" I begged.

"He said, 'To hell with the woman! Let the jackals and hyenas have her!'"

Dancing warriors of the Sosa tribe before a political
rally at Chitcharo, Cape de Leone.

Twenty Six

hy did Europeans go to Africa anyway? Was it only to exploit the continent, as African nationalists claimed, or were there more noble reasons? The word "colonialism" had a negative connotation even before I arrived in West Africa, but the notion of "missions" was much more accepted. Still, many nationalist leaders argued that Christian missionaries were merely there to foist their own beliefs and cultures on others and that this was, in its own way, a form of colonialism. But apologists were at least as persuasive. To them Christianity was a vehicle, not intended to uproot, but to build upon the African's traditions. In this sense, missions was not merely a guise to achieve economic or political results that colonialism couldn't because it had become an intolerable doctrine. Rather, missionaries, especially Christian missionaries, came to the continent to truly better mankind by bringing Christ to a world that hadn't had the opportunity to know of Him before.

It is ironic that we in the West have sent our missionaries off to convert millions of Africans when we have converted ourselves to the religion of politics and a consumer economy. I recognized this even in the 1950s. But if the West has suffered from a loss of spirituality, the nations of Sub-Sahara Africa have suffered even more from the failure to capture a common national identity or belief system. Because what I witnessed is this: when there are no commonly accepted standards of conduct (viz. no rule of law and no beliefs beyond personal aggrandizement by those who hold power), then cultures are endlessly in flux. Chaos—absolute, unequivocal mayhem—

becomes the norm and human life is accorded no more value than that of a mosquito!

I remember giving this so much thought because these were the very ideas that were discussed vigorously in Sub-Sahara Africa by every thinking person, black or white, who gave much thought to anything. I personally had the opportunity to think a great deal about these matters for three days as I sat in a jail cell in the basement of Parliament House in Grand Bassa.

The troops had transported me to Parliament House and gloatingly deposited me there. I apparently was a great "find." My life was now intertwined with this great national conflict whether I wanted it to be or not. On the one hand, Albert Mubarsoi claimed to be working to improve Cape de Leone, to see it evolve into more of a developed nation—with modern roads, schools, health facilities, and employment opportunities— but without the Western influence of law and commerce that colonialism had brought; on the other hand, he was diminishing the role of the chieftains, the traditional governing power that had existed for hundreds of years. Tannen and the paramount chiefs claimed that Mubarsoi had achieved little and primarily held power to pilfer the country's treasury for his own private gain. To add spice to the mix, Mubarsoi had promoted Islamic teachings and ideas without providing any undergirding philosophy of law.

My mind during those three days was also on less grandiose concepts, because I was sick from worry. How could Margaret have survived after my capture? Should I have turned her in where she would at least be with me in jail, not left to fend for herself in the African bush? Perhaps, again, I was to blame for a death.

On the morning of my fourth day in jail, a large, elderly guard arrived carrying a tray of steaming food—mush, African rice and vegetables and hot tea. Another guard opened my cell door and the first guard set the tray down on the cold, cement floor. I grabbed for the tray.

"You don't have much time to eat, Monsieur," said the guard. "You are to meet the big man in a quarter hour."

I was too starved to even bother asking what the guard meant. I gobbled the food, swabbing the bowl of rice and vegetables clean with my fingers. The two guards returned minutes later and opened my cell door. They handcuffed me and led me out of the cell. "Who is this big man?" I asked.

Neither of the guards responded and my heart raced. Had I just eaten my last meal? Was I going to the executioner?

The guards escorted me from the basement, up the stairway and through a doorway that opened into Parliament House. We walked down an ornately decorated hallway and then stopped in front of an office door. The first guard knocked on the door twice, opened it, unlocked my handcuffs, and pushed me inside.

"Mister O'Connor," said a deep, thick African voice. I glanced up at the opposite end of the room and saw a large man in a military uniform sitting behind a desk. "Please come in."

The man stood and walked towards me. I had seen his picture a thousand times in newspapers, national magazines, and posters. "I'm pleased you could join me," the large general added.

He shook my hand and then motioned for me to take a seat. In back of his desk, hung on a dark paneled mahogany wall, was a large portrait of my host dressed in the same military regalia he now wore. He took his own seat behind his imposing desk and smiled.

"I hope your accommodations have been satisfactory," he said. "I apologize for any inconvenience. More time than I would have liked has been devoted to dealing with a troubling conflict in the inner country. I believe you know a little something about that."

I said nothing and watched the general closely. He was about forty, very muscular, and extremely dark, with a powerful looking upper body. He had a square jaw and his teeth flashed very white, straight, and capped. He had a fuller face than I remembered from his pictures, but it wasn't heavy or sagging in any way. He looked at me momentarily as though he was studying me.

"What do you know about this woman Margaret Mahoney?" he suddenly asked.

"Nothing," I said.

"You know something, Mr. O'Connor. We needn't play cat and mouse about this." My host pulled out a drawer from his desk and from it a newspaper. He placed the paper in front of me. It contained the article and picture about Margaret and me published on the front page of the *Grand Bassa Daily-Times*, the picture being the one taken in Burguna with the burning bodies behind us. "Yes, I know her," I said, pushing the newspaper back at him. I gave him basic biographical facts about Margaret.

"I see," said Mubarsoi, "and how did you meet this priest, Francis Tannen?"

"Who?"

"Are you having another memory lapse, Mr. O'Connor? Come now, why continue to play games? You've been working with Reverend Tannen for at least the past year. I know that much."

"We met here, also."

"But Tannen's Australian, isn't he?"

"Originally."

"Why, of course," said the President, "that makes perfect sense. The bush of interior Cape de Leone is the natural meeting place for three English-speaking Caucasians from three separate parts of the world. I should have guessed. Not London, not Cairo or New Delhi, but rural, isolated West Africa. Yes, this explains everything. How could I have possibly been so stupid?"

Mubarsoi's sarcasm led to indignation.

"Tell me, Mr. O'Connor, why would three foreigners, none of whom have any ties to Cape de Leone, try to destroy my government?"

"I don't believe I understand, Mr. President."

Mubarsoi jumped up from his chair, pounded his powerful fists against his desk and moved his head within inches of my face.

"Mr. O'Connor, I'm tiring of your ruses! I could have you shot this minute for your activities as a Christian missionary and there would be no questions asked. Do you understand that, sir? Now I want to know, what's the purpose of these acts your so called "Christian Peoples Party" has against me? I've done nothing to you."

"Does corruption, crimes against fellow country men, failure to hold elections, and illegal expropriations of tribal lands ring any bells, Mr. President?"

His face scowled and he pushed his large, heavy desk towards me, budging it several inches. "I've heard it before and it's all lies! There's nothing to it! We have a constitution, Mr. O'Connor. I've done nothing against our constitution!"

"But you wrote the constitution, Mr. President, just like the President you overthrew wrote the constitution he served under. Doesn't it seem slightly self-serving that under the new Leonean constitution that only one chamber of Parliament and one party—yours—is allowed? Doesn't it seem peculiar that there is no mention of any election for the office of President or that the judiciary is all appointed by you without any approval required of Parliament or any other body?"

"Why do you Westerners always insist that there is only one model for governing? These are apocalyptic times, Mr. O'Connor. You and I will have much to answer for if this country self-destructs. Ninety percent of my people are illiterate. Fifty percent are dead before the age of forty. Half still worship stone idols. Judgment is not just being passed on Cape de Leone but on all of Sub-Sahara Africa whether it can survive without foreign intervention. What complaint does Tannen have with me? Why is he trying to overthrow my government?"

"Why did your troops destroy the village of Burguna, Mr. President? Did you have any thought for life when your soldiers slaughtered several hundred innocent women and children?"

Mubarsoi's chest expanded and his eyes darted wildly around the room before fixating on me. He picked up his telephone and

spoke quickly, summoning someone—I couldn't discern who—
to be brought in. He then slammed the telephone down and said,
"I know what you think of me! I can tell your mind is made up.
But before you—"

There was a knock on the door interrupting Mubarsoi's
warning. A slender Arab man entered wearing a flowing white
robe. I had seen him before, but I couldn't recall the circumstances.
When the man approached us, Mubarsoi introduced him as
Mahomet Ali-Said and I then remembered him from when he
served as an adviser to Chief Faramha. Mubarsoi then addressed
Ali-Said, "Tell Mr. O'Connor what you know about the attack on
the village of Burguna."

Ali-Said looked surprised by Mubarsoi's abrupt command,
but spoke. "We believe that members of the Mbulu tribe
committed the atrocity, Mr. O'Connor. Many years ago they
were enemies of the Tambe. They live primarily in Liberia. They
came across the southern border and committed the killings in
Burguna. We heard this from some of the Mbulu themselves.
They were given uniforms to wear to make them look as though
they were from the Leoneon military."

"At whose direction, Mr. Ali-Said, was the attack ordered?"
exhorted Mubarsoi.

"By the direction of the Christian Peoples Party, your
Excellency. Reverend Tannen in particular," Ali-Said replied.

"I don't believe it," I replied. "Why would the CPP do that
to one of its own villages? Tannen lived there himself for ten
years. It's the only permanent home he's known in Cape de
Leone. What purpose would it serve?"

"Perhaps you should ask him, Mr. O'Connor," Mubarsoi said.
"I suspect it has something to do with trying to legitimize his
plot to overthrow my government." He leaned into my face. His
breath was unbearable, but that was the smallest of my problems.

"I am growing very impatient with your CPP, Mr.
O'Connor! My country is being torn apart by your proselytizing
and the raids of your soldiers. It's costing my government

millions of leones each week to fight the CPP! You tell Reverend Tannen that I want peace. I will guarantee him, Miss Mahoney, and you safe transport out of the country if you leave now. But if he refuses my generous offer, sir; if he continues this fractious effort to overthrow my government, I promise Reverend Tannen that he will regret it! I will drive him to Hell and rip out his heart with my own hands! If Tannen wants the complete annihilation of this nation, it will be at a price too dear for him to ever repay, even with his immortal soul!"

Mubarsoi ordered one of the guards into his office and he escorted me out of the room. I was taken immediately to a Mercedes Benz waiting outside of Parliament House. We sped to the outskirts of Grand Bassa, where I was dumped out at the CPP headquarters. They obviously knew where it was. How could any of us be safe?

My concerns were lessened when I found that nearly everyone had vacated the temporary headquarters. A young soldier on sentry told me that nearly all of the troops had gone to a large village in the central part of the country named Chitcharo. A rally would be held there the following day that included all of the tribes and chieftains who aligned themselves with the CPP. I hitched a ride on one of the last trucks traveling to the village.

When we arrived in Chitcharo a few hours later, a large, flat area had been cleared on the edge of the village. There was no sign of Tannen, only young soldiers dressed in military khakis— many barely of high school age. Depleted from worry and lack of food, I finally found a shade tree behind a large mud hut and collapsed from exhaustion. But soon I was in custody again, a rifle shaft poking me at the back of my head. The young CPP soldier marched me to a large mud hut with a thatched roof.

"Tell the Secretary I have the stranger," yelled the soldier, who prodded me to the edge of the hut. A door opened and the soldier pushed me through the door. I stepped in to see Francis Tannen behind a desk. He was examining a large map spread over a desk top. He looked up, seemingly annoyed at being disturbed, and said, "What do you want, lieutenant? Oh, it's you, Eugene. It's all right, lieutenant," Tannen said. "I know this man. You may leave."

The young officer quickly saluted and closed the door behind him.

"Sorry about that, Eugene," Tannen said. "I was informed there was a stranger. Didn't know it was you. Can't be too cautious these days."

"Yes," I said. "It seems you're a wanted man."

Tannen looked up at me with a proud smirk. I told him that I had been captured and brought before Mubarsoi. He let out a long sigh and then glanced at me and sneered. "Peter or Judas, Eugene?"

"What?" I asked.

"Peter or Judas?"

"I don't know what you mean, Francis."

"Oh, I think you do. Either you denied knowing me or you've come to betray me. It's that simple. Am I to expect Mubarsoi's troops to ransack our camp tonight?"

I never liked the priest and now he had become intolerable. "I met Mubarsoi and was released to bring back a message to you. That's all, Francis."

"But why would Mubarsoi release you if you didn't give him something in exchange?"

"I gave him nothing; no information. I can assure you. He told me to tell you he wants peace. He told me that if you stop the efforts to overthrow his government, he won't seek retribution. He's willing to guarantee that Margaret, you, and I can leave the country safely."

"And that's all he wants?"

"He wants peace, Francis!"

"You believe that?" Tannen retorted. "You're more than a traitor, Eugene. You're a simpleton! Mubarsoi wants our heads! He won't settle for anything less!"

"I can't believe you won't at least consider—"

"I had hoped for more loyalty from you, Eugene, but I see I was expecting too much. You desert Margaret to save your own skin and now you're willing to sacrifice me and the success of our cause."

I stood dumbfounded while Tannen yelled near the top of his voice. "Lieutenant Kabill, come in!" The door quickly opened and the officer stepped inside. "See to it that Mister O'Connor is escorted outdoors, Lieutenant. Oh, and don't allow him to enter this building again. I don't want him anywhere near here!" Tannen starred at me. "I could have you arrested, Eugene, but I won't out of deference to what you've done for the party in the past, but I'm sorely disappointed in you. I had hoped for more."

The guard grabbed my left arm and started to pull me away. "Why are you doing this, Francis?" I exclaimed. "I've done nothing against you." The guard tugged at my arm harder, but I resisted. "What do you know about Margaret," I begged, adding, "I didn't desert her. I was captured!"

But the guard dragged me out of the large hut without Tannen saying another word. I had no where to go and simply wandered around the makeshift camp ground full of troops from the CPP. The hot afternoon sun burned my skin. The sky was a distant blue and the ground dry and dusty. Young soldiers in faded and dirty khaki uniforms milled about the village joking and smoking cigarettes. The cigarettes were French ones. I could tell from the sweet smell of the tobacco. Because of the drought, water was scarce and canteens were passed around carefully to conserve the precious liquid.

After about thirty minutes, I met the young officer, Major-General Charles de Gaulle, who had headed up the rescue of us after the Burguna massacre. He was hesitant to help me, but he finally did after I explained to him that I had no where to go. The young major-general told me that Tannen had ordered some CPP soldiers shot that day for committing crimes against one of the villages. Tannen was attempting to instill law and order throughout the ranks. It was because of this that de Gaulle thought Tannen might have been so hostile and curt to me.

The next day I stayed around the canteen area and repeatedly asked individual soldiers if they had seen a white woman. I received one negative response after another. By mid day, more than three thousand additional tribesmen arrived in the village for the rally. They initially camped inside the area in front of the platform, surrounded by military trucks. But by late afternoon, the throng of tribes overflowed beyond the circle of trucks. Thousands of tribesmen were dressed in colorful native dress, while others wore simply a Spartan loin cloth. The individual tribes remained segregated. As I walked by each tribe and heard their multiple languages, I thought that this must truly be a modern Tower of Babel.

Dusk descended and there was much chanting and dancing going on amongst the tribes. I was hungry, so I decided to walk down the center of Chitcharo to find something to eat. I turned down a narrow, dusty path, for no reason other than I thought I might possibly find a village woman willing to feed me in exchange for some trinkets I had been given by General de Gaulle. Money was useless outside of the capital city; everything was bought and sold in the villages by barter. The path was crowded with villagers resting on their haunches, looking forlorn and talking to one another.

Half-way down the path, I looked out and I saw Margaret bending down consoling a small child that was sitting in the dusty path and crying. It was a dream I told myself—a vision. But then Margaret glanced up, saw me, and smiled. It was as though she had expected me to come walking through this crowded village.

"Gene!" she said. She kissed the child on the cheek and stood up. "Can you believe we've found each other again?" She stepped toward me. "It's like a dream, isn't it?" Margaret said, hugging me tightly. The villagers stopped talking and gawked at us while we embraced.

She told me that she had been rescued by CPP soldiers and brought to Chitcharo three days before. We continued our conversation over a bowl of rice and vegetables. A village woman, whom Margaret had befriended, served the meal to us and refused to accept anything in exchange. When the natives had so little, it amazed me how generous they could be. During our meal, I rubbed my face and felt the prickly sensation that a five day old beard produces.

Margaret was unusually tan and her hair matted. For the first time I noticed small wrinkles around her eyes and mouth. I could tell she was under a lot of stress and probably hadn't been getting much sleep. During our meal I told her about meeting Mubarsoi, his offer of safe transport for us, and that Mubarsoi and Mahomet Ali-Said blamed the massacre at Burguna on the CPP. She refused to believe it, too.

"I don't trust Mubarsoi to tell anyone the truth," Margaret said. "Least of all to one of us. He's intentionally polarizing the whole country. Have you heard about his conversion to Islam? He's now ordering that every citizen should become Muslim and that Islamic shari'ah law will be applied throughout the country. Why would he do this if he truly wants peace? How are the tribes that have recently converted to Christianity supposed to react?"

When Margaret told me this, my mouth dropped open from disbelief. Margaret shook her head slowly. Her face took on a worried, sullen expression. We sat together and said nothing to each other for a short time. I finally glanced down the path and noticed the movement of several hundred villagers. They were walking away, going to the political rally.

Margaret and I followed, arriving at the edge of Chitcharo. Villagers sat surrounding the soldiers and tribal members. The troops sat near the platform, while the tribal members stood in back, chanting and dancing. Drums pounded wildly. The whole atmosphere was like one of a carnival or religious festival with overtones of war-mongering. The air was charged, electric with anticipation that something special was about to happen!

As time passed, the chanting became louder and louder. It became dark and floodlights were turned on, illuminating the stage. Soon after about fifteen tribal leaders walked on to the platform. Following behind the chieftains were Jeremiah Bantu and Francis Tannen. The chieftains, dressed in florid, brightly colored robes, stood on the stage in a single line and waved in large circles to the tribal members and villagers. The crowd roared with applause and cheered. The chieftains then proceeded to sit down on chairs. One by one, each stood, walked to the podium, and spoke in his native language through a microphone to the riotous crowd. Of course only the tribe they belonged to understood them, but it seemed that the entire multitude of rally-goers cheered at the appropriate time. The chieftains spoke of the injustice of being ruled by Mubarsoi, of how their tribal rights had been taken away, and that the only way to reclaim those rights was to fight the evil dictator.

Next Jeremiah Bantu was introduced. The elderly, sagacious looking leader stood and addressed the crowd. He appeared very tired and spoke in a dry, monotonous voice, but he, likewise, criticized Mubarsoi harshly and called upon all lovers of a free nation to support the Christian Peoples Party.

Finally Tannen was introduced, being the last one to speak. He wore all of his priestly regalia, appearing somehow transformed from his normal, human appearance into royalty, something divine. When Bantu introduced him, all of the soldiers and tribal members jumped, applauding and chanting wildly; the deafening drum beats rolled with a savage abandonment. An additional spotlight illuminated Tannen, making his large profile even more impressive against the row of chieftains and the dark backdrop of the night.

Tannen spoke of Mubarsoi's injustices, bringing the crowed to a fever pitch. He first spoke in English, but then he began to repeat what he had just said into the language of the Mandingo. After that he repeated himself again in perfect Lagolese, then in the language of the Hoisa, and then in the language of nearly every tribe present. Amazement covered the faces of the tribal peoples. The villagers gazed at him as though the priest was indeed a messenger from God, come specifically for the purpose of communicating to them. Not since the great Nineteenth Century British explorer Sir Richard Burton had the African continent heard an interpreter of such linguistic ability. Tannen then returned to English and to the continuation of his speech which called for the rejection of Allah and Mubarsoi and the acceptance of the Christian God and the CPP.

Again Tannen began to translate into the different languages. But this time, during the several minutes it took for him to repeat himself, a few dozen soldiers began passing out an ornament of some kind. It was a necklace and they were showing the villagers how to put the necklace on around their necks. When they came to us, we saw that the chain contained the Christian cross. The thunderous, adulatory response from the natives sent shivers down my spine. The crowd's reaction caused Tannen to become even more demonstrative, more convinced of his own persuasive powers and greatness.

"The salvation of our villages and way of life depends upon your sacrifices!" Tannen finally bellowed. He waved his arms effusively and contorted his face into a look of anguish and pain. "For those who fight the tyrant, Mubarsoi, for those who sacrifice their lives for the cause of our party, as Christ sacrificed His life for ours, their sins shall be forgiven and they shall enjoy the promise of eternal life! War against the Muslim infidels is extremely pleasing to God! Do not worry about your possessions or about your families! Let every believer in the Christian God wear the cross into battle that we may be free of the tyrant, Mubarsoi, and his false god, Allah! We must fight and repel the infidels back into the sea!!! God wills it! God wills it! God wills it!"

After he translated this last message into the various tribal languages, Tannen continued yelling this last phrase until the entire mass of people—troops, tribal members, villagers, and chieftains alike—were repeating it in unison at the top of their voices: "GOD WILLS IT! GOD WILLS IT! GOD WILLS IT!"

Drums beat wildly; villagers shouted themselves hoarse. A power as electric as lightening, as burning as the African sky at sunset, had taken over. As I witnessed the pandemonium, I recognized the awesome power that this man had over the soldiers and tribal members, including the chieftains, and that Tannen knew a fundamental fact about human nature: that armies aren't moved so much by aggression as by devotion. I then realized that Tannen was a racist of the worst kind, not seeking separation from the West Africans because of a feeling of superiority, but, rather, arousing in them a sense of unity in order to exploit them for his own ignoble, egotistical ambitions. And Margaret and I had played right into his hands. We had helped accomplish exactly what he wanted by working to convert the tribes.

And then the haunting words of what John Stivonovich told me about Tannen came back into my mind, and I realized that it was likely that Tannen had given the order for the attack and slaughter of his own adopted village as Mahomet Ali-Said had told me. In the midst of my reflection, the chanting, the beating drums, and the war-dancing reverberated louder and louder! Tannen was now waving wildly to the crowd, basking in the applause, the adulation, the fever of the moment!

I glanced at Margaret and sensed from her frightened, bewildered expression that she, too, was thinking what I was: that this was the beginning of the end; that only pain and misery would befall us all; and, that the Reverend Francis Tannen, S.J. was a very dangerous man!

Twenty Seven

One number in many ways foretold of the horrific fate of the country: from late July to late September 1959, 400,000 Leoneons were slaughtered, mostly sliced and hacked to death by soldiers using machetes. The rate of killing was so great during this time period that the nation's dead accumulated at nearly three times the rate of Jewish dead during the height of the Holocaust. By another comparison, it made Pol Pot and the Khmer Rouge's killing of two million Cambodians in the 1970s look like nothing more than a leisurely bloodletting.

Mubarsoi had recruited youth militia and armed them for the purpose of defending the Islamic state against "heathen Christian sympathizers." "Let whatever is smoldering erupt," stated an editorial in the *Jihad*, "because the flow of Christian blood is the only thing that will cleanse the nation!" Of course, most Leoneons couldn't read a newspaper. But strongly worded diatribes of this kind gave legitimacy to military and religious officials who incited their troops and worshippers into killing their fellow villagers when there was even the slightest hint they were Christian. It was, in effect, the law of the land.

If the militia and Islamic civilian population had the support of the state to justify their acts of atrocity, rebel CPP troops initially possessed revolutionary idealism as their rationale to commit butchery in kind. The innocent civilians who were caught in the middle tried to flee into overcrowded, filth-ridden refugee camps in Guinea, Liberia and Ivory Coast. But for too many, they didn't run soon enough and they ended up in body piles, bloody heaps of heads, torsos, legs and arms—carrion for vultures and hyenas.

I lived each day and night during these few months in fear

that Margaret and I would be caught and skewed with a spear or hacked to death with a machete. Some soldiers said they were only fighting over diamonds, but it wasn't that simple. It was true that the sale of diamonds extracted from the northern mines helped fuel the fighting. The sales aided both sides in obtaining foreign currency to finance the purchase of arms. But the rank-in-file soldiers didn't kill for this reason alone. Rather, they were young men bound by the African tradition of obeying authority. Tell an uneducated and testosterone-driven teenage boy, the most likely perpetrator, that it is his duty to kill and then give him the means—a rifle or a machete—and he'll obey!

But the death raids also took on a dimension that political mass violence just can't explain. Eliminating enemies was one thing, but why the brutal sadism, such as the dismembering of limbs, the gang-raping and disemboweling of pregnant women?

Margaret and I wandered like zombies around the country, following Tannen's forces because we couldn't think of any other possible option. There was always an immediate need to provide comfort, to bandage wounds, to scavenge food and water for the troops or their victims. Most of all, Margaret wouldn't leave Frances and I wouldn't leave Margaret. During this time, the thought of what Albert Mubarsoi had told me kept coming back into my mind, because the chaos and terrible crimes against humanity were exactly what he had promised if Tannen and the CPP continued their attempts to overthrow his government. I stayed awake many nights out of anger at my inability to convince Tannen to heed Mubarsoi's warning. But then there was another side of me that knew there was nothing I could have done. Tannen was too determined to proceed according to his plans regardless of the costs.

I further realized that the war that now raged—Islam versus Christianity, Christianity versus Islam—wasn't a religious war at all. It had little resemblance to the terrible crusades of past centuries. The violence based purportedly upon religious fervor was really fueled by warring tribal brutality. Tribal identity ran deeper than any political or religious affiliation. And now I realized that Justin Perry was right when he told me years before "you'll destroy them before you change them." That's exactly what I feared Tannen had it mind simply for the scholastic satisfaction of seeing if it could be done.

By late September 1959, any shred of idealism in the CPP soldiers had died as the indescribable savagery continued. The revolutionary zeal they had exuded just ten weeks before was now completely extinguished. Even the younger soldiers— ammunition exhausted, zeal worn out, who had earlier brandished their rifles with cockiness and bravado—now crept about with guarded, scared looks. They still carried the now worthless weapons, but the rifles no longer served as a potent phallic symbol but as a club or prop to lean against while waiting for something to happen.

As for the progress of our cause, we had surreptitiously returned to the outskirts of Grand Bassa by the end of September. The capital and port city of normally 350,000 residents was nearly devoid of human life; only empty tattered huts and surly, sickly dogs were left. Already the stench of rotting corpses had faded away after they that had been picked apart and devoured by large birds of prey.

That is what I saw as I scanned the southern rim of the capital city. The fighting up until this time had been so diffuse throughout Cape de Leone that it was unclear who was prevailing—government troops or CPP's.

Despite the heavy losses, Tannen traveled around the city's outskirts in a chauffeured driven British truck appearing ebullient, at the height of his glory. He didn't seem to be experiencing any of the same burdens of thirst, exhaustion, hunger, and fear that penetrated the bodies and spirits of CPP troops and those of us who were camp followers.

CPP troops now surrounded the outskirts of Grand Bassa. They had been there for up to three days before our arrival, not allowing anything or anybody to enter into or go out of the center of the city. Mubarsoi and several thousand government troops were holed up in Parliament House and surrounding government buildings. Tannen had given orders the night before that an attack was to be made this morning. I had been given the task of working in the area of communications. Margaret had talked to Tannen about me. As a result, his attitude had changed completely from the time he ordered me out of his office in the village of Chitcharo. I was now included in Tannen's small entourage of conspirators, leaking bits of information and strategy to the rebel commanders on an as-need-to-know basis. I would have easily fled the country and the horror of the war, except I had decided long before that I wasn't going to leave the country again without Margaret, even if it cost me my life.

The sun had just risen and there was a stillness that came over the deserted city, the same sort of stillness that precedes a violent storm. A small group, including Jeremiah Bantu, Tannen, six paramount chiefs and me, stood in front of a free standing house that served as the temporary nerve center for the rebel troops. Each of us held binoculars. We were on the southeast edge of Grand Bassa, on top of a small hill and approximately three-quarters of a mile from Parliament House. Approximately 5,000 of our troops were located in a semi-circle about a half mile in front of us. They stood, forming a long line that curved inward, three to four men deep. Tannen wore headphones and spoke into a portable telephone, exchanging information with three commanders. The three were located, respectfully, behind Parliament House, and to the west and south of the capitol building.

"Tell General Lelinka to order his men in," Tannen said calmly into the mouthpiece of his telephone.

Pause.

"Yes, I know our troops on the south flank aren't yet in place, but you're ordered to go in. Do it!" Tannen yelled.

The paramount chiefs looked on in amazement as Tannen spoke into his cordless machine. About thirty seconds later, we heard the beginning of shooting. Quickly the reverberations of shots became closer together and louder. In the distance we could see our troops moving up the back gardens of Parliament House, but the large Victorian capitol building blocked our view to most of the action that was taking place behind it. The scene was stimulating, exciting, but the action also seemed somehow surreal, like play-acting on a very large scale.

Tannen ran inside the small house behind us and emerge with two flags—a yellow one and a green one. He glanced at me angrily and threw me the flags. It had been my responsibility to have the flags in hand, but I had become so engrossed in all the activity that I had forgotten to retrieve them. "Wave the yellow one, Gene!" Tannen screamed.

I waved it in large circles and about a half-mile directly west of us, a soldier, who also held a yellow flag, then began to wave it in large circles. The signal told the troops who were positioned to the south of Parliament House to start their attack.

"Are you in yet, General Lelinka?" Tannen hollered into the telephone.

Pause.

"Don't worry about casualties!" Tannen screamed. "Don't pull back. You're getting relief from the south flank. We need your men to go forward. You understand, general?"

Suddenly several hundred government troops poured out of Parliament House. They lined themselves behind the large stone fence that stood about chest high and that ran the entire length of the capitol building. They began shooting at our troops who were positioned to the left and front of us. These troops had not yet fired a single shot or left their reclined positions. Tannen tossed me the green flag and motioned for me to stand in front of him about fifty feet. "Now, Gene!" he exclaimed.

I waved the flag up and down exuberantly and the troops, who had waited with discipline, broke lose from their ranks. They charged up the front gardens of Parliament House. Many of them didn't even have rifles but raised machetes over their heads and screamed at the top of their lungs. A rush of adrenaline raced through my body as I wished I was one of them.

"General Lelinka, where do we stand?" Tannen yelled into his telephone.

Pause.

"Excellent!" Tannen exclaimed. He turned to Jeremiah Bantu and the chiefs. "We're in, Mr. President. We're in!"

Bantu and the paramount chiefs smiled broadly. But the celebration lasted only momentarily as we saw several of our soldiers hit by ground fire before getting even half way to Parliament House. We had more men than Mubarsoi's forces, but they had superior artillery and a higher position. Tannen kept ordering the troops from all three different directions to keep fighting.

We could see the presiding officer about a half-mile from us. He stood briefly, motioned for his men to charge, but most of the soldiers simply stayed where they were. Pathetically, they were being picked off one by one by enemy fire. Our squadron that had attacked from the west emerged from Parliament House with several captured P.D.F. soldiers. The government troops held their hands behind their heads. Our soldiers held guns on them, marching the captured troops away from the center of the fighting along a stone path that curved around to one of the few paved roads in the entire city. There must have been about 100 prisoners.

"Secretary Tannen," yelled a soldier who had just run up from the squadron from the west. He was breathing hard. "Colonel Hubuto has been trying to reach you over the radio, sir. He wants to know what to do with the prisoners."

Tannen seemed annoyed, distracted. All of us looked over at the squadron that the soldier referred to. Our troops were not doing anything except pointing their guns at the captured government troops. "Sir, what do I tell Colonel Hubuto?" the messenger repeated.

"Kill them!" Tannen snarled. "Kill them all!"

The soldier looked frightened, uncomprehending.

"That's my order, soldier! Do it. And then Colonel Hubuto needs to get the hell past here to the north flank. Additional troops are needed there! Go tell him!"

The soldier saluted and then sprinted back to his squadron. We could see the face of the colonel as he received the order from his messenger. The officer's expression appeared to be one of disbelief. Tannen ran out about seventy-five feet from the house, appearing to have no fear for his own safety. He waved to grab the colonel's attention. Tannen then made a large gesture, taking his right hand and slashing it across his throat. The colonel turned around to his troops and gave the order. The CPP soldiers pointed their rifles at the heads of the prisoners and fired.

The battle, now being waged on two fronts—north and south—had deteriorated into complete chaos! Several of our troops had broken through the first line of enemy defense, but they were being fired upon from both the front and back. Tannen continued to shout commands into his telephone, but the fighting was so intense, so chaotic, that none of his orders were being followed. Suddenly mortars exploded less than 100 yards from us. The explosions shook the ground. Mubarsoi's forces were now aiming at us! Tannen was oblivious of the near misses, being so intent on the progress of the battle. We now both stood about fifty yards in front of the house. But when I glanced behind me, the six paramount chiefs were obviously frightened by the attack against us personally. They frantically started to gather their possessions and then suddenly a huge explosion hit the house behind us!

"What happened next?" Reuben asked. He implored me to continue. We had been in the air for a couple of hours since our departure from Mauritania. Fifteen minutes earlier, our jetliner had dipped to about three hundred feet above the rugged tree line. Reuben hadn't told me, but I suspected we had already entered into Cape de Leone airspace and were flying low to avoid radar detection.

"What happened, Professor?" Reuben begged to know. "I've never spoken to anyone directly involved in the battle."

"I woke up several hours after the explosion in a small house on the outskirts of Grand Bassa," I replied. "After we were hit, Tannen's chauffeur had carried Francis, me, and the lone surviving paramount chief to his truck and transported us to the house. Justin Perry and Margaret were there. They had converted the house into a makeshift hospital and were trying to care for several of the troops who survived but who were in bad shape. Jeremiah Bantu and the other chiefs had been killed in the mortar attack. Tannen and I were far enough in front of the explosion that we were knocked unconscious but not badly hurt. I lost some hearing in my left ear. Tannen had some shrapnel lodged in the back of his head and left shoulder. Perry operated on him and within a few days he was back on his feet. But the army disintegrated. Mubarsoi was still in power, although he lost as many men as we did.

"We came within a cat's whisker of toppling him. You were right about that. Tannen was furious that the CPP generals weren't able to keep the troops together when we were so close to victory. But there was too much devastation, too many casualties to keep the squadrons intact. Most of the surviving soldiers were starving and hadn't seen their families for months. Still, the cause wasn't over yet."

I next told Reuben my version of the cattle killing incident, which lead to the death knell of any hope that Tannen still had to defeat Mubarsoi.[4] Within a month of the final battle at Parliament House, many of the refugees who had fled the country started to return. But then one of the most bizarre events to ever plague the African continent began to unravel. A village chieftain by the name of Solanjoi, who had been influenced by Christianity and who called himself a prophet, pronounced that "he had been to Heaven and had talked to God." God, according

---

4 Adapted from Noel Mostert, *Frontiers, The Epic of South Africa's Creation and the Tragedy of the Xhosa People*, (New York: Alfred A. Knopf, 1992), pp. 1187-1200.

to Solanjoi, was extremely angry with the Leoneon people, the civil war, and all the killing. He demanded a sacrifice of the largest dimension to atone for the spilling of so much blood and to remove the sin that had crippled the country.

If Solanjoi had been the only soothsayer, then perhaps even the highly superstitious natives would have dismissed the self-appointed "prophet of God" as delusional, a charlatan. But then several other "prophets" from throughout the country—most notably another chieftain from a larger tribe—declared that God had spoken to them as well. The respected chieftain said that God told him that the people were guilty of great sin. That in order to atone for their wickedness, they must slaughter all their cattle and destroy their crops. Only then would God forgive them.

The chieftain traveled throughout Cape de Leone and preached that the survivors of the great civil war must kill their cattle and destroy their crops in order to save themselves, restore the nation to order, and to be free of sin. If these prophecies were followed, the chieftain proclaimed, prosperity and abundance of food would spring forth—God's way of demonstrating His forgiveness of the Leoneon people.

At this time drought continued mercilessly! It hadn't rained in more than a year, during the entire civil war and now past the end of the fighting. Lakes and watering holes had dried up; animals had died of thirst trudging to river beds that were cracked and desolate. The land had become scorched, barren, devoid of life. Picked over carcasses of rhinos, antelopes, and other animals were found along dusty, cracked paths. Between thirty and forty percent of all the cattle, the primary measure of wealth and means of sustenance, had already died during the drought. Peasants themselves were dying of the long-term effects of the war and the terrible heat and endless days and nights of no rain.

The people became desperate, searching for anything that would provide relief to their suffering! And out of their suffering, even those who had previously been unbelievers in these visions began to embrace the prophecies. They started killing their cattle and destroying what little grain still existed in hopes of ending their misery. The mass slaughter of cattle, the frenzy for survival, rose to a crescendo at the new moon which began in early November 1959. For days throughout the country, the people destroyed thousands of cattle. By the end of November more than 500,000 cattle—nearly the entire remaining herds—had been destroyed. But the drought continued! And death by starvation followed.

From October to December, Margaret and I went from village to village to try to lessen the suffering. We advised the villagers not to kill their cattle or if they did, to eat them quickly so as to not let the meat spoil. But our efforts seemed futile. We had little to offer and had become so weak ourselves from not having sufficient food, water, and rest, that we risked our own survival by continuing.

We had last seen Tannen in the village of Ciskei. He was still determined to reorganize an army to challenge Mubarsoi. I had pleaded with Margaret for weeks for us to flee Cape de Leone. I told her my own life was in her hands. After repeatedly resisting my pleas, she finally agreed one morning to my plan for escape.

We traveled northeast by foot for a day and a half towards Cape de Leone's eastern boarder with Guinea. We finally came across a small village that had formerly been home to a British trading company. I believed that nothing more could shock us, but when we arrived I found I was wrong. There in the center of the dusty village, we found approximately twenty-five natives alive but within hours of death. It was as though we had stepped into Hell itself!

The villagers sat in the center of the ghost-town beneath the shade of large palm trees. They looked like nothing more than shadows of human forms. Flies swarmed over their faces and sores covered their bodies. As we walked up to the natives, they remained immobile—angles of bones and skin weighed down to the dusty, orange soil by starvation and disease. Black, motionless eyes, recessed into gaunt faces, starred at us.

Margaret and I moved from one poor suffering soul to another. We had nothing more than a prayer to offer. Margaret looked up at me and whispered, "I can't go on, Gene. It's too far to the border and there's no guarantee that we can make it. I want to go back. I want to find Francis."

"We have no other choice but to go on," I replied. "Can't you see? If we don't get out of the country, we'll end up just like them."

Margaret shook her head. "I want to go back, Gene! If you must go on, I understand, but I can't. Not without Francis!"

I had feared that she might change her mind. Now it had happened. It was risky if we continued our escape attempt across the border because we weren't certain what we would find; it was risky if we tried to return to Grand Bassa. Either way starvation or being murdered was a high probability.

But go back we must. I simply couldn't leave her. If I'd been married to Margaret, I couldn't have been bound to her with any tighter cords. We left the villagers much as we found them—suffering ghost-like underneath the grove of palm trees. We left feeling totally deflated, realizing we could do nothing if we stayed but watch each die one by one. We then headed back towards Grand Bassa. It took us the better part of two days to reach the outskirts of the city. The evening of the second day we finally found the house that had been converted into a makeshift hospital where Tannen and I had been taken after we were injured. We forced our way through one of the side windows that had been boarded up. We began to forage for anything to eat. We were near the point of starvation.

Remarkably we found some canned food in the back of a kitchen cupboard. We ate right out of the cans, neither of us saying anything to the other. When I finally looked up at Margaret, I now saw dark circles around her eyes, hair that had not been washed for weeks, skin that had been tarnished by a scorching sun and blowing dust—harsh conditions that had all worked to diminish her physical beauty. But I loved Margaret more at this very moment than I could ever recall before.

We immediately collapsed from exhaustion. Margaret slept in the bedroom and I fell asleep on a cot in the main room. I'm not sure how long we were asleep, but I heard a knock and then a voice called my name. I walked to the door and cracked it opened. A young African soldier stood holding a rifle in his left hand.

"Colonel Kawachi sent me, sir. I've come to tell you that you're in danger. There's fighting going on in this area. Also, sir, Colonel Kawachi told me to tell you that Secretary Tannen has been killed. He said you would want to know."

Margaret came to the door before I could stop her. "What did you say, soldier?" Margaret asked, standing beside me.

"Secretary Tannen was killed this afternoon, madam. A truck he was in was ambushed. Everyone in the truck was killed. Colonel Kawachi wanted me to tell you. It's not safe for you to stay here. P.D.F. troops are patrolling the area. You must leave."

Margaret slumped to her knees, covering her face with her hands. I kneeled beside her and tried to shut the door, but the young soldier stuck his foot and leg in the doorway to prevent me from closing it.

Through the doorway, he scooted his rifle and pulled out a handgun from a holster fastened to his army belt. "These are for you," he said. "Please, Mr. O'Connor. Leave while you still can. There's no one left to protect you. You're in great danger."

The soldier then stepped back and vanished into the darkness. I turned back to Margaret and she was still on her knees, now sobbing. A sudden, unexpected cool air blew through the doorway. The night sky was pitch dark and thunder rumbled in the distance. The wind picked up and it felt like it was going to rain.

Twenty Eight

"" A fter you learned that Tannen had been killed, how were you captured, Professor?" Reuben asked. "Margaret and you were expelled, so obviously that meant you had to be captured by Mubarsoi's troops."

We were still flying over the northern part of Cape de Leone when Reuben asked this question. I was just about to tell Reuben what really happened, but it occurred to me that he didn't know the truth about Tannen's death, so I lied to protect Margaret, whoever she was to him–aunt? mother? None of it seemed to matter in this bizarre, out of control situation.

"Yes, Nigel. In fact, we were captured almost immediately after learning of Tannen's death."

But the events of what truly occurred flashed through my mind like lightening.

That night, after we had been told that Tannen had been killed, I carried Margaret into the bedroom and laid her on the bed. Despite the young African soldier's warnings, she was in no condition to flee. I returned to the main room and sat next to the table where I placed the rifle and handgun we had been given. I was too afraid to sleep myself, too afraid that we might be attacked by P.F.D. troops at any moment. I could hear Margaret weeping in the bedroom and later went to try and comfort her. I don't believe she ever fell asleep and morning seemed like an eternity in coming.

At daylight, I got up and went outside and urinated. The air was already hot and sticky. Despite thunderous threats the night before, it still hadn't rained. When I returned to the house I began to search through the cupboards for any food that we might have missed the night before. I found none, but instead came across an old battery operated radio and turned it on. The radio was tuned to the government's station, which was then the only station that still broadcast in the country. The BBC had stopped operations several months before when it decided it was too dangerous to keep its staff in Grand Bassa. The crackling broadcast was on for no more than a few minutes when a news analyst came on with a bulletin that Frances Tannen and four rebel soldiers had been killed the day before. It would surely end the civil war, the reporter said. Out of the corner of my eye, I saw Margaret enter the room. Her face was flushed and I could tell she had overheard the broadcast.

"We need to find out where they have Francis," she said. "I want to make sure he receives a proper burial."

I turned off the radio and went to her. "That's impossible, Margaret. If we try to locate Francis' body, we might as well just turn ourselves in and be killed, too. You're blinded by grief. Don't you see? We have to find a way out of the country as soon as possible."

Margaret didn't argue, but walked to the table and plopped down on a chair, looking up with puffy eyes that had dark circles around them. She looked ghastly.

I unfolded a tattered map of Cape de Leone that I had carried and laid it out on the table. "I figure we can either go northeast," I said, tracing the route on the map with my right index finger, "back the way we came two days ago, and try to enter Guinea, or else we can go north, northwest along the coast into Senegal. That's more direct, but it's probably more dangerous, too, traveling along the coastline."

Margaret appeared distracted and uninterested. She raked her fingers through her disheveled hair. "Whatever you think is best, Gene. It doesn't matter to me."

Suddenly the front door was kicked open and two CPP soldiers bolted in with machine guns pointed at us.

"Are you alone?" asked one in broken English.

Margaret and I stood stunned, immobile, speechless.

"Are you alone?" the soldier screamed.

I nodded, but the other soldier ran to the bedroom and banged the door open. He quickly scoured the rest of the small house and returned. Then both soldiers dropped their machine guns to their sides and scooted backwards, exiting the house.

Before Margaret and I had even a moment to grasp what was happening, the front door flung open again and a man walked in wearing a witch doctor's mask. He pulled it off and, to our mutual amazement, it was Francis Tannen! We just stood there stunned. Margaret ran to Francis and threw her arms around him and jabbered. But he was impatient. Francis didn't have time to hear Margaret expound about how upset she'd been to hear the news of his reported death.

"Where have you two been?" Tannen exclaimed.

"We tried to find a way out of the country," I answered. "We're all going to die if we don't get out immediately. There's already been a report that you were killed in an ambush. We got news of it last night from a CPP soldier and then we just heard it again on a radio broadcast a few minutes ago. Surely you're aware of it."

"Aware of it?" the priest retorted. "Hell, yes, I'm aware of it! I concocted the story and had it planted. I want it reported as widely as possible to all the tribes and villages. But I had no way of letting you know."

"But why would you do such a thing, Francis?" Margaret asked.

"To mislead Mubarsoi, right?" I answered. "To make Mubarsoi think you're dead so you can hit him with a surprise attack. At the very moment he thinks you're completely out of the picture, he'll let his defenses totally down. Then you're going to blind side him. That's it, isn't it, Francis?"

"Good guess, Eugene," Tannen replied, "but wrong! No, the next time I go up against Mubarsoi he'll know that I'm very much alive. I want him to know who and what has smothered him."

"Then why the hoax, Francis?" Margaret implored.

"Because Margaret," he said, "I'm counting on your teaching of the Scriptures to be our salvation! In two days there will be a large rally of tribes supportive of the CPP in Chitcharo. They will believe they're coming to honor the great fallen leader Francis Tannen, spiritual guru of the CPP who has given his life so that they may be free of the tyrannical Mubarsoi. It will be reported that my body was stolen from Mubarsoi's forces and that I'm to be buried in a cemetery for CPP heroes. I'll be carried in a casket into the center of the ceremony and mourners will be encouraged to walk by the open coffin. There will be wailing and the display of anger over the death of their great rebel leader. But then miraculously who will rise from the dead?"

"The resurrection," I answered. "What genius! The resurrection of Francis Tannen, who will lead them in a new assault on Mubarsoi!"

"Precisely, Eugene, just as Christ rose on the third day after death to fulfill the prophecy of the Scriptures, so shall the fallen leader Francis Tannen!"

"But what's the purpose, Francis?" Margaret pleaded. "Why go through this charade to trick the natives into believing something that's not true? It's blasphemous!"

"Because Margaret, after this the tribes will never question my authority again. Do you understand? If I tell them to fight until death, they'll fight until death! Mubarsoi may have won a few rounds, but the war is ours!"

"But think of all the killing, Francis!" Margaret exclaimed. "Isn't a half million lives enough for you? Isn't destroying a nation sufficient? What's it for? What's the purpose?"

Margaret was becoming hysterical, and for the first time I saw concern in Tannen's eyes. He tried to console her.

"We can't let the people suffer any more under Mubarsoi's rule, Margaret. Can't you see? This is the opportunity to finally bring peace to the tribes, to preach fully the gospel without threat of persecution and suffering."

"Without suffering?" Margaret begged. "You want to stop their suffering by waging more battles against Mubarsoi? My God, Francis, have you actually visited the villages? The natives are dying of starvation, disease, lack of medicine. And you're going to bring peace? You're going to fulfill the Gospels by continuing this inane war? Oh, my God, Francis! You've lost your mind!"

Margaret stepped back and looked down on the table. She seized the hand gun and pointed it at Tannen. He started to walk toward her.

"Get back, Francis!" she yelled. "The killing has got to stop! You can't just manipulate other people's lives like this!"

But he kept moving forward and suddenly the revolver went off. The shot cleared Tannen's head. The priest grinned as if nothing had happened. He continued inching forward.

"Please give me the gun, Margaret," he said. "Just hand it over to me."

But the gun went off again, the shot striking Tannen in his left shoulder, jerking him back half a step. The gunshot wound didn't stop him, and he smiled at Margaret until he doubled over at the waist and his right arm clenched his shoulder. Blood spurted out of his mouth and he tried to say something. Tannen fell on the bamboo floor. Margaret and I dropped down and knelt beside him. And then a most remarkable thing occurred. Suddenly Tannen turned black all over! He had apparently suffered a heart attack. His blood had rushed to the surface of his skin and he became a deep bruised color. He groaned a couple of times and then stopped breathing.

"Margaret," I shouted, grabbing her by the hand, "we have to run!"

But she wouldn't leave Francis. I tried to pull her away, but she fell to the floor and placed her arms around his neck. She laid her face against his and started calling his name time and time again, begging Francis to wake up, to forgive her. I couldn't pull her away!

By that time the soldiers protecting Tannen had rushed in from outside. We never had a chance to escape. They were on top of us almost immediately. I quickly grabbed the pistol from the floor and blurted that I had shot Tannen. One of the soldiers swung at me with the butt of his rifle, striking my face. I was flattened and didn't come to until we were intercepted by P.D.F. soldiers later that day and jailed again in the basement of Parliament House.

I had no more than completed this last thought, none of which had been shared with Reuben, than we landed at a small paved air strip cut out in the middle of a forest. We had been flying so low for so long that the sudden descent and landing caught me totally by surprise.

Our two traveling companions, Thombi Smith and Karim Jones, walked in front of us, carrying our luggage. They threw our bags into the trunk of a Mercedez-Benz sedan. An identical second car was parked in front of the Mercedez-Benz and two men, apparently drivers, stood beside each vehicle. As Reuben and I approached the drivers, they first saluted Reuben and then, as we reached them, they in turn hugged him, conveying an odd sense of having both an official regard for my host as well as one based on friendship. Perhaps now my questions would finally be answered. Behind us, the small jetliner quickly flew off. Reuben and I sat in the back seat of the first vehicle.

"How far are we from Grand Bassa?" I asked.

"About twenty miles."

"But why here?"

"It eliminates any problems," answered Reuben. "That's all. It's just simpler."

"Is Margaret in Grand Bassa?"

"Yes." He looked out the side window, but said nothing more. The sun was setting but in this part of the country there were no long shadows; we were in a valley and light simply peeked out from the rim of the surrounding hills. Reuben glanced at me, yawned, and scooted down in his seat.

"You never finished your story, Professor. How did you get caught by Mubarsoi's forces?"

It was obvious that Reuben didn't want to answer any more questions. But the landing, actually being in the country, caused me to have more faith in his own accounts. The anticipation of seeing Margaret again stirred me, causing me to share the balance of my story after we had been taken back to Grand Bassa.

"Nigel, we were captured by P.D.F. forces," I said. "I was beaten and transported to a jail cell in the basement of Parliament House again, but I didn't know what they had done with Margaret. When I woke the next morning, I was taken to a large room also in the basement of the Parliament building where there was a huge curtain draped across one end of the room. I was placed on a chair at the opposite end of the room. Bursting through the door, Mubarsoi came up to me. And from there I shared with Reuben the conversation that took place between the dictator and me.

"So we meet again, Mr. O'Connor," Mubarsoi said. "I had so hoped this wouldn't happen, but when men are resigned to follow their own desires, they unfortunately must be willing to suffer the consequences. It's a pity you didn't take my advice several months ago."

Mubarsoi sighed, looked down and then nodded to a guard that had accompanied him. The guard pulled me up from the chair and struck me in the abdomen with his club. I doubled over in pain and fell to my knees. The guard pulled me up again, forcing me to stand. Mubarsoi pinched me hard on the cheek.

"And now the question is, what do I do with you, Mr. O'Connor? After you and your colleagues have destroyed my country, what is the fitting retribution? An eye for an eye as your Bible commands? One life for the million your cause has taken? That doesn't seem quite equitable, does it, sir?"

Mubarsoi nodded again to the large, burly guard who flailed the club into my stomach a second time. The blow forced out all the air in my abdomen and I gasped and fell again to the hard cement floor. The guard pulled me up and steadied me on my feet. Mubarsoi motioned for another guard to open the large curtain at the end of the room. And what I saw next has haunted me ever since: there were Margaret and Justin Perry swinging from the ends of ropes. Toppled chairs lay beneath them. A third empty noose above an upright chair was to the right of Margaret's dangling body. Of course, I assumed quickly that it was intended for me. The curtain closed and then the guard closest to Mubarsoi struck me in the head and I fell to the floor, too beaten and weak to get up on my own.

Mubarsoi crouched, put his hand on my shoulder, and spoke very deliberative. "Mr. O'Connor, some must suffer death, like Dr. Perry, because of the sin of greed. Others, like Miss Mahoney, because of misguided loyalty. What is your failing, sir? For what must you die for? Failure to heed wise counsel?"

"But Margaret, Perry, they both—" Reuben interrupted.

"I was certain they were dead, Nigel," I said, stopping him in mid-sentence. "When you told me otherwise back at the university, I didn't believe you because I had seen them with my own eyes dangling from nooses.

"Mubarsoi's guards took me back to my cell," I continued. "And then later that night they transported me to a ship docked at the wharf. I was certain they were going to shoot me and dump me in the ocean. But they carried me by a stretcher onto the ship and placed me in a small cabin. And then to my amazement, after they threatened me if I tried to leave, they left me alone! I kept thinking the guards would return and beat me again or torture me, but they never returned. So it wasn't Justin Perry and Margaret I saw?"

"Oh, it was them all right. Margaret told me they had to pretend to be dead in order to convince you. Somehow Perry and she had been suspended by shoulder harnesses under their clothes to make it look like they were hung. It was a deal they struck with Mubarsoi in order that you would be freed."

"So I could be freed! But why?" I begged. "Why didn't Mubarsoi just kill all three of us? What good were we to him alive?"

"I don't know for certain," answered Reuben, "but I have some theories. One is that if Perry and Margaret had actually been killed, the British would have intervened in Cape de Leone, very possibly militarily. As you know yourself, Perry had several influential friends in the British government. Also, Margaret was still the wife of my uncle, Derrick Reuben. I don't know if Mubarsoi realized the significance of it, but my uncle still had considerable power and connections in Dublin and London. Killing Margaret would have brought even more pressure to do something militarily in Cape de Leone.

"Another theory," continued Reuben, "is that if you three were killed along with Tannen, you would have been considered martyrs. It might have caused the tribes to rally again and clearly Mubarsoi didn't want that.

"In any event," Reuben continued, "Perry was deported back to England. He eventually returned to Africa and settled in Rhodesia. He married a Dutch woman and survived the country's political change over to Black rule in 1980. He died just two years ago."

"And Margaret was sent to the monastery in Spain?"

Reuben nodded. "She remained there for the next thirty years."

I glanced outside the back seat window and saw we were now driving on a paved road towards Grand Bassa. Small bungalows dotted the roadside. We were entering into a populated area.

"I've arranged a hotel room for you for the night, Professor," Reuben said. "It's nothing luxurious, but you should find it suitable."

"But when do I see Margaret?" I asked.

"It's been a very long trip, Professor. You need to get some rest and I'll pick you up in the morning."

"No," I replied. "I want to see Margaret tonight. You've said all along how sick she is. I don't want to squander any more time."

Reuben appeared peeved by my insistence but said nothing. We traveled on. As we came to the outskirts of Grand Bassa, I thought I recognized some of the buildings and surroundings. It gave me an eerie feeling. When I looked up, I saw a billboard. It was a huge profile of Albert Mubarsoi, illuminated by ground lights. It was obviously an old picture because he looked about the same age as when I had met him in the late 1950s. The billboard had a simple, pedestrian message: "Vote for President Mubarsoi, our Nation's Leader!"

We drove another mile into the center of Grand Bassa. A few street lamps cast dim lights along the roadway. The downtown area reminded me of the drab environs of a city in a communist country. Soldiers with machine guns patrolled the square containing Parliament House.

"With the elections Sunday, there's extra security," Reuben said.

Our car stopped on a side street in front of a small hotel. "We're here, *Mr. Engels*," Reuben announced.

We got out of the back seat and Smith also emerged from the car behind us. He carried my one piece of luggage and we went into the hotel. Reuben took care of checking me in and then he turned to me, handing me a key and a scrap of paper with scribbling on it.

"If I'm needed, you can reach me at this number. Otherwise, I'll see you at 9:00 in the morning."

"And that's when I'll see Margaret?"

Reuben nodded. He then shook my hand and said, "Mr. Engels, please keep your official passport on you at all times. You'll notice it's properly stamped, verifying your entry into the country. Also, I recommend you stay in the hotel tonight. It's not safe outside. Too many soldiers wanting to ask too many questions. There's room service available."

Reuben then left and a bellhop escorted me to my room. There appeared to be few other guests in the small, European-style hotel that had peeling wall paper and worn, thread-bare carpet. It was obvious that at a much earlier time the hotel had been an up-scale, elite British establishment, but through neglect and normal wear and tear it had become shabby. My room was located on the second floor and looked out at a very uninteresting brick wall. I unpacked my suitcase, brushed my teeth, and fell into bed. I was sure that I would quickly fall asleep, but out of no where the remainder of my story, which I had been unable to complete while with Reuben, flooded uncontrollably out of my mind.

My presence on board of the ocean liner in late December 1959 was simply a conundrum. I stayed in my room for a day, nursing my injuries the best I could, afraid to death to leave the small compartment. At this time I was also trying to deal with the emotional and physical trauma of my last encounter with Mubarsoi. I had nightmares of seeing Perry and Margaret swinging at the ends of ropes. I was afraid to sleep, knowing that the ghoulish visions would come back to prey on me if I did. I was numb, in shock, a zombie.

Why should I be spared, I kept asking? Why should Margaret be put to death, when I was as guilty as her of Christian proselytizing? Why only her and Perry when I had furthered the war efforts through my own union with Tannen and the CPP? Or had I, in my effort to protect Margaret by saying that I had killed Tannen, inadvertently only saved myself?

When we arrived in New York, I couldn't think of what else to do except to take a bus back to Indiana. Uncle Paul and Aunt Betty were ecstatic to see me, but my return offered me little consolation. I tried to tell them what had happened, but it soon became clear to me that it was impossible for them to understand what I had been through. For more than a month I merely survived at Blessed Acres and did little of nothing. Every time I tried to read, my mind reverted to the last time I saw Margaret alive. Every time I sat down to lunch or dinner, all I could remember is when Margaret and I scrounged for food our last night together. Every time I went for a walk, all I could recall were the evening saunters Margaret and I would take in the village of Burguna. I couldn't get her out of my mind!

Fortunately, in the spring of 1960 something happened that, in many ways, became my salvation. The new editor of *The Prophet* called me up and said that he had heard I was back in town. He asked if I would write about my experiences in Cape de Leone for the newspaper. I first refused, but he was insistent. And so I wrote a series of articles about my time in West Africa. Later I received a telephone call from a regional editor of *The Cincinnati Enquirer*. He said that the wife of a college friend had sent the articles to him. He wanted to reprint them verbatim for the *Enquirer*. Soon after his newspaper hired me to write a series of articles about Mexican migrants who were seasonally employed in eastern Indiana. From there I traveled to South Florida to write about the flood of Cubans who had relocated in the Miami area after Fidel Castro had overthrown the dictator Fulgencio Batista. And then came the chance to travel to Chile and write about the killing of several Americans that the U.S. State Department had taken little interest in.

From then on, one opportunity to report on intrigues followed another. From 1961 to 1985, I traveled throughout much of the world on assignment for *The Cincinnati Enquirer* and later *The Chicago Sun-Times*. In tiny countries I covered coups by illiterate, but power hungry despots. The traveling and writing clearly beat a job at the Lisbon Glass Works or farming Blessed Acres, so I took assignment after assignment.

My travels also took on a personal significance because I continually remembered Margaret's story about her own decision to leave Ireland after her brief encounter with God. I longed for that same Road to Damascus revelation. Its constant anticipation had kept Margaret in my thoughts even after believing, for thirty years, that she was dead. But now I had even more to hope for, because in the morning I would see Margaret herself! That comfort was more than enough to allow me to fall asleep.

Twenty Nine

The next morning Karim Jones and I left the hotel and climbed into a silver Mercedez-Benz parked in front. Thombi Smith sped us away. The heat was already suffocating, prompting me to remove my suit coat and unloosen my tie and shirt collar. Strewn garbage and open sewers lined the streets; terrible smells of decay and human waste stung my nostrils.

Smith drove us down side streets full of open markets and roaming natives and I couldn't get over how shabby the city looked. We finally arrived at a shop that appeared to be a general store. A large, hand painted sign hung over the entrance door: **"GRAND BASSA BUSINESS & HOUSEHOLD SUPPLIES," Askia Muhammad, Proprietor."**

I looked up the street and saw we were only about a half block from Parliament House. Even in the unbearable heat, soldiers dressed in green khaki uniforms paraded in front of the capitol building with machines guns slung across their shoulders. Jones opened the front door to the shop and gestured for me to enter.

"Please wait inside, sir. Mr. Muhammad and Mr. Reuben will be with you shortly."

Jones and Smith then followed me in and disappeared through a flap of tarp-like material that separated the front of the store from the back. I scanned the cluttered shop and saw a hodgepodge of new and used business and household supplies: typewriters, adding machines, vacuum sweepers, dishes, desks, chairs. There were also dozens of other items, including sculptures, figurines, and canvas paintings of all sizes and shapes.

"Mr. Engels," said a deep, unfamiliar voice from behind me.

"How pleased I am that you've come to our small, backward country."

I turned around and noticed a slender, but distinguished-looking man with a closely cropped beard. He obviously was Arab. He extended his hand. "My name is Askia Muhammad. It's a pleasure to meet you. You do honor to my humble establishment."

"It's good to meet you, Mr. Muhammad," I replied, shaking his hand. "I understand you're interested in my kitchen ware."

Muhammad's face brightened and he smiled. "Indeed, Engels' kitchen products have an excellent reputation. They should sell well here, Mr. Engels, *especially under the right political regime*," he added, winking his right eye. "Can I get you some tea, Mr. Engels?"

"Yes," I replied. "And would you have any bread or something to eat. I'm afraid I over slept this morning and missed breakfast."

"Of course, Mr. Engels. I'll arrange for something immediately. Mr. Muhammad led me through the flap that opened to the back of his shop. We navigated through a room that contained dozens of business machines and household appliances setting on tables and on the floor. We then went through a side door and entered into a magnificent room.

"I'll leave you here alone for now, Mr. O'Connor," Muhammad said, winking again at me. "Mr. Reuben should be here any time. He's been waiting for you."

I walked over to a large table located in the center of the room and sat down. Placed on the table top was a large, thick leather bound binder. I opened it and on the inside cover of the binder read in hand printed letters, "La Propiedad de Margaret Mahoney Reuben, Convento de Sante Theresa, Cordoba, Espana."

The first document I came to was simply a copy of a newspaper, the *Grand Bassa Times*. It was dated 2 April, 1989, just five weeks before. I unfolded it and to my amazement there was a picture on the top of the front page that included Reuben, Albert Mubarsoi, and a small girl! Underneath the picture read a caption: "President Albert Mubarsoi and Social Services Secretary Robert Peters receive flowers from village girl in appreciation for new health clinic."

There was a brief article underneath the caption and it, too, referred to the man in the picture with Mubarsoi as Robert Peters, not as Nigel Reuben. I put the newspaper down and there I found another newspaper article. This one also contained a picture of Reuben, a formal pose. The caption underneath the photo read: "President Mubarsoi Names English Diplomat to Cabinet."

I quickly scanned the clipping. It was dated 25 March, 1987. It was about Mubarsoi naming a "Robert Peters," a long-time British diplomatic officer, to the post of Secretary of Social Services. The article cited Peters as being one of Great Britain's most distinguished civil servants. It went on to say that Peter's appointment came about at the urging of Great Britain's Prime Minister Margaret Thatcher. I vaguely recalled reading about the unusual arrangement two years before.

I turned the first page of the large binder and there to my even greater astonishment was an article I had written back in 1961 for *The Cincinnati Enquirer*. I quickly turned the remaining pages and found probably more than fifty clipped stories I had written for one newspaper or another.

"I'm glad you could join us this morning, Professor," I heard a voice say from the edge of the room. "I hope you're feeling rested."

I looked up. It was Nigel Reuben, or was it Robert Peters? He smiled and looked down at the binder I was holding.

"I see where you've found Margaret's scrapbook of your work," the man added. "You've undoubtedly also seen the newspaper clippings about me. I suppose you must be wondering about them."

I was in mild shock.

"Margaret had to know I was alive if she kept copies of my articles," I replied.

"Oh, yes, there's no question of that, Professor."

The man I had assumed all this time was Reuben walked closer towards me.

"But why have you kept so much from me, Mr. Reuben?" I exclaimed. "Or is it Robert Peters?" I picked up the paper, unfolded it to reveal the picture of Mubarsoi and him, and then threw it on the table as though an attorney tossing down his final piece of evidence before a jury. "Is this a mistake? A joke? Tell me now, Mr. Peters, if that's who you really are! Why have you lied to me repeatedly from the first time we met on Monday? Why would you be associated with President Mubarsoi and then bring me back under false pretenses knowing the history between us two?"

I grabbed Peters by the collar, but a voice came from the main entrance to the room.

"Hold it, Mr. O'Connor! I'm the one who should answer you, not Secretary Peters."

A stranger with terrible facial scars appeared in the doorway. He looked to be in his fifties. He walked quickly to where Peters and I were standing and separated us. The stranger looked at me squarely in the eyes.

"I had hoped we might have a leisurely lunch where I could attempt to explain everything, Professor O'Connor. But your reporter's curiosity has gotten the best of you. Please sit down."

The stranger put his right hand forward to shake mine. "My name is Nigel Reuben," he continued. "I'm Margaret Reuben's son. You knew her as Margaret Mahoney."

"Then you are Robert Peters," I exclaimed, turning to my traveling companion for the past two days.

"Yes, Professor," he answered. "I apologize for the deception, but you'll understand now why it was necessary."

The real Reuben spoke next. "Secretary Peters is the Minister of Social Services here in Cape de Leone, Professor. More importantly, he is a close confident of President Albert Mubarsoi. You're well aware of Mubarsoi, Mr. O'Connor? The most devious, most evil dictator in Sub-Sahara Africa!"

"Yes, of course," I answered.

"But if we're successful," the newly revealed Nigel Reuben said, "we'll soon have a new Acting President of Cape de Leone."

I felt totally confused. Both men looked at me and smiled. Reuben then pulled out a picture from his wallet and addressed me.

"Professor O'Connor, this is a photograph of my mother and me. I know it's been thirty years since you've seen her, but trust me, it's her. This is when she visited me when I was a student at Oxford in 1958."

I examined the picture. It was indeed a photograph of Margaret, at about the time I knew her. She had her arm around the shoulder of a young man who looked to be in his late teens, perhaps early twenties.

"Yes, this is Margaret," I said looking up. "But is this you, Mr. Reuben? I mean—" I stopped in mid-sentence, unable to finish.

"You mean my scars, Professor? Surely you can see beyond the scars. A man's life sooner or later shows up on his face. Mine just happens to now be disfigured. But the condition of my face is part of the reason why we wanted you here so badly—for you to see for yourself the thirty-five years of horrible scars that Albert Mubarsoi has imposed on this country by his rule."

"Professor," interjected Peters. "I came here to Cape de Leone two years ago at the direct request of Prime Minister Thatcher. Then, as now, the country was in desperate straits. President Mubarsoi only accepted me because the Thatcher government offered fifty million pounds in direct humanitarian aid if I was given a position in his cabinet to oversee how it was used. Mubarsoi was desperate for foreign support. He needed it to try and avoid a civil war that's been brewing for several years. You're familiar with the facts. We've talked about them ever since we met on Monday."

"Yes," I said. "I know he's been barely able to hold on. But that's why I was so surprised when Mubarsoi called for an election several weeks ago. He's as vulnerable now as ever. Surely he can see this."

"But the election, if it goes forward, can only help him, Professor," said Reuben.

Peters nodded. "That's exactly right. It's all a front. Mubarsoi is merely holding the elections to get England to pay the balance of aid that it offered under the original agreement. Great Britain gave twenty-five million pounds to Mubarsoi's government in 1987 when he first appointed me as Social Services Secretary. It promised to give the balance when he held elections. He's held off as long as he can, but now things are so bad that he has to have the aid. Government employees haven't been paid in six months and there's terrible starvation going on in the interior part of the country. Nearly fifty percent of adults are unemployed and teenage gangs are going around defacing buildings and looting stores just because they have nothing better to do. The nation is going to implode soon if something isn't done.

"So Mubarsoi agreed to hold the elections on Sunday, but there's little risk to him," Peters continued. "He'll win in a landslide. There's no possibility that Josiah Kimba can defeat him. Kimba has been in hiding the past two months, afraid that government troops will kill him if he openly campaigns. And so are the people. The only ones who will vote will be the few villagers who support Mubarsoi. Everyone else will be intimidated into staying home."

"But surely the Thatcher administration isn't going to give Mubarsoi more aid just because he wins a sham election," I exclaimed.

"We're not certain of that, Professor," said Peters. "I've kept my superiors in London informed of what's happening and they're very leery of giving Mubarsoi anything. But that's a decision that's still to be made depending upon what happens in the next few days. And when it is made, it will probably be decided at the highest level. My government might still give aid simply to try and avoid a full-scale civil war. Such an outbreak could destabilize the entire region, including Liberia under Samuel Doe's government."

"And whether England gives the money or not," added Reuben, "that still doesn't get rid of Mubarsoi. Even if he does step down, his son is ready to replace him. Albert Mubarsoi is an old man. We could possibly wait until he dies in office if we absolutely had to, but with Angel Mubarsoi waiting in the wings to take over from his father, that's totally unacceptable. We have to get rid of the entire family for this country to ever heal itself."

"But how do I fit into this plan, gentlemen?" I asked. "Why would you spend your time to bring me here to tell me all this? I've come to see Margaret. I can't do anything about what you're talking about."

"But you can, Professor," Reuben replied. "You can play a critical role in two ways. First, we need the support of the U.S. Government and other foreign nations. We need others to know what Mubarsoi has done to brutalize this nation, how he's stolen it blind! We have proof of the monies he's skimmed from the treasury and placed into his own private foreign accounts. Sadly, the corruption here is worse than in all of Africa, but no one seems to care much.

"Professor," Reuben continued, "the nation remains the poorest in the world. We're not just talking about the poorest in West Africa. In terms of infant mortality, life spans, health care, education—by any measure, Cape de Leone is at the bottom of the pile."

"Even if I agree with everything you've just told me, what can I do?" I pleaded.

Reuben picked up the large binder and flipped through the pages of my articles.

"We need someone to tell the world of what's happening here, Professor! We need a highly respected, Pulitzer prize-winning writer to document what we know to be true and to justify a temporary government until legitimate elections can be held. Can't you see how desperate we are to get our story told? We pleaded with the U.N. to send observers to monitor the election scheduled for Sunday. And what did we receive by way of a reply? A response from the Commission on Human Rights saying it was sorry but that it didn't have the funds to send a team of observers.

"We've had members of Amnesty International document the human rights abuses. We've begged the Red Cross and other relief organizations to come and see for themselves. But we're still not getting our message out. You could play a critical role. You're the only leader left of a coup that nearly defeated Mubarsoi thirty years ago. If you stay to help us now, can't you see the possibility for world wide attention you could bring to our plight?"

I rose from my seat and started to pace along one end of the room. A thousand thoughts ran through my mind.

"I appreciate the confidence you've expressed in me," I replied. "But gentlemen, you're grossly overestimating what I could accomplish even if I accept your challenge. Besides, you keep referring to ousting Mubarsoi. What do you mean by this? What specific plans do you have to remove him?"

Reuben and Peters exchanged guarded looks. Reuben then cleared his throat.

"At nine o'clock Friday morning, Professor, two days before the election, Secretary Peters and five other members of Mubarsoi's cabinet, all Leone natives and sympathetic to our cause, will meet personally with President Mubarsoi and demand his resignation."

I couldn't help myself and laughed. "Excuse me, Mr. Reuben, but what happens at 9:15 a.m. after Mr. Peters and these five Cabinet officers have been lined up and shot? Do you have a plan for that?"

"Not exactly, Professor, because we believe we will be successful. The British government and a number of other Commonwealth nations are going to denounce the election today for what it is, a total sham. Beyond that, President Mubarsoi will be told that unless he resigns, that within twenty-four hours a British naval battalion will enter Grand Bassa to wipe him and his family completely off of the face of the earth. A small fleet of British ships left three days ago from England to come to Cape de Leone. They will be anchored off of the coast Friday morning when Mubarsoi is approached. It will be easy for him to verify the existence of this small armada."

"And if he does resign, then what happens?" I asked. "Are you just going to let Mubarsoi walk away, no trial for his crimes, no attempts to recover the millions you've said he's stolen for himself?"

"That's exactly right," replied Peters. "We believe there is more than enough evidence to try him for crimes against his own country, but that would merely prolong the suffering that is going on here. In fact, we're willing to let him fly out of Cape de Leone untouched in his own private jet. My government has already negotiated a deal with Libyan leader Mommar Khadify for Mubarsoi to fly into Tripoli. Khadify will grant him and his family total immunity and safe haven."

"Well, gentlemen, then it sounds like you have it all settled," I replied. "Excellent! You'll have accomplished your goal and you won't need me. Isn't that right?"

"I wish it were that simple, Professor," said Reuben. "If we succeed, we still need to convince the people of Cape de Leone and foreign interests how we can justify a British diplomatic officer and an Irish businessman being part of a new government. We're trying to remain behind the scenes, but there simply isn't a native leader that we presently feel comfortable with now to assume the Presidency, even if it's only temporary.

"If we turn the government over to Josiah Kimba, we believe it will only be a matter of weeks before he would be overthrown by one of a half-dozen tribal leaders waiting in the wings to take power. In that case, the country probably wouldn't be any better off than if Mubarsoi continued.

"At the same time, we need to act now! We can't wait! We can't let the election occur without first forcing Mubarsoi out. It will be much more difficult after the election is held to try and persuade him to leave."

"But you've just said a British battalion will be in Grand Bassa within a day if Mubarsoi doesn't resign," I insisted.

Peters stood and paced about the room, turning back to me. "Well, that's a bit of a stretch, Professor. While the British government is sending a small fleet of ships to give the impression that it is prepared to go to war, there is no guarantee that it will invade if Mubarsoi doesn't resign. My government," said Peters, "hasn't yet committed to an actual invasion. We're still negotiating with Whitehall on this issue."

"I see," I replied. "In other words, gentlemen, your threat may be all bullshit?"

Both Reuben and Peters nodded their heads solemnly.

"And what happens if Mubarsoi doesn't accept your bluff?" I asked.

"Then there's a chance we'll end up in front of a firing squad, Professor, as you suggested," Peters answered.

"Yes, I would imagine that's a definite possibility." I paused. "You're playing very high stakes poker, aren't you, gentlemen?"

Reuben and Peters sat down at the mahogany table and I now paced before turning back to them. "Why couldn't you, Mr. Peters, just have told me who you are? And why masquerade as Margaret's nephew and not her son? Or why didn't you," I said facing Reuben, "contact me and explain all this? Why send Mr. Peters?"

"I couldn't risk leaving Cape de Leone, Professor," answered Reuben. "I haven't been out of this building for the past month. I'm enemy number one on Mubarsoi's hit list. He knows I'm in the country. He knows that Margaret Mahoney was my mother. He knows I lost my wife in a raid involving his soldiers two years ago. His government is looking for me, and I'm dead if he finds me. And even if I was successful in leaving the country, it would have been very risky to try and reenter."

"And I was in Washington, D.C. over the weekend, Professor," Peters added. "I was there for the purpose of meeting with your country's Undersecretary for African Affairs, Chester Crocker, at the U.S. State Department. I wanted to see what the reaction would be from your government if Mubarsoi is overthrown. We need its support."

"So you didn't just fly to the States to retrieve me?"

"No," said Peters. "I flew into the States last Friday, into Washington, D.C. like I said. But I came to Indiana last Sunday to bring you back here."

There was an awkward pause. Then Peters continued.

"Professor, I had to try and convince you based on the only grounds that we believed you would come—loyalty to Margaret. After we read in her diary about how close the two of you were, we believed you might be willing to return. And of course we were right. We felt that until you could actually see how valuable you could be that we wouldn't be able to convince you to help us."

Peters stopped speaking, hesitated, and then looked over at Reuben. Reuben continued. "There's another way you can help us, Professor. Please come with Robert and me. I've something to show you."

The three of us went to the back of the room and out a side door. The opening led out into a beautiful garden, a lovely landscape of African flowers and bushes that was totally unexpected. A high iron rail fence surrounded the garden. The building we had been in was to our right, and we walked northward through this exquisite patchwork of green. Looking north through the blossoms of African tulip trees, I saw the dome of Parliament House. Reuben led our advance, glanced around and continued walking until he came to two piles of dirt. Behind them were two large canvas tarps covering something above ground. Reuben glanced again behind him and up to where troops were marching in front of the capitol. The soldiers were totally unaware of us, as we were behind the iron rail fence and hidden by the thick tulip trees. Reuben, Peters, and I walked up to the piles of dirt. Reuben then reached down and pulled the tarps off gently, respectfully.

Two headstones were revealed, but only one grave was filled in. The headstones read:

Rev. Francis G. Tannen, S.J.	Margaret Mahoney Reuben
1905 - 1959	1909 - 1989
Priest, Scholar, Founder of	Devoted teacher, nurse,
the Christian Peoples Party	Christian missionary, and friend
	to the People of Cape de Leone
Deuteronomy 4:37-38	John 15:17

"But your mother's grave is empty, Mr. Reuben," I blurted out. "Margaret's alive?"

Reuben looked down, not at me. "Professor, we were able to locate Father Tannen's remains by a tip from a native who knew where he was buried. We secretly removed his remains and reburied them here last week. As for my mother, she passed away of ovarian cancer in Spain six weeks ago. One of her last requests was that she be buried in Cape de Leone, but with Albert Mubarsoi still in power, it has been impossible for us to follow her wishes. If we succeed this Friday in removing him, one of the first things that will be done is that my mother's body will be exhumed in Spain and she will be reburied here, next to Francis Tannen. I think she would have wanted it that way. Tannen was the love of her life."

"So you lied about that, too," I said. I couldn't look at them. The appearance of Margaret's headstone brought tears to my eyes. Over the past three days and despite the terrible news about Elizabeth Brownlie, the thought of seeing Margaret again had given me renewed hope and life, had excited me beyond belief! But just now I had gained the cruelest kind of knowledge: that Margaret had been alive during the past thirty years—years that I could have been with her, cared for her, loved her—but that I didn't know it.

I turned back slowly to Reuben. "Do you know why your mother never contacted me? If the scrapbook inside is truly hers, then she had to know that I was alive."

"She told me once," Reuben answered, "that Albert Mubarsoi had threatened that if she ever tried to contact you, there would be a death squad looking for you immediately. Her mail at the convent was constantly intercepted and read. She was afraid to try and communicate with you. Mother felt responsible for Francis Tannen's death. She didn't want to be responsible for yours as well. She followed your career by having me search the newspapers for your stories."

Reuben's scarred, puffy face looked up at mine. "There's more for us all to fight for, Professor. In my mother's will, she left everything she owned—about thirty million pounds she inherited from my father—to establish schools for young girls throughout Cape de Leone. That was a goal of hers when she lived here in the fifties and it never changed. Today most of the girls in the country still have no opportunity for education. Less than 20% of all children over the age of five ever attend primary school. There aren't the resources or the mindset to make this happen, but with what my mother did, I believe we now have part of the problem solved. Can you possibly understand what this means?"

"It's tremendous what your mother did, Mr. Reuben," I said. "A tribute to her own life and a hope for the nation's children."

"Yes, and Robert and I want you to head up the program to establish the schools. That is the second critical role you can play if we can get rid of Mubarsoi and establish a new government."

Reuben didn't wait for me to respond, but stepped forward, gathered the two large tarps and covered up the graves. He glanced around in all directions and then we walked back inside the building, back to the ornate room.

When we returned to the mahogany table, I found a small note written in calligraphy next to a decorative plate of eggs, hash browns, and toast: "Mr. O'Connor, Bon appetit! Askia Muhammad."

I pushed the plate aside. "Nigel," I said, "I must confess that I didn't know that Margaret had a surviving son. Why wouldn't she have mentioned this to me?"

"My father didn't treat my mother very well, Professor," Reuben replied. "He admitted that to me before he died. As I think you know, my parents were separated most of their married lives. Their relationship was very complex, perhaps as complex as hers and Francis Tannen's. My mother left Ireland when I was only four years old. She tried to take me with her, but my father wouldn't let her. He made sure that I was never left alone with her when she returned to visit me.

"And then many years later, when I was older," Reuben continued, "I learned that my mother had followed Francis Tannen, first to the States and then here to Cape de Leone. I never met the man, but I learned through others that my mother had fallen madly in love with him. She apparently couldn't live without him. Do you know how that made me feel, Professor? For my mother to leave my father and me in order to follow this egocentric, unbalanced priest?"

I saw deep sorrow in Reuben's eyes. Added to the death of his wife was the passing of his mother. I tried to offer sympathy, but he wouldn't let me pity him.

"Professor," he continued. "I apologize for bringing you here under false pretenses, but I hope you now understand why we did it. You can be extremely valuable in what we're trying to accomplish. It would be the fulfillment of my mother's dreams for the country. But those dreams can never be a reality as long as Mubarsoi and his family remain in power."

There was a pause and it seemed that both men were waiting on me to respond.

"Mr. Reuben," I replied, "I'm very impressed with what you're trying to accomplish here, but I need time to think this over."

Reuben looked as though his sails had just been tightly furled. "Yes," he said. "Yes, I understand. Of course, this is a major decision. You need time." His eyes darted around the room as if to give himself a few moments to collect his thoughts. "But we're hoping to move on this in two days, Professor. We're trying to get everything in place."

"I understand that," I replied. "Please give me until tomorrow morning, Mr. Reuben. That will allow me this afternoon and this evening to think it over. This is more excitement than I've experienced since my days as a reporter."

Peters smiled. "When you talked about that long chapter of your life on our flight here, Professor, I could tell you missed it. That's another reason why we thought you might be willing to help us. All those factors that you shared—danger, intrigue, rooting out evil—they're all here!"

"Professor," Reuben interrupted. "I need to go now. Thank you for your willingness to listen. I hope you can help us." Reuben shook my hand and stepped through the tarp that separated the back of the store from the front.

Peters added, "I need to return to my own hideaway as well, Professor. I've intentionally kept a low profile for the past few weeks. But I'll see that Thombi and Karim drive you back to your hotel. I would ask that you wait until after dusk so as to be as inconspicuous as possible. I hope you understand."

I nodded and smiled. I liked Peters. Although he had totally misled me, ironically I felt now that he was a man I could trust.

"Oh, Professor," Peters added. "I need to mention something else. During our flight here, I sensed that you thought I might somehow be involved in the death of your goddaughter. After what you've learned today, I hope you don't still believe that. I can assure you that I had nothing to do with it. But I pledge my total support to try and find out what happened if we can only get through the crisis that's looming here."

By raising the matter of Elizabeth's death, Reuben's attempt to comfort merely caused my heart to plummet again.

"Professor," Peters continued, seeming to sense my despondency. "I'll leave you alone. If there's anything I can do, anything at all, I'm at your disposal. Askia Muhammad knows how to reach me."

Peters started to walk out of the room, when I suddenly thought to call to him. "Mr. Peters, there is one thing. Would you know if there are any direct flights out of Grand Bassa back to the States?"

"Pan American has one flight a week into New York City, but that was this morning. There won't be another until next Wednesday."

"No other airlines?" I asked.

"I don't think so," Peters answered. "I can check, but I'm fairly certain that's it. There's a direct flight to London on Mondays and another to Paris on Saturdays. Everything else goes first to an African city. But if you're thinking of flying out this week, I wouldn't recommend it."

"Why not?" I asked.

"Because the airport is swarming with security guards right now. That's another reason I didn't want to land there last evening. It's too dangerous. Too many guards. Too many chances for questions. You need to lay low. All of us do."

"Would you do me a favor and see what flights leave tomorrow, Mr. Peters? I just want to know what my options are, that's all."

Peters nodded and pulled the door closed.

I sat reading for a few hours and allowed the afternoon to pass. In the early evening, I walked outside again, back to the beautiful garden, back to the graves sites, one for Tannen and the other intended for Margaret. It was about an hour before dusk. I heard the cry of a muezzin, calling for evening prayer. His songful, cadenced voice came from atop a minaret, which stood near Parliament House. I pulled off the canvas tarp that covered Margaret's empty grave, and the sight of her head stone was more than I could bear.

I walked quickly back inside the building and Thombi Smith drove me back to my hotel. In my room, a porter brought me a tray of food. While I sat eating, I mulled over everything that Reuben and Peters had told me that afternoon, everything about how I was so needed. But I couldn't make myself care about their cause. At a certain intellectual level I knew what they were saying was true—if Mubarsoi was going to be removed, this was the time for it to happen. But I didn't care. I simply didn't care because my world—the one I had been either forced to live in or chose through options that weren't at all clear to me—had been shattered.

Don't they see how little difference I could make? If the scourge of genocide in countries like Uganda, Rwanda, and Zimbabwe has not shocked the world into caring about the inhumanities going on in Africa, how are a handful of stories from me going to make a difference? And even if Reuben and Peters succeed in ousting Mubarsoi, do they really think they are going to make life for the average native substantially better? And what about my life?

Then thoughts about the misfortunes that had recently occurred, notably Elizabeth's death and the discovery of Margaret's, flooded my mind. How could the ironies be any greater? That an Indiana farm boy would end up, after punishing himself endlessly for the denial of his father's affection and for causing the death of his mother and brother, believing he could recapture some past love that he had once experienced with an Irish woman he had met in a West African village? How could anything be so inexplicable as the fact that this farm boy had both strangely and unwittingly played a part in bringing into existence a beautiful young girl (Elizabeth) and then just as inexplicably be accused of causing her death? The rest of my story flowed through my mind as I lay on the bed in my small hotel room and tried to make some sense of my life.

Some time in 1961, a little more than a year after I returned to Lisbon shell shocked from Cape de Leone, Irene Brownlie became pregnant. Her husband, Merlin Brownlie, was in his late-fifties. Many townspeople smirked and expressed surprise that

Merlin could even impregnate his wife. The unfunny impediment to a possible conception between the two was that the farm implement dealer was in very poor health and had been forced to retire. While Merlin had swore off the bottle years before, the result of decades of hard drinking had finally caught up with him.

Irene nursed Merlin and took care of her husband as only a devoted wife could. But poor Merlin suffered and lingered for the next fifteen years, before finally succumbing to dementia and liver cancer. It was a slow, agonizing death to endure for Irene and her now teenage daughter, Elizabeth.

Living off and on at Blessed Acres, I would often see Irene before Merlin's death. I occasionally attended some of Elizabeth's school events such as her softball games, her admission into the high school's honor society, and the junior class play in which she played the lead in *The Diary of Anne Frank*. Elizabeth had a bit of tom-boy in her, but she was also very attractive and bright like her mother.

Before Merlin Brownlie's death, my Uncle Paul, who died himself of cirrhosis of the liver from his own bout with alcohol, told me a very short, but interesting story. I don't believe it was any deep, dark family secret. Rather, it simply came up after Uncle Paul had been to The Roanoke County Bank one day and happened to run into the bank's president.

According to Uncle Paul, when my mother was still sixteen and working in the Lisbon Glass Works, she had quite a crush on a young fellow worker. Mother and this man worked side by side in the boxing department at the Glass Works while they were both still in high school.

"Do you know who he was, Gene?" Uncle Paul asked out of the blue. "I'll tell you. It was Randall Shore, that's who," Mutt replied, answering his own question. "That's right, your mom had a real crush on Randall Shore. They made a handsome couple. But you could tell he was college material, wanted to spread his wings a bit before he came back to Lisbon. Your mom went and married your dad on the rebound. I don't mean to say anything bad about your father, Gene, but that was a real shame. Your mom would have been good for Randall. He's a dandy gentleman. He doesn't flaunt his wealth and power like some who's got it."

And so I learned the reason that Randall Shore took an interest in trying to help me better my life. For a brief period in their teenage years, Mr. Shore and my mother had been sweethearts. Apparently he never quite got over her, or at least he wanted to show respect or appreciation for my mother by extending an act of kindness towards me. I had always liked the man but from then on I had an even warmer feeling towards him. But that is only part of my story.

In 1977, Merlin Brownlie died. Irene had been extremely devoted to him. In the last year of Merlin's illness, Irene left her job at the electric company in order to be his full-time nurse. When I was home from assignment, I would occasionally stop out to their house and visit with Irene and Merlin and try to lift their spirits. It was during this time that I became even closer to Elizabeth.

Then a very strange thing occurred immediately after Merlin's funeral. I had left Irene and Elizabeth after the funeral luncheon, having first offered to take them home. But Irene kindly refused, saying she needed to spend time with Merlin's family. So I went on home to Blessed Acres. But later that day, Irene drove down the long lane and parked under the shade of one of the large weeping willow trees. It was a chilly, September afternoon, and farmers were just starting to harvest some of their crops.

Although I hadn't expected her, I invited Irene into the living room and learned the news that makes my story more complete. It seems that Irene had kept something to herself that had nearly drove her crazy, and with Merlin's death she could no longer contain the secret. As she explained to me, after she and Merlin had married, she quickly learned that he was in much poorer physical condition than he had led her to believe. In fact, it was because he needed someone to look after him that he wanted so badly to get married, and Irene was the willing candidate.

"We never had relations, Gene," Irene said in a low voice. "You know, the kind of relations that husbands and wives share together. Merlin wasn't capable. He just couldn't function in that way. The alcohol had made him very sick and he was too proud or embarrassed to go to a doctor to see if something could be done."

Before I could even think to formulate the next question, Irene shared the rest of her secret. "Gene, I've never told this to anyone, but Merlin wasn't Elizabeth's father. Not even Merlin or I talked about it when I became pregnant. It was like we had a silent understanding—as long as I said nothing and continued to take care of him, he accepted Elizabeth as his daughter. It was our own private, secret pact."

"But then who—"

"I think Merlin thought all along it was you, Gene," Irene said. "Merlin knew we had dated for a number of years. And later, after Elizabeth's birth, you're the one who would come and visit us. You're the one who took an interest in Elizabeth's school activities." She paused and then looked at me sadly. "Gene, Elizabeth's real father is Randall Shore. Randall and I got to know each other while working on a Red Cross project together in the early sixties."

I'm sure that a look of total disbelief must have come over my face. Irene took my hand. "Please don't be upset with me, Gene. Randall is such a kind, considerate man. Every month he sends me a check to help with raising Elizabeth. I would have never been able to quit my job and care for Merlin without Randall's generosity.

"Oh, Gene, I just had to tell someone," Irene continued. "Now with Merlin's death, with Elizabeth soon coming of age, I knew this day would come, but now I don't know what to do. Elizabeth should know who her real father is, shouldn't she? Oh, Gene, I am so scatter-brained right now, so upset! Things are such a mess! Of course nobody here knows. This is Lisbon and

Randall's a bigger hero than the Civil War soldiers on the monument of the Courthouse square."

Then Irene fell apart and cried for the next several minutes. I sat beside her on the living room sofa and held her as she poured out her heart and wept. I knew why Irene had to be so secretive. We lived in the heart of Midwest Puritanism! Oh, it was understandable if a local teenage girl got pregnant by her hormonally-driven boyfriend. But a totally different standard existed for a man of Randall Shore's stature. There were still townspeople who would withdraw all of their money from Shore's bank for a lesser moral offense.

And so Irene sat crying. She had buried a husband in the morning and divulged the identity of a one-time lover in the afternoon, and it was quite unclear which was the more difficult for her to do. Here is where I came in. Here was the reason for Irene reaching out to me of all people to share her most secretive confession. For in the next breath Irene asked me to go to Randall Shore, to ask, now that Merlin was dead, whether he would allow Irene to tell Elizabeth who her real father was.

> And so Irene sat crying. She had buried a husband in the morning and divulged the identity of a one-time lover in the afternoon, and it was quite unclear which was the more difficult for her to do.

And so against my initial protestations, I went to see Shore with this sole question in mind. And he, at the age of seventy-one, a life-long bachelor who was one of the kindest and most distinguished men I have ever known, received me, I suspect, without ever having the faintest idea of the purpose behind my visit. And when I shared with him that I knew of Elizabeth's true father and that not even Merlin Brownlie knew himself, Randall Shore's breathing stopped momentarily. He fell back into his dark leather chair and he sighed for several seconds. Then he gave me my answer: Elizabeth shouldn't be told and she should continue to be led to believe that Merlin was her father.

But Shore wouldn't totally forego his parental obligations; he had established a large trust fund for Elizabeth. She would come into half of it at age eighteen and the other half at age thirty. Elizabeth would be told by the bank, which would serve as the trustee, that a relative on her father's side of the family had left the money to her on condition of him remaining anonymous. And that was it!

So I dutifully reported back to Irene. She sadly accepted Randall Shore's decision, and life resumed much as before. But then came my own involvement and decision, one of the most heartfelt, if rash, that I've ever made. At the time, I could only think how sad it was that Elizabeth didn't have a father. I had known the loneliness over the lack of such a relationship, and so I offered to marry Irene and to be the father to Elizabeth that Randall Shore refused to be.

Irene shook her head. How could I possibly think of such a thing at that moment? But weeks later, during one evening's walk along Lisbon's uneven sidewalks, she shared that despite her feelings for me, she was unsure whether marriage between us would ever be a good idea as long as my work required long absences from Lisbon. But she agreed that Elizabeth needed a father figure. And then she encouraged me, if I still wished, to become more involved in Elizabeth's life. And so I did. I attended Elizabeth's remaining school events, I took Irene and Elizabeth to movies at the Muncie theaters; I went shopping with them at Christmas in Indianapolis. And with the passage of time, I believe I succeeded and Elizabeth accepted me, though more as an uncle than a father.

It was at this point that my career as a writer had reached a plateau. It was sufficient to provide a meager living, but nothing more. It also required me to be gone from Lisbon approximately half of each year. Thus, with no work-related benefits and no retirement plan, I had reached the point where my career held little promise of achieving any greater financial rewards, and I had long ago stopped writing for the thrill of seeing my name on a by-line.

I had seriously considered becoming an agent for an insurance dealership in Lisbon when I received a telephone call one morning in April 1985 that changed my life. It was from a gentleman who said that he served on the Pulitzer Prize committee from Columbia University. The stranger announced that I had been selected as that year's recipient of the Pulitzer Prize for reporting on international affairs. The committee specifically cited a series of articles I had written for the *The Chicago Sun-Times* about the devastating affects that the war in Nicaragua were having on the indigenous tribal population of the country. And so after being an obscure, foreign correspondent from a Midwest town that no one had ever heard of, I suddenly became a known writer, at least in a small but influential circle of newspaper editors and publishers.

After the Pulitzer, I received several job offers as a reporter for a number of newspapers. I was flattered by the offers, but then the dean of the journalism department at Indiana University called me about a new opening. He informed me that a wealthy attorney from Elkhart, Indiana, had recently endowed a newly created professorship in writing. It would be a joint appointment with the Department of English. He asked if I would be interested in the position. How could I hope for more at the age of fifty-seven and without a college degree myself?

And so in the fall of 1985, I began my second career as the "John R. Rehm Professor of Writing" at Indiana University. Each semester I was responsible for teaching two classes in the Journalism Department and an undergraduate writing course in the English Department. In the meantime, Irene had won a second term as Auditor of Roanoke County. Elizabeth, after teaching three years of high school English in Fort Wayne, Indiana, decided to enroll in 1986 in the journalism Ph.D. program at Indiana. With the professorship, came the opportunity for me to have one student assistant and, of course, Elizabeth was my choice. From 1986 to the present, Elizabeth worked for me as was needed, occasionally teaching a course and grading papers. At the same time she completed her qualifying examinations for her doctorate.

And this, in brief summary, has been the story of my life. But now in this tattered, sorry excuse for a hotel, I thought not of the past but of the future. A year away from retirement, I had planned to call it quits in 1990 at the age of sixty-three. College teaching hadn't been as fulfilling as I had hoped and I had made few friends in either department. I looked forward to returning to Blessed Acres, to Irene, and to writing my memoirs. But then came this terrible week and the turn of events that I couldn't have forecast in several lifetimes.

How could I ever face Irene again, knowing that I was implicated in her beautiful daughter's death? How could I ever find refuge in living at Blessed Acres, knowing that less than five miles away, in the Limberlost Cemetery, was entombed a young lady of twenty-seven who died mysteriously with me as the prime suspect? And now that I had learned the truth about Margaret, who had been the love of my life, it all seemed too overwhelming. At this point the hotel room seemed to close in on me. I couldn't help myself and tears rolled from my eyes. I climbed down from my bed and kneeled beside it, facing the door to my room. I began to pray to God, sobbing uncontrollably like a child. I hadn't prayed on my knees since Philip and I had shared a bedroom together at Blessed Acres. And as I sobbed, this tremendous sensation of doom and loss came over me again: the same sensation as that first night after mother's and Philip's deaths; the same sensation as the moment when I learned it had been Randall Shore, not my father, who had sent me the note and five dollar bill after their funerals; the same sensation as when I first saw Margaret hanging from a noose, convinced that her life had been taken.

It was as though God had completely abandoned me and had done so with an especially sadistic glee—by placing me in space to drift in time forever, but with the cruel knowledge that my price for eternal life would be eternal solitude. And then I realized, I think for the first time, that what I feared most was not death, but of being alone! And the loss of Elizabeth, the loss, again, of Margaret, and the knowledge that I would soon lose Irene, too, because of being implicated in Elizabeth's death—it all came crashing down upon me!

At the height of my heaving, I heard a knock on the door. I wiped away the tears before I answered.

"Go away, whoever you are!" I yelled between sobs. "Please go away!"

"Professor O'Connor, it's Robert Peters," a voice called back. "Are you all right? Is there something wrong?"

At that precise moment, Peters opened the door and stumbled in. I had failed to lock it.

"Professor," said Peters. "You're on your knees. What's wrong? Are you ill? Can I get you a doctor?"

"No, I'm quite all right," I replied, refusing to admit that I wasn't.

"Then what are you doing down there on the floor?"

"I'm praying, Robert. I'm praying to know what to do for I feel as though God has abandoned me and I'm destined for ruin."

"Oh, I can't believe that," said Peters. "Please don't be so despondent."

When I didn't respond, Peters continued. "I'm not an especially religious man, Professor, but I don't believe our fates are controlled by whim. I couldn't risk my own situation here if I didn't believe that what we're going through isn't worth it. You're being too hard on yourself."

Peters looked at me befuddled, seeming not to know what to say next. He then pulled out a small note book from his breast pocket and glanced at it.

"I wanted to get back with you about whether there are any flights out of Grand Bassa to the U.S. this week. There aren't. The only other option I know of is that tomorrow morning there is a train departing for Dakar, Senegal, at 6:30 a.m. From there you can catch a flight to New York. The flight leaves from the Dakar International Airport tomorrow afternoon at 4:00 p.m. It's the only option I can think of."

"I see. I appreciate you checking," I said standing up. "Would it be possible to have a taxi take me to the train station tomorrow morning at 5:30?"

"If that's what you want, I'll have Karim Jones drive you there," said Peters.

I stood up and glanced down at his shoes. "I know I told Nigel that I would give him an answer tomorrow as to whether I would stay or not. But my mind is already made up. I'm sorry, Robert, but I have to return to the States as soon as possible. I need to try and exonerate myself. I'm apparently the prime suspect in my goddaughter's murder."

"But how can that be—"

I interrupted him. "I know Margaret would probably be disappointed in me. Everything she and I planned for is wrapped up in your cause. But just as this isn't her fight any more, it isn't mine either. At least not at this moment. I have to deal with the deck I've been given."

Peters was deeply disappointed, but he said he understood. He next walked towards me and shook my hand. "In the morning Karim will be here to take you to the train station. You'll not need to say anything to him. He'll have your ticket to Dakar and your plane ticket to New York. I'll see that both are taken care of yet tonight."

Peters walked to the door and then turned back around. "Professor, I have but one small request before I go."

"Yes, Robert. What is it?"

"If you find yourself talking to God again, will you say a prayer for what we're about to do here. We could use some divine intervention."

"Yes, of course," I replied. "What Nigel and you are trying to accomplish will be at the top of my list."

Thirty

The next morning Karim Jones picked me up at the hotel promptly at 5:30 just as Peters had promised. Jones drove me to the train station where we passed pockmarked store fronts plastered with political graffiti and gunshots. The streets were nearly empty. Jones and I entered into the train station and we walked onto the platform next to the train. The station was one of the grander structures in Grand Bassa, being a large steel-framed construction similar to Victoria Station in London. As we approached the platform, a dingy, dented sign read: "Departure - Dakar 6:30 a.m."

"Wait here, sir," said Jones as he took my suitcase. "Please don't move. I'll return for you."

Jones disappeared for several minutes and I started to look up and down the corridor between the station and the train. There were two African guards holding machine guns down at the other end where the engine idled. There were also about fifteen to twenty other passengers waiting to board. The guards had just finished going through a passenger's suitcase. They started to walk past the others towards me, and I became very nervous. I fidgeted for my Engels' passport in my left breast pocket and couldn't find it. "Where in the hell is it?" I muttered under my breath. I searched the rest of my pockets, all the time trying not to draw attention to myself. My heart raced and I started to perspire. Did I leave my passport in the bag that Jones just took? The guards continued walking my direction. I didn't know what to do and an impulse to flee ran through my body.

Suddenly there was a small explosion at the other end of the platform! It sounded like fire crackers. Waiting passengers screamed and a lady near the outburst fainted, slumping to the ground. The guards turned and raced towards the fallen woman. Then before I knew what was happening, Thombi Smith grabbed me from behind and pulled me towards him. "Come with me, Mr. O'Connor. Please hurry!" he exclaimed.

Smith dragged me from the train platform and into a room near the ticket counter. The room was dark and had a musty odor to it. As soon as I was inside, Smith slammed the door shut and locked it behind us. He held his hand over my mouth. "Don't talk yet, sir."

Lights flickered on. I glanced quickly around the room and saw that it was used for storage, being filled with railroad supplies and other equipment. Thick blinds covered the window, preventing any light from escaping.

"I'm sorry if we frightened you, Professor," said a voice from behind me. I turned around and saw Nigel Reuben. He wore a fake mustache and horned rimmed glasses, but his scarred face was unmistakable. "I thought it would be safer in here until the train leaves," he said. "I had intended to catch you at the hotel this morning, but I had to retrieve someone and it wasn't possible to meet you before you left." Reuben was surrounded by large burly men, apparently body guards. He reached out and put his hand on my shoulder. "Are you sure you won't stay, Mr. O'Connor?"

It took several seconds for me to regain my composure. "It's not that I'm unsympathetic to your cause," I blurted out. "Surely you know that. It's that I have business I have to attend to back in the States."

He nodded in a knowing way. "Please wait, Mr. O'Connor. I have someone for you to meet."

Reuben walked to the edge of the cluttered room. There, sitting alone, was a beautiful young African woman dressed in colorful native costume of orange and purple. She was absolutely striking. She stood up and the two of them walked back to me.

"Professor," resumed Reuben, "do you know who this is?"

I shook my head, befuddled.

"You once saved my life, Professor O'Connor," announced the woman. She reached out and embraced me and then smiled broadly.

I withdrew from her unexpected hug, but she wouldn't release me completely, determined to hold my left hand. She held it tightly and tears trickled down her beautiful, full cheeks. "My name is Falaba-Marabella Nalinga, Professor. I was told by the nuns who raised me that Margaret Mahoney and you found me in the bush. You were with my mother when she died, Professor. Margaret named me."

"Falaba-Marabella?" I said, remembering with deep pleasure the small child Margaret and I discovered. I hugged her this time, exclaiming, "I can't believe it! You're so beautiful, so grown up and beautiful!"

"This is her, Professor," said Reuben. "No imposter, no fictitious person. Falaba-Marabella is now married to a young man who is a chieftain of the Khumran tribe in the southern province. He is an outstanding chief and will be a great leader of this nation, I predict, in a few years. Falaba-Marabella is highly educated and is an outstanding leader in her own right. She will do much to make the women of this nation better educated and more self-reliant. She has a strong faith."

"Professor O'Connor," said Falaba-Marabella passionately, "we need to share the message of Christ's love with the Leoneon people! But to do this, President Mubarsoi must be removed. Won't you please stay? I'm not asking for myself, but on behalf of the people of this nation who are without a voice. You could do so much to help us spread our vision for the country!"

Reuben and Falaba-Marabella looked at me with great hope in their eyes. How could I disappoint them? And yet I knew what my answer had to be.

"It's impossible for me to remain," I replied. "I have to go back and get the matter involving my goddaughter's death cleared up. But perhaps," I exclaimed, "I can be of benefit in another way. I will write about what has gone on here. I can use what little influence I have to bring attention to what you're trying to accomplish. Please don't think that I'm not interested just because I must leave."

Reuben extended his hand and placed it on my shoulder. "I can tell you are sincere, Professor. Whatever help you can give us will be greatly appreciated. I won't pressure you to change your mind."

Falaba-Marabella hugged me. "You are a kind man, Professor O'Connor. God-speed be with you. I pray that you will one day return to us and help the Leoneon people realize their greatness."

"Professor," Reuben added, "the offer is still on the table for you to return to help establish the schools that my mother envisioned."

"If you are going to go, sir," said Karim Jones, interrupting, "then you must board now. The train could depart at any time. We have secured a private compartment for you, but you must board now so as not to raise any suspicion. We cannot create another diversion, sir."

Falaba-Marabella pulled something from a satchel that she picked up from the floor. It was a picture and she handed it to me.

I examined the picture and saw an elderly woman, looking tired but still with a spark in her eyes. In the picture, Falaba-Marabella kneeled beside her, her hands cupped over the woman's hands.

"It's Margaret, isn't it?" I asked.

"Yes," Falaba-Marabella replied. "I was with her during the last two weeks of her life. There was never anyone like her."

"Then you got to know her?"

"Oh, yes, Professor O'Connor, very well. Several years ago I searched for Margaret and found her. Each year from then on I traveled to Spain and would spend several days with her. It's because of Margaret that I was raised and educated in a very fine Catholic girl's school in Ghana."

"I'm so glad that you got to know Margaret, Falaba-Marabella."

She nodded and smiled. I went to hand her the picture back. "No, please keep it, Professor. I want you to have it."

"I also have something for you," said Reuben, handing me a wrapped package. "I found it when I went through my mother's possessions. It's personal, but then you were closer to her than even me. Please accept it."

Reuben cleared his throat, holding back emotion. "My mother loved you very much, Eugene," Reuben said, for the first and only time calling me by my Christian name. "I don't have to be a romantic to know this from how she wrote about you. I think you can tell yourself," he said pointing to the package. "And Falaba-Marabella has something else for you, too."

"Here, Mr. O'Connor," interrupted Falaba-Marabella. "Just before she passed away Margaret asked that I see that you received this. I think she held out the hope of giving it to you herself someday."

"Mr. O'Connor, please come," Karim Jones pleaded.

I shook Reuben's hand and hugged Falaba-Marabella one last time before darting through the door and straight onto the train. A small compartment, just in front of the caboose, had been reserved for me. I noticed that the time was now 6:45 a.m. We were already fifteen minutes late in leaving. We finally pulled away. There were no well-wishers at the station, just the two armed guards who now sat on benches, machines guns draped across their laps, appearing bored.

The train creaked away as though it was a freight train straining to pull car-loads full of coal or grain. We rolled slowly through the northern suburbs of Grand Bassa, past the back sides of pitiful looking shanties. The train lumbered along and the scenes outside passed-by as though we were moving in slow motion. At this speed, it seemed we would never make it to Dakar in time.

The sun streamed in from the east through dirty, streaked windows. I looked down at the package that Reuben had given me. I opened it and saw that it was Margaret's diary. I flipped through the pages and read entries dated in the 1950s when we were together teaching in Burguna. I saw the mention of my name several times. Just at this time, a squat, elderly African women opened the door to my compartment and walked in. She looked very sad. She fanned herself, saying something to me in Jula or in another language I couldn't understand, and sat down. I suspected that she couldn't read the sign outside my compartment that read "Reserved."

I next pulled the wrapping off of the gift that Falaba-Marabella had given me. I noticed it was an old book, faded and frayed. I then recognized its cover. I opened it to the front page where an inscription in slightly smeared blue ink read: "Presented to Dorothy Hamilton for seven years of faithful Sunday school attendance, King of Glory Missionary Church, Lisbon, Indiana, signed this 25th day of June, 1920, Reverend Clarence Hogarth." I had long ago thought that it had been lost or destroyed. Mother's Bible had now come home.

I leafed through the Bible and there I found an envelope addressed to me. Even though it had been decades since I had seen Margaret's handwriting, I knew immediately it was hers. I opened the envelope and found a letter and a pressed dried flower contained within it. And then it struck me that this was the African violet that Margaret had plucked on Mount Dugaga, the one which she said she would save to remind her of me.

I noticed the sad eyes of the elderly, African woman staring at me. I sensed that she could tell I was upset, and I began to look outside again to avoid her stare. As I gazed through the compartment's window, I noticed we were now entering into a different type of terrain. We were miles from Grand Bassa and at the beginning of a very flat, grassy land known as savannah. There were few trees. The rains had not yet come and the earth radiated a golden hue that was both picturesque and noble. From a distance, I could see laborers walking out into the fields for morning work. They were wearing the same type of worn, tattered clothes as when I worked with the villagers in Burguna in the 1950s.

The train, if anything, seemed to move more slowly. My concern at arriving late into Dakar and missing my flight to New York grew greater. I just had to get back in time for Elizabeth's funeral and to straighten out the mess I was in! The flight out of Dakar to the States was my only hope! I was just beside myself, torn with emotion from the prospect of reading Margaret's letter and feeling overwhelmed by what awaited me back in Indiana. Why are we so limited in seeing what lies before us? I thought.

And then I recalled, out of nowhere, one of my favorite passages that I often read when Margaret and I would share devotions together: *First Corinthians 13, verses 8 to 12.* I picked up mother's Bible and flipped to the verses. Saint Paul's message spoke to me clearly: there is so much we don't presently understand, but when we are one with Christ, we shall see all! And then I smiled with a passing thought: wouldn't it be remarkable if one day Falaba-Marabella became a great leader and prophet to the Leoneon people? That through a small orphaned child, plucked from the African wild, Margaret's dream for an educated and Christian nation might be realized.

And I also knew that, if I could get the terrible mess cleared up about Elizabeth's death, I would return to Cape de Leone, regardless of whether Reuben, Peters, and their associates overthrew Mubarsoi or not. If they weren't successful, I would mount a campaign to take out the tyrant myself. And if they were, I would become Margaret's champion, because the greatest tribute to her would be to complete the work she had never been allowed to finish. I smiled at the thought that because of Margaret's vision, a young baby girl being born in the African bush today might have an education and become another Falaba-Marabella.

And then I also remembered Margaret's story about her driving along the Irish countryside, distraught and prepared to do herself in, and of her finding God when she least expected it. I looked out through my window. We chugged around a curve that opened into another plains area that seemed boundless. I prayed with hope and anticipation that I, too, might still personally experience God one day along such a clearing.

The early morning sun pierced the streaked windows forming a spectrum of colors. Time momentarily stood still. The old African woman across from me had fallen asleep, her eyes closed and her hands folded across her lap. I looked out again at the golden savannah. And as we slowly crossed the arid, West African landscape, I saw a beautiful blue sky stretch endlessly above the grasslands to meet the horizon beyond.